THE FRIEND ZONE

ABBY JIMENEZ

PIATKUS

First published in the US in 2019 by Forever, an imprint of
Grand Central Publishing, a division of Hachette Book Group, Inc

First published in Great Britain in 2019 by Piatkus

1 3 5 7 9 10 8 6 4 2

A CIP catalogue record for this book is available from the British Library.

ISBN 978-0-349-42340-1

Printed and bound in Great Britain by Clays Ltd, Elcograf S.p.A.

Papers used by Piatkus are from well-managed forests
and other responsible sources.

Piatkus
An imprint of
Little, Brown Book Group
Carmelite House
50 Victoria Embankment
London EC4Y 0DZ

An Hachette UK Company
www.hachette.co.uk

www.littlebrown.co.uk

This book is dedicated to all the people who lifted me up while I was writing it. And Stuntman Mike.

THE FRIEND ZONE

ONE
JOSH

I glanced down at the text while the light was red.

Celeste: I'm not giving you a dime, Josh. Go screw yourself.

"Goddamn it," I muttered, tossing the phone on the passenger seat. I knew she was gonna do this. Leave me with my finger in the dam. *Shit.*

I'd left her the contents of the whole house, and all I asked was for her to pay half of the Lowe's bill. Half of three thousand dollars' worth of appliances I'd generously given her instead of selling them, despite the card and payments being in my name. And of course, *I* was somehow the asshole in all this for leaving the state for a new job three months after we'd broken up.

I had it on the highest authority she was now hooking up with some guy named Brad.

I hoped Brad enjoyed my Samsung stainless gas range with the double oven.

Asphalt-scented heat drifted in through my open windows as I sat in Burbank's slow-moving morning gridlock. Even on a Sunday, there was traffic. I needed to get my AC fixed if I was going to survive in California—another expense I couldn't afford. I should have walked to the grocery store. Probably would have gotten there faster at this rate, and I wouldn't have wasted gas—another thing that cost twice as much as it did in South Dakota.

Maybe this move was a bad idea.

This place would bankrupt me. I had to host my best friend's bachelor party, there were moving expenses, the higher cost of living…and now this bullshit.

The light turned green and I pulled forward. Then the truck in front of me slammed on the brakes and I hit its bumper with a lurch.

Fuck. You've gotta be kidding me.

My day had been officially ruined twice in less than thirty seconds. It wasn't even 8:00 a.m. yet.

The other driver turned into a Vons parking lot, waving out the window for me to follow. A woman—bracelet on her wrist. The wave somehow managed to be sarcastic. Nice truck though. A Ford F-150. It still had dealer plates. Kind of a shame I'd hit it.

She parked and I pulled up behind her, turned off the engine, and rummaged in my glove box for my insurance information as the woman jumped from her vehicle and ran to look at her bumper.

"Hey," I said, getting out. "Sorry about that."

She turned from her inspection and glared up at me. "Yeah, you know you have one job, right? Not to hit the car in front of you?" She cocked her head.

She was small. Maybe five foot two. Petite. A dark wet spot cascaded down the front of her shirt. Shoulder-length brown hair and brown eyes. Cute. Impressive scowl.

I scratched my cheek. Irritated women were a particular specialty of mine. Six sisters—I was well trained.

"Let's just have a look," I said passively, putting on my calm-in-a-crisis voice. "See what we're dealing with."

I crouched between the back of her truck and the front of mine and surveyed the damage as she stood over me, her arms crossed. I looked up at her. "I tapped your trailer hitch. Your truck is fine." Mine had a small dent, but it wasn't anything major. "I don't think we need to get our insurance companies involved."

I couldn't afford to have an accident on my driving record. It wasn't good for my job. I pushed up on my knees and turned to her.

She leaned over and tugged on the hitch. It didn't wiggle. "Fine," she said, obviously satisfied with my assessment. "So, are we done here?"

"I think we can be done."

She whirled, darting around to the passenger side of her truck as I started for the grocery store. She dove into the cab, her legs dangling from the seat as she leaned in on her stomach. Her flip-flop fell off into the parking lot with a plop.

She had a nice ass.

"Hey," she said, twisting to look at me as I walked past. "How about instead of staring at my ass, you make yourself useful and get me some napkins."

Busted.

I put a thumb over my shoulder. "Uh, I don't have any napkins in my truck."

"Think outside of the box," she said impatiently.

Feeling a little guilty for openly admiring her assets—or rather for getting caught doing it—I decided to be helpful. I went back to my truck, opened my gym bag, and grabbed a tee. When I handed her the shirt, she snatched it and dove back into the cab.

I stood there, mostly because she had my favorite shirt, but also because the view wasn't anything to complain about. "Everything okay?" I tried to peer past her into the front seat, but she blocked my line of sight.

A small, light brown dog with a white chin growled at me from the window of the back seat. One of those little purse dogs. I scoffed. It wore actual clothing.

"I spilled coffee in my friend's new truck," she said from inside. She lost her other flip-flop to the sweltering parking lot and was now barefoot, her red-painted toes on the running board. "It's everywhere. So no, it's not okay."

"Is your friend a dick or something? It was an accident."

She pivoted to glare at me like I kicked her dog. "No, he's not a dick. You're the dick. You were probably texting."

She was feisty. A little too cute to scare me though. I had to work hard to keep my lips from turning up at the corners. I cleared my throat. "I wasn't texting. And in all fairness, you *did* slam on the brakes for no reason."

"The reason was I needed to *stop*." She turned back to the mess.

I suspected the reason was she spilled coffee on herself and hit the brakes reflexively. But I wasn't going to poke the bear. Well trained.

I slipped my hands into my pockets and rocked back on my heels, squinting up at the Vons sign in the parking lot to my left. "Okay. Well, good chatting with you. Leave my shirt on the windshield when you're done."

She climbed into the passenger side of the truck and slammed the door shut.

I shook my head and chuckled all the way into the store.

When I came back out, she was gone and my shirt was nowhere to be seen.

TWO

KRISTEN

Shawn planted a chair smack in the middle of the fire station living room and straddled it backward, facing me. He did this so he could harass me as close as humanly possible.

I sat in one of the six brown leather recliners parked in front of the TV. My Yorkie, Stuntman Mike, stood in my lap, growling.

Shawn bounced his eyebrows at me under his stupid pompadour hair. "'Sup, girl. You think about what I said?" He grinned.

"No, Shawn, I don't have any Mexican in me, and no, I don't want any."

The fire station captain, Javier, came down the hallway into the kitchen as I leaned forward with a hand on my dog's head. "Shawn, I want you to know that if I needed mouth to mouth, and you were the last paramedic on Earth, I prefer donations made to the ASPCA in lieu of flowers at my funeral."

Javier laughed as he poured himself a coffee, and Brandon chuckled over his book from the recliner next to me. "Shawn, get lost."

Shawn got up and grabbed his chair, mumbling as he dragged it back to the table.

Sloan breezed back in from the bathroom. She had on that white linen skirt she got when we were in Mexico last summer and sandals that laced up her calf. She looked like Helen of Troy.

My best friend was gorgeous. Blond, waist-length hair, colorful tattoos down her left arm, a glistening rock on her ring finger. Brandon was her firefighter and equally hot fiancé.

It was Sunday. Family day at the station when the four guys on shift got to bring their friends and family to have breakfast with them if they wanted to. Sloan and I were the only takers this morning. Javier's wife was at church with his daughters, and Shawn didn't have a girlfriend.

Imagine that.

Technically I was here for Josh, the fourth member of the crew, though I'd never met him before.

Brandon's best friend, Josh, just transferred from South Dakota to be the station's new engineer. He was Brandon's best man, and I was Sloan's maid of honor for their April 16th wedding in two months. Josh had missed the engagement party, so it was some all-important thing that we meet each other *immediately.*

I checked my phone for the time. I was starving and getting irritable. Breakfast was on Josh today. He hadn't shown up yet though, so nobody was actually making anything and all I'd had was coffee.

He was already pissing me off, and I hadn't even met him yet.

"So," Sloan said, sitting in the recliner next to Brandon. "Are you going to tell me where you got the shirt?"

I looked down at the black, men's Wooden Legs Brewing Company T-shirt I'd knotted at the waist. "Nope."

She eyed me. "You left for tampons, and you came back wearing some random shirt. Is there some particular reason you're hiding this from me?"

Brandon glanced up from his page. He was a pretty level-headed guy. He didn't usually let things work him up. But explaining that I'd christened his new truck with my black Sumatra drip would probably earn me a stern disapproving look that would somehow be worse than if he cussed me out.

I opted against it.

I'd cleaned it up. I'd managed not to damage the bumper in the fender bender I'd caused slamming on the brakes when I spilled it everywhere. What he didn't know wouldn't hurt him.

Since my top was already ruined, I'd used it to clean up the mess and changed into Parking Lot Guy's shirt instead.

"It's Tyler's," I lied. "It smells like him. I just missed him." I put my nose to the top of the collar and made a show of breathing in.

Damn, it smelled good.

That guy had been kind of sexy. A nice body under those clothes, I could tell. Good-looking too. That clean-shaven boyish face I always gravitate to.

I needed to get laid. I was starting to fantasize over strangers. It had been too long. Tyler hadn't been home in seven months.

Sloan's face went soft. "Awwww. That's so sweet. It's sad you can't be with him on Valentine's Day tomorrow. But just three more weeks and you'll have him for good."

"Yup. His deployment will be done and we'll officially be living together." A twinge of nerves twisted in my gut, but I kept my face neutral.

Sloan smiled and put a hand to her heart. She didn't much like Tyler, but she was still a romantic.

My cramps surged and I clutched my stomach with a grimace. I was in the throes of another epic period. This, coupled with hunger, the events from earlier, and the 3:00 a.m. police drama at my house that I wasn't telling Sloan about, had me in a fine mood. I was so tired I'd just tried to plug my charger into my coffee cup instead of my phone.

Sloan checked her watch and then wordlessly rummaged in her purse and shook two Aleve into her hand. She handed me her glass of water and gave me the pills in a well-rehearsed routine we'd perfected during our five years as roommates.

I swallowed the pills and turned to Brandon. "That book any good?"

"It's not bad," he said, looking at the cover. "Want to borrow it when I'm done?" Then he peered past me and his eyes lit up. "Oh, hey, buddy."

I followed his look to the door and my jaw dropped. The handsome jerk from Vons stood there with bags of groceries.

Our gazes met from across the room, and we stared at each other in surprise. Then his eyes dropped down to my—*his*—shirt, and the corner of his mouth turned up into a smirk.

I stood, putting Stuntman on the chair as the guy set down his groceries and walked toward me. I held my breath, waiting to see how he was going to play this.

Brandon laid his book over the arm of the recliner and got up. "Josh, this is Kristen Peterson, Sloan's best friend. Kristen, Josh Copeland."

"Well, hello—it's so nice to meet you," he said, gripping my hand just a little too tightly.

I narrowed my eyes. "Nice to meet you too."

Josh didn't let go of my hand. "Hey, Brandon, didn't you get a new truck this weekend?" he asked, talking to his friend but staring at me.

I glared at him, and his brown eyes twinkled.

"Yeah. Want to see it?" Brandon asked.

"After breakfast. I love that new-car smell. Mine just smells like coffee."

I gave him crazy eyes and his smirk got bigger. Brandon didn't seem to notice.

"Got any more bags? Want help?" Brandon asked. Sloan had already dived in and was in the kitchen unbagging produce.

"Just one more trip. I got it," Josh said, his eyes giving me a wordless invitation to come outside.

"I'll walk out with you," I announced. "Forgot something in the truck."

He held the door for me, and as soon as it was closed, I whirled on him. "You'd better not say shit." I poked a finger at his chest.

At this point it was less about the coffee spill and more about not wanting to reveal my brazen attempt at covering up my crime. I didn't lie as a rule, and of course the *one* time I'd made an exception, I was immediately in a position to be blackmailed. Damn.

Josh arched an eyebrow and leaned in. "You stole my shirt, shirt thief."

I crossed my arms. "If you ever want to see it again, you'll keep your mouth shut. Remember, *you* rear-ended *me*. This won't go over well for you either."

His lips curled back into a smile that was annoyingly attractive. He had dimples. Motherfucking *dimples*.

"*Did* I rear-end you? Are you sure? Because there's no evidence of that ever happening. No damage to his truck. No police report. In fact, my version of the event is I saw a hysterical woman in distress in the Vons parking lot and I gave her my shirt to help her out. Then she took off with it."

"Well, there's your first mistake," I said. "Nobody would ever believe I was hysterical. I don't *do* hysterics."

"Good info." He leaned forward. "I'll adjust my story accordingly. A calm but rude woman asked for my help and then stole my favorite shirt. Better?" He was smiling so big he was almost laughing.

Jerk.

I pursed my lips and took another step closer to him. He looked amused as I encroached on his personal space. He didn't back up and I glowered up at him. "You want the shirt. I want your silence. This isn't a hard situation to work out."

He grinned at me. "Maybe I'll let you keep the shirt. It doesn't look half-bad on you." Then he turned for his truck, laughing.

THREE
JOSH

In honor of the new-guy-cooks rule, I made breakfast for the crew on C shift. A Mexican egg skillet, my specialty.

I was on probation—the probie. Even though I was five years into the job, I was only five shifts into this station. That meant I was the last one to sit down to eat and the first one to get up and do dishes. I was practically a servant. They had me cleaning toilets and changing sheets. All the grunt work.

Sloan and Kristen opted to help me, and Brandon took pity on me, so they all stood in the kitchen wiping counters and scraping food off plates while I washed the dishes and Shawn and Javier played cribbage at the table.

Kristen had glared all through the meal, but only when she didn't think anyone was watching. It was kind of funny, actually. I kept ribbing her. From what I gathered through my prodding, she'd told everyone the shirt was her boyfriend's.

I wasn't going to say anything. Brandon didn't need to have the thunder stolen from his new truck by learning it had already been defiled, but I was drawing untold amounts of enjoyment from giving Kristen shit. And she didn't take any of it lying down either. She matched me tit for tat.

"So, Josh, you drive the fire truck, huh?" Kristen asked casually, wiping down the stove.

"I do." I smiled.

"Are you any good at it? No problems stopping that thing when you need to?" She cocked her head.

"Nope. As long as someone doesn't slam on the brakes in front of me, I'm good."

Glare. Smirk. Repeat. And Sloan and Brandon were oblivious. It was the most fun I'd had in weeks.

Sloan handed me the cutting board to wash. "You'll be walking Kristen down the aisle at the wedding." She smiled at her friend. "She's my maid of honor."

"I hope you walk better than you drive," Kristen mumbled under her breath.

I grinned and changed the subject before Sloan or Brandon asked questions. "What's your dog's name, Kristen?"

The little thing had sat on her lap all through breakfast. Occasionally his head popped up over the table to look at her plate, the tip of his tongue out. He looked like a fluffy Ewok.

"His name is Stuntman Mike."

I raised an eyebrow over my sink of dishes. "Tarantino?"

She raised hers. "You've seen *Death Proof*?"

"Of course. One of my favorite movies. Kurt Russell as Stuntman Mike. And your dog has issues?" I asked. The little Yorkie wore a shirt that read I HAVE ISSUES on it.

"Yes, they're mostly with Shawn."

I chuckled.

Sloan swept cilantro stems into her hand and tossed them in the trash, and Brandon pulled out the bag and tied the top. "Kristen has an online business called Doglet Nation," Brandon said. "She sells merchandise for small dogs."

"Oh yeah? Like what?" I asked, setting a casserole dish into the rack to dry.

Kristen pulled out the coffee grounds and dumped them into the compost bag. "Clothes, bags, gourmet dog treats. Sloan bakes those. Our big-ticket item is our staircases though."

"Stairs?"

"Yeah. Little dogs usually can't jump up on a high bed. So we make custom staircases that match your bedroom set. Stain, carpet, style."

"And people buy that?" I set the last bowl to dry in the rack and peeled off my rubber gloves.

"Uh, yeah they buy that. Why would you drop a couple grand on a nice Pottery Barn or Restoration Hardware bed, only to have some hideous foam staircase next to it from PetSmart?"

I nodded. "I get that, I guess."

"Which reminds me—I'm out a carpenter," she said to Sloan.

Sloan's brow furrowed. "What? Since when?"

"Since Miguel quit on me last week. He got a union job at Universal doing set work. Dropped me like I was radioactive. I have three stairs on order."

Sloan shook her head. "What are you going to do?"

Kristen shrugged. "Put an ad on Craigslist. Hope the guy doesn't end up being some kind of pervert out to kill me to sell my organs on the black market."

I snorted.

Brandon nodded at me as he put a new bag into the trash can. "Josh is a carpenter. He's pretty good at it too."

Sloan looked at me. "Really?"

Brandon was already fishing out his cell phone. I knew what he was pulling up. The tiki bar I'd built in my backyard. Celeste's tiki bar. *Brad's* tiki bar.

"Look," he said, handing around the phone. "He built this."

Sloan nodded in approval. Then the phone went to Kristen, and she glanced at it before her eyes shot up to mine.

"Not bad," she said begrudgingly.

"Thanks. But I'm not looking for any side work," I said, waving them off. I didn't need to build dog stairs for pennies on my day off. The living room of my new apartment was still full of boxes.

"Yeah, who needs an extra two hundred dollars for three hours of work?" Kristen said, flipping a hand dismissively. "Not Miguel apparently."

I froze. "Two hundred dollars?"

Sloan sprayed the counter with lemon-scented all-purpose cleaner. "Sometimes it's more—right, Kristen? It depends on the style?"

Kristen stared at her best friend like she was telling her to shut up. Then she dragged her eyes back to me. "The stairs run four to five hundred dollars apiece, plus shipping. I split the profits fifty-fifty, minus the materials, with my carpenter. So yeah. Sometimes it's more."

"Do you have a picture of the stairs?" I asked.

Kristen unenthusiastically handed me her phone and I scrolled through a website gallery of ridiculous tiny steps with Stuntman Mike posed on them in different outfits. These were easy. Well within my ability.

"You know, I think I do have time for this. I'll do it if you don't have anyone else." A few of these and I could pay off my Lowe's card. This was real money.

Kristen shook her head. "I think I'd rather take my chances with the organ thieves."

Sloan gasped, and Brandon froze and looked at Kristen and me.

"Is that right?" I said, eyeballing her. "How about we talk about this over *coffee*."

Kristen narrowed her eyes and I arched an eyebrow. "Fine," she said like it was physically painful. "You can build the damn stairs. But only until I find a different guy. And I *will* be looking for a different guy."

Sloan looked back and forth between us. "Is there something you guys want to tell us?"

"I caught him staring at my ass," Kristen said without skipping a beat.

I shrugged. "She did. I have no excuse. It's a great ass."

Brandon chuckled and Sloan eyed her best friend. Kristen tried to look mad, but I could tell she took the compliment.

Kristen let out a breath. "Give me your email address. I'll shoot you the orders. When you're done with them, let me know and I'll generate and send you the shipping labels. And I'll be inspecting every piece before you take them to FedEx, so don't try and half-ass anything."

"Wait, you don't have a shop?" I asked. "Where am I supposed to build these?"

"Don't you have a garage or something?"

"I live in an apartment."

"Shoot. Well, it looks like this won't work out." She smirked.

Sloan stared at her. "Kristen, you have an empty three-car garage. You don't even park in it half the time. Can't he work there?"

Kristen gave Sloan side-eye.

I grinned. "He can."

A loud beeping came over the speakers throughout the station followed by the red lights. We had a call. Kristen held my stare as the dispatcher rattled off the details. Too bad. I could have hung out with my cranky maid of honor a little longer.

No luck.

Brandon leaned in and kissed Sloan goodbye. The girls would probably be gone by the time we got back. "We'll finish cleaning up," she said.

"Get my number from Brandon," Kristen said to me, crossing her arms over her chest in a way that I think was meant to keep me from offering her a hand to shake.

Since the call was medical, we didn't have to put on our fire gear. So Brandon and I headed straight for the apparatus bay where the engine was parked. I could feel Kristen's eyes on my back and I grinned. She hated me. An ongoing theme with the women in my life at the moment.

Besides Celeste, all six of my sisters *and* my mom were pissed that I'd moved. Even my little nieces were giving me the cold shoulder when I called. Seven and eight years old and they'd already mastered the little-girl passive-aggressive equivalent of "I'm fine."

"What'd you think of Kristen?" Brandon asked through a grin as we climbed into the engine.

"She seems cool." I shrugged, putting on my headset.

Brandon and I had spent a year together in Iraq. He knew me well. Under normal circumstances, Kristen was my kind of woman. I liked petite brunettes—and women who tell me to go fuck myself apparently.

"Just cool?" he said, putting on his headset. "Is that why you were checking out her ass?"

Javier took his seat, chuckling to himself at Brandon's comment and Shawn hopped in, catching the tail end. "Kristen's hot as fuck. I check out her ass every time she's here." He put his headset on. "That dog bit me once though."

We all laughed and I fired the engine to life.

"She's not into me. She's got a boyfriend. And I'm not looking right now anyway." I hit the switch to open the garage door. "I'm not done paying for the last one."

Literally.

FOUR

KRISTEN

The interrogation began on the drive home.

"What the hell was going on between you and Josh?" Sloan asked as soon as we pulled out of the fire station parking lot in her crappy Corolla. "Since when do you get offended because a guy looked at your ass?"

I didn't. Nothing offended me except for cauliflower and stupidity. I just didn't want this particular ass-man anywhere near me because if he looked, I was going to have a very hard time not looking back.

Josh was the human version of ice cream in the freezer when you're on a diet. He was my type, and I was sex deprived and not a particular glutton for punishment. Few men could spar with me when I was at my saltiest, and running that gauntlet was practically foreplay for me. I didn't feel the need to torture myself unnecessarily by subjecting myself to it on a daily basis.

"If I tell you the truth, will you tell Brandon? Where do your loyalties lie now that you're engaged?"

She laughed. "Tell me."

I came clean about the spilled coffee and the shirt.

"Oh my God," she said, turning on Topanga Canyon Boulevard. "Brandon can never know. Like, ever."

I scoffed. "Yeah, no kidding. He loaned me his truck for five minutes for an emergency tampon run and I manage to spill coffee in it *and* get into a minor accident with his best friend."

I'd have taken Sloan's car, but it was impossible to start. It came with a volley of instructions. Jiggle the key while pumping the gas, put your shoulder into the door to get it open, don't let the screeching belts startle you. I hadn't wanted to find myself bleeding to death in a grocery store parking lot because I couldn't get the engine to turn over. I could have spilled coffee and gotten into an accident in her car and nobody would have been the wiser. I could have totaled it and it would have probably been an improvement.

"Why does Brandon get a new truck *and* a motorcycle and you have to drive this piece of crap?"

"I *like* my car." Sloan twisted her lips up on one side. "Josh's cute, huh?"

"If I didn't have a boyfriend, I'd get under him."

She gasped and looked over at me, wide-eyed. Sloan was a lot more sexually conservative than I was. Shocking her was one of my favorite hobbies. I never missed an opportunity.

I shrugged. "What? I haven't gotten laid since last year. And this shirt smells incredible." I dipped my nose back inside the neckline. "Like testosterone and cedar. And did you see him washing those dishes? He looked like Mr. February in a sexy firemen calendar. Guys like that are the exact reason why my grandmother always told me to wear clean underwear in case you get into a car accident."

She shook her head. "I swear to God you're a man."

"I *wish* I were a man. Then I wouldn't have to deal with all this faulty plumbing." I cramped again and winced, rubbing a hand on my stomach.

She looked over at me as she stopped for a red light. "Is it getting worse?"

It *was* getting worse.

"No, same as always."

Sloan didn't need to know the truth. She was the kind of person who carried other people's problems on her shoulders—especially the problems of those she loved. I had no intention of telling her what the doctor said until she was back from her honeymoon. Let her be ignorant and happy.

It didn't need to ruin both our lives.

~

Tyler called while I was going through my emails, an hour after Sloan dropped me off at home. I was still cramping and feeling generally like shit. I stared at the chiming phone for four rings before I picked it up.

"Hi, babe." I put more enthusiasm into my tone than I felt. That was the thing about military relationships—you didn't get a lot of calls. Maybe one a week. You had to take them when they came, whether you felt like taking them or not.

And today was a *not*.

"Hey, Kris," he said in that sexy accent of his. A little French, a little Spanish maybe? All his own. "I got the care package. You're a lifesaver."

I set my laptop on the coffee table and went to the kitchen with Stuntman trotting behind me. "Good—I worried it wouldn't come in time."

"Got here Friday. I can't wait until I can get chocolate-covered espresso beans whenever I feel like it."

"Yeah." I grabbed a bottle of Clorox and a rag and opened the fridge. Usually I paced when I was on the phone. But I cleaned when I was stressed.

Stress won out.

I started pulling out Tupperware and juice cartons and setting them on the floor, holding my phone with my shoulder. "I'll buy some so you'll have them in the pantry when you get here."

The pantry. It would be *our* pantry. I don't know why this weirded me out so much. I dragged the trash can next to the fridge and began tossing old take-out boxes.

"It's Valentine's Day tomorrow," he sang, poking me.

I made a dismissive grunting noise into the fridge. I hated Valentine's Day. He knew that. Total waste of money. "I hope you're not planning on sending me flowers," I said dryly.

He smiled through the phone. "What would you like me to send you then?"

"Something practical that I'll get use out of, like a dick pic."

He laughed. "So what's going on at home?" he asked.

I reached to the far end of the top shelf to pull down a two-liter bottle of flat Sprite. "Not much. Hey, do you know anything about working with wood?" I opened the bottle with a *pith* and turned it upside down in the sink and waited for it to drain.

"No. Why?"

"Oh, it's just Miguel quit," I mumbled.

"What? Why?"

"He got another job. I need a new carpenter. I have this one guy, but he's not the best option." I muscled the rack filled with condiments from the door. "He doesn't have a workshop like Miguel so he has to do it out of my garage."

"I don't know the first thing about woodworking, Kris. Hey,

if you put an ad out, wait for me to get home before you do interviews. There are a lot of perverts out there and you're home alone."

My mind went to my 911 call this morning. I wouldn't tell Tyler about that. It would just worry him, and there wasn't a thing he could do about it.

I carefully unloaded the mustard and ketchup bottles and started washing the empty rack in the sink. "So what's the game plan when you get out? How long until you get hired, you think?"

It wasn't like he had to worry too much about finances. Tyler came from money. But if he didn't have a job to go to every day, I didn't know how I'd handle all the togetherness.

We'd been dating for two years, but he'd been deployed the whole time. I'd met him at a bar when he was on leave. Long-distance was all we'd ever known. Two weeks of leave every year, full of sex and eating out, was one thing. Having a live-in boyfriend who was going to sit around and hang out with me for an indeterminate amount of time was something else entirely.

The whole damn thing triggered me. I was going from having a man who was almost invisible to having one that would be here 24-7.

And this was *my* idea.

He'd wanted to reenlist and I'd told him if he did, I was out. I couldn't do another deployment. But lately I was afraid I couldn't do *this* either. It's not that I didn't love him. It was just a huge change.

"I've got an interview with the State Department as soon as I get back," he said. "Might take a while before I get in. And I'll get to spend lots of time with you until I'm out of background checks."

My lips pursed. I put the shelf upside down to dry. "Yeah. Maybe we can rent a cabin up in Big Bear or something while we wait. Catalina Island. Make it fun."

"Think bigger. Why stay in Cali when we can go somewhere we've never been?"

He loved to travel.

I smiled, weakly, and went in for the next rack. Stuntman barked. He got excited when the fridge was open. I never fed him human food, but I think Sloan had been sneaking him pieces of turkey whenever she was here.

"Is that my little arch nemesis?" he asked. "That dog better not bite me again."

I pulled on the shelf. It was stuck. "Or *what*?"

"Or he's going to the pound." He laughed. He was kidding. But it annoyed me just the same.

"How do you deal with armed insurgents when you can't handle one four-pound Yorkie?" I gave the shelf a hard yank and it came away from the door with a clatter of condiment jars.

"If that fat ass is four pounds, I'll eat my helmet." He chuckled.

I laughed and felt myself soften a little. "He's just fluffy."

"I know. I'm just playing with you. You know I love your dog." He paused for a moment. "*Mi amor*?"

Our game. My lips twitched into a smile and I stayed silent. I set the condiment rack down on the kitchen table and closed the fridge door.

"*Amore mio*?" he said in Italian.

Still, I waited. I wanted one more. Maybe two.

"*Meine Geliebte*?"

German maybe?

"*Mon amour*?"

Ugh. That did it. The French always got me.

Tyler had been a military brat. His parents were diplomats and had been stationed all over the world. He knew four languages by the time he was old enough to talk. Now he knew nine. He was an interpreter. He was also one of the most intelligent men I'd ever met.

He specialized in simultaneous interpretation, a skill set all its own. He knew Arabic and Farsi too, which made him a particular asset in the Middle East. They'd lobbied hard to keep him in service. It said a lot about his feelings for me that he was willing to leave all that.

I put my back to the fridge door and slid down to the floor, a grin on my face. "Yes?"

"I know you're nervous about me coming home. I can hear you cleaning."

He knew me too well. "And you're not? I mean, let's be honest here—this is a little crazy, right? We've never spent more than fourteen days together at a time and now we're moving in together. What if I drive you insane? What if on day fifteen you want to kill me in my sleep?"

What if I want to kill you in yours?

On paper it made perfect sense. He didn't have a place of his own. Why get one? He'd be over here all the time anyway. And if he was going to be over here, shouldn't he pay rent?

This move-in thing had been in the works for six months. Tyler and I had decided on it back when Sloan and I moved out and I got my own place. It was hardly a new development. It just felt like it was barreling toward me all of a sudden.

"Kris, the only thing insane would be me spending another two years half a world away from you. It wasn't just you who couldn't handle it anymore. It's going to be great. And if it's not, you'll tell me to go fuck myself and make me move out."

I snorted and put my forehead into my hand. God, what the hell was wrong with me? "Tyler, do you ever see yourself acting crazy, but you can't stop because you're not a quitter?"

"You're the least crazy woman I know. It's my favorite thing about you. It's normal to be nervous. It's a big step." He changed the subject. "How are you feeling? Do you have a surgery date?"

"Two and a half months from now. The week after Sloan's wedding. I'm not anemic anymore," I added.

"Good. I wish I were already there to take care of you."

"Oh yeah? Are you going to buy me pads when I need them?" I asked wryly, knowing this errand was an affront to his very manhood. Men were so dramatic about buying feminine products. I never understood what the big deal was.

"Now, let's not get ahead of ourselves."

I rolled my eyes with a smile. "Lucky for you, there's only one need I want you to take care of. I'm climbing the walls."

He laughed. "As long as you're not climbing anybody else."

My mind flickered traitorously to Josh.

Tyler didn't have anything to worry about. I didn't cheat. Never had, never would.

Cheating was a completely avoidable scenario as long as you operated with the barest amount of common sense.

Like not putting yourself into vulnerable situations, such as hiring a hot fireman-carpenter to spend hours working in your garage.

Josh would be an endurance test of my willpower.

"Look, Kris, I gotta go. I'll try to call you again in a few days. No more stressing. I can't wait to see you. And I'm gonna tear you up when I get there," he added.

Now he had me in a better mood. Of course, how much

he could tear me up depended entirely on where my wacky cycle was at the moment. But I liked the offer. "I can't wait." I grinned.

"I love you."

"I love you too."

We hung up and I surveyed the chaos I'd pulled from the fridge. Stuntman sat in the middle of it, looking up at me. His little white chin looked like the beard on a nutcracker.

This is fine. It's all going to be fine.

But I spent the next three hours scrubbing the kitchen just the same.

FIVE

JOSH

Two days after our fender bender, I knocked on Kristen's door. Yapping started on the other side. I'd just gotten off my shift, and I had a heaping pile of building materials in the bed of my truck. Brandon let me raid his garage for power tools. Thank God. This job was temporary—I didn't need to be buying shit.

Kristen opened the door, wearing a pink robe and a green mud mask. "Hey. Come in."

Stuntman Mike bounced off my shins. I reached down to pet him, and she stopped me. "Don't. He bites."

"We've already met. He let me hold him at the station," I reminded her.

"He's got a misplaced sense of ownership over me and his memory is stored in a brain the size of a peanut," she mumbled. "Wait a few minutes until he calms down. Then it'll be safer."

I looked down at the little fluff ball. He growled and wagged his nub of a tail at the same time. I followed her into the house and leaned down and gave Stuntman Mike a pat while she wasn't looking.

A teetering stack of FedEx boxes sat piled by the front door. The coffee table was covered in carefully organized piles of paper. A laptop sat in the middle of it with a beer next to it, still cold. The glass bottle was perspiring. "Already drinking, huh? It's breakfast time."

"I had a Pop-Tart with it," she grumbled.

I snorted.

Her house was clean. Sparse, but clean. Smelled a little like bleach. There was a huge vase of flowers on her credenza. From the boyfriend for Valentine's Day, I guessed. I hated that holiday. Just an excuse to spend money on overpriced shit. I was glad I was single for it this year.

"Here's the garage." She opened a door off the laundry room.

A tiny lacy black thong hung from a hanger over the dryer at eye level. I looked at it longer than was probably appropriate.

I hadn't been with anyone since Celeste. I'd been too busy and worn out from the new job and the move. And to be honest, I'd been enjoying not having to deal with a woman. It was a reprieve.

It had been my experience that all women, even the ones you're only having sex with, are on some level exhausting. I wasn't in any particular hurry to get back to it.

I came up behind Kristen and peered into the garage over her shoulder. It was cavernous and mostly empty except for a few containers stacked against the far end and a newer black Honda parked in the last bay. She hit a button on the wall and sunlight shafted under the opening garage door.

She turned to me, the green mask starting to crack around the edges. "Bathroom is down the hall. Sodas are in the fridge. Holler if you need something. I'll get you a fan. It's a hundred and fucks degrees out here." She left me standing there.

Well, the reception was chilly, but at least she'd let me in.

I backed my truck up and started to unload, and she came

down the stairs and set a fan in the middle of the floor. Then she walked out into the driveway, green mask and all, and put my folded shirt into my hands. "Here. I washed it."

"Thank you." A car rolled by and the driver stared at her. I looked back at her with an arched eyebrow. "Don't you care what people think?"

"Do I look like I care?"

"No."

"There you go." She turned and went back into the house and I smiled after her.

Kristen had crossed my mind a few times over the last two days. I'd actually found myself somewhat looking forward to coming over and getting further abused.

I'd asked Brandon about her boyfriend. Not straight out—I'd asked him why she didn't have *him* build the stairs. Just an excuse to find out more about her.

Brandon only met him once, almost a year ago. Didn't have much to say about it, other than the guy seemed all right. But he *did* say Sloan didn't seem to like him for some reason. I'd pressed for more, but he just shrugged and said she wasn't a fan.

Two hours later I poked my head into the living room. "Where'd you say the bathroom is?"

She'd changed into sweats and a T-shirt and she lay on the couch with a heating pad on her stomach. Her mud mask was gone.

She answered with her eyes closed. "Down the hall, second door. Put the seat back down." She winced.

"You okay?"

"Fine."

She didn't look fine. She looked like she was having the period from hell.

"Have you taken anything yet?" I asked.

"I took two aspirin at four a.m." Even her words sounded painful.

I looked at my watch. "You can alternate with Motrin. I have some in my gym bag."

I went out to the truck and got two pills and brought them back with a water bottle from the fridge and handed it to her. She took them gratefully.

"You get a lot of calls for period cramps?" she asked, lying back against the cushions, closing her eyes.

"No. But I grew up with enough women to know the drill. Also, I'm a paramedic. You shouldn't be taking aspirin for cramps. Aleve or Motrin is better."

"Yeah, I know. I ran out," she muttered.

"I'm going to get some lunch. Want something?" I figured if I was going to eat, might as well ask her too.

She opened an eye and looked at me. "No." Then she sat up with a grimace. "I need to go to the store."

"What do you need? I'll get it. I'm going out anyway."

She clutched the heating pad to her belly and eyed me. "You don't want to buy what I need. Trust me."

I scoffed. "What? Pads? Tampons? I have six sisters. This isn't my first rodeo. Text me what you want." I turned for the garage before she could object. I couldn't care less about buying the stuff, and she didn't strike me as the kind of woman to be embarrassed by feminine products—or anything, for that matter.

She wasn't. She sent me a long list. It was all heavy-duty. Ultra this and overnight that. I grabbed her some Motrin too.

I stopped at McDonald's and got her food, figuring she was probably too sick to make something for herself.

When I got back, I dropped the bag of tampons at the foot of the couch.

"Thanks," she said, sitting up to peer into the top of the bag. "I'll write you a check. I've never met a guy who was willing to buy that stuff."

"What, your boyfriend gets worried the cashier will think he's got his period?" I said, plopping onto the couch next to her with the McDonald's bag in my lap.

She gave me a little smile. She already seemed to be feeling better. The Motrin must have been working.

I started pulling food from the bag. "Fries," I said, putting the red container in her hand. "And a hot fudge sundae." I put that in the other hand.

She looked from her hands back to me in confusion.

"My sisters always wanted something salty and sweet when they were on their periods," I explained, digging out the rest of the food. "Fries and hot fudge sundaes. They'd send me out to McDonald's. I bought it on autopilot. There's a Big Mac and two cheeseburgers too. I didn't know what you wanted."

Her face softened, and for the first time since I'd met her, it looked unguarded, like she just now decided to like me. I must have finally tamponed my way into her good graces.

"Six sisters, huh? Younger? Older?" she asked.

"All older. My parents stopped when they finally got their boy."

Dad said he'd cried from happiness.

"Wow. No wonder you ply menstruating women with ice cream. I bet when their periods synced they sat around glaring at you and making prison shivs."

I snorted. "Big Mac or cheeseburger?"

"Cheeseburger. So, how'd you meet Brandon?" she asked, setting the sundae down on the coffee table and eating one of the fries.

I handed her a yellow paper-wrapped cheeseburger. "The Marines."

She arched an eyebrow. "You were a Marine?"

"Once a Marine, always a Marine," I said, taking the Big Mac and opening the box.

She looked me up and down. "How old are you?"

"Twenty-nine. Same as Brandon."

Stuntman Mike jumped up suddenly from the couch and started barking frantically at nothing. He startled the shit out of me, but she didn't even flinch, like this was a daily occurrence. He stared at nothing, seemed satisfied that whatever it was was gone, and then he spun a few times and lay back down. His shirt today read I MISS MY BALLS.

"How old are you?" I asked.

"Twenty-four. Like Sloan."

She was mature for her age. But then I always thought Sloan was too.

"Hmm." I took a bite and chewed thoughtfully. "You seem older."

A sideways smile told me she liked that I thought that.

"How are you liking the new fire station?" she asked.

She must have seen the answer on my face.

"Really? It's shitty?" She seemed surprised.

I shook my head. "I don't know. It's all right."

"What? Tell me."

I twisted my lips. "It's just at my old station, we didn't get shit medical calls. I mean, we only got, like, three a day—"

"How many do you get here?"

"Twelve? Fifteen? It's a busy station. But the calls are bullshit.

Drunk homeless guys. Crap that should be a trip to a walk-in clinic. I went on a call yesterday for a stubbed toe."

"Well, most people are pretty fucking stupid." She ate a fry.

"My granddad used to always say, 'Even duct tape can't fix stupid,'" I said, putting my straw in my mouth.

"Hmm. No. But it *can* muffle the sound."

I burst into laughter and almost choked on my soda. I liked her wit so much more when I wasn't the brunt of it.

"You know, I never thought about firefighting being like that," she said after I'd gotten hold of myself. "It's so romanticized. Every little boy's dream," she said sarcastically.

I looked into my fry box. "It is not what everyone thinks it is—that's for sure."

I'd questioned all my life choices in the last week. So far there wasn't much that I liked about any of it. Reduced to a probie, paying through the nose for everything, running calls to put Band-Aids on idiots. Except *this* was turning out to be interesting...

"Why did you move?" she asked.

I shrugged. "I had a breakup. My girlfriend of three years, Celeste. Figured a change of scenery was due. Thought I might like the busier station. And it was getting a little too much living so close to my sisters. I realized that I liked them better when I was deployed," I said dryly.

"The breakup her idea or yours?" She unwrapped the cheeseburger and took out the pickle and ate it first. Then she dragged the bun on the paper to scrape off the onions.

"Mine," I said.

"And why?" She took a bite.

"A lot of reasons. The biggest one being that she didn't want to have kids. I did. It wasn't negotiable."

She nodded again. "That's a big one," she mumbled.

There were a lot of big ones at the end. I also didn't much enjoy supporting her shopping habit or her inability to actually work in any of the many career paths she'd chosen. She was a perpetual student, jumping from one pursuit to another and never graduating. Paralegal, vet tech, dental assistant, nursing assistant, EMT—she was the most partially educated waitress in South Dakota.

"How about you? Boyfriend, right?" I asked, looking around her living room for a photo. When I'd gone to Sloan and Brandon's to pick up tools, Sloan had photos and art and shadow boxes all over the place. Kristen didn't have anything on her walls. Maybe Sloan took it all in the move.

"Yeah, Tyler. He's coming home in three weeks. Moving in. He's a Marine too."

I took a swallow of my Coke. "First time living with someone?"

"I lived with Sloan. But yeah, first time living with a boyfriend. Any tips?"

I pretended to think about it. "Feed him and give him lots of sex."

"Good advice. Though I'm hoping that's what he does for me," she said, laughing.

Her laugh transformed her face so instantly I was immediately taken by how beautiful she was. Natural. Long thick lashes, smooth flawless skin, warm eyes. I'd thought she was pretty the other day too, but a scowl is an unflattering filter.

I cleared my throat, forcing myself to look away from her. "So doglets, huh?" I nodded at Stuntman Mike. He had his head on her lap. The tip of his tongue was out. He didn't even look real. Like a stuffed animal. "You know, he doesn't seem like the kind of dog you'd own."

She looked at me curiously. "What kind of dog do I look like I'd own?"

"I don't know. I guess I just had a preconceived notion about what kind of people own dogs like this. Paris Hiltons and little old ladies. Is he the reason why you started the business?" I took a bite of my Big Mac.

"Yeah. There were things I wanted to buy for him that I couldn't find online. So I started making them. People go nuts for their little dogs. The business does well."

That I could believe. Just with the amount of orders she'd already given me, I could tell she made a decent living. It was pretty impressive.

I tilted my head. "They're kind of useless though, aren't they? Little dogs don't really do anything."

She scoffed. "Okay, first of all, he can hear you. Second of all, he's a working dog."

"What, a personal support animal?" Everyone seemed to have one these days. "Doesn't count. A dog that hangs out with you isn't a working dog. That's not a job."

"And what exactly would count?" she asked.

"A police dog. A search-and-rescue or service animal. A protection dog. A hunting dog."

She looked at me, dead serious, and put a hand on Stuntman Mike's head. "He's a hunting dog."

"I'm pretty sure that's an insult to hunting dogs everywhere." I dug for my cell and pulled up a picture of my buddy's Lab with a duck in his mouth. "*This* is a hunting dog."

She looked unimpressed. "Yeah, that's a dog that hunts ducks. Stuntman hunts women."

I snorted.

"What? I'm serious. He's lady bait."

I glanced at him. He *was* pretty cute.

She put her cheeseburger on the coffee table and pulled her dog into her lap like a floppy teddy bear, cradling him like a baby. His tongue rolled out and hung from the side of his mouth. "How about this? The next time you go to the store, take him with you."

I shook my head. "I can't take him to the store."

"Why?"

"Uh, because he's not a service animal?"

She laughed. "Stuntman can go anywhere. He's wearing *clothes*. He's not a dog—he's an accessory."

I chewed a fry thoughtfully. "So I just walk him in on a leash?"

"No, you put him in a bag."

I shook my head with a laugh. "I'm cool buying tampons, but I'm not walking a tiny dog into a store in a purse."

"It's not a purse—it's a satchel. And if this were entirely dignified, don't you think all the guys would be doing it? It's a core part of the strategy. Men don't own dogs like this. They own dogs like *that*." She pointed to my phone. "It's adorable. Trust me. You'll be a chick magnet."

I didn't care about being a chick magnet, but I liked the idea of having an inside joke with her for some reason. "Okay. You've piqued my interest. I'll test your theory."

"And if I'm right?"

"Then I'll tell you that you were right."

She twisted her lips to one side. "No. Not good enough. If I'm right, you pose in some website pictures with my dog satchels. I need a male model."

Oh God, what have I gotten myself into? "Somehow this whole deal feels like I'm the loser." I chuckled. Whatever. I was a good sport.

"How are you the loser? I'm giving you the opportunity to use my highly trained hunting dog to lure scores of women into your bed."

I smirked. "You know, without sounding like an asshole, I don't really have a hard time getting women."

She tilted her head. "Yeah, I can see that. You have the whole sexy fireman thing going for you." She waved a hand over my body.

I took a drink of my soda and grinned at her. "So you think I'm sexy, huh?"

She pivoted to face me full on. "There's something you should know about me, Josh. I say what I think. I don't have a coy bone in my body. Yes, you're sexy. Enjoy the compliment because you won't always like what I say to you, and I won't care one way or the other if you do or don't."

~

Two days later I was back at the station. I'd just sat down in the living room after cleaning up the kitchen by myself for half an hour. The rest of the crew liked to hit the gym after dinner. There weren't enough weight benches for everyone. As the probie, I had last right to anything, let alone the limited workout equipment, so TV it was.

Brandon came into the living room with a water bottle and dropped into a recliner. "Shawn lost the book I loaned him."

"What book?" I asked, flipping the channels.

"*Devil in the White City.* I swear to God, every time I loan that guy something, he either loses it or damages it."

"Did you check the bathroom?"

"It's the first place I looked. Keep an eye out for it, yeah? I bet he set it down in the apparatus bay or something. I'm probably going to have to buy a new copy," he grumbled.

"Why'd you let him have it?"

He waved a hand. "Eh, I don't know. Shame on me, right?" He shook his head. "Hey, how's the side job?"

I smiled, thinking about Kristen. "She's cool as hell. She hung out with me in the garage a few times both days, just bull-shitting. She's hilarious."

No offense to Brandon, but Kristen was turning into my favorite co-worker. And if I had to get bossed around, I'd rather it be by her any day.

He laughed. "Uh, I was asking about the job. But I can see where your mind's at." He grinned like he'd just won some bet. "I knew you'd like her."

I gave him a sideways smile. "What do you know about her?"

Brandon was probably the one guy friend I could talk to about this. He wouldn't give me shit. And God knows I'd sat through enough talks about Sloan.

He shrugged. "What do you want to know?"

Everything.

"I don't know. Just tell me what you've seen. You've known her as long as you've known Sloan."

He thought about it for a second. "Well, let's see. She's smart."

I could see that about her. Good with math. I'd watched her figure out the totals on a few phone orders in her head, tax and all.

"She's competitive. Doesn't like to lose. The couple of times Sloan and I hosted poker, Kristen played and she made it to the final table both times. And those guys are pretty good. She's driven."

"How solid do you think her and her boyfriend are?" I asked. "They're moving in together, so it's serious, right?"

This was what I really wanted to know.

He gave me a raised eyebrow. "I know she's faithful to him, buddy."

I wasn't implying that I hoped she would cheat. But now I was curious. "How do you know?"

"I mean, I've never seen anything to lead me to believe she's ever messed around on him. And she doesn't seem like the type. She's too principled."

I liked that she was loyal. A lot of women cheated when their men were deployed. I saw it often enough when I was on tour. The long separations took their toll. It said something about her character that she stayed the course, but at the same time, I didn't like that it meant they were probably pretty serious.

"You think she'll marry him?"

He grinned, shaking his head. "All right." He picked up the remote from the arm of my chair and put the TV on mute. "You want to know what I think?" He leaned forward with his elbows on his knees and clasped his hands, going into squad leader mode. He was about to level with me. "I think she's not as into this guy as she could be."

Now here was something. I sat up. "What makes you say that?"

"I don't know. A hunch. Body language. *Sloan.* Any relationship that doesn't have the best friend behind it is going to have challenges. And I didn't get the impression Kristen was super in love with him. It seemed one-sided between them. That's just what I got when I saw them together. But that was almost a year ago. Things might be different now."

I tapped my finger on the armrest and stared at the Marine

Corps tattoo on Brandon's forearm. Mine was on my chest. We'd gotten them at the same time. "She doesn't have any pictures of him in the house. Not one." Girls like to put up pictures. It had to mean something that there weren't any.

"Eh, there's plenty on her Instagram."

I deflated again.

He gave me an amused smile. "Look, buddy, you know how it goes. You come off tour and you don't have a place of your own so you move in with your girl. It could just be that. Convenience. *Or* it could be they're really in love. You want my advice?"

I waited, looking at him.

"Stick around. One of two things is going to happen when this guy comes home. They'll either break up or they'll get married. And if they break up, you'll be the first to know. There's no deadline. You like hanging out with her." He shrugged. "So hang out with her. Be her friend."

Her friend. I could do that. That was easy enough. Anyway, what choice did I have?

SIX
KRISTEN

I stood in the door of my garage, holding a plate, looking at a shirtless muscular back bent over a half-constructed staircase. This was why I hadn't wanted him here. I knew it was going to be a problem. I had a boyfriend and I was attracted to this guy and now Josh was going to be out here, half-naked and sweaty every time I needed something from the garage.

This was a pleasant upgrade from Miguel, for sure.

Josh had been working for me for a week. He'd already done five orders and he'd done them well. He was a fairly decent carpenter. I got four more orders last night, just enough to keep him busy and shirtless in my garage until he went back to his real job for a forty-eight-hour shift the day after tomorrow.

He turned and gave me one of his million-dollar smiles. Straight white teeth, crooked upturned lips on one side. His hair had that messy thing going on, like a grown-man version of a cowlick. Then he saw what I was holding, and he deflated like a popped balloon. I made my way down the steps and shoved the plate in front of him. "I made lasagna."

He looked at it suspiciously. I couldn't cook. I didn't pretend I could. He was well aware of this. This was a Stouffer's lasagna that I'd heated up, so technically I *did* make it.

I'd made a few things I'd shared with him over the last week. Some very soggy mac and cheese, a sad-looking sandwich, and a hot dog I'd boiled in water. I mean, if I was cooking for myself, I wasn't going to not offer him some. That would be rude. After all, he'd fed me once and he was in my home.

Or maybe the rude thing was making him eat my cooking. I couldn't tell which was worse.

"Thanks." He took the plate. "It smells good," he said almost hopefully. He always ate what I gave him, but he'd also brought a lunch today and announced it loudly when he got here.

"Want to come inside and eat at the table?" I asked.

He checked his watch and wiped his head with the back of his hand. I'd set up the fan, but it was still easily eighty-five out here, even with the garage door open. "Sure."

He handed me back the plate and turned to put on a shirt while I watched the contoured muscles of his broad back disappear under the gray fabric. I averted my eyes when he turned back to me so it didn't look like I had been staring the whole time.

On the way inside, Stuntman jumped at his feet. Josh scooped him up and held him for a minute, letting him lick his face.

The little thing was a roller-coaster ride of emotions. He seemed to take to Josh though. He *hated* Tyler. In fact, I was worried how it would play out once Tyler moved in. Stuntman wouldn't even let him sit on the bed. Even thinking about how that was going to go launched me into a manic cleaning spree.

I wondered if Stuntman would let Josh sit on the bed. I bet he would.

That thought made me want to clean too.

Josh washed his hands in the kitchen sink, grabbed a Coke

from the fridge, and pulled up a chair at the table. He took a bite and made a face.

"What?"

"It's still a little frozen." He gulped hard, wincing.

I got up, collected his plate and stuck it in the microwave.

He wiped his mouth with a napkin and swallowed some soda, looking like he was trying to get the ice crystals from his teeth. "Why don't we make a deal? While I'm here, I'll do all the cooking."

I shrugged, leaning on the counter. "I'd be offended if I wasn't so fucking practical."

He laughed and his dimples creased. God, he was a good-looking man. I, on the other hand, looked like a bum.

My guilt response to the attractive male in the house was to make as little effort at looking presentable as humanly possible.

I had no way of controlling what thoughts about Josh ran through my head. That runaway train had already left the station. But I *could* control what I projected. My clothes were my outward way of saying, "Nope, not interested," while internally my imagination was naked and disrespecting my relationship with Tyler in every way possible.

My hair was in a sloppy pile on my head and I had dressed like I was about to play a mean game of volleyball. I picked the shirt with the hole in the armpit on purpose.

"Hey, I wanted to ask you for a favor," Josh said. "Can I use your guest bathroom to take a shower later?"

Josh, naked in my shower. "Sure."

"I've got a date, and I don't want to have to drive home and back."

"And do we have Stuntman to thank for this date?" I asked, hoping I sounded adequately unaffected by this news. *As I should be.* The microwave beeped and I handed him back his plate.

"You were right. He's a hunting dog," he mumbled.

"What was that? I couldn't hear you." I grinned.

He gave me a sideways smile. "He's a hunting dog. Are you happy?"

He'd taken Stuntman to the Home Depot on my challenge and he'd come back saying only, "Let me know when you want to do the photo shoot."

He put an exploratory finger into the center of the lasagna, testing the temperature, and seemed satisfied. He put his finger in his mouth to suck the sauce off it and started eating. I put my own plate in the microwave and leaned back on the counter to wait.

My cell phone pinged.

Sloan: Are you behaving yourself with your cute carpenter? 😊

I grinned mischievously.

Kristen: Nope. He just put a finger in my lasagna.

Sloan: WTH?!

I snorted.

Sloan: Okay, now my eyelid is twitching. Thanks.

Triggering Sloan's nervous eye twitch was like hitting the bell on a strongman game. I loved it. You'd think after twelve years she'd be desensitized to my sense of humor, but she never failed to get flustered.

Sloan: Remember, you can look but you can't touch. Unless you break up with Tyler 😀

I narrowed my eyes. She'd love that.

Kristen: Not a chance.

Sloan's prejudices against my boyfriend boiled down to, "I just don't see it."

It wasn't him and me she couldn't see. It was him and *us*.

I guess I kind of got why. I mean, Tyler didn't ride a motorcycle. He didn't hunt. Didn't care for poker. Preferred an expensive glass of wine to whiskey or beer. Liked theater over movies. Brandon and he had very little to discuss the one time they met except for the Marine Corps, and Tyler's job was so specialized they couldn't even really connect on that front.

Tyler didn't fit into Sloan's vision of our future, full of pool parties and barbecues. He was more of a cocktail-party and charcuterie-plate kind of guy.

I didn't like charcuterie plates. They always had weird stuff on them.

I took my lasagna from the microwave and sat down across from Josh.

"That party is coming up soon," he said. "Do you mind if I got ready here then too? It's thirty minutes in the wrong direction if I go home."

Sloan had a dinner party planned for stuffing wedding invitations into envelopes and putting together the wedding favors. It was a mandatory bridal party activity and in typical Sloan fashion, she wanted everyone dressed to the nines to take pictures for Instagram.

"Sure. Wanna share an Uber? I want to drink."

"Yeah, sounds good."

I smiled. I liked that we were going together. Aside from being fodder for my fantasies, Josh bore the distinction of being one of the few people who didn't annoy me. I liked spending time with him.

A dangerous circumstance to be sure.

My cell phone rang and I answered it, leaning over in my

chair to grab my order clipboard off the counter. I wrote the order down and hung up.

Josh gave me an amused smile. "Wow, you're so different on the phone. So professional."

"I only cuss on business calls when I'm upselling my Son of a Bitch and Crazy Little Fucker shirts."

Josh chuckled and cut another bite of lasagna with the side of his fork. "What did they order? Any stairs?"

A part of me hoped he asked because he liked coming over and wanted a reason. That same part of me purposely dropped lasagna on my shirt as penance. If I had one more inappropriate thought about Josh, I was going to have to see if I had some old curlers to put in my hair.

"He has my stairs in every room of his mansion already," I said, wiping the red sauce stain with a napkin. "Dale's my best customer. He's got six Maltese and millions. He owns a strip club in downtown LA. Spent two years in prison for tax evasion. I love the guy. Every month he orders twenty-four shirts for his dogs. He likes me to deliver them in person."

His handsome brow furrowed. "You deliver goods to a felon by yourself?"

I gave him a cocked eyebrow. "He's eighty-three. He's lonely. And how dangerous can an arthritic old man with a ponytail and a dog named Sergeant Fluff McStuffs actually be?"

He chuckled. "Fluff McStuffs? Do all little dogs have stupid names?" He took a drink of his soda.

I balled up the saucy napkin and picked up my fork. "You should name any dog according to how it will sound while yelling his name and chasing him down the street in a bathrobe."

He laughed so suddenly Coke dribbled down his chin. He choked a moment and I handed him a napkin.

"So have you planned the bachelor party yet?" I asked once he'd recovered.

"I'm working on it. It's not for another month and a half, so I have time. How about you?" He was still smiling and shaking his head.

"We're going to a day spa first. Then Hollywood in a limo to go barhopping. And I'm making her a suck-for-a-buck shirt," I said.

His forehead wrinkled. "A what?"

"Hold on—I'll get it." I went to my room and grabbed the shirt I'd been working on. When I came back out and held it up, he stared.

"Are those Life Savers?"

I'd sewn the candies onto the shirt every inch or so apart. "Yeah. Random guys pay a dollar per candy and they have to bite it off her. The ones on her nipples are five dollars. She's going to hate it."

He started laughing again.

"Where are you taking Brandon?" I draped the shirt carefully over the back of a chair and sat back down.

He chewed thoughtfully. "I'm thinking Vegas. No strip clubs. Maybe a nice resort, a round of golf. A steak house. This job is definitely helping me with the budget."

You'd never find Brandon in a strip club. It spoke to their friendship that Josh knew that. I could see Brandon going to be a good sport, but that wasn't his scene. He was kind of introverted. He didn't like dancing, wouldn't go near a karaoke bar. "He'd probably like a straight-razor shave. Maybe a bourbon tasting."

He gave me an approving nod. "I like that. Anything else?"

"Can you get a motorcycle? He loves his bike. He'd want to ride there."

That earned me a dimpled smile. "You're good at this."

"I'm full of ideas. Too bad they'd never let us do something fun for the walk down the aisle. Sloan wants it all dignified." I rolled my eyes.

"What did you have in mind?"

"I don't know. Something viral video–worthy. Maybe the lift from *Dirty Dancing* or something."

"We still could. It could be a surprise. You know they'd love it once they saw it."

I eyed him. "Do you have those kinds of dance moves?"

"Hell yeah, I've got those moves. Nobody puts Baby in the corner. Let me know when you want to start practicing."

God, those dimples.

The corners of my lips turned up. "You and I might just be the perfect best man–maid of honor match ever."

He smiled at me a flicker of a second too long and something fluttered in my stomach.

I couldn't help but think we were well matched in more ways than one.

And mismatched in the worst way possible.

SEVEN

JOSH

Why I'd decided to go on this date was beyond me. There was nothing wrong with Amanda. She was beautiful and nice, but my heart wasn't in it.

Kristen had been right: Stuntman Mike was a hunting dog. He was like a decoy, a call, and a retriever all in one.

I had stopped at a sandwich place before the Home Depot. It was by a yoga studio where a class had just gotten out, and I'd been approached by almost every woman within a fifty-foot radius. For being such a crazy shit, Stuntman Mike sure was in his element with the ladies. The little dog was all swagger and charm, letting them hold him while he licked their faces. Kristen had dressed him in a shirt that read I LOVE MY DADDY, and it had tipped the scales.

Amanda and I sat at a bar about ten minutes from Kristen's house. I'd asked her to drinks instead of dinner so I could bail if we didn't hit it off. She wore a pink, fitted dress and she smelled like peaches. Long brown hair, killer legs, nice eyes.

Too much makeup. Ordered some fruity, skinny martini with an umbrella in it. Doesn't eat cheeseburgers.

She put the tips of her fingers on my knee. "I'm going to run to the ladies' room." She bit her lip, her hair falling in a cascade over her shoulder. "They have really great salads here. Want to get a table?" She winked at me and slid off the stool.

The ice cubes clinked in my tumbler as I took a swallow of my old-fashioned and watched her walk to the bathroom.

I wondered what Kristen was doing.

I pulled out my cell phone and scrolled to her number. She picked up on the second ring. "Hey. What's up?" she asked. I could hear her fingers tapping on her laptop.

"What're you doing?" I leaned on the bar.

"Invoicing. Same thing I was doing when you left half an hour ago. That was quick. Unless you're calling me to see if you and your date can use my guest room..."

I smirked. "Can I?"

"If you change the sheets," she said without skipping a beat. "So what's our story, then? I'm your sister? I'll need details if I'm going to wingman you properly. And if she ends up being some crazy bitch who keeps showing up over here looking for you, I'm taking a hundred dollars off your paycheck per infraction."

My laugh made the bartender turn around. "I don't need your guest room. But thanks for the offer. I'll keep that in mind. She's in the bathroom."

"You're calling me while she's in the *bathroom*? Oh my God, you're bored as fuck."

I chuckled. "I just spent twenty minutes listening to the benefits of an organic, vegan diet. I haven't eaten dinner yet, and I'm craving pepperoni now. I'm, like, ten minutes from you. Want to share a pizza in a half an hour?"

"I could eat."

I grinned. The color pink approached from my peripheral vision. "Text me what you want on your pizza," I whispered.

"Gotta go." I hung up and swiveled back to my date. "I just got called in." I pulled out my wallet and put a few bills on the bar. "I'm sorry to have to take off on you."

She looked disappointed, but she seemed to believe me, which at the very least lessened my guilt at running out on her. I should have never asked her out in the first place. I just wasn't ready. I wouldn't make that mistake again.

I picked up a pizza and some Stone Brewing dark ale and headed to Kristen's, actually looking forward to going back over.

It occurred to me that this was what I should have been doing tonight from the very beginning. I didn't have to work at hanging out with her.

When Kristen opened the door holding Stuntman Mike, she was in curlers.

If I ever had any question whether she was remotely into me, her complete and utter lack of an attempt to impress me was the answer. She did not give a *fuck*.

I actually liked that she was herself in front of me. But the implication didn't thrill me. It meant her feelings toward me were totally platonic. For all intents and purposes, I might as well have been the gay friend, or a brother or something. I was friend zoned, *hard*, and this was the proof. The more I got to know her, the more this bothered me.

She must really be serious about Tyler.

She plopped down onto the couch and put her laptop on her lap. "Wanna watch something?"

After moving her neat invoice pile, I set the pizza down on the coffee table. "Sure." I sat down next to her and opened a beer for her.

There was something intimate about being in her house at night. The energy was different. The light was dimmer, and things seemed quieter. And I wasn't there to work, which was a definite change in dynamic.

She took the beer I opened for her. "Thanks." She gave me the remote. "I've gotta finish this billing though."

"How about *Death Proof*?" I asked, opening the lid on the pizza box. "You've already seen it, so you won't miss anything."

"Perfect."

I scrolled through Netflix and found it. We sat there with Stuntman Mike between us wearing his BITCHES LOVE ME shirt, drinking beer and eating pizza through the first half hour of it. Then she did a final tap on her laptop and shut the lid.

"So what was wrong with her?" she asked, propping her feet up on the coffee table.

"Who?"

"Your date."

I shrugged. "Nothing in common. And I'm just not ready to date, I think."

"Then why'd you ask her?" She looked at me, balancing her beer on her thigh.

"She was a yoga instructor. Yoga pants." I bounced my eyebrows.

"Well, you *are* an ass-man."

"Plus, I was being mobbed. I panicked."

She snorted. "Do you realize how bendy she probably was?" She took a swallow of her beer. "You messed up, dude."

I smiled, putting my beer to my lips. "Eh, I'll be all right. Besides, women like that are too much work. The better looking they are, the crazier they are." I'd had far too much experience with this.

"That's not a universal rule. Sloan is hardly crazy at all and look at *her*."

I shook my head. "I don't know. She seems like she could go off the deep end if the right guy pushed her. Brandon's just too mellow to unleash the fury, I think."

She laughed. I loved it when she laughed. Like a little reward.

"Well, your yoga instructor was a vegan, so at least you know she wouldn't have boiled your rabbit. You smell good, by the way," she said, like an afterthought.

"Thanks."

She smelled good too. When she'd given me back my shirt, some of her perfume still clung to it, even though she'd washed it. Tart apples. I didn't want to admit how many times I'd put that shirt to my nose. I didn't want to admit that I'd wished a few times I could put my nose to her neck to see if it smelled different on her skin.

I reminded myself that she was taken. The good ones always were.

What I had sitting next to me was the "cool girl." That rare woman who was gorgeous without being nuts. The girl in high school who hung out with all the guys, but she never dated any of them because none of them was mature enough for her. That girl who had a boyfriend who went to college and picked her up in his car after school. She could beat you at beer pong and had a football team who would kick your ass for saying one wrong word to her, but she'd never let them because she could handle herself.

"What?" she asked. "You've never seen a woman in curlers before?"

I was staring. Just sitting there, staring at the side of her face like a fucking creep. "I was just wondering what you were like in high school."

"Less sarcastic. Skinnier."

I smirked. "Drama club? Sports?"

"Orchestra."

"I pictured you as head of the debate team for some reason."

She nudged me. "What about you?"

"I wasn't into sports. I just kind of got through it. Not very memorable." I drank my beer. "What kind of guys did you date?"

She looked back at the TV. "College guys, mostly."

I knew it.

A cell phone rang from the end table to my right and Kristen bolted up straight. She put her beer on the coffee table and dove across my lap for her phone, sprawling over me.

My eyes flew wide. I'd never been that close to her before. I'd only ever touched her hand.

If I pushed her down across my knees, I could spank her ass.

She grabbed her phone and whirled off my lap. "It's Sloan. I've been waiting for this call all day." She put a finger to her lips for me to be quiet, hit the Talk button, and put her on speaker. "Hey, Sloan, what's up?"

"Did you send me a *potato*?"

Kristen covered her mouth with her hand and I had to stifle a snort. "Why? Did you get an anonymous potato in the mail?"

"Something is seriously wrong with you," Sloan said. "Congratulations, he put a ring on it. PotatoParcel.com." She seemed to be reading a message. "You found a company that mails potatoes with messages on them? Where do you find this stuff?"

Kristen's eyes danced. "I don't know what you're talking about. Do you have the other thing though?"

"Yeeeess. The note says to call you before I open it. Why am I afraid?"

Kristen giggled. "Open it now. Is Brandon with you?"

"Yes, he's with me. He's shaking his head."

I could picture his face, that easy smile on his lips.

"Okay, I'm opening it. It looks like a paper towel tube. There's tape on the—AHHHHHH! Are you kidding me, Kristen?! What the hell!"

Kristen rolled forward, putting her forehead to my shoulder in laughter.

"I'm covered in glitter! You sent me a glitter bomb? Brandon has it all over him! It's all over the sofa!"

Now *I* was dying. I covered my mouth, trying to keep quiet, and I leaned into Kristen, who was howling, our bodies shaking with laughter. I must not have been quiet enough though.

"Wait, who's with you?" Sloan asked.

Kristen wiped at her eyes. "Josh is here."

"Didn't he have a date tonight? Brandon told me he had a date."

"He did, but he came back over after."

"He came back *over*?" Her voice changed instantly. "And what are you two doing? Remember what we talked about, Kristen..." Her tone was taunting.

Kristen glanced at me. Sloan didn't seem to realize she was on speaker. Kristen hit the Talk button and pressed the phone to her ear. "I'll call you tomorrow. I love you!" She hung up on her and set her phone down on the coffee table, still tittering.

"And what did you two talk about?" I asked, arching an eyebrow.

I liked that she'd talked about me. Liked it a *lot*.

"Just sexually objectifying you. The usual," she said, shrugging. "Nothing a hot fireman like you can't handle."

A hot fireman like you. I did my best to hide my smirk.

"So do you do this to Sloan a lot?" I asked.

"All the time. I love messing with her. She's so easily worked up." She reached for her beer.

I chuckled. "How do you sleep at night knowing she'll be finding glitter in her couch for the next month?"

She took a swig of her beer. "With the fan on medium."

My laugh came so hard Stuntman Mike looked up and cocked his head at me.

She changed the channel and stopped on HBO. Some show. There was a scene with rose petals down a hallway into a bedroom full of candles. She shook her head at the TV. "See, I just don't get why that's romantic. You want flower petals stuck to your ass? And who's gonna clean all that shit up? Me? Like, thanks for the flower sex, let's spend the next half an hour sweeping?"

"Those candles are a huge fire hazard." I tipped my beer toward the screen.

"Right? And try getting wax out of the carpet. Good luck with that."

I looked at the side of her face. "So what *do* you think is romantic?"

"Common sense," she answered without thinking about it. "My wedding wouldn't be romantic. It would be entertaining. You know what I want at my wedding?" she said, looking at me. "I want the priest from *The Princess Bride*. The mawage guy."

I took a swallow of beer. "I'd put my wife in a chair when I'm supposed to pull off her garter, and I'd dance around her to 'Stuck in the Middle with You' like in *Reservoir Dogs*."

"Yes! And I'd want my husband to show up at the last minute all red like in *The Hangover*. The pictures would be awesome."

I turned back to the show with a smile.

This is the date I should have been on tonight. This was a date I would have gone home with.

"Hey," she said, leaning her head back on the couch and looking at me. "I'm sorry I was rude to you when we first met."

I chuckled. "So you're going to stop giving me shit about my driving?"

"No. You're a horrible driver. I meant that stuff."

I laughed.

"I had a bad week. You caught me on a really rough morning."

"Why?" I took a drink of my beer.

She paused for a moment like she was debating whether or not to elaborate. "Well, you know Miguel quit on me. And my period was pretty crappy. I haven't really been sleeping, and that morning I met you, someone tried breaking into my house—"

"Wait, *what*?" My mood changed in an instant. I sat up and set my beer on the coffee table. "Someone tried breaking in here? Who?"

My reaction seemed to surprise her. "Look, you can't tell Brandon about this. Sloan doesn't know. She's all into these crime shows and her imagination would just run wild. I don't need her freaking out on me."

"Did you call the cops?"

"Of course."

"Did they catch him?"

She shook her head. "They found a couple of cigarettes in the backyard and a beer can. It was three in the morning. Stuntman started barking. I walked the house and came around to the back door just in time to see the doorknob jiggle. The door was locked and they took off when I turned on the porch light. What?"

The look on my face must have been as pissed off as I felt.

This was not fucking okay. She was here by herself, all 110 pounds of her, and somebody tried coming in here to do God knows what to her. "Do you have an alarm system? A gun?" Why was she so fucking blasé about this?

"No. But soon I'll have a Tyler. Nothing better than an armed Marine, right?"

I frowned. "You shouldn't be here alone."

"I'll be fine." She waved a hand at me. "I didn't tell you to get you all worried. I just wanted you to know why I lost it on you. It was kind of the final straw in a week from hell. There was that and then Miguel quitting, and I was just exhausted and annoyed and you're such a bad driver, hitting people at intersections—"

"Have the police followed up with you? Has anyone else reported break-ins?"

"No. But last night—" She stopped like she caught herself.

I waited. "Last night *what*?"

"I found another can and two cigarette butts out there this morning."

My jaw clenched. That was it. "I'm staying the night here until Tyler comes back." I was dead serious. And no wasn't an option.

Her face went soft. "While I appreciate the gallantry, you're at the station half the time anyway."

"And on those days, you go to Sloan's. If you don't, I'm telling Brandon what's going on."

She blinked at me.

"Look, if this were one of my sisters, I would hope that someone would do the same thing for her. You shouldn't be here by yourself with nothing but the dog equivalent of a rape whistle to protect you. This fucker obviously knows you're here alone.

What if he would have gotten inside? Or grabbed you while you were walking the dog?" I got up.

"Where are you going?"

"*We're* going. I'm not leaving you here while I run home."

"Run home for what?"

"To get my gun."

EIGHT

KRISTEN

Josh put a hand out to me, his face stern. I didn't take it.

"This isn't open for negotiation. Let's go," he said, unblinking.

I didn't budge. "Tyler is not going to be okay with this."

"The next time he calls, hand me your phone."

"What?" Was he serious?

"Any man who would allow his girl to be unprotected in this situation is either uninformed or an asshole. Which one is it?"

Damn, he was good.

I pressed my mouth into a line. "He's seven thousand miles away. He doesn't need to worry about something he can't do anything about."

That's how you managed military relationships—you kept the bad things from each other. He didn't tell me when an IED went off under a Humvee or when a suicide bomb detonated at a checkpoint, and I didn't tell him when a creeper was coming into my yard at night to have a beer and a smoke. We kept our conversations light and fun, and that was the rule. Otherwise you lost your mind.

"That's what I thought," he said. "I'm not leaving you alone here. So you have a few choices. Call Sloan, tell her what's going on, and stay over there until Tyler comes home. Get a hotel. Or let me sleep here, in the guest room." He looked at me, stone-cold serious. "This is no different than having a roommate. There's nothing inappropriate about it. You can't be here by yourself with this shit going on."

I let out a resigned sigh. Of course he was right. And honestly, I *was* pretty scared. The first time I was moderately bothered but just figured it was a onetime deal. But this morning really freaked me out. I'd been super jumpy when Josh left on his date and I was alone in the house again. I'd been stress cleaning all day.

I couldn't go to Sloan's. A pipe had burst in her guest room last week and the bed was still dismantled. I wasn't sleeping on a sofa and I wasn't paying for a hotel. Fuck that.

"Let's go," he said.

"Do I have to put on a bra? Because if I have to put on a bra, I'm not going." I blinked at him matter-of-factly. I also wasn't taking the curlers out, for reasons already covered.

My comment earned me a break in the serious expression. I let him pull me from the sofa and I made him wait while I popped two more Motrin for the road. I was on day eleven of my period and there was no sign of it letting up, but at least it had finally downgraded from ultras to regulars.

I tried to see the silver panty liner whenever I could.

~

Josh's apartment was a studio full of boxes. He had a mattress on the floor with a sleeping bag for a blanket and a single lamp next to it that constituted all the furniture in the room. It smelled faintly like him: clean cedar.

He was opening boxes labeled "bedroom" while I waited, leaning against the kitchen counter.

"You still haven't done much unpacking," I said, looking around. I peeked into a cabinet by the microwave and found it empty.

He closed the lid to the box he was in and ripped open the next one. "I work forty-eight-hour shifts and then I go to your place and build stairs for tiny dogs. I haven't exactly had time."

He pulled out a black metal box and unlocked it. He reached in and came out with a small hand cannon.

"Wow. That's a big gun."

"You know, you're not the first woman to tell me that." He smirked, shaking out a few bullets from a box and loading it while I watched.

Goddamn it was sexy.

My phone pinged.

Sloan: Is Josh still there?

I thumbed in a reply.

Kristen: Sloan, some serious alpha male shit is going on right now. I need to focus.

Sloan: What are you talking about?

Kristen: He's pulled out his gun and he's showing it to me. It's HUGE. I'll call you tomorrow.

I turned off my ringer, imagining the horrified look on Sloan's face and grinning to myself.

I looked back at Josh. "Brandon should come help you unpack."

He put the gun back into the box. "It's fine. It's just clothes. I'll get to it eventually. Celeste took everything in the house." He stood up.

"You let her?" I asked, sliding open a drawer by the sink.

A single plastic fork and two ketchup packets sat inside. "This place is depressing." No wonder he hung out after he was done working in the garage.

"I didn't feel right leaving her with an empty house. She stuck me with some bills that I would have liked to leave her too," he said, looking around the room like he only now realized how the place must look. "She's dating a guy named Brad."

I scoffed. "Brad? I bet he wears pink cargo shorts and smells like Axe body spray."

He laughed and leaned against the counter across from me, crossing his legs at the ankles.

I cleared my throat. "My futon really sucks. Are you sure you want to do this?"

Not that I wasn't appreciative of the gesture. I *would* feel better having him there.

If Tyler wasn't moving in, someone like Josh would be the perfect roommate. He had a stable job. He was gone half the week, so I'd still have alone time, and he was really cool to hang out with.

The attraction I had to him was a major issue. I couldn't live long-term with a guy I'd want to hook up with—because I probably *would*. It would just be way too convenient. But I'd always liked the idea of a male roommate. I'd never had the option because I'd lived with Sloan right out of high school, which was great. But in another universe, I would totally have lived with a man.

He crossed his arms over his magnificent chest. "Yes, I want to do this. If something happened to you because I didn't, I couldn't live with it."

I cocked my head, my curlers shifting. "When did you stop drawing penises on stuff?"

He snorted. "What?"

"Like, how old were you when you stopped drawing penises on stuff? I was just thinking how great a guy roommate would be and I realized the only downside would be finding penises drawn in the steam on the bathroom mirror."

His dimpled smile made me grin.

"I just drew a penis on Brandon's truck the other day."

I laughed. "So men never outgrow it. Nice."

He smiled at me. "Is this really what you're standing there thinking about?"

"Welcome to my brain. Strap in and keep your arms inside the ride at all times," I said, peering into a drawer I'd pulled open with my finger.

Inside sat a photo next to a spare set of car keys and a pen. I picked up the picture. It was framed by four sloppily painted Popsicle sticks, like a kid made it. The magnet had broken off the back and sat in the drawer. It was Josh, on his hands and knees with a boy on his back riding him like a pony. I laughed and he cleared the space between us and leaned against the counter next to me.

"My nephew, Michael. Two years ago. He gave me that for my birthday."

My smile fell the tiniest bit. "You like kids, huh?"

"Love 'em."

He was standing just a little too close. He crossed his arms and it made his muscles push out and press into my shoulder. God, he smelled good.

That yoga instructor messed up running him off. If she would have just shut up about tofu, he might be over there instead of here.

Her loss.

"Do you want a big family?" I asked, already guessing the answer.

"Oh yeah. I loved growing up in a big family. I want at least five myself. I kind of thought I'd have kids by now, actually."

"Why don't you?"

He shrugged. "Didn't get out of the military until I was twenty-two. I wasn't ready yet. And then I was with Celeste. She never wanted kids, but she was a lot younger than me. I thought maybe she'd change her mind as she got older, you know?"

"And she didn't."

He shook his head. "Nope. She was fucking pissed at me for breaking things off too. That's why I gave her everything. It wasn't her fault. I was the one who changed the rules. I just couldn't stay in a relationship that was a dead end like that."

"I see." *A dead end.* "And are you going to make your wife give you all these kids you want, or are you going to adopt some of them?"

"Nah, I want them the old-fashioned way."

A disappointment I had no right feeling dropped into my stomach.

He looked at me with those deep-brown eyes. "How about you? Big family?"

I shook my head, looking away from him. "I'm an only child."

"But do you like kids? Wanna have them?"

I handed him back his photo, hoping he couldn't see the crack in my heart through my eyes. "Yeah. I do."

It wasn't a lie.

It also wasn't ever going to happen.

NINE

JOSH

She hadn't been kidding—her futon really did suck. Hard as a rock. When we got back to Kristen's, I changed into pajama bottoms and a T-shirt. I was standing over the brick of a bed, debating whether the couch was a better option, when she knocked on the door.

She stood in the hall in her curlers, wringing her hands, with Stuntman Mike at her feet looking up at me. I thought for a second she'd seen someone in the yard and had come to tell me.

"Josh? Can you come to my room?"

My wolfish grin broke some of the tension on her face.

"Oh, stop. There's a spider. I need you to kill it. Please. Before it disappears and I have to burn my whole house down."

I laughed. "Should I get my gun or . . . ?"

She bounced nervously. "Josh, I'm serious. I hate them. Please help me."

I pulled a few tissues from the box on my nightstand. "You know, you seem too fearless to be afraid of spiders."

"A black widow killed my schnauzer when I was a kid. Embracing a lifelong debilitating fear of spiders is cheaper than therapy." She stopped in the doorway of her room like there was an invisible force field, and I almost bumped into her back.

"Well? Where is it?"

She pointed to the wall on the other side of her bed. It was a decent-size spider. I could see why she was distressed.

Her room was surprisingly girly. I don't know what I was expecting. She had tons of throw pillows and a soft-looking blanket draped off the footboard. It smelled like the perfume she'd had on the day she wore my shirt—green apples.

Stuntman Mike climbed a mahogany staircase that matched her bed frame and plopped down on the pink floral bedspread with his tongue out.

The brown spider scurried a few inches and Kristen spun and did a little jumpy thing, burying her face in my chest.

I'd never liked spiders more in my life.

I put my hands on her shoulders and delicately moved her out of my way. "What would you have done if I wasn't here?" I asked, as I pressed the tissues to the wall firmly, ending the siege.

"I would have gone to Sloan and Brandon's." She squeezed herself against the door frame as far as she could go while I walked the dead spider to the toilet in her guest bathroom.

I flushed the tissues and turned to her. "Let me get this straight. You'll pack up and leave for a spider, but you have a prowler in the backyard and that you just ride out?"

"My priorities feel straight." She looked around me at the toilet like she wanted to make sure it actually went down.

"That spider looked pregnant, by the way. Thank God you called me when you did."

She flapped her hands and squeaked a little and I laughed at her. I crossed my arms and leaned in the bathroom doorway. "We got a call for a spider last week. Believe it or not, it was one of the least stupid calls we went on."

"I actually get that. I was close to calling 911 myself."

I chuckled at her.

"Well, thank you," she said. "If I can ever return the favor, let me know. Like, if you ever need a porch plant killed, I'm your girl."

I smiled and we both just stood there. Neither one of us made a move to go, even though it was late.

A mischievous grin crept across her face. "Are you tired?"

I liked the glint in her eye and I had no intention of ending this night if she didn't want to, no matter how tired I was. "No."

"Do you want to go TP Sloan and Brandon's house?"

My laugh made her eyes dance.

"I know it's a little tenth-grade retro," she said. "But I've always wanted to do it. And you can't TP a house alone—it's a rule."

"We'll have to show up there tomorrow and help them clean it up. Pretend it's just a lucky coincidence," I said.

"Can you borrow a tool from Brandon? I can text Sloan in the morning to tell her we're going to pick it up. She'll cook if she knows we're coming. Then we'll get breakfast *and* atone for our sins." She grinned.

A half an hour later I was crouched behind my truck two houses down from Brandon's, game-planning with Kristen. She still hadn't taken out her curlers.

"If they wake up," she whispered, "we scatter and reconvene at the donut place on Vanowen."

"Got it. If you're captured, no matter what they do to you, don't break under interrogation."

She scoffed quietly. "As *if*. I can't be broken." She snatched her roll and darted from behind the truck.

We made short work of it. Operation TP Sloan and Brandon's was completed in less than five minutes. No casualties. We got back into the truck laughing so hard it took me three tries to get the key in the ignition. Then I noticed she'd lost a curler.

I got unbuckled. "No curlers left behind. It's Marine Corps policy." We got out for a recon mission on Brandon's lawn.

I located the fallen curler under a pile of TP by the mailbox. "Hey," I whispered, holding it up. "Found it."

She beamed and jogged across the toilet-papered grass, but when she reached for the curler, I palmed it. "You're injured," I whispered. "You've lost a curler. The medics can reattach it, but I'll need to carry you out. Get on my back."

I was only about 50 percent sure she would go for this. I banked on her not wanting to break character.

She didn't skip a beat. "You're right," she whispered. "Man down. Good call."

She jumped up and I piggybacked her to the truck, laughing the whole way.

Those thirty seconds of her arms around my neck made my entire night.

Once we officially made our getaway and were driving from the neighborhood, she turned to me. "Hey, you wanna see something cool?"

I wanted to do anything that meant I got to spend more time with her. "Yeah, sure."

"Okay, turn left here," she said. "It's a surprise."

We drove a few miles and then she directed me into a vacant parking lot in a strip mall on Roscoe Boulevard near her house. "Park there. This is it."

I pulled into the empty lot and put the truck in park. "Well? What's the surprise?"

None of the businesses were open. It was almost 1:00 in the morning.

She unbuckled herself and sat facing me, her legs tucked under her on the seat. Her eyes sparkled. "Look." She pointed out the windshield to a run-down pawnshop in front of the truck.

"What?"

"You don't know what that is?" She grinned.

I looked back at the storefront. Just a tired shop. "Nope. What?"

She leaned over and whispered in my ear, "I ain't through with you by a damn sight. I'ma get medieval on your ass."

My eyes flew wide. "No fucking way." I jumped out of the truck and stood in front of the pawnshop, examining the windows and sign. She climbed out after me.

"Is this . . . ?" I asked in awe.

"Yup. The pawnshop from the gimp scene in *Pulp Fiction*."

I grinned up at the yellow sign. "Wow."

"I know."

I knew the movie had been filmed in California, but it never occurred to me to look for the landmarks.

"Are there more?" I asked.

"Yeah. There's the street where Butch runs over Marsellus. And the outside of Jack Rabbit Slim's is actually a vacant bowling alley in Glendale. We could drive by that sometime if you want. Most of the landmarks are gone though. The restaurant from the Honey Bunny scene, the apartment where Vincent gets killed—all torn down."

I furrowed my brow, but not because of the demolished landmarks.

This was the best date I'd ever been on. And it wasn't even a date.

I looked at her, balancing on the balls of her feet off a concrete parking lot divider. She had no makeup on. Sweats. Hair in fucking curlers. Hell, she didn't even change out of the shirt with the enormous lasagna stain on the front before we left the house. And she was a thousand times better than the drop-dead gorgeous yoga instructor from a few hours earlier.

Fun. Witty. Smart. Beautiful.

The cool girl.

And nothing that I could have.

TEN

KRISTEN

My cohabitation situation with Josh was on day five. I stayed in Mom's empty beach house the two days he went to work. It wasn't ideal. My inventory was at my house and I had to be there to get any work done. The commute was two hours. But he was right—I couldn't be in my house alone at night. It just wasn't safe.

Josh and I had developed a sort of routine. We ate almost every meal together, watched marathons of shows, took turns walking Stuntman, and did late-night food runs. I had planned to stay away from him as much as possible, but there was only the one TV in the living room and the coffee table was my unofficial office. And if we both needed to eat, it didn't make any sense to do it separately. So we just kind of fell in together.

Every morning he'd patrol the yard for evidence of my creeper. It was seriously fucking hot. Then he'd make us eggs and we'd sit at the kitchen table talking until he had to get to work.

He had just come back over for another two-day stretch. I sat on the steps of the garage talking to him. I wore a tie-dyed shirt I'd made at summer camp, like, nine years ago with Sloan. I also wore the matching scrunchie. I'd been digging deep to maintain my homeless-chic wardrobe. It was becoming more and more necessary.

I liked him. I liked him a *lot*.

He was fun. When he left for his two-day shift, I *missed* him. Big-time.

This wasn't good. I needed Tyler to come home.

Josh was telling me about a call he went on, and I zoned out watching him carve an ornate design into the side of a step. I loved that he worked with his hands. It was beyond sexy. I wondered how those hands would feel on my bare skin. Strong and rough.

I thought about that stupid piggyback ride so much you'd think it was foreplay. The press of those back muscles and the warmth of his skin against my breasts. The way he smelled. How easily he'd lifted me. I bet he could do push-ups with me sitting on his back. Then I imagined him doing push-ups over me while I lay on a bed under him.

God. I'm going straight to hell.

I stuck a finger in a tiny hole at the waist of my shirt and made a tear.

Tyler called. Coincidence? Or did he feel the threat from halfway around the world?

"I gotta take this," I said.

The phone call was like an emergency broadcast test breaking into one of my favorite shows. I'd sit through it because I had to, waiting impatiently for it to be over so I could go back to watching what I was before the interruption.

It sucked that I felt that way.

I *liked* talking to Tyler. I just didn't like talking to Tyler when it meant it took away from talking to *Josh*. I knew this was wrong. I knew it was unhealthy. And I also couldn't stop myself from feeling this way.

I hit the Answer Call button and got up and went out to the sweltering sunbaked driveway, out of earshot. "Hey, babe."

"Hi, Kris. What are you doing?"

"Hanging out with Josh in the garage. What are you doing?"

"Getting ready to see *you*. Eight days." I could hear the smile in his voice.

Yes. Eight days. Then it would be the *Tyler Show* I was watching.

"I know. I can't wait," I said, forcing enthusiasm. I studied a crack in the driveway and rolled my foot over a dandelion growing from the crevice, smooshing it onto the concrete, bleeding yellow and green.

"Have the cops gotten back to you? Any updates?"

Once the danger had been neutralized by Josh's presence in my guest room, I came clean to Tyler about the attempted break-in. "No, I haven't heard anything."

"And Josh is keeping his hands to himself?" he asked.

I gazed into the garage and Josh's eyes flickered away from me like he'd been watching.

I wondered if Josh ever thought of me the way I thought of him, or if my attempts to turn him off were successful. He seemed to enjoy my company, but he never crossed any lines with me. That was a good thing. Because if he ever did, I'd have to make him leave. Permanently.

"Josh is very well behaved," I said, telling the truth. "I mean, I wouldn't have even agreed to this if he wasn't Brandon's best friend. He was prescreened." All true.

I left out the part that I had a major crush on him and was enjoying my time with him more than I should.

"What does that guy look like anyway?" Tyler asked.

"Josh? Hot fireman." No point in lying to him. He'd see for himself soon enough. And Tyler was never shocked by my bluntness.

"Not hotter than me, I hope." He was giving me that cocky grin of his right through the phone. The guy knew he was gorgeous. He didn't sound particularly worried.

"It's kind of a crapshoot, actually. The two of you would really rake it in at one of those 'save the children' fund-raisers where the guys get auctioned off."

I'd go broke at that fund-raiser. For the kids, of course.

He laughed. "Well, tell him I appreciate him looking out for you until I get home."

"I will. So what's going on over there?" I wanted to change the subject away from Josh.

"Oh, I've got a story for you, actually."

I arched an eyebrow. Tyler's stories were great. "Montgomery?"

"Hansen," he said.

He had two buddies over there, Montgomery and Hansen, who never failed to produce good stories.

"Hansen just got back from leave. You won't believe what this guy did."

"Tell me," I said.

He launched into an animated story about Hansen's exploits and I smiled, remembering why Tyler and I were able to make a two-year long-distance relationship work. He was great on the phone. I breathed a sigh of relief that I felt drawn in again and wasn't impatient to hang up and get back to Josh.

"He's got three squad cars and a Bentley parked in front of his house at three in the morning," he said.

"Fucking Hansen."

"I know. He had pictures of the whole thing." I could imagine him shaking his head, those piercing green eyes laughing. "The guy kills me." He chuckled.

I sighed. "What are you gonna do when you're not hanging out with these guys anymore?" Both Hansen and Montgomery had reenlisted.

He went quiet for a beat too long. "We'll stay in touch. I'm not worried about it." But something in his tone had flattened. "Hey, I was thinking we could take a trip to Spain when I get back. I'd love to show you where I lived when I was a kid."

We talked for a few minutes about Spain. Then the phone muffled, like he was talking to someone else. "Kris, I need to get going. I'll give you a call in a few days."

"Tyler?"

"What's up?"

I shot a look at Josh. "I really need you to come home. I miss you."

"I miss you too, Kris. Talk to you in a few days."

We hung up and I stood in the driveway for a moment, looking in at Josh.

I did miss Tyler. The thing was, even though I missed him, I couldn't really *remember* him.

Tyler dimmed for me during these separations. It was like a dying fire. But it always blazed back up the second he was with me again. And I knew at least some of what I was feeling for Josh was because what I felt for Tyler had become fuzzy and hard to recall over so many miles and so much time.

Josh was present and clear. Of *course* he felt more distracting to me. Right? Tyler was a season I hadn't seen in eight months, and Josh was brighter than the sun at the moment. That's all it was. It wasn't that Josh was anything special. How could he be?

Josh and I had a divide between us so large we might as well be a different species. He wanted an enormous family, and I…

I just needed Tyler to come home. That's it. I needed him to come back into my life and blot out the sun.

I needed an eclipse.

Josh looked over at me and gave me his stunning, dimpled smile, and I felt my disloyal heart reach out for him.

Yes, I needed an eclipse.

But then I'd just be in the dark, wouldn't I?

ELEVEN

JOSH

Kristen and I never touched. Not since the piggyback ride almost two weeks ago.

I wanted to touch her. Hell, I thought about it almost constantly. But her boundaries were well laid. She never sat too close. I never caught her looking at me. She never gave me even the smallest indication she was interested.

And why would she? She had *Tyler*.

The second day I'd stayed the night, he'd called, and I heard her tell him the entire situation about the prowler and me staying in the guest room. She was honest with him. He didn't seem to get upset.

He trusted her.

He had every right to, at least as far as *I* was concerned. I clearly wasn't a threat.

How had I gotten myself into this? Falling for an unavailable woman. And that's exactly what I'd done in the last two weeks. I'd fallen.

I'd fucked up. I was going to pay for this when her boyfriend came back and it all ended. I should have been more careful, spent less time with her, said no sometimes when she wanted to hang out. I should have gone on dates, looked at other options.

But I couldn't do it.

Even as I felt myself tumbling down this rabbit hole, I couldn't stop myself. I didn't even fucking want to.

Today she'd taken off for a hair appointment at 10:00 in the morning and hadn't been home all day. We had Sloan and Brandon's wedding invitation thing later tonight.

It was boring without her here. She'd left Stuntman Mike, wearing his DOGFATHER shirt, and he'd become my work buddy. He mostly slept, but once in a while he'd jump up barking at phantom sounds. It kept things interesting.

At 5:00, Kristen still wasn't home when I got in the shower in the guest bathroom to start getting ready for the party. But when I came out, dressed and ready to go, my breath caught the second I rounded the corner. She sat at the kitchen counter, looking at her phone.

She was a fucking *knockout.*

She'd been pretty before, even under her baggy T-shirts and sweatpants. But now? Dressed up? My God, she was sexy as hell.

She wore a black fitted cocktail dress and red heels. Her hair was down and curled and she had her makeup on. Bright-red lipstick.

When she glanced up, I tried to act like I hadn't been frozen in the doorway.

"Oh, hey. Will you zip me up?" she asked, sliding off the stool still texting. She didn't even give *me* a second look.

I cleared my throat. "Uh, yeah. Sure."

She turned and gave me her back, still looking at her screen. The zipper to her dress was all the way down and the lacy top of a light-blue G-string peeked out. Her perfume reached my nose, and I could almost taste the tart apples on my tongue.

Fuck. This is torture.

I pulled the zipper up, my eyes trailing the line of her spine. No bra. She was small on top. Perky. She didn't need one. I stopped to move her hair and my fingers touched her neck as I gathered it to one side. I had the most incredible urge to put my lips to the spot behind her ear, slip my hands into the sides of her dress, around her waist, peeling it off her.

She has a boyfriend. She's not interested.

I finished the job, dragging the zipper to the top. She'd looked at her phone the whole time, totally unaffected.

Kristen wasn't shy or conservative. That much I'd seen over the last few weeks. She probably didn't even think twice about any of this. But I practically panted. I was getting a hard-on just standing there. I hoped she didn't look down.

She turned. "Okay, I got an Uber. He'll be here in five minutes." She looked up at me full-on for the first time since I'd come into the room. "You look nice."

I stared at her. "Thanks. You too."

My heart pounded so hard I thought she might be able to see it through my shirt. The tips of my fingers buzzed with the memory of touching her skin.

Stuntman Mike strutted over to me and plopped at my feet. I reached down and scooped him up, happy to have something to distract me. "Hey, little guy."

Kristen beamed, dazzling bright-red lips over perfect, straight teeth. "God, he really likes you. I just can't get over it."

"Yeah, we hung out all day today." I kissed the top of his head. I liked him, but this was for her. I loved the way her eyes always sparkled when I was affectionate with her dog. I pressed him to my cheek, and she melted.

She sighed. "He doesn't like anyone. He hates Tyler."

Yeah. I get that. Because I'm starting to hate Tyler a little myself.

TWELVE

KRISTEN

The party was at Luigi's, under the stars. We had the entire outdoor patio of Sloan and Brandon's favorite Italian restaurant for our night of activities. First we'd do dinner followed by a few hours of stuffing wedding invites into envelopes and putting together the favors—a hundred and fifty small jasmine-scented votive candles. Each one needed a label, a box, tissue paper, a hangtag, and a ribbon.

The caprese salad, chicken marsala, and penne pasta were served buffet style beneath a white lattice dripping with grapevines and fairy lights. Frank Sinatra crooned over the speakers.

The whole thing was *so* Sloan. She was doing her Pinterest obsession proud.

We were all seated at a long wooden farm table with fresh flowers and flickering votive candles every few feet. Sloan and Brandon's mom and his sister, Claudia, took the end of the table. Sloan's cousin Hannah got stuck next to Shawn, where he'd probably hit on her the whole night. Josh sat by Brandon, and I ended up next to Sloan, across from the two of them.

It was a perfect March night. The air was fragrant and warm.

And the spot on my neck where Josh's fingers touched me—that was still warm too.

God, he looked incredible tonight. It took everything in me not to stare at him. The second I saw him, I think an entire ovary detached and floated down into my useless uterus to wait.

I was done lying to myself. Over the last week I'd come to terms with the fact that I was more attracted to Josh than I was to Tyler. By a landslide. By a tsunami. And that was saying a lot because Tyler and I didn't exactly lack chemistry.

And it wasn't just Josh's body. It was *him.* There wasn't anything about him I didn't like. I wished there were.

He was easygoing and funny. My moods didn't scare him. He just kind of shrugged them off. He was down for anything. We hated all the same stuff—artsy indie movies with endings that didn't have any closure, pineapple on pizza, daylight savings time. Sometimes he said something right as I was going to say it, like our brains worked on the same wavelength.

Every day I searched for some fatal flaw so I could stop having these feelings. Sometimes I purposely grilled him on things, just to see if his answers would irritate me.

It never worked.

I felt good today. I wasn't cramping or bleeding for once. My nineteen-day period was finally gone, and I'd spent the afternoon getting waxed and polished at the salon. I did it because I knew I was going to this thing with Josh tonight. I was supposed to be dressed up, and for once looking half-decent wouldn't betray my feelings for him. I wanted him to think I was beautiful, just one time.

Even if I was just teasing him, just to see if I could.

Josh and Brandon were deep in conversation across the table, going on about duck hunting, and Sloan leaned in and whispered over her tiramisu. "Josh has been looking at you all night."

I picked up my sangria and took a sip. As if he intended to prove her claims, Josh glanced at me and smiled.

If I was a woman who blushed, I would have.

I hadn't talked to Tyler in days. He'd called yesterday and I didn't answer because I was watching *Casino* with Josh and didn't want to stop hanging out with him to talk to the man I *should* be talking to.

It was shameful.

But I only had two more days until Tyler came home. That was it. And then Josh would vanish back into the garage. An imaginary clock had been ticking in my mind for days, and I was panicking again that Tyler was moving in. Only this time it had more to do with losing Josh than worrying Tyler and I wouldn't work out.

I nudged Sloan. "Bathroom." I slid my chair out and set down my wineglass. Sloan got up and followed, the red petticoat swishing under her polka-dot dress.

Once in the safety of the ladies' room, she cornered me in front of the sink, grinning. "That guy is so into you."

Her pause dared me to deny it. Maybe he *was* a little into me. It didn't matter though.

Unchallenged, she went on, her eyes twinkling. "And you know what else? Brandon won't talk about it. You know what that means? It means Josh is saying stuff to him that he doesn't want to tell me." She looked positively thrilled at this bit of information.

I couldn't look her in the eye. I stared at the colorful collection of tattoos on her arm. "I like him, Sloan. Like, a lot. I haven't felt this way in a really long time." *Maybe ever.* I glanced back to her.

She broke into one of her dazzling beauty-queen smiles. "Are you going to break up with Tyler?"

And there it was.

I shook my head. "No. Josh and I are never going to be a thing."

She wrinkled her brow. "Why not? It would be awesome. Me and Brandon, you and Josh. The Ramirezes and Copelands could buy houses next door to each other, raise our kids together..."

I scoffed. "Well, that escalated quickly."

As if I hadn't thought about how easy it would be. How perfect. But it was impossible because I was no different than his last girlfriend.

I needed to tell her. I couldn't keep this from her anymore. Not now that Josh played into it.

I should have told her weeks ago, but Sloan couldn't compartmentalize like I could. It would upset her. I mean, it upset me too, but I was able to accept it as one of the shitty things that happens in life that you can't change, and go on with my day. But I couldn't explain why I couldn't be with Josh without coming clean. And I really needed to be able to talk to her about this.

"Sloan, there's something I need to tell you."

Her beautiful expression fell. She knew my tone. She knew this was bad.

I tucked my hair behind my ear. "You know I've had to give up a lot because of my periods."

She knew. We'd been friends since the sixth grade. She was well aware of my three-week-long menstruation nightmares. I got an ulcer junior year from taking too much ibuprofen for the pain. I'd missed prom because my cramps were so bad I couldn't even stand up. She'd driven me to the ER more times than I could count.

"I didn't want to drop this on you before the wedding, and I'm sorry if it messes with you."

I rallied myself to just say it, to tell her what I'd been dealing with for the last six weeks on my own.

"I'm having a hysterectomy."

Sloan's face broke instantly. Her hand flew to her mouth. "*What?*"

I'd finally gone for the nuclear option. I was done hemorrhaging for weeks at a time, suffering needlessly, not living my life. Enough was enough.

"They don't normally recommend one for women my age. It's elective. But the fibroids are severe and affecting my quality of life. The chance I'll ever be able to actually carry a baby is almost nonexistent."

"How did it get so bad?" she asked, almost in a whisper.

"Sloan, it's *always* been this bad."

She looked away from me, her eyes searching the floor. "Oh my God, Kristen. Oh my God. Why didn't you tell me? I . . . I would have gone with you to the doctor. I would have . . ." Then her mouth opened and her eyes came back up. "You'll never have a baby," she breathed.

I shrugged. "I'd never have one anyway."

She looked stricken. "But there is a chance you *could* get pregnant someday, right? Even if it's a small one, there's still the chance. If you do this—"

"Sloan, my uterus is a wasteland. It always has been. It's been one thing after another since my very first period, and now it's a fibroid-riddled holocaust too. I have the womb of a fifty-year-old and I've tried everything—you know I have. I spent the better part of the last six months bleeding myself into anemia again. The IUD I got as a last resort hasn't done a thing. I still have bleeding and cramps almost all the time. The birth control pills that were supposed to help made the tumors get bigger. That's it. I'm out of options."

The defeat moved across her face as the reality of what I was saying settled in. This wasn't some spontaneous thing I'd decided to do on a whim, and she knew it. I'd weighed my options. I'd seen multiple specialists. I'd read the "grieving my uterus" brochures. I'd talked with other women who were having the same issues and had gone through it.

"I'm not going to get better, Sloan."

I looked down at my stomach and smoothed my dress over the small, firm, distended mound that was my abdomen. I looked three months pregnant. That had been the final straw. The thing that tipped the scales. The tumors had begun to distend my uterus.

Google searches had shown me women with my condition with stomachs so full of growths they looked six months pregnant. That was it for me. The final insult to my injury. I couldn't let this continue until it got that bad. I'd given up enough dignity already.

"The doctor said they could get so big they'd make it hard to breathe. Push my other organs around. Look. Look at my stomach, Sloan."

She stared at the triangle between my fingers. "When?" Her brown eyes blinked back tears.

"April. I scheduled it for the Thursday after your wedding. I'll still have my ovaries so I don't go into menopause. I can do a surrogate pregnancy if I can ever afford it. So there's that."

She sniffled. "I'd carry a baby for you."

"And you think Brandon would go for that?"

She pulled a paper towel from the dispenser and pressed it under her eyes. "I'm sure he'd be okay with it."

I doubted that. Brandon was a good guy, but I didn't picture him being cool with his wife carrying another man's baby or loaning her body to something so serious for so long. It wasn't entirely her choice to make.

I'd already looked into it. It was no small thing in gesture, cost, or practice.

A professional surrogate would run me around fifteen to twenty thousand dollars and the in vitro another twelve grand. The success rate for IVF was only 40 percent, and my insurance wouldn't cover a dime. So basically, barring a lottery win and a lot of luck, my rust bucket of a womb was going to leave me barren and childless. I'd probably end up being that crazy aunt who wore veiled hats and smelled like mothballs with ten small dogs.

I smiled at Sloan, even though I knew it didn't reach my eyes. "Well, let's cross that bridge when we come to it. Tyler doesn't even want kids. But I appreciate the offer."

"Tyler doesn't want kids?" she asked, furrowing her brow.

I shook my head.

She blinked at me. "Are you serious? Why are you with him, then? You want kids, Kristen."

I looked away from her.

"Kristen!"

"Sloan, stop."

"What the hell are you doing? Why are you settling?"

The bathroom door opened, and some lady came in. She smiled at us, and Sloan and I stood there awkwardly while she went into a stall.

"I'm not settling, Sloan," I whispered. "The man is a ten. He's driven and ambitious. He's smart. He makes good money. We have things in common. And let's be honest here—I have to choose a man that doesn't want kids. That's just the reality of my situation. Josh wants kids. He broke up with Celeste because she didn't want them. And in the best possible case, if all the stars align, maybe I might have *one*. One baby, if I'm rich and lucky. Tyler and I are just more compatible."

She stared at me. "Oh my God, you're doing the thing. The spreadsheet thing that you *always* do. You don't pick a boyfriend like you pick what car to buy, Kristen." She crossed her arms. "You don't love Tyler, do you?" she hissed quietly. "You're not even remotely in love with that man. I knew it. I knew it when I saw you guys together the last time he came out."

"I *do* love him," I insisted.

Was it some head-over-heels, sappy Sloan-and-Brandon thing? No. Was it what I felt brewing for Josh? Definitely not. But it was love. It felt a little faded at the moment, sure. But that's because he'd been gone so long. It would come back into focus. It always did. I was mostly sure.

She shook her head. "Love is not a checklist of pros versus cons. It's a *feeling*. What are you doing, Kristen?"

What I was doing was being smart. Tyler made sense for me. He was the path of least resistance. He was exactly the kind of man I needed.

"And what if I *am* being a little rational about Tyler? More people *should* be rational about their relationships. If they were, we wouldn't have so many single moms with deadbeat baby daddies and cheating spouses who destroy their families. What the hell is wrong with being practical and looking at things logically?"

"Break up with him." She pressed her mouth into a line. "Break up with him before he moves in."

The woman came out of the stall, washed her hands, and Sloan and I stood glaring at each other in silence. The lady tore off a towel, dried her hands, and left.

"Why?" I asked once the door was closed. "What is the point in breaking off a perfectly good relationship with a decent man I care about whose lifestyle fits my own?"

"Uh, happiness? So you can maybe have a shot with Josh? Or someone like him who wants kids? How can you act like this isn't something you want?"

"Who *cares* if it's something I want?" I threw up my hands. "It's completely irrelevant. I can't have it."

She glared at me.

"So I move on Josh. And then what? We fall in love? Why? So he can maybe decide to settle? So he can date me for a few years until he feels resentful enough to leave me? After wasting a few good years when he could be with someone who can give him a family? Or worse, he stays and always wonders what if? Gives up on what he wants? That's assuming he'd even look at me twice after he finds out I don't have a fucking uterus."

She shook her head. "At least give him the chance to make the decision himself. What if he's okay with adopting?"

I blew out a slow breath. "He *did* make the decision, with the last one, who he loved and was already living with. And that man doesn't want to adopt—he wants his own kids. I *asked*."

"Okay, well maybe you *can* get pregnant. You've never tried. You can't know if you don't try, and you can't try if you don't have a uterus," she snapped.

I cocked my head. "I never used protection with Tyler. Not *once*. Not with any of my serious boyfriends going back to junior year. I've been playing baby Russian roulette for eight years, and I don't see any kids running around." I threw my arms out and looked around the bathroom. "And it's worse than it's *ever* been."

The puff of air she let out told me she knew she was losing the argument. "Just... have an honest conversation with Josh. Maybe—"

"*No.*" For the first time since we'd started talking about it, anger bubbled inside of me. "Do you think discussing my deficiencies as a woman with a man that I'm half in love with is something I want to put myself through?"

My voice cracked at my admission, and I needed a moment to regain my composure. I bit my lips together until the tightness in my throat went away.

"Why would I tell him, Sloan? To humiliate myself? To have him look at me with pity? Or worse, to get rejected? There's not going to be any rejection, because I won't be making an offer. There's no point. I'd like to spare myself this one indignity, if that's okay with you."

We stood in silence—her looking wounded and me trying to understand why something so rational felt so shitty.

I let out a long breath. "Do I have feelings for Josh? Yeah. I do, okay? He's fucking wonderful and I fucking hate that I can't pursue it. But I *can't*. I can never guarantee that I can give him kids. In fact, I can almost guarantee that I *can't*. I know how this goes and I'm not going there."

My pause let the words settle. When I continued speaking, my voice had gone so weary I didn't even recognize it as my own. "This isn't a man who wants one or two kids, Sloan. He came from a huge family. You know what he told me the other day?" Bitterness rose in my chest. "He said he wants a whole baseball team of kids. It's all he wants. And it's the one thing I can't give him. Not really. Not in any way that's close to what he has planned for himself."

I bit the inside of my cheek until it hurt and I looked away from her. "He couldn't sit with me in the bathroom and watch the little pink line show up on the stick or put his hand to my belly and feel his baby kicking. He wouldn't be able to come with me to ultrasounds or hold my hand while I push. This is a man who wants to be a daddy, Sloan. And I'm never going to be a mommy. It just is what it is."

Her bottom lip trembled and she looked like she might start sobbing.

Sloan was always the emotional one. This was why I didn't want to tell her about it. Now it was going to cast a shadow on what should have been a carefree time for her before her wedding. I should have never said anything. It was selfish of me.

I sighed. "Sloan, you're a romantic. You have some vision in your head of us being pregnant together and the four of us going on vacations and pushing jogging strollers around the block. You'll just have to adjust."

She swiped at her eyes with her thumb. "I hate this. I hate that you have to give up so much."

"I'm not. Don't think about what I'm giving up. Think about what I'm getting *back*. The thought of never having to have another period for the rest of my life makes me want to fucking cry from happiness. I'm so ready to be done."

She looked so miserable you'd think *she* was having the hysterectomy. I hated it and I loved her for it.

I put my hands on her arms. "You know what I really need? I just need you to listen and support me. That's it. Tell me you can do that."

Please. Be my friend. I need you.

She nodded, closed the space between us, and hugged me. The familiar smell of her honeysuckle perfume—of my best friend—grounded me, and I realized how hard it had been not being able to talk to her about it, or tell her how Josh made me feel.

"Sloan?" I said after a moment, my chin over her shoulder.

"Yeah?"

"I TP'd your house with Josh."

She sniffled. "I know."

I laughed a little and squeezed my eyes shut.

"The Josh thing would have been so cool," she whispered into my ear.

It *would* have been cool. But men like Josh weren't for me anymore. They'd never be for me again. Men who wanted pregnant wives and big families, sons that looked like their dads—these men weren't the ones I could choose from. I could have Tylers. I could have more dogs. A bigger career without kids to distract me. I could have more disposable income and a clean house without crayon on the walls and dirty diapers to change. I could be the cool aunt.

But I couldn't have children.

And I could never, ever, have Josh.

THIRTEEN

JOSH

Sloan and Brandon had said goodbye to their guests. Just Kristen and I stayed behind fulfilling our maid-of-honor and best-man duties helping them load the finished wedding favors and invitations into Brandon's truck. Kristen, Sloan, and I stood on the patio watching the busboys blow out candles and clear the table while Brandon signed the charge draft.

"Good party," Kristen said to Sloan. "We got it all done."

Brandon handed the check to the server and came up behind his fiancée, wrapping his arms around her shoulders. Sloan smiled, leaning into the kiss he put on her cheek.

Kristen got out her phone, and I watched her pull up the Uber app.

"Want to go get something to eat before we go home?" I asked her, hoping she'd go for it.

We'd been working on our projects for the last three hours, so it *had* been a while since we ate dinner, but my invite was just an excuse to stay out with her because I wasn't staying the night tonight.

Or any other, probably ever again.

The backyard intruder had been apprehended. Some kid from the neighborhood, fucking around in people's yards. I hadn't told her. I needed to, but I just couldn't bring myself to say it yet. The second she knew they caught the guy, I wouldn't have any reason to sleep over tonight. I had work the next two days and when I came back, it would all be over. Tyler would be home.

This was my last night with her.

I tried not to let the disappointment darken my mood and ruin the little time I had left.

"Sure. But I can't find an Uber," she said, looking at her screen. "The nearest one is twenty-three minutes away. The bars must be getting out."

"You can take my car," Sloan said, hugging Brandon's arms to her chest. "We took two cars over since I had to get here early. I'll just ride home with Brandon."

Kristen shook her head. "I'm not driving that thing."

"I can handle it," I said. "I can drive anything."

"Can you?" Kristen eyed me.

"Ha ha. Give me the keys. I have work tomorrow. I haven't had anything to drink besides the champagne toast."

Sloan handed them over and we said our good-nights. Something was off with Sloan. She gave Kristen a hug that was a little too long to be casual, but Kristen's face was unreadable.

"So where do you want to eat?" I asked as we walked out into the parking lot to the click of Kristen's red heels.

"Tacos. I know a late-night place."

This made me smile to myself. She always knew exactly where she wanted to eat. She wasn't one of those women who gave you the "I don't care" speech and then rejected every suggestion you made. When I pointed this out to her last week, she said she's already thinking about what she wants for dinner while she's eating breakfast. I loved that about her.

I loved a lot of things about her.

When I opened her door for her, it creaked miserably. Sloan drove an old Corolla. It looked like a car you'd find in a junkyard. It was a serious piece of shit.

The door on the driver's side stuck, and I had to muscle it open. I got it started, but just barely, and I pulled out of the lot to the squeal of belts. Kristen pointed for me to turn left.

I looked at her. She was so beautiful tonight. The subtle hints of gold in her hair, the depth of her eyes, the fit of her dress. I had to drag my gaze back to the road. "Everything okay with you and Sloan? You guys spent a long time in the bathroom earlier."

"Fine." She looked out the window.

She wasn't going to tell me. I dropped it.

"Hey. I forgot to tell you something," I said reluctantly.

She turned back to me, and I thought I saw the flicker of something sad or tired in her eyes. "Tell me what?"

"I'll be out of your hair tonight. Today, when you were out, your neighbor across the street brought his son over. Apparently he and his little friend were stealing beers from his dad's fridge and drinking them in your backyard. They tried to get into your house to steal liquor. The good news is you've got a kid whose dad is making him mow your lawn for the next month."

I looked over at her, and the expression on her face looked like disappointment.

Disappointment.

Could she feel the same way about this that I did? Was it possible she didn't want me to leave either?

"Oh. Well, I'm glad the mystery is solved and you're off the hook," she said.

"Can I be honest?" I paused, debating what to say. "I liked

hanging out with you." It was the closest thing that I could bring myself to say to her without feeling like I was crossing a line.

"I liked hanging out with you too," she said quietly.

The silence between us was heavy.

Why did I feel like we were breaking up? I guess in a way, we were. The two of us as we knew it was about to be over.

On Monday when I got to her house, I'd have to meet this guy. Shake his hand. See them together. I didn't think I could do it. I really didn't. I was going to give her my notice. I'd help out until she found someone, but I couldn't stick around after this.

The taco place ended up being a food truck. It sat in a vacant parking lot in the seediest part of Los Angeles with poor lighting and grass poking out from the cracks in the asphalt.

It made me wish I had my gun.

Tents on the sidewalk lined the outside of the lot's fence, and the streetlight over the entrance flickered.

"Are you sure you want to eat here?" I asked, turning off the engine and scanning our surroundings, not liking at all what I was seeing. Buildings with broken windows, graffiti on the walls. I responded to calls to areas like these frequently. None of them good. Stabbings, overdoses—*rapes.*

"Why? You don't have to parallel park. What's the problem?"

I scoffed. "Really? Parallel parking is the only thing that would keep you from eating here? Look at this place."

"These are the best tacos in the city," she said, getting unbuckled. "And don't pretend you know how to parallel park. We both know how well you drive." She grinned at me.

An old homeless guy who had been sitting on the inside of the fence shambled toward the car. "Nope. Let's go." I said, turning the key in the ignition. It made a weak cranking noise that I didn't have time to process because Kristen opened the door and got out.

"Shit," I mumbled, quickly following. The door didn't close all the way when I slammed it, but I didn't have time to fix it. The homeless guy was almost to the car, and Kristen was... *walking toward him*?

"Hey, Marv," she said as I bolted in front of her to put myself between them. I threw an arm across her chest and a hand out to stop the toothless man's advance.

"Hey," Marv said, ignoring me and talking around me to Kristen like I wasn't there.

She rummaged in her purse and handed him two dollar bills over my arm.

"Enjoy your food. Your door's open, son," the guy said before shuffling back to the fence.

Kristen turned to me. "He's the guy who watches the lot. Come on." She motioned to the taco truck.

My heart still thrummed in my ears. "Are you serious? The guy who 'watches the lot'?" I followed her, looking over my shoulder back at the man.

"Yeah, it's a thing. Kinda the Skid Row version of valet. He picks up trash, keeps the shady guys out. He does a good job. Look, no needles anywhere. And that guy'll shank somebody for so much as looking at our car. Not that it's anything to look at." She gave me a crooked smile.

I shook my head. "You have no survival instincts, do you? You deliver dog sweaters to a felon, hunker down when you've got a prowler in the yard. Now you're paying off homeless guys who 'watch the lot.'"

"Hey, my instincts are spot-on. The prowler turned out to be a nonissue. And anyway, I already know how I'm going to die."

We stopped in front of the truck window. The generator made a whirring noise, and the scrape of spatulas on a sizzling grill clinked from inside.

"How?" I asked.

"Spider bite. Or being sarcastic at the wrong time."

I chuckled as two more cars pulled into the lot in quick succession. A nice SUV and an older model Honda. The rest of my guard dropped.

"Do you like everything?" she asked. "Onions? Hot stuff?" The smell of cooking meat drifted out of the window, and a gray-haired man in a dirty white apron waited for our order as moths fluttered around the light over the whiteboard menu.

"I eat everything," I said.

She ordered for us, and I paid, putting a twenty through the window before she had a chance to object.

"This isn't a date," she reminded me, trying to hand over her own cash. She never let me pay.

"Yeah, but you paid for our protection," I argued.

She didn't look pleased, but she accepted my excuse. I watched her standing there, and a twinge of regret that this *wasn't* a date washed over me.

I couldn't believe I had to give her up.

When our food came out, she gave three tacos to Marv and we sat on the hood of the car to eat.

"That was pretty sexy back there when you went Marine Corps on that guy," she said as she pulled off her heels and chucked them through the open sunroof.

"I wouldn't have let him touch you." I wouldn't let anyone hurt her, ever.

She took a sip of her Sprite. "I know. That's what was sexy about it."

For all her claims that she found me sexy, it did me no good whatsoever. She didn't want me. None of this would continue once her boyfriend was here. I wouldn't be able to take her out for tacos or show up with pizza. I wouldn't even be able to sit in her living room with her.

I wondered if this thought had any effect on her, or was she just happy that her boyfriend was going to be home?

Probably that last one.

I sat looking out over the lot, a sucking sense of loss pulling on my heart.

She was like a unicorn. A mythical creature. An honest, no-drama woman who didn't bullshit and drank beer and cussed and didn't care about what people thought of her. She was a unicorn, tucked in the body of an attractive woman with a great ass.

And I couldn't have her. So I should just stop thinking about it.

We finished eating and got back in the car. I didn't want to take her home. Or rather I *did*, but not to drop her off.

I considered asking her to go do something else, just to make it last, but it couldn't be anything that felt like a date. She wouldn't agree to that. But I didn't know Los Angeles. I had no idea what was open. And there was only so far I could take this without it verging on inappropriate for a woman with a boyfriend and healthy boundaries. So I reluctantly prepared to take her home.

This was it. The last time I'd have her alone. The final moments.

I'd had all I was going to get.

I turned the key in the ignition and the engine didn't turn over. My eyes flitted to hers and I tried it again. The cranking turned into a click.

"Shit," I said, rejoicing internally at the idea of being stranded with her in a dodgy parking lot in the middle of the night.

"Do we need a jump?" she asked, peering at me with her pretty brown eyes.

"Probably," I grumbled, doing my best not to seem pleased at this development. I got out and flagged down the guys in the Honda still eating in their car. One unsuccessful jump start later and I was calling a tow truck.

"I'm going to give Brandon so much shit for this. Sloan should not be driving this thing," I said, getting back into the driver's seat to wait. That part was true, but for the sake of extending our night, I couldn't be happier that Sloan drove a piece of crap. I had to slam the door three times to get it to shut, and I was more than happy to do it.

"She's sentimental. This was her first car. Sloan can never bear to part with anything." She lowered her seat all the way back until she was lying down, and she turned on her side to face me, her arm tucked under her head. "She still has the ticket stubs from the first movie we went to, like, twelve years ago."

The way she was lying showed off the curve in her hips. I could almost picture her like that next to me in bed. Her lipstick was gone, but the stain was still on her lips, making them look pink and supple. I wanted to put a thumb to her mouth, see if it felt as soft as it looked.

She looked out of place in this shitty car with torn, faded fabric on the seat under her, duct tape on the glove box. Like an elegant leading lady right out of a black-and-white movie, dropped into a scene that didn't make any sense.

I tore my gaze away, afraid she'd notice me staring.

"Lie down with me," she said. "We have what? A forty-five-minute wait? Might as well be comfortable."

I lowered my seat and stared up through the sunroof at the Los Angeles version of stars—the planes lining up to land at LAX.

We sat in silence for a minute, and I thought of that scene in *Pulp Fiction*, when—

"You know what this feels like?" she asked. "That scene in *Pulp Fiction*, when—"

"Comfortable silences. When Mia Wallace says, 'That's when you know you've found somebody really special. When you can just shut the fuck up for a minute and comfortably share silence.'"

She made a finger gun at me. "Disco."

We smiled and held each other's gaze for a moment. A long, lingering moment. And then, just for a second—a split second—her eyes dropped to my lips.

That's all it took.

In that moment, I *knew*. She'd thought about kissing me just then.

This isn't one-sided.

It was the first hint I'd seen that she was interested. That she thought of me as more than just a friend.

Encouraged, my heart launched into rapid fire as I started debating my options.

The boyfriend.

My threshold for being respectful to this lucky, absent bastard was evaporating. I was going to make a move on her. If I didn't, I'd never forgive myself for not trying. If there was even the slightest chance she might be into me, I *had* to try.

But how? Should I just try to kiss her? Would she tell me to go to hell?

Probably.

What if I slid my hand over hers? Would she yank it away? She would. I knew she would.

I needed something else. Something less. More subtle. Something that could go either way to test the waters. Something that could *lead* to something else.

"Hey, I give a decent foot massage if your feet hurt." I nodded to the center console where her heels still sat after being dropped through the sunroof.

To my surprise, she pivoted until her back was against the door, and she swung her legs over into my lap. She put an arm behind her head and leaned back. "Go for it. Those heels were killing me today."

I grinned inwardly that my strategy worked and put my back to the door while I took her tiny foot in my hand. "I'm a foot massage master. 'I don't be tickling or nothing,'" I said, giving her a *Pulp Fiction* line.

She snorted. "I'm exfoliated and pedicured. *Someone* should touch them."

I thought about what Vincent Vega says in the movie, that foot massages mean something. That men act like they don't, but they do and that's why they're so cool.

This meant something, and I knew she knew it. She was as familiar with that movie as I was. She had to be making the connection.

And she'd allowed it.

I reveled in the chance to touch her and at the unspoken meaning behind her letting me do it.

"So, Foot Massage Master, what other tricks do you have in your bag?" she asked, giving me a sideways smile.

I pressed a thumb into her arch and circled it around with a smirk. "I'm not giving you my trade secrets." *What if I need them?*

She scoffed. "Your gender doesn't have any secrets that every woman hasn't already seen by the time they're twenty."

I arched an eyebrow. "Ever heard of the naked man?"

She rolled her eyes. "Oh God, the naked man. That one's the *worst.*"

I laughed. "Why? Because it works?"

She scrunched up her face. "I have to admit it *has* worked on me in the past. I mean, the guy's naked. Half the work is done for you already. It's kind of hard to say no. But when it doesn't work, it's so cringey."

I tipped my head from side to side. "It's risky. I'll give you that. You have to know your audience. But big risks can reap big rewards."

"Waiting for your girlfriend to leave the room and then stripping naked to surprise her when she gets back is so unoriginal though. You men have no new material. I swear you could go back twenty thousand years and peek into a cave and find cavemen drawing penises on everything and doing the naked man and the helicopter."

I pulled her foot closer and laughed. "Hey, don't knock the helicopter. It's the first move we learn. It can be a good icebreaker."

"The helicopter should be banned over the age of eight. I'm just going to spare you the illusion right now. No woman is sitting around with her girlfriends going, 'Gurl, it was the sexiest helicopter I've ever seen. Totally broke the ice.'"

I chuckled and ran my hand up her smooth calf, rubbing the muscle. I pictured that delicate ankle on my shoulder where I could kiss it, run my palm down the outside of her thigh, pull down those light-blue lace panties...

She smiled. "Have you ever seen the buttback whale?"

"No."

"Now *that's* a rare sighting."

I took her other foot and started working on it. "What is it?"

"It's when you're in a pool or a lake or something and you—You know what?" She waved me off. "It's just better if you see one in person. I'm not going to ruin it."

I laughed. "What? You dangle buttback whale in front of me and then just take it away?"

She shook her head. "It's too magical. If I tell you, it's just going to take the wonder from it when you finally see one."

I started to tickle her. "Tell me."

She shrieked and tried yanking her foot away, and I held her tighter. "What is the buttback whale, Kristen?"

"Okay! Okay! I'll talk!" She twisted and giggled and I stopped tickling her, but I kept her foot.

Her dress had inched up her thighs in the struggle, and I gave the bare skin an appreciative glance. She saw me do it.

She smirked at me and tugged the fabric down. "All right, the buttback whale is when you pull your swim trunks down under the water and then you come out like a whale breaching the surface, flashing whoever is in the pool with your butt."

I grinned. "How have I never heard of this?"

She shook her head. "No idea. You men are always looking for ways to moon each other. I'm sure it was a man's idea."

"I'm going to do it to Brandon the next time I'm in a pool with him."

She put her arm back behind her head. "Oh, well make sure you give me a heads-up. It's been years since I've seen a buttback whale." She gave me a wry grin.

I hoped it meant she wanted to see my bare ass.

When I pressed both thumbs into the ball of her foot, she bit her lip. "Damn, you're good at that."

You should see what I could do with the rest of you.

I kept circling my thumbs. "So what about you? Any tricks of the trade?"

She snorted. "I'm a woman. I can go into a bar penniless wearing sweats and a questionable rash and come out with left-overs and a buzz."

I was laughing at this when her cell phone rang. She reached for her purse and fished out her phone. "It's Tyler." She didn't answer it. She turned off the ringer.

"You're not going to answer it?" She didn't answer the last time he called either.

She didn't make eye contact with me as she put her phone back. "Nah."

When she finally looked at me, we gazed at each other for a moment.

"Why?" I asked.

One little three-letter word. Such a loaded question. I didn't want to talk about Tyler. I wanted to talk about why she was ignoring him when she was with me.

The first time had been noteworthy. But this was a statement. Even if she was busy, she still should have answered, just to make sure it wasn't an emergency. He was in a war zone.

She pulled her feet from my lap. "I just didn't think you'd want to sit here and listen to me on the phone." She shrugged.

I wasn't buying it. I called bullshit. "And what about the other day? That's two calls you missed. It's hard to call on deployment."

"We were watching a movie," she said defensively.

A weak excuse. A movie we'd both seen half a dozen times. We weren't even paying attention to it when he'd called. We'd been talking.

"Why aren't you answering his calls when you're with me?" She was too honest to deflect a direct question.

I might be reaching. I might hate the answer. I might be totally out of line, but I had to ask it. I had to know if time with me was as important to her as it was for me.

For me, even the seconds mattered.

She stared at me, her lips slightly parted. I could see her struggle with the answer.

Tell me.

Then she looked over my shoulder.

The tow truck had pulled into the lot.

FOURTEEN

KRISTEN

Thank *God*. Saved by the tow truck.

Josh gave me a long look before he put his shoulder into the door to get out and meet the driver.

I knew this wasn't over. He was going to keep asking. I couldn't do it. I wasn't going to lie, but I wouldn't answer. The truth wouldn't be fair to anyone. What was the point in telling Josh I was hoarding every moment with him? Why?

My feet still tingled where he'd touched them. It radiated through my body like electricity, turning on everything as it went up. The memory of his strong, rough palms made my breath shudder. It was too easy to imagine those hands slipping under my dress.

I'd wanted him to touch me, and he'd offered me a chance to let him do it. I couldn't say no. I'd let him because it was all I'd ever get.

I put my heels back on, grabbed my purse, and got out to join Josh by the truck. He watched me as he talked to the tow truck driver, and I felt his eyes on me like they were hands.

It was getting chilly. Past midnight. I stood hugging my arms as Josh signed some paperwork on a clipboard. He turned back to me and closed the space between us as the tow truck guy started hooking the car up to the hoist.

"Cold?" Josh peeled off his jacket before I could answer and threw it around my shoulders in a halo of his cologne. I had to fight to keep my face neutral. The jacket was warm from his body, like it was him wrapped around me.

"Thanks," I said. "I'm sorry this happened. You have work tomorrow morning."

"I'll be okay." He rubbed my arms over the jacket, trying to warm me.

He never touched me, and now he'd touched me twice in a matter of minutes, like some unspoken boundary had dissolved.

I wished he would slip his arms around me. He looked like the kind of man who gave great hugs. Bear hugs. The kind that enveloped you.

For a second I wanted to ask him if I could hug him. I bet he wouldn't say no. But I'd already played with enough fire for one day, and that would be crossing a line.

The foot rub had been crossing a line.

But God, I wanted the hug. I wanted it so badly the pull toward him felt physical, like the ocean dragging against your ankles when the tide pulls back.

But I had to maintain boundaries. For so many reasons—Tyler being the least of them.

Josh nodded to the car. "I'm having it towed to a shop by your house so we can get a ride with him and then just walk the rest of the way home."

The tow truck guy spoke over the sound of clinking chains. "You kids are gonna have to lap sit. I got my dog with me."

My eyes flicked to Josh's, and I shook my head quickly. "No. I can't sit on your lap."

The words were coming out of my mouth before I knew what I was saying. But I couldn't. I *really* couldn't. If I sat on his lap, the temptation would catapult me. "I'll look for an Uber."

I started punching into my phone, opening the Uber app.

"What? Are you serious?" he asked.

"Yeah. We don't fit in there, so no choice."

He made an impatient noise. "Look, I've gotta be at work in a few hours. I'm still an hour from getting home if I leave *right now*. Can we just do this?"

I shook my head, staring at my phone. I got an Uber. Then the driver immediately canceled the trip. *Fuck!* It was the area. Nobody wanted to come to this part of downtown this late. It was too dangerous. "Then go. I'll be fine here. I'll call a cab."

Josh's eyes bored into me. I could feel them, but I didn't dare look up.

"Kristen, we're practically in Skid Row. I'm not leaving you here. If you stay, I stay. And if you make me stay, you're making me lose sleep."

I looked up at him, my eyes pleading. "I can't sit on your lap," I said again. I didn't bother with an excuse. I didn't like to lie. Let him think this was about Tyler.

He raked a hand through his hair, shaking his head. "I don't get this, Kristen. You're way too practical for this. We have a ride. He's here. *Now*. We'll be at your house in fifteen minutes. I don't care if you sit on my damn lap."

"I've got a boyfriend." Not an excuse. Not a lie. Completely factual.

"Well, I'm not going to tell him this story if you're not. Let's go." He started for the door of the tow truck, his tone final.

It was wrong. It was wrong because how much I wanted it made it wrong. A fifteen-minute ride sitting on Josh's lap—it would be an eternity. And I would love every second of it and hate myself for it.

I looked around desperately, like a cab might suddenly appear from the shadows. Instead, the taco truck tapped its horn as it drove past us, leaving the lot. Even Marv had disappeared. The vacant lot with its dim lighting and wall of tents immediately looked menacing. We didn't even have a car to sit in and wait while I tried to get a taxi to come get us.

He was right. We had to take this ride.

I let out a breath, steeling myself for what I had to do.

Josh got in first, sliding in next to an old white-faced golden retriever who took up most of the cab.

I was hot suddenly. *Really hot.* I took off his jacket and folded it over my arm and climbed in after him. He pulled me onto his knees, strong hands on my waist, and I draped the jacket over my lap.

Josh leaned over to close the door, his chest pressing into my body, and I held my breath at the contact.

Fuck, I can't do this.

It was sensory overload. So much of him at once I felt dizzy. I wanted to leap off his lap and into the parking lot where I would be safe from myself. But he was the sun. His gravity was too strong, and now that I was so close, I couldn't get out of his pull.

He slammed the door and sat back against the seat while I perched sideways on his knees, my back stiff, trying to keep my breathing steady. He made an exasperated sound, like I was being ridiculous, and pulled me closer until my shoulder pressed into his chest. He wrapped the seat belt around us, folding into me as he did, and buckled it in.

The cab smelled like dog and gasoline.

And Josh.

His breath tickled my cheek. "There. Is that so bad?" he asked, his voice low.

It was terrible. So fucking terrible. Because it was wonderful and it was so much more than I could handle. He was warm and firm, and he smelled incredible. It made me want to rest my head on his shoulder and nuzzle his neck with my nose, and if I did, and he tipped his head down, I'd kiss him and there would be no stopping me.

I couldn't even look at him. We were so close together that if I did, I was afraid our lips might touch.

I tried to relax. I leaned back into him, acting like none of this was a big deal while I secretly obsessed over every point of contact—the back of my thighs on his, the hand that he had set on his knee where his fingers absently grazed my leg, the arm he had casually wrapped around my waist.

It felt like we sat there for hours before the guy got in and started the engine.

Part of me relished every second, sitting there so close to Josh. The other part of me was tortured—teased.

If things were different... if my uterus didn't make us an impossibility, if I didn't have a boyfriend—I'd have kissed him right there where he sat, in front of Tow Truck Guy and Old Dog, and I wouldn't have thought twice about it.

But things weren't different. They were what they were.

The truck lumbered out of the lot and Josh held me in place, the muscles of his strong arm keeping me steady.

The roads were empty, the occasional cop car the only sign of life.

I tucked my hair behind my ear and licked my lips, not knowing where to look. I glanced over at Josh, expecting his eyes to be forward, looking out the windshield, but instead they looked at my mouth.

So I looked at his.

Our gazes flicked back up at the same moment, and our eyes locked.

Oh God, Sloan was right. He was into me. And I was into him.

And now he *knew* it.

The truck swayed and the driver fiddled with the radio, and Josh looked at me, his brown eyes hooded. I could feel his soft, warm breath on my face, the steady in and out of his chest, and my resolve wavered. I couldn't hold my ground. How could I? I couldn't even pull my eyes away.

His lips parted and the arm encircling my waist wrapped around me another fraction. The fingers by my leg slid over my knee until his warm palm cupped my bare skin.

The movements were subtle. So minor they almost seemed insignificant. The tow truck driver wouldn't even have noticed it if he'd been looking right at us. But to Josh and me, they were milestones. Questions and answers. Risks and permission.

When I didn't make him stop, his eyes dropped back to my lips, his expression darkening in a way that made me lose my breath.

He wants to kiss me.

Would he do it? Right here in this tow truck?

Yes. He would.

Because if I were him, unattached and without reasons not to, I would too.

My already pounding heart launched into fluttering. If he leaned in, I was physically incapable of turning away. I would let him close the space between us and press his mouth to mine.

I wanted to know what he tasted like. What his lips would feel like touching me. I was losing sense of time and reality as everything closed in around us and became him, smaller and smaller, nothing but his face, those eyes, his head tilting, noses touching, breath on my bottom lip—

You're not a cheater.

I jerked back before I lost the power to do it, turning my face hard to the windshield, gasping for air.

The spell was broken.

He pulled his hand away from my knee. His grip around my waist loosened. I could feel the disappointment in the set of his body.

I wondered if he could feel it in mine.

Finally the tow truck pulled into the parking lot of the auto shop. I unbuckled us and scrambled off him, hopping out as soon as the wheels stopped turning, and started walking the three blocks toward my house without waiting for him.

"Kristen, stop!"

I kept walking.

He had to deal with the tow truck driver, and I needed to put space between us and that ride. I needed to put *Tyler* between us, where he belonged. Tyler, who didn't care if I couldn't give him kids. Tyler, who wouldn't be affected one way or another if I had my uterus yanked.

I pulled out my cell phone to play the message he left me, hoping the sound of his voice would smack me back into reality, ground me again, make me realize that no, I didn't want Josh—I wanted my boyfriend.

But it wouldn't.

Sloan was right. I had settled. Because anything less than Josh would be settling.

How did I get here? How had I fallen so far into this fucked life that I didn't even want? I was a frog in a pot of boiling water.

I dialed my voicemail, struggling to catch my breath, emotion sucking up all the air. I called to hear Tyler's message like it was my duty. Like it was something unpleasant I had to get through out of sheer obligation.

"Hi, Kris..."

Would Tyler and I share comfortable silences? Would he annoy me when he was here day in and day out?

He would annoy me because he couldn't be Josh. Because he would make Josh disappear. And it would change the way I felt about Tyler. It wouldn't even be fair to him, but I knew it would happen. I would resent him.

My throat got tight. I was a horrible person. It was traitorous to feel this way about another man, but I couldn't stop the landslide. I couldn't remember what Tyler smelled like. Couldn't remember the way his arms felt around my body.

Everything was Josh.

"...I probably won't be able to call you again for a few days and I really hoped we could talk tonight..."

I forced myself to keep the phone pressed to my ear, forced myself to endure the decisions I'd made as they tumbled over me and buried me in rubble. Every choice was another stone on the pile. The hysterectomy. *Boulder.* Asking Tyler to move in. *Boulder.* Spending so much time with Josh, letting myself fall in love with him. Boulders, heavier and heavier.

"...I've been trying to reach you and haven't been able to get you on the phone..."

I wrapped my arm across my stomach and walked as quickly as I could in heels. I knew Josh was behind me somewhere and I needed more distance.

I ran up my front steps and dug my key from my purse, got the door open, and pushed inside holding the phone to my ear with my shoulder. I was going to lock myself in my room and not say good night to him. I couldn't be face-to-face with him again. Not alone.

"... You mean so much to me, Kris, and I love you..."

As much as I recognized that Tyler wasn't what I really wanted, I knew, without a shadow of a doubt, that he was the only safety net I had between me and Josh. That he had to stay in place, or I'd plummet. There was no question in my mind. If there was no Tyler, I would crash into Josh so hard my heart wouldn't survive the impact.

I just needed Tyler to get home. *Now.* I needed him to protect me from myself and remind me why we were together. To distract me and make me fall back in love with him and—

"... I reenlisted."

I stopped so fast my heel wobbled and I almost rolled an ankle.

What???

My fingers fumbled, and I dropped my cell with a smack on the hardwood floor. I scrambled to pick it up, and I held the phone in front of me with shaking hands and played the message again on speaker.

Then I listened a third time just to be sure I heard what he said.

He reenlisted.

He broke up with me.

It was over between us.

No more net...

I became an instant danger to my own heart. I tossed the phone onto the sofa, took off my heels, and bolted to the door.

Josh was already coming up my steps at a jog. As soon as he saw me in the doorway, he started in on me. "You can't go walking around alone in the middle of the night, Kristen. It's not sa—"

I collided with him, throwing my arms around his neck, and crushed my lips to his.

He didn't even pause. Not for a second. He kissed me back.

His mouth was urgent and didn't ask questions, like he knew this moment was a gift and he didn't want to risk having to return it. But I needed him to know. I broke away, gasping for air, my forehead to his. "Tyler and I broke up. He left me a message. He reenlisted. I told him if he did that, we were through. And he reenlisted."

I didn't care. In that intoxicated moment, I did not give one fuck that Tyler and I were over.

He studied my face for a split second before he answered by kissing me again.

He was like slipping into warm sheets. It was everything safe and perfect. All the tiny, stolen, fragmented pieces of him that I'd collected over the last few weeks, his smell, the feel of his breathing against my body in the tow truck, the contours of his shirtless chest in the garage, the roughness of his hand on my bare knee, the study of his mouth when he wasn't looking—all came together into a familiar and exhilarating rush as he pressed against me and kissed me.

Hands plunged down my back to cradle my ass and he ground into me.

Only sex. That's all it can be.

"Do you have a condom?" I breathed.

He shook his head, trailing his lips down, ravaging the side of my neck.

I tipped my head back and closed my eyes. "I haven't been with anyone in over six months and I have an IUD."

He kissed me roughly under my jaw.

"Have you been with anyone since Celeste?"

"No." His eyes came back up to mine and I could see the desire, like smoldering embers in his irises. "And I'm good without one if you are."

This man wanted me. We wanted each other. I was in that rare window of time when the bleeding had stopped. That once-a-month respite from my period hell.

And I'm in love with him.

I was going to sell my soul to have him. I would fly too close to the sun.

But I would do it with conditions.

"Okay, no condom. I don't like them anyway. But Josh, this is just sex. Nothing else," I whispered. "You have to agree or it stops now."

My eyes drowned in his. My breasts pressed into his chest, his breath rolled over my lips, his hands pulled me into him, and I was small and protected, nestled into his firm body. It was better than the hug I'd envisioned. It was paralyzing.

Say yes.

He didn't answer. He smiled against my lips, wrapped my legs around his waist, and carried me straight to the bedroom, devouring my mouth as he staggered through the door.

My dress pushed up around my hips and his hands held my naked thighs against him. The straining in his pants, pressed into my panties, drove me almost mad. I felt like a crazed animal. I wanted to rip his clothes off him with my teeth.

He set my feet down in the middle of the room and I tugged at his shirt, desperate to run my hands along his bare chest. He kicked out of his shoes and peeled off his shirt, and his warm masculine scent ensconced me as I grappled with his belt buckle. The metallic clink was like a mating call that made us both frantic.

I fumbled with the zipper and he took over, his fingers quicker than mine, pulling his pants down. He sprung free and I gasped. "Oh my God..."

The man was a bull.

It was the most beautiful penis I'd ever seen. I stared at it, holding my breath, wondering if it would even fit.

If this was a Copeland family trait, no wonder his mom had seven kids. I'd never put this away. I'd make this damn thing my screen saver.

My wide eyes came back up to his, and he bounced his eyebrows and grinned. Then he turned me and gathered my hair to the side of my neck and kissed along my shoulder, pressing the length of that enormous thing against my ass as he unzipped my dress, letting it fall around my ankles. I panted like a dog in heat.

"Don't touch my stomach," I breathed. "I have this thing and it makes it bloated and..."

He nodded against my neck and his hands came around to cup my breasts, grinding into me again from behind.

I ground back.

He moaned, slipping a hand down the front of my panties. "Tell me what you like," he whispered against my ear, moving against me.

Oh my fucking God...

What *didn't* I like? It had been so long and I was so deprived I was afraid he was going to finish me right there. My body began to tremble at the build. I couldn't take it anymore. He seemed to sense it because he pulled his fingers back right before I disintegrated in his hand, and he laid me down on the bed, sliding over me. He hovered on his forearms and ran a thick, muscular thigh up between my legs until it hit my core and I sucked in air against his lips.

Oh my God, he was so good at this...

And he fucking *knew* it.

He smiled and kissed me, his tongue darting in my mouth, his rough hands canvassing my skin like he wanted to feel every inch of me.

I did the same.

It felt so good to touch him. My eyes had spent so much time learning his body, and my hands wanted to map him. I ran fingers along his chest, over the curve of his broad freckled shoulders, down the muscles of his back, along the valley of his spine. I breathed in his scent as I grabbed his firm ass and pulled him into me and he groaned, rubbing hard against my leg.

I couldn't believe this was real, that I got to touch him, that he was kissing me, that there was nothing between us but my thin G-string. His bare skin pressing into mine was the most exquisite feeling of my life, a million nerve endings connecting with his, little electrical shocks that merged into one huge surge.

He sat up and kneeled between my legs, picking up my foot and putting it on his shoulder.

The view was fucking *spectacular*.

The definition of his chest continued down with a line of hair into a V muscle that pointed at his divine penis like an arrow. I reached out and took him in my hand and his breathing went ragged. My gaze came back up to his hooded eyes. He kissed my ankle and I watched him do it, biting my lip, stroking him, my need unraveling into something so starved I wanted to beg him to have mercy on me and just fuck me already.

I thought of the way he'd touched me in the car, his strong hands massaging my calf, and I couldn't help but feel like he was continuing something he started earlier. He ran his palms from my ankle, behind my knee, up my thigh, and he hooked my panties in his thumbs and pulled them down and off. Then he balled them in his hand, shut his eyes, and put them to his nose, breathing in.

When his eyes opened again, they'd gone primal.

He came at me like a wild animal.

He lowered onto me, his jaw clenched tight, every muscle of his body tense, and I lifted my hips. He held my gaze as he eased himself in, slow and deliberate, and I wrapped my legs around his waist, feral with need, frantically urging him deeper.

One…

Two…

I wasn't going to last a minute and it was all overload, his naked body pressed to mine, the feel of him inside me, rhythmically thrusting against my core, deeper and deeper, his quivering breath over my collarbone, his hips grinding between my legs, his scent, his sounds, the heat of his skin, the rocking of the bed, the moaning in my throat—my back arched and I fell apart at the same time he did, clutching at everything, pulling him into me, pulsing with his release.

He collapsed on top of me and I was decimated.

I lay there like a rag doll, twitching with aftershocks.

He gasped for breath, his face by my ear. "Holy… fucking… shit," he panted.

I just nodded. I couldn't even speak. I'd never had sex that good. Never in my *life*—and I'd had my share of good sex. It was like we'd been foreplaying for weeks and I'd been sexually malnourished, starving, waiting for him to feed me.

He looked up at me after a few moments, the storm in his eyes quieted, and he kissed me slow and languidly while he caught his breath, putting soft pecks along my jaw, brushing the hair off my forehead with his fingers.

I loved it.

It was so sweet and tender. And I couldn't allow it. "Can you get me a towel?" I asked, putting a stop to it.

He kissed my forehead. "Sure." He got up and I watched him walk across the room, his perfect naked body silhouetted by the light coming from my bathroom. He came back in a second later and smiled at me as he handed me a towel.

My heart yearned for him. I wanted to cuddle with him. I wanted him to stay. "Okay, time to go."

He got under the covers. "Nope." He scooted in and threw an arm over me.

"What do you mean 'nope'? We're done here. Thank you, and go home now."

This was the price. The payment for what I stole. I couldn't have it all. I tried lifting his arm off me. It weighed, like, a million pounds. God, he was muscly.

He rolled me onto my side, pulled my back into his chest, and snuggled me. "Nope. I'm staying the night. You took time off my sleep schedule. I'm not driving a half an hour to my apartment just to lose more sleep before a forty-eight-hour shift."

"Well, you're sleeping in the guest room, then," I said, pulling at his hand.

He went into a vise grip over my rib cage. "Nope. Your futon sucks."

It wasn't that I didn't want him there. I *did*. I'd never wanted anyone to stay the night more in my life. And that's exactly why he needed to leave.

This had to be sex and only sex. This wasn't a relationship. It couldn't be. Ever. I could never let him mistake it for one. I had to be crystal clear about that. I was a dead end worse than Celeste, and if he ever developed feelings or things ever got fuzzy, I'd have to end it.

He needed to go.

"Josh, we're not cuddling. This is a sex thing." I tried to wriggle away from him and he laughed, nuzzling my neck.

"Knock it off. We're two grown-ass adults. We can share a bed for a night. And I'm not cuddling you—I'm using you as a body pillow."

I gave him side-eye that he couldn't see. "Well, I'm not making you breakfast in the morning."

"Thank God."

I smirked. "Fine. *Stay.* But don't go catching feelings. I mean it. We are not a thing. Got it?"

"Using me for sex. Got it." He pulled me closer and kissed my shoulder.

"Stop!"

"Good night." I could tell he was smiling.

I gave up my struggles and tried to relax. The rise and fall of his chest moved rhythmically against my back, and with every exhale, I sank deeper into him, like I belonged there.

Like I was loved.

I squeezed my eyes shut, trying to push the feelings down.

This was a bad idea. I didn't know if I could compartmentalize this like I thought I could. Especially if he was going to be pulling this shit.

And why *was* he pulling this shit? Didn't guys prefer noncommittal sex-only situations? Didn't he say he wasn't ready to date? I was making this easy for him.

My tired mind drifted off into sleep, and while I was somewhere in the fog, buried in his strong arms, he put his nose to my hair and breathed in.

FIFTEEN

JOSH

We stood in her kitchen eating cereal, looking at each other. She ate hers out of a measuring cup because she "likes the handle." It made me smile.

"Don't smile at me." She gave me a warning glare. She'd been feisty from the moment she woke up. It was adorable.

Her hair tumbled wild around her face, still curled a little from the party, and she wore nothing but an oversize sweatshirt that bared one shoulder and the light-blue lace G-string I'd gotten to take off her last night. She was beautiful. So fucking sexy.

"I can't even smile now?" I grinned at her. My heart was so damn happy.

Waking up with her was like Christmas when you see you got everything you wanted. I woke up with a grin on my face, and then she'd gotten up and jumped me again.

It had been a good morning.

"I need to make sure you're clear on the rules here," she said over her cereal. "This is a booty-call situation. That's it. Friends with benefits."

Yeah, she'd said that last night—a few times actually. I'd been so focused on the sex part of that statement I hadn't really processed the rest of it. I'd been a little distracted at the time.

Now that we were clothed, and my brain was working properly, I was ready to address this.

"What if I don't want to be just friends with benefits?" I smiled at her.

"Then we'll only be friends." Her face was stony.

Wow. Okay.

Was she really bent on this booty-call thing? I'd half thought she was just giving me shit last night with the whole "thanks for the sex, get out now" bullshit. She liked to give me a hard time—it was her thing. I didn't think she was entirely serious.

I decided to poke her.

"Oh yeah? So we can see other people, then?" I took a bite of my cereal with a smirk.

Something flashed in her eyes. "Of course. Bone whoever you want." She shrugged, looking away from me.

I studied the side of her face. Her forehead wrinkled the way it did when she was frustrated. It bothered her—I could see it. So if it bothered her, why was she insisting on it?

"Well, we should probably start using condoms, then," I said casually, calling her bluff.

"Fine. We probably should have used them anyway." She put her cereal in the sink.

This was *not* the answer I had hoped for. She didn't like condoms, so I'd been expecting something snarky along the lines of, "Well, *I'm* not the one who wants to see other people."

Now I'd just talked myself into using a condom. *Fuck.*

I set my cereal down on the counter. "Well, you're on birth control. And of course, if we agreed to be exclusive, we could keep—"

"Nope. Condoms are fine."

She walked out of the kitchen, and I watched her go with a

wrinkled brow. But I didn't have time to get further into it with her. I had to be at work in twenty minutes. I'd slept all of two hours last night. I was exhausted and work was going to suck because of it.

It had been worth it.

I washed my bowl and went looking for her. She sat on the couch with Stuntman Mike, her laptop on her lap.

"I gotta go to work," I said. I'd talk to her about this later.

I put my hand on the back of the couch and leaned down to kiss her, and she jerked her head back. "No. We don't kiss unless we're fucking."

The comment gave me a small, unexpected jab in the heart. "Why?"

"Because this is a sex thing, Joshua. It will only ever be a sex thing. We're not dating. There are not going to be any public displays of affection or hand-holding or any of it. If you can't deal with that, then let's stop this right now."

I stared at her, and she looked back at her screen, emotionless.

"Okay." I straightened up. "Well, I'll see you in a few days. For *sex*."

"Bye," she said, talking to her computer.

I gave her one more lingering look. She never raised her eyes.

A wall. An enormous wall had suddenly come up between us. *What the hell?*

I didn't understand it. Could she actually be serious about this? She didn't want to date me? At all? *Ever?* Why?

This wasn't some girl I wanted to call at 2:00 in the morning to bang and leave. I liked her. I more than liked her—I wanted to be with her. I'd been hoping this was the start of something between us. If she'd wanted to be exclusive, I would have slapped on the boyfriend title in a second.

Could this be about Tyler? I mean, I guess I just thought by how quickly she'd thrown herself at me that she wasn't too upset over the breakup.

We hadn't talked about it—*I* certainly wasn't going to bring up Tyler if *she* wasn't, and she hadn't broached the subject. She didn't really filter, so if he'd been on her mind or the breakup was fucking with her, she'd say it, right?

But the only thing she was saying was that she didn't want *me*.

It ate at me the whole way to work.

Once I got to the station, Shawn put me through a two-hour list of shitty probie chores. By the time I had a chance to talk to Brandon, he was working out.

The gym was a large gray-carpeted room off the apparatus bay. One treadmill, a bike, and an elliptical that nobody ever used sat in a row facing a mirrored wall. Three weight benches, a punching bag, and a rack of weights lined the other wall with a view of the fire engine through a large window.

I grabbed a cup of water from the watercooler by the door and took a weight bench next to where Brandon sat doing curls. "Hey. Sloan's car broke down on us last night. Stranded us in a fucking parking lot in Skid Row." I leaned forward with my elbows on my knees, holding my water cup between my legs. "And I hooked up with Kristen."

Brandon finished his set. "Well, I can't say either thing really surprises me." He pivoted to face me and grinned, bouncing his eyebrows.

I took another swallow of my water. "She broke up with her boyfriend last night."

"Good." He started doing curls on his other arm. "Sloan'll be happy."

"Well, I'm glad someone's getting what they want out of it. She doesn't want to date me. Sex only."

"Okay. What's the problem?" He set his weight down with a thump. "I thought you didn't want to date. Didn't you blow off that yoga instructor?"

"This is different. I like Kristen. A lot. And we get along. We get along fucking great. And the weird thing is I know she likes me too—I can tell. Something doesn't feel right." I finished my water and crushed the cup, tossing it into the trash can by the towels.

"Hmm. How was the sex?" he asked.

I scoffed. "Fuck, it was the best sex I've ever had. Not even kidding."

She'd pounced me like a hungry tiger that escaped its cage. The way she smelled, the way she tasted—even thinking about it made my dick twitch.

Shawn came through the door and tossed a gym towel onto the weight rack. "What up, fellas?"

Brandon and I nodded at him.

"Just ask her what her deal is," Brandon said. "It's probably because she just broke up with what's-his-face. Kristen's pretty blunt. I don't imagine her not telling you exactly what she's thinking if you asked."

Shawn sat on the other bench next to Brandon. "You talking about Kristen? Sloan's friend? She's single now? She's hot as fuck. I'd hit it." He lay down and scooted under the weight bar.

I grabbed his towel and threw it at him. "Hey, asshole, she's taken."

Shawn laughed, dragging the towel off his face. "Not by you."

"Yes, by me." *Sort of.*

He paused with his hands on his barbell and looked over at me. "Damn! You're crushing that? She's gone slumming, bro!"

I gave him the finger.

Brandon chuckled. "Do you want me to ask Sloan?"

"No." Kristen and Sloan would see that shit a mile away. "Don't ask. Don't tell her what I said, yeah?"

He picked his weight up and started doing curls again. "Just see how it goes. Give it a few weeks."

Shawn grinned. "Can't nail that shit down, huh?"

I ignored him and stood up to grab weights for my barbell. I wasn't getting into this with him. Relationship advice from Shawn was the last thing I fucking needed. He'd had his car egged by girls so many times we'd had to start locking the gate to the fire station parking lot.

Shawn grunted through his set and put the bar back on the rack with a clang. "She probably wants to get back with the ex."

"He reenlisted. It's why they broke up," I said, wanting to put that theory to bed. "He's not coming back."

Brandon spoke up. "Her idea to break up or his?"

"Hers. Or maybe his. I'm not sure." He reenlisted knowing she'd leave him if he did.

I hadn't thought of that. Even if she'd broken up with him, her hand had been forced. So in a way, he'd done the leaving.

Shit, maybe that changed things.

Shawn sat there catching his breath. "He's gonna miss those care packages and titty pics and come begging. Trust me, dude. And in the meantime she's gonna revenge fuck her way through her contacts list." He reached down and grabbed his water bottle, taking a drink. "Looks like she just got to the *j*'s."

Jealousy surged at the thought of Tyler trying to get her back. Now I wished I *had* brought him up earlier so I knew how she felt about it all.

Brandon chuckled and switched arms. "She probably just needs time, bud."

Shawn snickered, scooting back under his bar. "She probably just needs the *d*, and not just yours."

"Fuck you," I said, tightening my weight on the bar.

Brandon laughed. "Come on, it's been what? Twelve hours since they broke up? You can't expect her to just dive right into another relationship, no matter how amazing *you* might be."

Brandon had a point. But maybe Shawn did too. She'd been tied down for two years. Maybe she *was* happy to be single and wanted to see what else was out there.

I didn't like that. At *all.* I didn't like anything Shawn was pointing out.

Suddenly my forty-eight-hour shift felt too long.

The red lights flashed through the gym. We had a call. All three of us were up in an instant.

The voice of the dispatcher came over the loudspeaker. "Person down. Engine ten respond to sick person at four thirty-seven Palm Drive with medic unit six hundred seventy-four."

We streamed out of the gym into the apparatus bay and climbed into the engine as Javier came out of the crew quarters.

"I almost got to eat a sandwich," Javier said, getting into the front seat with the laptop.

I climbed into the driver's seat. Shawn sat behind me next to Brandon and put on his headset. "Hey, Javier, Josh's fucking Kristen."

Javier paused mid–seat belt and looked at me. "Really? Isn't she engaged?"

I turned on the ignition and the engine rumbled to life. "No. She broke up with him last night. She doesn't want to date me though. And I'm not fucking her. I *like* her, asshole," I said over my shoulder.

Shawn snorted. "Naw, she's fucking *you.* Hey, man, for real though—if you're a dick in a jar, you better not rock the boat."

I put on my headset. "What?" I hit the button to open the bay doors and turned on the lights.

"You're a dick in a jar. Chris Rock? 'Break in case of emergencies.' She had an emergency, dude," Shawn said. "If you start getting all stage-five clinger, she's gonna replace your ass and get a new jar."

Brandon laughed. "I think what he's saying is to give her space."

Javier opened up the laptop. "Normally I'd disagree with any and everything Shawn says, but as an old married guy with two grown daughters, I have to agree with him. It's too soon. Let things happen naturally."

Javier looked at the laptop and got the specifics for the call. Vague. Sick person, possibly unconscious.

More bullshit.

A toothache. Drunks. So, so many drunks. Hell, this call was probably a drunk. "Sick person" was the universal code for "no idea, but probably someone shit-faced."

I closed the bay door behind us and fired up the sirens.

Shawn didn't drop it. "Hey, maybe she'll get a brown jar next. I got a jar she might like."

"Oh yeah?" I said, turning onto Victory. "They make jars that small?"

The guys laughed and Javier talked to his screen. "I met the love of my life at nineteen. Never got to play the field. Kind of wish I did. Be single. Date around in the meantime."

"I've dated around," I mumbled.

Nobody was like Kristen. Witty, beautiful. Smart. She made me laugh. I loved talking to her, loved seeing what she thought about things. Over these last few weeks, she'd become my other best friend. And dating around wasn't an option—it was a waste of time.

We pulled up to a tired apartment complex. When we got inside, I was right. More bullshit. A lady pretending to be unconscious after a fight with her husband. She wanted him to think he'd given her a heart attack. A nice little guilt trip.

These theatrics seemed to be a relatively common affliction here. I'd gone on five calls like this since I'd gotten to California. Someone pretending to have a medical emergency to get attention. A waste of time and resources.

We didn't get calls like this in small-town South Dakota. We got a fraction of the calls they did here, but when we did get them, they were legitimate. People didn't call 911 unless they needed to fucking call. They didn't use us as props for their dramas. Small-town people had pride.

I couldn't wait to tell Kristen about this shit. She loved hearing about my calls. It was the first thing we caught up on when I would come back over after a shift. She'd have something hilarious to say for sure. Last week I'd single-handedly wrangled three drunks into the back of an ambulance, and she'd called me the Idiot Whisperer.

On the way back to the engine with the crew, I spoke low to Brandon. "How do you stay so fucking patient with these people?"

Brandon shrugged. "It's just the job. You do your best to educate them when you can."

"Does it work?"

"No," Shawn said with a laugh, and Javier chuckled behind him.

I shook my head. "You know, I considered the Forest Service before the move. I'm starting to think I should have looked more into that."

Shawn snickered. "What? You wanna be a fucking gardener?"

"The Forest Service isn't that bad," Brandon said, loading his gear back into the engine.

"Not having to deal with people?" I said. "Being outside, in nature? What's not to like?"

Shawn climbed into the engine. "You're just fucking clearing brush. Smokey the Bear shit."

"And that's worse than *this*?" I asked. "We just revived a woman who wasn't unconscious. At least I'd be actually accomplishing something."

I climbed back into my seat and put on my headset. Javier had snagged someone from the complex about the trash in front of the fire hydrant, so we all sat and waited.

Fuck. What was I doing with my life? Did I really want to do this shit for the next twenty years? I didn't know if I had the patience. Sure, I got to go on some cool calls sometimes. I delivered a baby last week, and I put out a car fire. But most of it was crap like this. And the probation made it worse.

I could have applied for the Forest Service. Maybe tried Northern California. Lived near wine country and the redwoods where I could have hunted and owned some land.

But then there was Kristen.

If I'd moved somewhere else and come here for Brandon's wedding and met Kristen then, I would have wished I lived here by the time the night was done. I knew I would. She was special. She wasn't just some girl. I think I'd known that the day I met her.

I pulled out my cell phone and scrolled to her name, looking at the blinking line, waiting for me to type a text. *And tell her what?* She wouldn't even let me kiss her goodbye this morning. Why would she want to hear from me?

My whole life was one big probationary period at the moment. I was in limbo, waiting to see if things got better.

There was only one way to get through it. Put my head down. Do a good job. And do what I'd been told.

I'd just have to bide my time.

SIXTEEN

KRISTEN

Josh's forty-eight-hour shift gave me withdrawals. I felt like some sort of addiction had started, and now I craved him. I needed to see him like a fix. I actually got in the car to drive past the fire station like a stalker, and I had to talk myself down.

I debated texting him but decided against it because why? So we could be closer? Get to know each other better? If anything, I should have been figuring out ways to see him less. Looking for another carpenter, maybe even breaking off this booty-call thing altogether before I was in so deep I'd never get out.

Ugh. What have I done?

I texted Sloan to see if we could have lunch, but her stepmom was throwing her a small bridal shower at her dad's house in San Diego, and she was going to be gone both days of Josh's shift. I didn't want to drop the whole "I banged Josh" thing on her over the phone. So I sat through my two days without him, alone, watching the clock and missing him as I scoured my house from top to bottom.

When his shift at the fire station was done and he finally headed back over to work on the orders I had for him, I waited for the sound of the garage door opening like a dog waiting for his master to come home.

I'd done my hair and makeup and dressed in normal clothes for once. Nothing too cute—leggings and an off-the-shoulder shirt. I didn't want to send the wrong message. The message that broadcasted how I *really* felt.

Once I knew he was here, I scampered back to the living room sofa and put my laptop onto my lap so he wouldn't know I'd been waiting like some kind of fangirl.

It was so lame.

"Hey," he said, coming into the doorway with a smile. Stuntman bounced at his feet wearing his I'M LITTLE AND I HATE EVERYONE shirt. Josh crouched and petted him. "I brought you a breakfast burrito."

Oh God.

How had he managed to get more attractive in the past forty-eight hours? He looked so cute in his jeans and gray T-shirt with that messy hair and the fucking dimples I loved, and the man had a damn burrito for me on top of everything.

Not to mention now I could picture him naked.

My heart thudded just looking at him. I wanted to run to him and jump on him, wrap my arms around his neck and kiss him.

"Hey," I mumbled, looking back to my screen.

He set the food down on the coffee table, his cologne and the smell of sausage teasing me.

"Thanks," I said, pretending to write an email.

He waited for a long moment as I tapped at my keys. "Well, I guess I'll get to work..."

I didn't breathe until I heard the laundry room door close.

Then he spent the day in the garage. I didn't hang out with him like I usually did. He asked me if I wanted to get lunch. Of course I said no.

And of course I totally wanted to.

He didn't try to touch me or kiss me. He was trying to follow my rules.

I hated my fucking rules.

At 4:00, he came back inside and sat next to me on the sofa.

"I'm on my period, so..."

He snorted. "Good to know. Thanks for the info." He opened a Coke with a *pith*. "So what're we watching?"

I stifled a smile. "I'm just returning emails. I wasn't really paying attention." I closed my laptop and slid a hand across his thigh. "You know, we *can* do other stuff..."

I was used to getting creative with my sex life. Three-week-long periods didn't give me much choice, and I didn't see why my partner had to abstain in the meantime. And I really wanted to touch him. Even if it was just sex. I just wanted to be close to him.

But when I reached for his belt buckle, he stopped me. "No. If you're not having fun, neither am I."

"Who says I won't be having fun?" I smirked, trying to get my hand free.

He held it firm. "Kristen, no. That's not why I'm here."

I looked at him. "Then why *are* you here?"

He gazed at me with those deep-brown eyes. "To hang out with you. You said we're friends with benefits, right? This is the friends part. I want to spend time with you."

My heart tugged.

He has to go.

"Well, I have plans tonight. So I can't hang out with you," I said, sitting back into the sofa.

The corners of his lips went down a fraction of an inch. "Okay. When are you leaving? Want to get some dinner? Or watch something before you go?"

I got up. "I'm leaving now, actually."

The light drained from his eyes, and I instantly wanted to throw my arms around him and take it all back, ask him to stay and snuggle with me on the sofa and eat Chinese food out of takeout boxes and be my boyfriend.

But I *couldn't.*

This. Could not. Be. A. Relationship.

He pushed up from the sofa. "All right. I'll see you tomorrow, then." He didn't look at me before he left.

I buried my face in my hands. What the fuck was I doing? I had to cut him loose. This was torture.

This was *ridiculous.*

I just wanted to be normal with him. I wanted to treat him the way he made me feel. Give him all my attention and kiss him and hug him.

Tell him I'm in love with him.

But that would be me luring him into a dead-end attachment that would be a waste of everyone's time. Or worse, him rejecting me once he knew the truth about my health issues. And neither of those was acceptable.

With Josh, I could have a sex-only arrangement with strict boundaries...or I could have nothing.

I grabbed Stuntman, got in the car, and went to Sloan and Brandon's house. She opened the door wearing her painting shirt, her hair piled on her head in a messy blond bun. "Oh, hey."

She went back to her stool in front of her easel in the living room. She was an artist. This painting was of a little girl in a poppy field.

"Where's Brandon?" I asked.

She pointed the remote to the TV and muted her crime show. "He's in the garage."

"I slept with Josh."

She whirled on me, eyes flying wide. "*What?!*"

"Yeah." I dropped onto the sofa, clutching my dog. "Tyler and I broke up. I slept with Josh. It was fucking incredible. His penis is glorious. I'm dick whipped and in love with him, and I don't know what to do. I think I fucked up."

She looked absolutely horrified. The color drained right from her face. She didn't know what to do with "dick whipped," I think. She'd never had a one-night stand or even slept with someone who wasn't her boyfriend.

I gave her a minute. I knew she'd catch up.

Once she rallied, she sat down next to me. "And you think you fucked up—why?"

I put my face into my hands. "I like him so much. So much, Sloan. And he's all sweet and wants to hang out with me. He asked me if we could be exclusive. I told him no, that it's purely a sex thing for me, which it's totally not. But what else can it be?"

I looked at her, and I could feel the desperation practically seeping from my pores. "I mean, if he actually likes me, I have to shut this thing down. We can't be together. He won't be with someone who can't give him kids. I'd rather die than tell him I'm about to have my uterus taken out. And I'm not in the business of leading men on, right? So I should end it, shouldn't I? Right?"

She stared at me like I'd gone mad. "God, I've never seen you like this," she breathed.

Maybe I *had* gone a little crazy. This was not my normal MO. Guys didn't get me worked up. *Ever.* Sloan was in virgin territory with me on this.

"You know what he did the other day?" I went on. "I went to FedEx to drop off some boxes. And when I came back, he was in the kitchen with Stuntman. I guess he knocked over a soda and Stuntman walked through it, so he needed a bath. So Josh washed him, and I come into the kitchen and he's standing there, no shirt, with Stuntman wrapped in a towel, and he's cuddling my wet dog. I swear to fucking God, Sloan, I've never seen anything sexier in my entire life. The man is literally perfect. How is it possible that I've managed to find the perfect man and I can't have him?"

She rubbed my back, looking at a loss for what to do.

I put my forehead into my hand. "I hate my uterus so much. Sex makes me bleed. I've been spotting for two days. And as if that wasn't bad enough, I had to tell him to ignore my swollen stomach. It was fucking humiliating."

She looked sympathetic. "Well, what did he say?"

I scoffed. "Nothing. He didn't give a shit. The dude was about to get laid. He probably wouldn't even have noticed it, but I felt like I had to explain it anyway in case he did, and found himself wondering if he was boning a pregnant chick."

The beginnings of tears tickled the back of my throat. I got up and went to the bathroom for a tissue. I blew my nose and flushed it down the toilet, and the toilet handle came off in my hand. I came out and held it up. Sloan rolled her eyes and got off the sofa.

Her house was a fixer-upper. Brandon was doing the repairs. He did a good job, but the place broke as fast as he could fix it.

She took the handle from me, and we stood there in the hallway, flanked by framed photos on the walls, having a silent exchange. We could practically read each other's minds. She hated this was happening to me. She wished she could take it away, make it better. But she couldn't, and she didn't know how to even start.

"So what are you going to do about him?" she asked.

"I don't know," I whispered. "You know what's so messed up?" My eyes started to sting. "He fits. Like, the first time I met you and we just clicked, you know? That's Josh. He clicks. And I was okay with this until him. I was at peace with my decision. And now..."

The unfamiliar lump that accompanied tears swelled in my throat. That tightness that I so rarely experienced because I was seldom moved to cry.

"The universe is laughing at me, Sloan. As soon as I think this can't get worse, it's like, 'Hold my beer.' At every turn the kid thing keeps coming up, just in case I forget how much it matters to him. These constant little reminders that I don't have what he needs."

My mind went to Josh holding Stuntman in the towel. Then I thought of him holding a baby there instead. But it wouldn't ever be mine. That wouldn't be my husband giving our baby a bath in the kitchen sink. He'd only get that moment with someone else.

That did it. The sobbing burst out of me. Sloan had me in her arms in an instant.

I wasn't an emotional person. In the course of our friendship, Sloan had only seen me cry once after a cramp-induced trip to the ER, and that was more from pain and frustration than despondency. This was a violent shift in our dynamic, the moment when Dad breaks down and wide-eyed Mom has to comfort him. Sloan's maternal instincts kicked into crisis mode, and she clutched me to her, shushing me and whispering in my ear, the way my own mom would never do.

I'd borne the decision for this hysterectomy with stoic practicality. But I couldn't do that with Josh. I just couldn't. There was absolutely nothing practical about the way that man made me feel. I let myself just fucking cry. And it made me feel out of control and hopeless.

Someone knocked on the wall. We turned to the sound to see Brandon poking his head around the door into the hallway.

"Oh. Uh, sorry to interrupt. Josh is here. Is it cool if he stays for dinner?"

Josh came up behind Brandon, holding Stuntman. My dog was licking his cheek. "Hey, Sloan. Kristen." His smile fell the second he saw my face.

I swiped at my tears, fled to the bathroom, and closed the door.

SEVENTEEN

JOSH

The crying caught me by surprise. It never occurred to me she might be *that* upset about breaking up with Tyler. I just thought—

Stupid.

Of *course* she was upset. I don't even know why I'd been confused about this. She'd dated him for two fucking years. He was supposed to move in with her, for God's sake, and he'd reenlisted without talking to her and broke up with her in a damn voicemail.

Shit, no wonder she didn't want anything serious with me. She was probably so messed up over Tyler she couldn't even think straight. I was probably just some rebound thing for her.

Shawn was right. I was a dick in a jar.

I felt like an asshole, asking her to be exclusive. I'd thought we'd had something, for a moment. That maybe she was into me too. But now I felt like I'd imagined the whole thing. Misinterpreted every signal. I should have listened to what she was saying instead of trying to grasp at things that didn't exist. She told me before any of this happened that I needed to be able to handle a sex-only situation, and this was clearly why.

And then I showed up here, the day after Tyler was supposed

to come home, when it was probably really starting to hit her and she was trying to cry about it to her best friend.

I should just give her space. I should leave.

"I'm gonna go," I said to Brandon, putting down Stuntman Mike.

I didn't intend to intrude on her night. I didn't know she was at Brandon's until I pulled up and saw her car in the driveway. And if I was being honest, after seeing her with makeup on and her hair done when I'd gone to her house, I was relieved to know that her plans had been with Sloan and not some other guy. Especially after everything Shawn said.

But that wasn't the only reason I was happy to see she was here—I was just happy to fucking see her.

I'd thought about her the whole time I was at work, and then when I finally came back over, it was such a disappointment.

Before, I could sit with her on the couch and bullshit with her. And now, I guess I needed a reason just to hang out with her in the living room. Now we had rules and everything felt stiff.

For a brief moment I wished we'd never hooked up. That we'd stayed friends until she was over this joker, and then maybe I would've had a shot with her, free and clear. Because right now I felt like I'd lost that thing between us, that easy friendship that was there before we crossed that line. Sure, I'd gotten sex out of it, but I wasn't sure it was worth the trade-off. Not like this.

Sloan came around the corner into the living room. She looked weary. "Babe, the handle to the toilet broke off." She put a metal piece in Brandon's hand.

"I'll fix it as soon as Kristen comes out," he said.

Sloan looked over at me as I pulled my keys from my pocket. "Are you leaving?"

"Yeah, I'm just gonna head out."

She glanced back at the bathroom and then looked at me full on. "Josh, *stay.*" She spoke low. "Stay for dinner."

Something in her eyes implored me. I looked back and forth between her and Brandon. He had no fucking idea what was going on. He was as lost as I was. He looked at his fiancée like he might be able to glean the information from the side of her face.

"Are you sure?" I asked.

"Very sure," she whispered, shooting a look back at the bathroom.

Maybe I was a distraction? Maybe Sloan felt like I could get Kristen's mind off Tyler? I had no illusions that Sloan didn't know we'd hooked up. Kristen would definitely have told her. So Sloan knew what she was asking.

I didn't want to leave. I wanted to be wherever Kristen was. And if Sloan thought it was okay that I stay, that's what I was going to do.

I stayed.

Brandon and I headed back to the garage. He had a few projects I could help him with, and the house felt like it was zoned for the women at the moment.

"What do you think that was about?" Brandon asked as soon as we were alone.

He was talking about Sloan's intervention, not Kristen's crying. Given Kristen's recent breakup, the crying was understandable.

I sat on a stool at the workbench and shrugged. "I think she's fucked up about Tyler and Sloan thinks I'll get her mind off it."

His brow furrowed and he reached for his beer. He held it in his lap and tapped it absently with his pinky. "I don't know. I'm a little surprised Kristen's having this reaction to it, if I'm being honest. I've never seen her like that. Not even when her grandmother died. She's pretty tough." He pulled on his beer, looking as perplexed as I felt.

We sat there, both of us looking confused, like we'd stumbled into some sort of foreign female territory.

Usually if I walked into a crying-woman situation that I wasn't directly the cause of, I'd back away slowly and let the ladies work it out among themselves. But it bothered me that she was hurting. I wished she would talk to me.

Fuck, she *used* to talk to me.

Brandon looked at me. "What happened when you went over there today?"

I shook my head. "She was the same. Kind of cold. Kicked me out. Said she was on her period so we couldn't have sex."

"Do you think it was an excuse?" he asked.

"No. I believed her." If Kristen didn't want to have sex, I had no doubt in my mind that she'd just come out and say it. I didn't think the period thing was made up, especially because she'd offered me alternatives. But that was twice in a month.

Maybe she had issues with her periods. My sister Laura did too, and she used the same heavy-duty stuff Kristen did.

Brandon set his beer down and went back to looking at the busted kitchen cabinet door he was working on. "Help me with this thing. I'm going to try to fix the hinge."

He had an impressive workbench with neon Corona beer signs hanging over it. Two large, red, rolling tool chests sat against the wall next to cabinets he'd built himself for all his power tools. It was a good thing he was properly equipped, because the house he'd bought with Sloan needed work.

We fiddled with projects for a half an hour. I kept looking

at the door that led into the house. I knew Kristen was on the other side, making dinner with Sloan. I could *feel* her.

On an impulse I got up. "I'll be right back."

I walked in to the smell of garlic and basil and found Kristen sitting at the kitchen table with Stuntman Mike. Sloan stood over a steaming pot. The girls both froze immediately.

Kristen and I stared at each other for a moment. "Can we talk for a second?" I asked, nodding to the living room.

Sloan shot her a glance.

Kristen stood, setting down her dog. "Sure."

I followed her into the living room and she turned to me, her arms crossed. "What?"

"Well," I said, crossing my arms too. "You and I are going to be spending a lot of time together in the next few weeks with the wedding and everything. I think we should talk about the elephant in the room—you following me over here."

I got her. Her lips twisted into a reluctant smile.

Her eyes were puffy. Red. She looked sad and beaten. I wanted to pull her into my chest and hold her, tell her Tyler was a fucking dick for leaving her. The urge was so intense I had to clench my fists to keep myself from reaching out. But I sensed she wouldn't let me if I tried. I didn't like the helpless feeling it gave me.

I realized, looking at her, that as much as it fucking sucked that all I was to her at the moment was a booty call, I'd take whatever she was willing to give me. If she wanted nothing but a friend with benefits right now, that's what I'd be for her, because the way I felt about her wouldn't let me refuse any chance at getting closer to her.

I cleared my throat. "I didn't know you were going to be over here. I wasn't trying to crowd you," I said a little more seriously.

"I know." She looked away from me, her smile falling a bit. "Josh, I'm not sure us hooking up again is a good idea." Her eyes flicked back to me.

Shit.

I could respect her wishes if she wanted to back out for her own reasons. But if she thought she was sparing me any grief while she got over Tyler, I needed to set her straight.

"Do I get any say?" I asked, tipping my head a little to catch her eyes. "You don't want anything committed right now. I get that. Let's just keep things casual. We like hanging out with each other. The sex is good. Let's not overthink it."

She looked up at me. "And you would be okay knowing that it's *never* going to lead to anything else?"

Why she felt the need to slap the word "never" onto it was a little much. She'd get over Tyler at some point. But it made sense that she didn't want to put a time stamp on it. And I had the feeling if I even alluded to the possibility of us one day being more, she would bail. For now at least, yes, I was fine with the current arrangement. I could wait it out.

"My expectations are managed," I said.

"And you're going to see other people."

She said it more as a statement than a question. Like she was confirming that I was aware this was an expectation of hers and I had to agree to comply.

"If I feel like it, yes." I wouldn't feel like it.

"And *I* will see other people. So you understand that."

This was harder. But I reasoned she would see other people whether her and I were hooking up or not, so it didn't change my decision. And part of me thought that if I stuck around, she wouldn't date anyone else. She'd enjoyed the sex as much as I had—that was pretty fucking obvious. I'd just have to meet all her needs, a duty I was more than willing to fulfill.

"You're single. I'd expect you to date other people too," I said.

She studied my face for a moment, like she was searching for a reason to say no. She must not have found one.

"Okay. If you think you can handle it," she said.

Neither of us moved. We watched each other. One of our comfortable silences.

My eyes openly roamed her beautiful face. Her thick lashes, dark hair that just grazed her delicate shoulders, a long, graceful neck. Full lips.

I wished I could kiss her.

And the funny thing was she was staring at my mouth too. But her expression was pained. Like just looking at me hurt.

Damn, Tyler fucked her up. I hated that fucking guy.

Sloan called out from the kitchen. "Dinner's ready."

Kristen turned without another word. I followed her in the soft flurry of her tart-apple perfume and took the chair next to her at the table.

Stuntman Mike plopped on the floor between us. I leaned over, petting his head, and whispered to Kristen. "I hear this place has great food. Why don't we eat here more often?"

If I was here to cheer her up, I was going to do just that.

Her face softened. "It's hard to get a reservation," she whispered. She glanced at my lips again before her eyes came up to meet mine.

"I know a guy," I said. "Although I heard they had to close for a few days after the place got vandalized a couple weeks back."

She raised her eyebrows. "Oh yeah?"

I nodded and looked over at Sloan before continuing, my voice low. "The worst TP'ing Canoga Park has ever seen. No leads. Probably an inside job."

She smiled, and I saw her mood lift before my eyes.

Brandon came in from the direction of the bedroom and sat down, sliding something across to me. "Look what I got."

Sloan moaned, setting a Caesar salad in the middle of the table. "Oh God. Not that thing."

"What is it?" Kristen asked, eyeing the circular wooden box.

"It's a turkey pot call," Brandon said, scooting in his chair.

"Yeah, and he's been practicing with it for weeks. In the *house*," Sloan said, putting a bowl of pasta on the table and sitting down. "Gobbling, all day long."

Brandon gave his fiancée an amused look. "Hey, if I don't practice, I'm never going to get better."

Sloan smiled. "Uh-huh. But in the living room though? When I'm painting?" She passed the French bread. "He's usually so quiet."

"He's right," I said, picking it up to get a better look. "He needs to practice. It takes skill."

It was a nice pot call. Wood with a turkey feather carved into the round lid and a matching cedar wand to make the scratch noise. The kind of thing you pass down to your son one day.

I nodded in approval. "Nice. You know, there are turkey-calling competitions," I said to Sloan. "People compete on a national level."

"Really? It's that hard?" Sloan asked, serving herself pasta.

"Oh yeah." I took off the lid and ran a finger on the black scratch surface. "There are tons of different sounds they make. The kee kee run, the spit and drum, yelps, purrs, cackles, clucks. You have to practice or you won't get any birds out there."

Sloan grinned at Brandon. "Well, he *does* keep my cooking blog pretty busy. I guess I'll have to just put up with him."

Brandon picked up her hand and kissed it, and both Kristen and I smiled.

Kristen turned to me. "Do you know how to use it?" Her question was a white flag. She was making an effort to talk to me.

Brandon picked up his beer and tipped it at me. "Josh is actually great at that. That's why he always bags a bird."

He was wingmanning me for Kristen. I just hoped she found dead turkeys sexy.

Kristen smiled at me. A genuine smile. "Have you hunted all your life?"

"Yup." I put the lid on the pot call and handed it back to Brandon.

Kristen poked at her salad. Then she looked back up at me, her eyes innocent. "Is it true that 'vegetarian' is a Native American word for 'bad hunter'?"

Brandon laughed so suddenly he choked. I smiled at her, happy to see her coming back to her old self.

"You know, I still don't have a car," Sloan said over her pasta after Brandon stopped laughing. "You two broke my Corolla."

Kristen snorted. "Really? You're going to put this on us? The hamster probably died."

"What hamster?" Sloan looked confused.

Kristen skewered a crouton. "The one running in the wheel under the hood."

Brandon and I laughed, and Sloan pressed her lips into a line, trying to look angry, but she couldn't keep a straight face.

"How can you let her drive that thing?" I shook my head at Brandon.

"I told her, I don't know how many times, that I'll buy her a new car," Brandon said, still chuckling.

Sloan shrugged. "I don't want a new car. That was the car I learned to drive in. I had my first kiss in that car."

Brandon gave her a mock serious look. "Well, then it definitely has to go."

Sloan smiled at him and leaned over and kissed him fleetingly on the lips. I watched my best friend look at her for a moment after she went back to her food. He really loved her.

I remembered the first time he started talking about her, three years ago. We were sitting in a duck blind in South Dakota, and he went on for hours about this woman he'd been seeing. I'd never seen him so into someone. I made a mental note to talk about that during my best-man speech.

"Hey, didn't you two meet on a call?" I asked, trying to recall the story he'd told me. "At a hospital or something?"

Sloan smiled sweetly at Brandon. "Yeah. I only gave him my number because he was in uniform."

I grinned. "Can't say no to a man in uniform, huh?"

I twirled my fork around my pasta. It was incredible. Some kind of venison Bolognese. Sloan was a great cook. Kristen and I really *should* eat here more often.

"No, I can," she said. "It's just I figured they wouldn't let a felon or registered sex offender into the fire department."

Brandon chuckled. "I was pulling the rig up to the emergency room entrance when I saw her coming out. Back when we had an ambulance at the station."

Now I remembered the story. The rest of the details positioned themselves. Sloan's roommate was in the ER, and she'd been there with her. That had to have been Kristen, then. "Wasn't it you in the ER?" I asked, looking at Kristen.

Kristen was the last person to go to the ER for nothing. In fact, she was one of those patients you could never get to go to the hospital when they actually needed to. Stubborn to a fault. Mom called it strong-woman syndrome.

Most of my sisters had the affliction.

Kristen didn't look up from her plate. "I passed out at a pep rally."

My brow furrowed. "Why?"

"I was anemic." She said it without emotion, but I noticed the way Sloan watched her as she told the story.

Anemic. *Bleeding.* Were her periods *that* bad?

"When is your car going to be fixed?" Kristen asked, changing the subject.

"It's ready now," Sloan said. "I just need someone to drive me to go get it. Brandon can't. He's helping his sister move tomorrow."

"Well, I can bring it to you," I offered. "Kristen, why don't I drive home with you tonight? I'll leave my truck here, and I can stay the night at your place. After I'm done with tomorrow's orders, I'll pick up Sloan's car and drive it back."

It was like the whole room held their breath waiting for her answer.

"Sure," Kristen said, shrugging.

Forks went back to clinking on plates.

I was sure I'd be forced into the guest room, but I'd banked on her practicality and won. She knew I'd be there tomorrow morning early anyway. We had a ton of orders. And why deny Sloan her car? I'd spent the night there plenty of times already, this wasn't anything out of the ordinary. I clearly knew her well enough to anticipate her thought processes.

So why, then, had it been such a surprise to me how upset she was about Tyler?

EIGHTEEN

KRISTEN

Just when I thought I might have the strength to get out, Josh pulled me back in.

We'd played games at Sloan's until almost midnight. Sloan forced Josh and me to be on the same team. We *destroyed* her and Brandon at charades.

By the time Josh and I left together, a half an hour ago, we were back to our old prehookup selves, laughing and joking. All the weirdness was gone.

I'd just brushed my teeth and changed into shorts and a tank top for bed when he knocked on my bedroom door. When I opened it, the crooked smile on his face told me immediately that male trickery was afoot.

"Joshua. What can I help you with?"

He stood there in a white T-shirt and gray flannel pajama bottoms. "Do you mind if I ask you a question?" He grinned mischievously.

"What?" His masculine cedar scent mixed with the mint from his toothpaste and teased me from the doorway. It was intoxicating.

I tried to hold my breath.

"Do you have problems with your periods?"

The question took me so by surprise I immediately thought Sloan had said something to Brandon and he'd told Josh. But he went on before I could ask.

"Because they've done studies that show sleeping next to a man every night can regulate your period. Did you know that? Now, I'm pretty busy," he said, looking down the hall and then back at me, his dimples popping. "But I think I can offer you my services tonight in exchange for not having to sleep on your futon."

I stifled a smile. "This sleepover was *your* idea. You knew you'd be in the guest room."

He made a show of straining to look around me into my room. "Hmm. Can I check your smoke alarm?" He leaned in the door frame and crossed his arms in that way that pushed out his biceps and made his chest press against his shirt.

My ovaries swooned. Damn, it was too bad I was spotting. I'd drag him right to bed and cash in on this friends-with-benefits deal if I wasn't.

I put an arm across the door and fought the urge to smile, pressing my lips into a line. "My smoke alarm is fine."

"Can I have the dog?"

I scoffed. "Why the fuck would I give you my dog?"

"So I won't be lonely." He gave me a mock sad face.

"Well then *I'll* be lonely."

"You can solve everyone's problems by just letting me in. If you turn me away, I'm just going to come back doing the naked man," he said seriously.

I snorted. Heaven help me if he came back with the naked man. I was in no way strong enough to turn away a naked Josh.

"I'm spotting." I reminded him, hoping that would shut him down.

Tyler wouldn't come near me with a ten-foot pole if I was bleeding. I'd had to be pretty creative to keep our sex life satisfying when his leaves fell within my three-week-period window.

His eyebrows shot up. "Spotting only?"

"Yeah."

He crashed into me, arms around my waist, lips right into my neck. "I don't care about spotting," he whispered, kissing under my ear.

His sudden proximity knocked the emotional wind out of me. "I care," I breathed, hands on his chest.

Do I? I do, right?

"Well, stop," he said huskily, smiling into my neck.

He backed me into the bed, his strong arm guiding me down. When he slid over me, I was hypnotized. Rendered completely helpless.

And he wasn't lying about the spotting.

He really didn't care.

~

I woke up the next morning naked with my cheek stuck to Josh's bare chest. I lay there for a moment, the light cracking through my blinds, listening to the sound of his steady heart beating.

I wanted to give myself another few moments of happiness before I had to kick him out of my bed and pretend I didn't care whether he was there or not.

He stirred and I closed my eyes and pretended I was still asleep. His body shifted like he was looking down on me, and I heard his heart pick up a little. I knew if I looked up, he would smile and I could kiss him good morning.

But I wouldn't. Because that's not what fuck buddies do.

Lips gently touched the top of my head, and his arms tightened around me. It was sweet and tender.

And a bad sign.

He said he could handle this, that the sex-only thing was okay for him. But I'd have to keep an eye on him, end it if I thought he was getting too attached.

My stomach growled. I wondered what time it was. There was a cafe that—

I bolted upright. "What day is it?" I looked desperately for my phone.

Josh propped himself up on his elbows and looked at me, his hair messy. "March eighth. Tuesday. Why?"

I found my phone on the charger: 10:13 a.m. "Shit!"

I swung my legs out of the bed and crashed painfully into the nightstand with my hip, stilling the wobble with my hands. I scooped up Stuntman from the end of the bed and pushed him out the sliding glass door before running to the bathroom.

Oh my God, how could I forget?

I had no Tyler, just-fucked hair and my naked carpenter in my bedroom with less than twenty minutes to get my shit together. One hand jammed my toothbrush in my mouth while the other one turned on the shower. I got in before the water had a chance to warm up and brushed my teeth while I wet my hair in the frigid stream.

The shower door slid open and Josh got in next to me. "Whoa, this is freezing."

I spit into the drain. "This is not your shower. Get out."

He laughed, grabbing the soap. "I have to use a separate shower now? You don't even let your poor exhausted fuck buddy clean up after he spends the night servicing you?" He lathered his chest, grinning at me.

Normally, Josh naked in my shower would be the realization of a long-running fantasy, but this morning he was just taking up room where I could be hurriedly shaving my legs.

"What's the rush, anyway?" he asked.

I bent down to grab my shampoo and bumped his thigh with my forehead. When I came back up, he was smirking at me.

"My mom. I have brunch with my mom," I said, scrubbing my hair frantically. "I forgot. She'll be here in fifteen minutes. She thinks Tyler is coming with me. She doesn't know we broke up."

I snatched the soap from him, rinsing my hair while I washed my body. This was a nightmare. A fucking nightmare. "Josh, you need to be in the garage when she gets here."

"I can't meet your mom?"

"No." Dear God, *no. Hi, Mom, Tyler and I broke up, but here's my fuck buddy, Josh. Isn't he cute?* Lord help me.

My hands were actually shaking from the adrenaline.

"I'm getting pretty cold over here," he said, slipping his hands around my waist from behind and kissing the side of my neck.

I wiggled. "Josh, I don't have time for this. I told you this wasn't your shower."

"Okay, okay." He let go of me with a laugh.

He wouldn't be laughing if he knew Evelyn.

"You sure I can't meet her? I'm good with moms," he said, while I smacked conditioner in my hair.

"No. You can't meet her. Just..." I viciously scrubbed my face and rinsed, doing a quick spin to get the soap and conditioner off. Then I jumped out, grabbing the closest towel. "Just don't come out. And don't let Stuntman back in the house either. He hates her worse than he hates Tyler."

I tripped all over the bathroom, plugging in my hair dryer,

slapping on lotion, putting on mascara. Josh got out and went into the bedroom to get dressed.

Ten minutes. I had ten minutes. If my hair was wet, she'd know I had forgotten. She'd be worse if she knew I'd forgotten.

Ugh. She was going to give me so much grief about Tyler. *Well, it was only a matter of time.* Or maybe, *You ruin all the good things in your life.* Whatever it was, it would be tinged with disappointment and judgment and I didn't have enough warning to get into the right headspace to deal with her.

I'd been so distracted, and Tyler was the one who'd saved the date in his calendar. And of course she wouldn't call me to confirm or let me know she was on her way like a normal person. She'd prefer it if I fucked up and got the date wrong or forgot. I turned on my hair dryer.

Dry faster, dry faster! Damn it, why did I even wash it?!

At 10:29 I came out of my room, ready to answer the door. She was never late. She'd be here exactly at 10:30. But when I came down the hallway, putting in my earring, Mom was already in the living room.

Talking to *Josh*.

NINETEEN

JOSH

The hair dryer was still running in Kristen's room when the doorbell rang on my way to the garage. I called down the hall, but she didn't hear me. Figured I might as well make myself useful, so I answered it.

The woman on the front porch wasn't what I expected. She could have been Kristen's grandmother. Maybe she *was* her grandmother. She looked like she was pushing seventy. Still good-looking though. Kind of regal.

I saw Kristen's high cheekbones, petite frame, and large eyes. Her gray hair was pulled tight into a neat bun. She wore pearls.

When she saw *me*, she gave me a raised eyebrow and looked me over like I was a wine list that didn't have her year.

"Well, hello. Is my daughter available?" Her eyes flicked coolly to my wet hair.

"She'll be right out. Come in. I'm Josh, her carpenter," I added, giving her a hand to shake.

"Evelyn Peterson." She shook my hand firmly and then looked around the living room while she fished a small bottle of hand sanitizer out of her purse and squirted some into her palm.

It was a little rude, but I watched this with amusement.

I saw where Kristen got her scowl from. Evelyn did *not* look pleased.

"I hope you don't take the state of this house as evidence of a poor upbringing," she said, rubbing her hands together and eyeing an empty beer bottle and dirty plate on the coffee table. "Kristen grew up with a housekeeper, but I'd like to think I instilled a sense of pride in her." She wrinkled her nose at one of Stuntman Mike's half-chewed bones on the floor. "Even if it's not always apparent."

Kristen's house was spotless. You'd be hard-pressed to find a dust bunny under the couch. Who gave a shit about a beer bottle and a plate?

She moved around the coffee table and picked up a green dachshund sweater from a stack Kristen had been inventorying. It read I SEE YOU LOOKING AT MY WIENER. Evelyn grimaced and set it down with two fingers.

My mom would have thought that shit was hilarious. Evelyn wasn't a wiener-joke kind of lady, I guess.

I was starting to get a little uncomfortable. Too pretentious for my taste. Still, I was kind of her host at the moment, and I had to entertain her until Kristen took over.

"Uh . . . can I get you something to drink? A water?" I asked.

Her steely gaze settled back on me. "Thank you, no. Where is Tyler?"

"I'm not sure. I just work here," I said. It wasn't my place to tell her about the voicemail breakup.

She narrowed her eyes. "Hmm."

Kristen came around the corner, her hand to her earring, and she stopped cold when she saw us together. Then she did something I have never, in the entire time I've known her, seen her do.

She turned *red*.

"I was beginning to think I needed to send out a search party," Evelyn said curtly.

I braced for Kristen's snarky retort, but to my surprise she didn't reply. Instead she stiffly kissed her mom hello.

"And where is Tyler?" Evelyn gave Kristen an air-kiss. "I hope we're not going to be late. You know how I hate being late." She glanced at a diamond watch.

Kristen's eyes flicked nervously to me. "Actually, Tyler won't be coming. We broke up."

Evelyn's lips pressed into a line. She waited a long beat before she replied with a cool, "I see." She turned to me. "Joshua, would you care to join us? Our reservation is for three."

Kristen spoke quickly. "He has a lot of orders—"

"I believe this was *my* brunch invitation," Evelyn said. "You've deprived us of our threesome and failed to inform me in advance so I could make the proper arrangements to fill the seat. I'd like to invite Joshua, and it's my invitation to extend."

Her tone had a finality to it. I looked at Kristen. She'd gone totally silent.

Kristen, *silent*.

This alarmed me more than I could comprehend.

Something protective told me not to leave her alone with this woman. This Tyler thing seemed to be some sort of hot button between them, and I got the impression a buffer was needed. Maybe that's why she asked. The empty chair might piss Evelyn off and just make things worse.

"Sure, I'd love to come."

Alarm ripped across Kristen's face.

I looked down at my clothes. "I'm not sure I'm dressed for it though."

I didn't know where we were going, but both Kristen and Evelyn were in dresses and heels and I was in jeans and a Burbank Fire T-shirt. I didn't have anything else to change into.

Evelyn sighed. "You'll fit right in with all the other underdressed millennials there, I suppose. I'm sorry Kristen didn't make it possible for me to give you more notice." She turned for the door. "Oh, Kristen? You really should put your trash cans where they can't be seen from the street. Curb appeal matters, dear."

Evelyn came in a black Town Car with a driver. On the twenty-minute trip to the restaurant, she picked lint off Kristen's dress and commented on her damp hair. In between the nitpicking, I learned she was a tenured law professor at UCLA and a judge.

Man, she was uptight. I wondered if she ever hugged Kristen as a child. I couldn't picture it. I couldn't even imagine her smiling. Come to think of it, she didn't even have laugh lines. Just two deep wrinkles between her eyebrows where she drew them down.

Kristen seemed paralyzed. It was the weirdest thing. I kept looking at her, trying to figure out what was wrong with her. She reminded me of a cornered animal so frightened that its fight-or-flight response had shut off and it just sat there, frozen and terrified.

The restaurant was in Simi Valley, and I was definitely underdressed. The other millennials were no help. They were in sport coats and button-downs. A hostess led us to a white linen-covered table with a small vase of roses on it by the window.

"We'll have menus," Evelyn said to the hostess in a bored tone. "I don't trust buffets," she explained. "Too many people pawing at it."

Kristen and I shared a look. The buffet looked incredible. We both wanted to hit that up. It had a damn ice sculpture on it and a Bloody Mary bar. A fat prime rib sat on the carving table and iced crab legs and shrimp flanked the omelet station.

But I didn't want to be rude. I was a guest. And Kristen didn't look like she planned on arguing either, so we took our menus.

I don't know why Evelyn let Kristen have one though, because when the server came, Evelyn ordered for her—eggs Benedict. Kristen didn't comment, but I happened to know she hated poached eggs. She didn't like runny yolks. And she *definitely* didn't like being told what to eat.

I didn't get this dynamic at all. Kristen was sitting there, but she was nowhere to be seen. Her flame was completely extinguished, like her mom drained all the fire right out of her.

Our drinks were delivered. I sipped an orange juice, and Kristen took a long swallow of her mimosa.

Evelyn pulled artificial sweetener from her purse and squeezed it into her coffee. "So, Kristen. What did you do to run off Tyler?"

What the fuck? My hand tightened around my glass.

Kristen carefully set down her champagne flute. "How do you know it wasn't me who broke things off?"

Evelyn looked amused, like the question was absurd. "Was it?"

Kristen sat rigid. A student in the principal's office. "He reenlisted."

"I see." Evelyn set her spoon down on the saucer. "Well, I can't say this surprises me."

Something angry flashed in Kristen's eyes, but she seemed to push it down. She pressed her lips together for a second. "And why is that?"

Evelyn raised her coffee cup to her lips and took a sip. "Well, a driven man like that wants the same in a partner, wouldn't he?" She turned to me. "And Joshua, what is it that you do? Or do you build dog merchandise full time?"

The question was condescending. For all she knew, I *did* build dog merchandise full-time. And what the fuck was wrong with that?

"I'm a firefighter and paramedic."

"Do you have any higher education?"

Why did I get the feeling the question was meant to be insulting? She had to know not many firefighters also held doctorates. An associate degree in fire science was about the norm. But if I had to guess, anything under a four-year degree wasn't going to impress her. I couldn't care less. I was proud of what I did for a living. But she clearly meant to highlight what she considered to be a shortcoming.

"I never went to college. I went into the military after high school. And then the fire academy, of course."

Evelyn spoke over her coffee. "And how long have you been sleeping with my daughter?"

"Mom!" Kristen stared at her, openmouthed.

I sat back in my chair and dragged a hand down my face. Well, Kristen's bluntness was definitely hereditary.

Evelyn set her cup on the saucer and put her hands together. "Really, Kristen. We don't need to play games. We're all adults." She gave me a disapproving glance. "I do hope this wasn't the reason why Tyler decided to search for greener pastures, however. For once I thought you were on the right track."

Kristen flushed again and my hackles came up. Was this lady for real?

"I didn't have anything to do with him breaking up with her,"

I said, feeling a little indignant. "And neither did she. It's been hard on her, and I'm surprised you're not more concerned about how she's feeling at the moment."

I felt Kristen's wide eyes on the side of my face.

I went on. "And if you bothered to ask her, she'd tell you that he broke up with her in a voicemail like a coward."

Maybe that would knock that joker off the pedestal Evelyn seemed to have him on.

Evelyn's expression remained placid, and she didn't get a chance to reply because the server came and started setting food down in front of us.

Kristen looked at her eggs with dismay. She was pretty picky about her food, and she got cranky when she didn't eat. I got the feeling she'd muscle through this because her mom seemed to have some sort of mind control over her, but she'd hate it.

You know what? Fuck this.

I picked up her eggs Benedict and gave her my French toast. "Kristen doesn't like her eggs like that," I said to Evelyn, not even trying to mask my annoyance.

Kristen looked at me like I'd just given her one of my kidneys. I put a hand under the table and squeezed her knee.

Evelyn watched the whole thing with unmasked distaste.

I couldn't fucking believe this was Kristen's mom. How did this lady raise someone so cool? If it wasn't for the uncanny family resemblance, I'd think this was some elaborate joke.

Evelyn draped a napkin over her lap. "Joshua, you might find my impatience with my daughter a little confusing. You haven't known her very long. The thing that you don't realize is that Kristen has a tendency to self-sabotage."

"I highly doubt that," I said, my jaw tight. It wasn't her fault Tyler reenlisted.

She chuckled. "You would. But then you're the most recent proof, aren't you?"

Kristen's fork hit the plate with a clatter. "I realize you're disappointed that Tyler and I broke up," she said with sudden vehemence. "But it is none of your business. Who I'm *fucking* is none of your business."

Evelyn's eyes smoldered. "Of course. Why would anything you do be *my* business? I raised you to be a prosperous person, poured myself into your development, and you've spent the last five years systematically undoing everything I instilled in you. First you stopped playing piano, turned your nose up at Juilliard. Then you walk away from Harvard so you can play house with Sloan. You discarded the elite college education I paid for by dropping out of law school to sell clothing for dogs..."

Piano? Law school??

Harvard???

Evelyn scowled. "Now you've botched the only relationship I've ever approved of. But of course, continue on, Kristen. See how far you can fall. You could have been making a respectable living, for God's sake."

I was beginning to lose my fucking cool. "She *does* make a respectable living," I snapped. Shit, she made twice as much as I did, easily.

Evelyn sent me a cutting glare. "Our opinions on what constitutes a respectable occupation are likely very different, young man. And I'll thank you to stay out of it."

Like hell I'm staying out of it. "She started her own successful business from the ground up. She gets to be her own boss and she gets to do it from her living room. I'd think you'd be proud."

"Yes, it's not exactly a meth lab that I'm running, Mother," Kristen said, smirking into her mimosa.

There's my girl. I put a hand on her shoulder. "Well, no one's saying you should give up your hobbies, honey bunny."

Kristen choked and spit her drink back into her glass, and we both launched into laughter.

Steam came out of Evelyn's ears and she glared at us. Kristen descended into a giggling fit, leaning into my shoulder.

The spell was broken. She was *back*.

Evelyn dabbed at her mouth with her napkin and raised a finger at the waiter. "Well, it's good to see that you've found someone to celebrate mediocrity with, Kristen."

Kristen grinned up at me, still laughing. "We *do* know how to celebrate, don't we, Joshua?"

"I'm all worn out after last night's celebration." I chuckled, wiping at my eyes. I slid my plate away from me and dropped my napkin onto it. "Ready to go?" I pulled out my wallet and tossed some bills onto the table. "Thank you for the invite," I said to Evelyn as I pushed out my chair. "Kristen?" I gave her my hand.

She didn't move.

Come on, Kristen—let's go. Don't stand for this shit.

She took my hand with a sideways grin and got up.

"Mom, this has been fun, as always." Then she grabbed the money I put on the table, tucked it into my back pocket, gave my ass a squeeze, and led me by the hand out of the restaurant.

TWENTY
KRISTEN

We burst from the restaurant into the warm noon air and made our way past the valet down the sidewalk to the fast click of my heels.

"Jesus, was she for real?" Josh asked, still laughing a little. We walked along a row of boutiques and salons. "I didn't think people like that really existed."

I scoffed. "Oh yes, she's for real. Sloan calls her the Ice Queen."

He shook his head. "Why do you let her talk to you like that? You don't actually believe that stuff, do you?" He looked at me, his thick eyebrows knitted.

I believed I disappointed her. And it was hard not to take what she said to heart. I *did* drop out of law school. I gave up on piano, which I was somewhat gifted at. Turned down scholarships. Considering what I could have been doing, what I was probably capable of if I wanted to apply myself and live a life I hated, yeah, I could be considered a disappointment. She had a point.

I didn't answer him.

"Kristen." He stopped me on the sidewalk and put his hands on my arms. "Hey, you know that nothing she said was true, right?"

I looked him in the eye. "She wasn't wrong about all of it, Josh." I was nothing if not self-aware.

He took a step closer and his warm eyes anchored me. "None of what she said about you is true," he said seriously. "You're one of the most driven people I've ever met. You're smart and successful, and Tyler's a fucking asshole for breaking up with you like that. That shit wasn't your fault."

Tyler.

He'd been calling almost every day since he broke up with me. I wasn't interested in hearing what he had to say.

I couldn't decide if the ruling emotion was guilt for falling in love with Josh while we were together, or fury that Tyler had ended two years by breaking all his promises and letting me know via voicemail.

He had to have known he was going to leave me, and he'd probably known for a while. He hadn't been any more forthcoming with his plans or reservations about our relationship than I'd been about my growing love for Josh.

I had feelings about this, and zero desire to explore them.

So I did with Tyler what I did with most of the shitty things in my life. I put him where I kept my hysterectomy and my childhood—in its own little room.

I tossed Tyler into his storage space, pulled the string on the light bulb, shut the heavy metal door, and latched the lock so I wouldn't have to look at the things that hurt, and I could go on with my life unaffected.

It was why I didn't cry. It was how I lived using only the left side of my brain.

But for some reason, compartmentalizing today didn't seem possible. I knew it the second I saw Josh standing in my living room with Mom. It was like things that happened with Josh couldn't be locked up. They just smeared all over, messy and impossible to put away.

The feeling was a little terrifying, like I'd lost my defense mechanism and I was naked and unarmed. With Josh's eyes looking into mine, I was emotionally exhausted and actually a little embarrassed about what happened today—and I didn't *get* embarrassed.

The tightness in my throat threatened to turn into crying. Crying. *Again.* For the second time in as many days. I didn't even recognize myself anymore.

He put a hand to my cheek as his stare wandered my face, and I was afraid he was going to kiss me. I was afraid because if he did, in that raw moment, I wouldn't be able to stop him. I had to keep that stuff under control. For both of us. I couldn't let lines blur.

But the side of his mouth came up into a smile. "You're hungry. Come on."

He pulled me into the nearest cafe.

Like, seriously. The nearest one. He didn't even look at the menu on the easel.

"What?" I said, horrified as he dragged me inside by the hand. "Aren't we going to at least check the reviews? What if it only has three stars?"

He held up two fingers to the hostess and turned to me. "You kill me, you know that? On one hand you embrace danger at every turn, and on the other you won't risk getting bad pancakes. And anyway, I'm buying."

I shook my head. "No, I'll pay for myself. We're not on a date."

"I know. Don't worry—I'm not trying to slip a date past you." He made a face like the idea was crazy. "I'd just like to buy you breakfast. I like feeding you."

"Why?"

He grinned at me and put his hands on my shoulders. "Because you're a lot nicer to me when you've eaten. It's more for me than you, really."

I cracked a smile and we followed the hostess through the restaurant to a table in a tiny enclosed patio. We had the space all to ourselves.

It was actually a little romantic. Mismatched bistro chairs and reclaimed wood tables with little vases of carnations on them. The patio was full of potted plants. Several fountains trickled along the vine-twisted brick walls that enclosed us. Throw pillows with Aztec patterns in the booths, Christmas lights strung over us. Intimate and lovely.

I was still going to check the reviews though.

Once we'd ordered, Josh started hitting me with questions. I think the brunch from hell was starting to process.

"I don't think I appreciated my mom enough," he said, taking the garnishes off his Bloody Mary and sliding them across to me on a napkin. "What was it like growing up with a mom like that?"

I nibbled on the pickle spear. "Like that brunch—but for eighteen years."

"She reminds me of that lady from that movie..." He snapped his fingers. "The one with Meryl Streep?"

I scoffed. "*The Devil Wears Prada*? She *might* be the devil. Nobody's ever seen them in the same room at the same time before."

He chuckled and I smiled weakly at him. God, he was my hero. In the last thirty minutes, Josh had done the modern-day equivalent of slaying a dragon. He saved me. *Twice.* Once from the Ice Queen and then again from starvation.

Food was my currency. Hungry was an emotion for me. I felt that shit in my soul.

I looked at the napkin he gave me. He liked all this stuff—celery, pickles, olives, shrimp. Either my hangry was truly terrifying or he gave it to me because he was taking care of me. He hadn't eaten yet either. He was hungry too, but he didn't even keep an olive for himself.

Josh was going to make a very good daddy one day. He was selfless and principled. Brave. Loyal.

He'd make a good husband to someone too.

I thought about how he'd given me his French toast earlier, and I had to clutch my heart through my dress.

"You okay?" he asked, watching me squeeze my chest.

I nodded. "Yeah."

It's just that you're perfect, and my heart hurts.

"Hey…" His eyes narrowed at my hand, and he reached for it over the table. "How'd you get this?" He ran a thumb along the purple mark just above my knuckles.

The touch gave me butterflies.

"Oh, it was a freak Pop-Tart accident while you were at work."

His thumb stilled, and he looked at me like I was about to tell him I was kidding. "A Pop-Tart accident? You got injured making a Pop-Tart?"

I pulled my hand back and feigned indignation. "Yes, I did. The middle of those things are like molten lava when they're hot. And me and this particular Pop-Tart had a run-in."

His eyes danced with amusement. "We really need to keep you out of the kitchen."

I shrugged. "So I cook the way you drive. Whatever."

He laughed.

"Hey," I said, after a moment. "I'm sorry she was insulting. It was meant to hurt me, not you."

He held his glass on the table. "You're very different around her."

Yes. Because she has the key to every room.

I'd never been able to keep her out.

Or lock her in.

I let out a long breath. "It's like the second I'm in her presence, I'm six years old, disappointing her at her dinner party with my Mozart concerto."

"How long did you play the piano?"

I reached down and pulled the backs off my heels. "Fifteen years. Every day for three hours, six days a week. Sunday was for tennis and whatever other activity she made me do."

He raised his eyebrows. "Wow. Why did you stop?"

"I stopped because she forced it on me."

He took a drink. "Were you any good?"

"Well, I'd hope so. You spend three hours a day doing anything for fifteen years, you better be good at it," I said, eating an olive.

I would play for him if he asked. And I didn't play for *anyone*.

Piano was symbolic for me. The shackles of my childhood, the chain I cast off when I finally had some control of my own life. Picking it up again, even though I was good at it, felt like acknowledging that her tyranny had merit. So my stilled fingers were my rebellion.

But for Josh? To have him look at me with admiration? I would play for Josh.

It was such an odd feeling wanting him to be impressed with me but simultaneously hoping he didn't like me too much.

"You got into Harvard? And you were in law school?" he asked.

I sighed. "Yes. I didn't see why I had to leave Sloan to go to

Massachusetts just to get a degree I didn't even want. So I went to UCLA. I was in my first year of law school when I dropped out. Obviously my mom was pissed about it," I mumbled into my coffee cup.

"You didn't want to be a lawyer?" He gave me a dimpled grin. "Arguing for a living? You? You were born for it."

I smirked. "I prefer to argue for fun."

Plus it had been too hard sitting in classes as my periods got worse and worse. The cramps, the anemia. Working from home was just easier on me. And I enjoyed having my own business. I was finally having fun with my life.

"Your mom is older than I pictured. How old is she?" he asked.

"Sixty-seven. She got pregnant with me when she was forty-three. A complete shock. She didn't think she could get pregnant." She'd had the same issues I did but less severe. "I basically ruined her life. Her career, her retirement plans—all put on hold."

I'd been a twin. She'd lost my brother in the fourth month of her pregnancy. If she had to be stuck with a baby, at least it could have been the boy so my dad could pass down the family name. But no. She'd gotten the girl instead. I disappointed her before I was even born.

How differently Josh and I had grown up. His parents had tried for a boy. He was exactly what they wanted when he came. And he was probably loved and cherished by every member of his family.

Like he was loved and cherished by me.

We were watching each other. Enjoying one of our comfortable silences. He was adorable. His hair was a little messy, his T-shirt tight over his broad chest.

For a moment I thought about whether or not I could keep

doing this. I didn't know if I could. Because even if I was successful at keeping him from loving me, I was failing miserably at not loving *him.*

I thought about waking up with my face pressed against his heart this morning, how he'd managed to finagle himself into my room last night.

Josh was my drug, my dealer, and that really toxic friend who's always pushing you into breaking your sobriety.

He was like that puppy that you swear will never sleep in the bed. It's so fucking cute, but you have to be the pack leader and lay down the law. Then it starts crying from the laundry room and you end up giving in the very first night.

"What are you thinking about?" he asked.

"Drug dealers and puppies in laundry rooms."

He laughed. "Of course you are."

"What are you thinking about?"

"I'm thinking that your dad must have been pretty cool." He took another sip of his Bloody Mary.

"What makes you think that?"

He shrugged. "A hunch. You lost your dad, right?"

"Yeah. When I was twelve. He had a heart attack. A few months before I met Sloan."

"What was he like?"

A little like you.

I let out a slow breath. "He was fun. And laid back. You'd have to be to live with a woman like that. He was a literature professor."

Mom had listened to him. He softened her. And when he died, she'd gone from difficult to impossible.

Our food arrived, and I breathed a sigh of relief. I didn't want to talk about me anymore.

My Spanish omelet actually looked pretty good. I pushed my hash browns over with the side of my fork and moved the toast so nothing touched.

"What's your family like?" I asked.

He grinned and puffed air from his cheeks. "Well, let's see. My parents are insanely in love. Dad worships the ground Mom walks on. They've got twelve grandkids so far, so holidays back home are like a Greek wedding. My sisters are all fiercely independent and competitive with each other. They fight over pretty much everything, but they're super cliqued up. Right now they're all united in their crusade to get me to move back home."

He salted his eggs. "Hey, Tyler didn't let her talk to you like that in front of him, did he?"

I took my first bite. It was perfect. I felt my mood improve almost immediately. "No. She didn't talk to me like that with him. She liked him."

It had been a reprieve. I'd *finally* done something right.

"Why?" he asked, putting ketchup on his hash browns.

"Tyler was sophisticated. She liked that."

"Oh," he said flatly, and I realized what I had implied.

But Josh *wasn't* sophisticated. He didn't like the theater—he liked movies, like I did. He preferred hunting, not art galleries. Pizza and beer to tapas and wine.

And he was perfect.

"Do you miss your family?" I asked, changing the subject.

He shrugged. "I'm glad I'm not there every day. It could get to be a bit much." He took a bite and chewed for a moment. "You know what I think the trick to dealing with family is? I've been thinking about this a lot lately."

"What?" I said, spreading strawberry jam on my toast.

"Marrying your best friend." He wiped his mouth with a napkin. "You marry your best friend, and at family gatherings you deal with your shitty relatives together. You laugh about it and have each other's backs. Share looks and text each other from across the room when everyone else is being an asshole. And nobody else really matters because you have your own universe."

He held my eyes for a moment. "That's what I want. I want someone to be my universe."

He'd have no problem finding that. No problem at all. Josh could have any woman he wanted. After all, he was the sun. Warm and vital. He would be the center of a big family one day, just like he wanted, and they'd all adore him.

And I was just some passing comet. Momentarily distracting. Useless and unimportant. I was nice to look at, fun to observe, but I'd never give life or be the center of anything.

I'd streak through and be gone, and Josh would forget me before we knew it.

TWENTY-ONE

JOSH

It was three and a half weeks to Brandon's wedding, two weeks since brunch with the Ice Queen.

Kristen and I had fallen into a new normal. When we hung out, it was like before. Friends only. No touching. No kissing. And occasionally, as long as we had sex first, she'd let me sleep in her bed and hold her. But only if we had sex. To her, the holding afterward was all part of it, I think. The second we left the bed, we had to shift back into friends-only mode. Of course this just made me that much more intent on making sure we ended up in bed. Not that I needed another reason to have sex with her, but now I was on a mission.

I wished I could put an arm around her on the couch when we watched TV or kiss her when we passed in the hallway, but her rules were rigid. I'd tried holding her hand once on a walk with Stuntman Mike and she fucking lost it on me. Didn't talk to me for three days, almost broke things off over it. Said I didn't "get" what friends with benefits meant.

After that, I didn't try to make moves on her outside of her rules. She obviously wasn't ready for an emotional relationship. It fucking sucked. But what was I going to do? It hadn't even been a month since Tyler. I guess I couldn't blame her for being hesitant to let me get close to her just yet.

She asked me all the time if I was going on dates, like she needed to make sure I was keeping up that end of the bargain. At first I was honest—told her no, I wasn't seeing other people. But she got really worked up about it.

Really fucking worked up.

Said if our arrangement was keeping me from dating, we should end it. I think she felt bad she wasn't ready to commit to me and didn't want me to miss out on finding someone who was. She knew I wanted to get married, have kids. That I already felt late to the game.

So I lied.

I'd say I was meeting someone for drinks and then I'd just go home for the night and sit around. Maybe go to the gym. When she'd ask me about my fake date, I'd just shrug and say we didn't have a connection. That seemed to placate her.

But the weird thing was, as much as she pressured me to see other women, I didn't think *she* was seeing other men.

She only ever sent me orders from her laptop. So when I was at the fire station and I got an order at 10:00 at night, I knew she was at home sitting on the couch going through emails. Not on a date. Then I'd wait an hour or so and reply with a dumb question about the order. If she replied right away, I knew she was still sitting on the couch working. She always replied.

On my days off, when I came over, she never did anything other than hang out with me. She never left the room to take calls, and she didn't disappear for mystery appointments or give me any reason to believe she was keeping to her promise that she'd date other people.

So why, then, didn't she want to be exclusive? Because by all accounts, I was the only man she was with. And that was a good thing, because I didn't think I could handle it if I wasn't.

I was just patiently waiting for her to move on from Tyler. I wasn't really sure I was actually making progress, but at least things didn't seem to be getting worse.

There was something to be said for that.

It was a little after 5:00 p.m. when a black SUV pulled into the driveway. Since I worked with the garage door open, I'd become the unofficial doorman for Doglet Nation. I signed for all the packages.

This didn't look like a delivery though. The driver was a man in sunglasses. He got out, and something told me I wasn't going to like who this was.

The guy was good-looking. Taller than me. He worked out—that much was obvious. He was well dressed, maybe my age.

He came straight into the garage with a confidence that told me he had official business here. Someone who'd been here before and had a right to come back.

"You must be Josh," he said, taking off his glasses and offering me his hand.

He had an accent. Not exactly Spanish, something else. More exotic, foreign. He wasn't a client. No way this guy owned a purse dog.

"I'm Tyler," he said, shaking my hand. "Is Kristen around?"

Hot, thick jealousy seared through me.

This was Tyler? This guy looked like an A-list actor in a goddamn action movie.

How *the fuck* had Brandon not said something about this? It was all I could do to keep my expression flat.

"She's in the house. Is she expecting you?" I crossed my arms over my chest, not making any move to take him inside.

He looked toward the door that led into the laundry room. "No," he said, his voice lowering. "She is not."

He seemed to notice my rigid posture, and he sized me up. "You were in the Marines." He eyed the Marine Corps tattoo on my bare chest.

"Infantry," I said.

"Gunny sergeant."

He outranked me. But then I wasn't a career military man like he was.

But he outranked me with Kristen too.

He seemed to be aware of this. Something in his eyes made me feel like I was the help. The lowly security guard giving him shit about his badge at a building he had full security clearance in.

His green-eyed stare was cool. "I want to thank you for staying with my girlfriend while the police worked out who was coming into the yard. It made her feel safe to have you there."

Possessiveness gripped me. "*Ex*-girlfriend. She's your ex-girlfriend."

His jaw flexed.

I didn't like this fucker. I didn't like that he was the reason why Kristen wasn't open to dating me. I didn't like that she obviously cared for him more than she cared for me. I didn't like that he was better than me, and I didn't like that he'd hurt her. I glared at him.

He glared back.

"Nice to meet you," he said stiffly, and he started for the door.

I put a hand to his chest. "*I'll* take you in."

He looked down at my hand, and I watched him bristle.

Make a move, asshole. I fucking dare you. Give me a reason.

His eyes came back up slowly, and I saw my own hatred reflected in his stare.

He knew. He knew I'd had her.

And he was the one who'd probably get her.

But in that moment we had an understanding. This was *my* house. At least right now it was. And if he wanted to go in, it would be me who took him.

I made him stand there for a tense couple of seconds before I turned for the door.

TWENTY-TWO
KRISTEN

The garage door opened, and I called out before Josh came around the corner. "Hey, do you want to try that Thai place in a minute? We could walk. They've got that tea you like."

I sat on the floor sorting my shipment of new plaid dog harnesses. The sizing seemed off. The extra smalls looked like smalls, and the smalls looked like mediums. I was pondering this as I looked up just as Josh walked in with Tyler directly behind him.

My breathing stopped.

Stuntman lost his ever-loving shit. He dove off the sofa and went right for Tyler's ankles. In one fluid movement, Josh scooped him up before he attacked.

My dog yapped and snarled, and Josh stood there for a moment before he finished depositing Tyler the way he dropped off a box when I was on the phone: He made eye contact with me, set him by the door, and left.

"What are you doing here?" I breathed.

Goddamn. He looked *good.*

I mean, he usually looked good. But that thing that always happened when he'd come back from leave, that moment of instant, primal attraction that smacked me in the face and reminded me what had drawn me to him in the first place—*that* thing happened.

He wore a long-sleeve striped button-down shirt rolled up at the elbows, with pressed black pants and a tan belt and shoes. His brown hair was thick and combed, and he had a five-o'clock shadow. He wore the silver watch I got him last Christmas.

"You won't answer my calls," he said, slipping his hands into his pockets.

He looked wounded. Slightly slumped. I'd never seen him anything but confident and smiling.

"Why would I?" I got up and crossed my arms. "We're over, so..."

Sadness flickered across his face.

For the first time since we'd broken up, it occurred to me that this had been hard on him.

I just thought his career was more important, and he was relieved he wasn't going back to civilian life. From his apologetic "I reenlisted without talking to you" message, I got the impression that while the breakup was an unfortunate by-product of his decision, he understood it was the choice he'd made and was at peace with it.

He took a step toward me. "Kris, can we talk?"

"Talk. Go for it," I said defensively. "But do it from there."

He glanced back toward the garage. "Let me take you somewhere. A nice restaurant. Where we can sit down and discuss things."

I scoffed. "I'm not going anywhere with you. You have two minutes. Say what you came to say and get out."

His jaw flexed. "Kris, I'm not leaving until we talk, and it's going to take a lot longer than two minutes for me to say what I came to say. So unless you plan on having *him* throw me out"—he nodded to the garage—"then let's go somewhere private."

The set of his mouth told me he meant it. He wasn't leaving until I let him talk. I thought of Josh, of him walking in and out of the house while Tyler and I had what was probably going to be a really shitty conversation.

I rolled my eyes. "Fine." I grabbed my purse off the coffee table. "Let's go."

He looked over my outfit. I was in shorts, flip-flops, I had a sweater tied around my waist, and I wore a T-shirt that read THE MORE I MEET PEOPLE, THE MORE I LIKE MY DOG.

Tyler liked expensive restaurants. The food on deployment was terrible, so when he came home, he wanted to treat himself. We'd probably end up at some fancy fusion place or something. I'd be epically underdressed, and I didn't give a shit.

"You're not going to get changed?" he asked.

"Nope." I marched past him to the front door. "You'll just have to make my excuses to the maître d'." I stomped outside.

He ran around me to the passenger side of his SUV and held my door open. I got in grouchily and stared into the garage as Tyler slipped into the driver's seat.

Josh stood over a staircase holding a nail gun with Stuntman leashed by his feet. Josh looked at me for a flicker of a second before he turned back to his project, his jaw tight. I wondered what he thought of all this.

Stuntman barked and strained against his leash as we pulled out of the driveway, and I couldn't shake the super weird feeling I was leaving my family behind.

Tyler's sandalwood cologne was more concentrated in the closed SUV. It blasted my face through the AC, familiar and new at the same time, stirring feelings of nostalgia in my heart.

"I missed you," he said. He reached for my hand, but I yanked it away.

The heavy-duty door that I'd stashed Tyler behind rattled and shook and then it burst open. A tornado of emotions rotated around me, and I couldn't process any of them. All I knew was that the general consensus was that I was pissed.

I felt indignant about him making his choice without the courtesy of even speaking to me first.

There was guilt that he was no longer the last man I'd slept with. That I'd jumped on Josh literally within minutes of us breaking up without so much as a twinge of regret.

Hurt that *he* seemed hurt.

Confusion as to why he was even here.

Surprise that seeing him made me wonder why I'd been so nervous about us moving in together.

Anger that he didn't have more of an effect on me when we were still together so Josh might have had less.

Outrage that he hadn't kept his promises so I would have to keep mine.

Pissed.

That was the muddied summary of how I felt. I was just pissed.

I glanced at Tyler. He seemed to be upset that I hadn't let him hold my hand. His face had darkened. "Are you sleeping with him?"

We both knew who he was talking about. There was no reason to act coy.

"That is none of your business," I snapped.

"Were you sleeping with him when we were together?" He didn't look at me, but his knuckles were white on the wheel.

I fumed. "You know what? Stop the car. Let me out." I unbuckled myself.

"Kris—"

"Fuck you, Tyler. I was faithful to you. And I didn't do this shit to our relationship. You did it. If you didn't want me sleeping with other people, you shouldn't have broken up with me. You gave up the privilege to be butt hurt the second you left me that voicemail."

He didn't stop the car.

"Okay," he said after a moment. "Okay, I apologize. I know you wouldn't do that. I just...seeing how he was about you, I...I'm sorry."

How was he about me? What the fuck happened in the garage? I wasn't going to ask, but what the hell?

We drove in silence for several minutes. When he finally spoke again, his voice was almost a whisper. "Do you love him?"

I ignored him. This answer was one that hurt to admit to *myself.* I turned to the window and tried to sort my feelings by staring out at the freeway.

As expected, he picked some ridiculously dim, hoity-toity seafood place in Malibu. Our table was under a stupid lamp made out of coral with a view of the ocean. He pulled my chair out for me and I refused to sit, glaring at him until he made his way around the table to his own seat.

I'd had enough of his chivalry. I wanted to get this over with. As far as I was concerned, this whole thing was too little, too late.

I sat and squinted at the menu. I was starving and irritable. The drive had taken forty-five minutes in rush hour. Josh and I would have been done eating dinner already. Josh never let me get this hungry. He would have put me in the passenger side of the car, closed the door, tapped the glass with his knuckle, and pressed a bag of chips against my window, grinning with those fucking dimples of his. Josh would have taken me somewhere *I* wanted to go, and he would have wanted to eat there too because we liked the same food.

A server put a bread basket between us. It wasn't even bread—just weird, jagged paper-thin crackers with sesame seeds on them. It totally triggered me, and I instantly felt hangry and more annoyed.

"The tuna tartare is supposed to be excellent," Tyler said, his tone conciliatory.

"Is it?" I slapped the menu closed and dropped it on the table with a smack. "Order for me because I have literally no idea what the hell I'm looking at."

"We could go somewhere el—"

"Nope. Let's do what *you* want. Always," I bit back. "Let's have a long-distance relationship that leaves me alone for months at a time while you do you. And let's eat what *you* want to eat. Because you're the important one here, right?"

It wasn't fair and I knew it. I'd signed up for a military relationship. But I wasn't rational at the moment—I was hungry.

I leaned forward. "Order oysters. I *dare* you."

All I needed was shells filled with snot set in front of us for me to completely lose my shit.

He pressed his lips into a line. He seemed to sense I was too hungry to be reasoned with. So when the server came back, Tyler placed our order, watching me the whole time from the corner of his eye like I might flip the table or something.

Afterward he tried again to reach for my hands.

"Kristen—"

"What?" I put my hands in my lap. "Say what you have to say, and do it without touching me."

"Kris—"

"You broke up with me in a voicemail. *Two years* and I get a voicemail."

Everything I did after that was fair game.

His thick eyebrows drew down. "I couldn't get you on the phone. I tried for days. Where were you?"

Hanging out with Josh. Panicking that you were coming home.

"You called twice, Tyler. I missed two phone calls, so you decided to replan our lives without discussing it with me?"

The indignation surged again. "Do you know what it's like to have a boyfriend you can't call? To not know where you are because it's classified? To never have a date for things? To go to weddings alone? I did this for you for *years*. And the first thing you're supposed to do for *me*, you bail on me."

I snatched one of the crackers from the bread basket and took a grumpy bite. "What about my surgery?" I waved the cracker around. "I could have had it months ago and had Sloan take care of me, but nooooo. You told me to wait. You wanted to be there for me." I put my fingers in quotes. "Thanks for all the months of extra needless suffering. And what about that big house you made me get so you'd have room for your things? I guess I'll just continue to foot that enormous rent, right?"

I glared at him, sitting back in my seat. "Oh, and you know, you really fucked me over with Evelyn too. Tossed me right into the lion's den. So thanks for that."

He let out a slow breath. "I know. And I'm sorry." He dragged a hand down his face. "I need you to know that this wasn't because I didn't want to be with you. It was never that. This just wasn't the life I wanted, Kris. The military is all I've ever known."

"Fine." I crossed my arms. "So you're doing what you want,

as usual. You made your choice. You did it without including me. Why am I here?"

"Don't you even miss me?"

The question hit me in the heart. His eyes begged me. *Begged* me to miss him.

Not really. Not until I saw you and I let you out of your storage room. Now I'm confused…

…Josh.

An urge to talk him out of wanting me took hold.

"You know, it's for the better anyway," I said, tossing a hand. "Because I'm not even myself around you. You would have hated living with me once you really got to know me."

He just looked at me, his eyes going soft like he knew what I was doing and thought it was cute.

"Okay, you don't believe me? This place—" I threw a hand up at the restaurant. "I don't like eating at places like this. What the fuck is squid ink pasta? I go to places like this with you because you like it and you only get to choose where you eat, like, fifteen days out of the year."

I put a hand to my chest. "I am very opinionated about where I want to eat. You don't even know that. That is a core part of who I am as a person, and you have never seen that side of me, Tyler."

The corner of his mouth came up into a small, amused smile.

"This is not funny. I'm being totally serious. I get very easily annoyed. I'm impatient and moody. I hate almost everyone. We don't even really know each other. All you've ever seen is me at my best, being agreeable and wearing makeup. That is not the real me."

Josh knows the real me.

I went on. "You reenlisted. It's done, and my position on another deployment hasn't changed. I'm not doing it. We are not getting back together. So I appreciate the explanation and the face-to-face. But none of this changes anything."

He leaned onto the table with his forearms and spoke directly to my eyes. "I love you."

My heart clenched.

I'd heard the words on the phone a hundred times. He'd written them in letters. But it had been almost a year since he'd looked me in the eye and said it to my face. And now that he did, there was no question that he meant it.

He waited, but I didn't say it back. I wasn't sure if I loved him.

I wasn't sure that I *didn't*.

Someone dropped off some weird salads while Tyler and I stared at each other tensely across the table. The green menagerie smelled faintly like seaweed, and I actually felt a little nauseous looking at it. The only thing I recognized on the plate was a cherry tomato, and even that was yellow instead of red. I pushed the plate away and crossed my arms, scowling.

I wanted to put out the stupid romantic candle flickering between us. I grabbed the glass votive and dumped my water into it, and Tyler wrinkled his forehead at me like I'd gone insane.

"What do you want from me?" I asked. "Closure? Forgiveness?" I picked up the sloshing votive and moved it next to the salt and pepper shakers.

His gorgeous green eyes canvassed my face. "Do you remember the day we met?"

I scoffed. "Of course. You were so lame. How could I forget?"

He smiled. "You'd convinced the piano player in that bar to let you play. It was incredible. I couldn't take my eyes off you."

The corner of my lip twitched. It was the last time I'd played. Two years ago.

I had a booth at a pet trade show in Orange County, and I was staying the night alone in a hotel. I had a few drinks in me, and nobody there knew me. The notes had soared from my fingers, and I saw him there across the room, under a light at a cocktail table like a scene from a movie.

Everything around him had blurred.

He continued. "I asked you your name, and then I wrote it in calligraphy on a napkin. And you laughed at me and asked me if that ever actually worked on anyone." He smirked a little. "It did, you know. It worked on every girl before you."

This made me smile, and I felt myself soften. "You were so well dressed I thought for sure you were gay."

He laughed, his eyes distant like he was pulling up a memory. "After you gave me a hard time for my stupid pickup tactic, I tried to buy you a drink. You said all you wanted was a new napkin. So I got you one, and I folded it into an origami swan. That *really* pissed you off."

I snorted. The damn origami swan. I still had it, though I'd never admit it. "I was pretty salty that day. I had no patience for desperate acts of origami."

He chuckled. "You told me if I could beat you at thumb war I could have your number."

Yeah. I hadn't seen that win coming. I'd never been bested. He had surprisingly agile thumbs.

I remembered how my heart had fluttered when our hands had touched. I'd been immediately attracted to him. The chemistry was instantaneous.

He shook his head. "I'd never met a woman like you before. You told me to go to hell and made me look forward to the trip."

He scooted his chair around so he was sitting catty-corner to me. Our knees touched, and a small thrill ran through me.

How close I had come to living with this man. To sharing my life with him. It could have been him sleeping in the bed next to me instead of Josh, my cuddly teddy bear.

Tyler's piercing eyes seemed to reach into my soul, and I couldn't look away.

"I couldn't throw my career away, Kris. I worked too hard to get to where I am. They dangled an opportunity in front of me, I panicked, and I did something stupid, and I've regretted it every day since."

He let out a shaky breath. "The morning after I left you that message, I woke up and I felt like I'd buried myself alive. I tried to call you right away and..." He shook his head. "This silence has been like a siege. I've been so desperate to get to you I almost went AWOL. You have no idea how hard it's been. I've been out of my damn mind."

He reached for my hand again. His expression was so raw I thought it might break him if I jerked away, so I reluctantly let him take it. His touch sent an unexpected jolt through me. A shiver of memory.

He looked down at our hands as he threaded his fingers in mine. My heart began to pound.

I remember you.

Tyler came flooding back to me like his touch broke a forget spell.

I knew this man. I knew the way he smelled and tasted. I could recognize his moods in a single word. I remembered the look in his eyes when we made love and the smile on his face in the morning when we'd lay in bed talking, sharing a pillow. I recalled the pain of kissing him goodbye at the airport and the emptiness when he left.

I remember.

He looked at our hands like it hurt him to touch me. His eyes moved back up to mine. "It's been a sucking void, Kris. Like some black hole that keeps getting wider and wider. You're the thing that I look forward to. The reprieve in the middle of whatever bullshit I'm dealing with. I have conversations with you in my head. I store things up to tell you. For the last two years, I've been on a countdown of nothing but you, living my life in the days between our talks and my leave."

He paused and studied my face. He was painted in regret and sadness.

"I messed up," he breathed. "I should have never done it. I should have just come home."

I let out a long breath. "And then you would have just resented me."

Fuck, was there no scenario in which a man could just be with me without having to give up on the one thing he wants for himself?

At the rate I was going, the only way I'd end up with someone for the rest of my life was if I choked on some queso and died on a first date.

Our food came, and we ate in silence. I stared at my plate, and he stared at me. When the dishes were cleared, my anger had officially run out. I replaced it with guilt.

"Tyler..."

He looked at me, his eyes hopeful at the change in my tone.

"I *am* in love with him. I think I've been in love with him from the day I met him."

I didn't see the need to lie to him. If he was going to be tortured over his choice, I didn't want him seeing me with rose-colored glasses.

He wiped a hand down his mouth and sat back in his chair,

his fist clenched on the top of the table. "I figured," he said finally, his voice low.

I wondered how he knew. What about me had given it away?

Maybe seeing *Josh* had given it away.

"Are you with him?" he asked.

I shook my head. "No."

He looked away from me. "Then he's a fucking idiot," he said, his eyes glassy.

"It's not his choice. It's mine. And I would be with him if I could."

He stared wearily at the bread basket. "But you don't love *me*?" His eyes went back to mine.

I shrugged. "I don't know," I said honestly. "I think a part of me was with you because you weren't really real, you know? You weren't here to deal with my shitty periods and get sexually frustrated like the boyfriends before you. You didn't want kids, so my issues didn't matter to you. Mom loved you. You were easy. And then we decided to make it real, and I was just so freaked out that you were coming home. I was scared to live with you and make that kind of commitment. But then when I saw you today, I..."

He hung on my words.

I let out a breath. "I saw you and I wondered why I was scared. I think I would have fallen right back in love with you the second you came home. But you never did."

And I needed you to. Because you were the only thing keeping me from throwing myself into the flames.

He squeezed his eyes shut. When he opened them, they were full of hurt. "And what about him?"

I shrugged. "What about him? I can't be with him. Ever. He wants kids. So that's the end of that."

He shook his head. "This is my fault," he said quietly. "All of it. I knew something was there with you two. I could feel it. And I fucking reenlisted anyway." He looked at me, the anguish etched deep in his forehead. "I did this. I practically handed you to him. I was so stupid."

"You're not wrong," I mumbled.

I wondered what would have happened differently if Tyler had just come home. If he would have moved in. Been there. *Reminded me*, like I was reminded now.

But deep inside, I knew Tyler never stood a chance against Josh. Josh would have hovered on the edges of any happiness I could have ever found with Tyler.

Josh would hover on the edges of my everything for the rest of my life, I suspected.

So I might as well get used to it.

Tyler paid the check and as we got up to go, he looked at me. "I want to take you somewhere."

He brought me to a hotel right off the beach. I thought we were going up to the roof—I'd seen a sign for a rooftop bar. But we got off on a guest room floor. When he pulled out a key, I realized he was taking me back to his room.

"Tyler—"

"Just . . . please, Kris. Just for a few minutes."

He opened the door into a sprawling space. An enormous panoramic window looked out over the ocean. He led me with a hand on my lower back into the room, and I realized it wasn't a room at all. It was a presidential suite.

A dining room table for eight sat to the left with a fresh flower arrangement on it bigger than I was. A spiral staircase led up to a loft with a library in it overlooking a gourmet kitchen.

A sleek black piano with flickering candles, two champagne

glasses, and rose petals on top of it sat by the open balcony door. Champagne nestled in shifting ice next to the piano bench.

He'd obviously had something romantic planned for us before I'd made it clear we weren't getting back together and I'd dropped the news about Josh on him.

The day hadn't gone the way he'd hoped.

It hadn't gone the way I'd hoped either.

"I wasn't sure if I should bring you here," he said. "I wasn't sure you even wanted to see me. It took me a while to find one that had a piano." He looked at me, his green eyes searching. "I was hoping you'd play for me. Like the day we met."

I looked back at the piano. I didn't want to reenact the day we met. I didn't want to perform for him or play these games.

What I wanted was to go home. I wanted to be with Josh.

We stood there in silence, the distant sound of the ocean crashing through the open balcony door.

He put a hand to my arm. "Kris?" He tipped his head to catch my eyes. "Will you play for me? Please? One last time?"

One last time.

So this was it. Our goodbye.

This was how it started, and this was how it would come to an end. Me, sitting on a piano bench while he watched me play. It was a fitting finale. I was glad we had it. Glad that he'd come and we'd said the things we needed to say. It was better this way.

I looked at him a moment. "All right, Tyler. One last time."

I took a seat, placing my fingers on the keys. A cool, salty ocean breeze rolled through the drapes, and I drew it deep into my lungs and began.

My mind disappeared into itself. I didn't feel Tyler sit next to me, and I couldn't tell you what music my fingers chose, or how long I played. Fifteen years of muscle memory made all the decisions.

When it ended, it felt like coming out of a dream. I put my hands in my lap and found Tyler sitting next to me, smiling gently, his eyes teary.

Then a hand came up under my jaw, and he was kissing me.

It was soft and careful, a closed-mouthed exploration. But it drew me up into him like a warm breeze lifting a kite. My arms found their way around his neck, and the memory of the shape of his mouth and the feel of his lips filled in the places that used to hold question marks and dark corners.

Yes, I remembered him. I remembered *us.*

But he wasn't Josh.

The scruff of his beard felt wrong. He was too tall. And while my heart pounded, it didn't reach out for him.

Maybe once, this would have been enough. I might have even mistaken this feeling for love.

But now I knew better.

He pulled away, a hand still cupping my cheek, and I looked at him, despair pouring over me.

This is as good as it will ever be.

If Tyler couldn't eclipse Josh, nobody could. And it made me start to cry because the whole fucking thing was completely and utterly hopeless.

His thumb moved along my jaw, and his eyes blinked back tears. He probably thought I was moved by the kiss. I guess I was. But not in his direction.

"I love you, Kris. I'm always going to love you," he whispered. "Please forgive me."

I looked away from him, wiping a tear from my cheek. "I can forgive you if you can forgive me back."

He wrapped an arm around my shoulders and pressed his cheek to the side of my head.

Our embrace was full of loss and regrets and what-ifs.

Tyler was a version of my life. A path I could have taken. But now I was so far off course I didn't even know where I was going anymore. All I knew was I was headed for a dead end.

And when I got there, I'd be alone.

"Kristen, have you ever heard of the red thread of fate?" Tyler said over me.

"No." I sniffled.

He turned me until I sat facing him.

"I've been studying Mandarin," he said, speaking to my eyes. "Learning a lot about the Chinese culture. And there was a story I read that really resonated with me."

He reached out and tenderly wiped a tear off my cheek with his thumb. "In Chinese legend, two lovers are connected by an invisible red thread around their pinky fingers. The two people connected by the red thread are destined lovers from birth, regardless of place, time, or circumstances. The cord might stretch or tangle, but it can never break."

His eyes moved back and forth between mine.

"You are on the other end of my thread, Kris. No matter how far apart we are, you're tied to me. I stretched us and I tangled us and I'm sorry. But I didn't break us, Kris. We're still connected."

He paused. That pause that he always did on the phone, the one that told me he was about to tell me the good part.

Then he pulled a tiny, black velvet box from his pocket and opened the lid.

My heart stopped dead. *Oh my God.*

"Marry me."

TWENTY-THREE

JOSH

I finished the last order Kristen had for me, but I stayed. I wanted to be there when she got home.

I wanted to see that she *did* come home.

The waiting was physically painful. My chest hurt like a bear trap was clamped over my heart. My mind ran wild. Where were they? At a restaurant talking? Or at a hotel, in his bed, making up?

No. She wouldn't. We'd just been together last night. She wouldn't, right?

Fuck, even the thought of her letting him hold her hand sent me into a meltdown.

He was here to get back with her—I had no doubt in my mind. The only thing I didn't know was what she was going to do about it.

Watching her leave fucking killed me.

But I had no right to her at all. I didn't even have the right to be upset. This was *the* guy—the one she'd been heartbroken over for the last month.

He was the guy, and I was no one.

I paced the garage. I paced the house. She was always home when I was there and the vacancy inside made my anxiety worse, reinforced the wrongness of it all. So I went back outside where at least I wasn't looking at her empty couch.

My stomach grumbled, but I couldn't eat. Even Stuntman Mike was worked up. He kept crying and looking at the driveway, following me around my workstation like he'd witnessed her kidnapping and was pissed I hadn't done anything to stop it. Finally I just put him in his satchel and carried him around with me.

6:00.

7:00.

8:00.

There was only so late I could stay before it became obvious I'd been waiting for her. I'd never worked past 9:00 p.m. before. But if I left and just went home, I'd never know when she came back, or *how* she came back. Happy? Sad? Tomorrow, wearing the same clothes?

And what if he didn't just drop her off? What if he came back to stay the night? I bet the fucker would love to rub that shit in my face. He'd probably do a goddamn victory lap.

Every car that drove by made my heart pound and head jerk up.

Maybe I should leave. I didn't know if I could handle seeing them as a couple. I told myself if she wasn't back by 9:00, I would go. Because the later it got, the more likely it was they were staying the night together—here or elsewhere. And either way it was better if I didn't know about it.

Finally, at 8:17, a maroon Nissan pulled into the driveway.

She came back in an Uber.

Alone.

My relief was a thousand-pound weight off my chest. I could finally breathe again.

Three hours. They could have just been in a restaurant. The drive there, the drive back—that easily could have been one hour of the three. She didn't stay the night with him. And after everything, she only gave him a few hours and didn't let him come back with her? Maybe this was a good sign.

I took off the satchel—I'd rather die than let her see me use her dog purse—and made it look like I was busy laying carpet on the already finished steps and not sitting in the garage waiting for her to come home like a lovesick puppy dog.

She got out of the car and came in through the garage, holding her sweater in her hand, dragging the sleeve along the driveway. Stuntman Mike ran to meet her, bouncing and crying at her feet, but she didn't reach down to pick him up.

"Hey," I said casually as she approached. "I'm just finishing up here."

She stopped in front of me and studied me wordlessly. I tried to figure out what happened from the way she looked.

She hadn't gotten dressed up to go out with him. That was good. But her lipstick was gone. Was that because they ate? Or because they'd been kissing? Had they fought the whole time? Is that why her shoulders were slumped? Her eyes were red. A little mascara smeared, like she'd been crying.

"Josh? Do you want to go sing karaoke with me?"

I blinked at her. "Karaoke?"

She sniffed, looking at me tiredly. "I feel a spree coming on. It's either a cleaning spree or a singing spree. Singing might be healthier."

I grinned at her. "Yeah. Sounds like fun."

She smiled weakly at me. "Okay. And you have to feed me. Like, soon."

I raised an eyebrow. "He didn't feed you?" She hadn't eaten before they left. They'd taken off over three hours ago. Damn, that fucker played with fire.

I hoped she was a nightmare the whole time.

"He kinda fed me." She grimaced. "I had some deconstructed Chilean sea bass ceviche tapenade thingy."

I scoffed. "Is that even food?"

"I have no idea. I'm starving," she mumbled, turning for the house.

It hadn't gone well. That was obvious. And they'd just been at a restaurant, like I thought—a shitty restaurant that she didn't like, on top of it. He hadn't scored himself any points with that rookie move.

Hope swelled inside me. Maybe this was the last we'd see of Tyler.

Still, she was down.

"Is everything okay?" I asked, standing.

She stopped with her back to me and let her head loll. "Fine." She paused for a moment. "He asked me to marry him."

The punch to my heart knocked the wind out of me. *What?*

I was grateful she wasn't looking at me because she would have seen it on my face. I couldn't catch my breath. I almost couldn't compose myself to answer.

I cleared my throat. "Oh yeah? What did you say?"

She waited a beat until she replied, talking over her shoulder. "I said maybe."

~

While she changed, I made her a sandwich—no mayo, only one piece of ham, provolone, no crust—the way she liked it. I handed it to her wrapped in a paper towel when she came out of her room. She looked like she wanted to cry when she took it from me. I hated seeing her so upset.

We called an Uber so we could drink.

And drink I planned to fucking do.

I said maybe.

He wanted to marry her and she was actually considering it. I felt sick.

In the Uber, she sat next to me with her leg tucked under her in the back seat, her knee poking through the ragged hole of her jeans. She'd done her makeup. She gazed wearily out the window.

I stared at her hand on the seat. Her ring finger was bare. *For now.* "Do you want to talk about it?" I asked.

She looked over at me. "You want to talk to me about my boyfriend?"

Boyfriend. She called him her boyfriend. Not ex-boyfriend. *Boyfriend.*

The knife twisted in my heart, but through sheer will I managed to keep my voice level. "Sure. I might be able to give you some insight."

I was torn between wanting to remain blissfully ignorant and needing to be informed. Morbid curiosity won out. I reasoned that whatever was going to happen would happen whether I knew the details or not. And if she talked to me about it, maybe I could sway her decision in my favor.

She took a deep breath. "Well, he reenlisted. Only this time he won't be in war zones. He'll be translating for dignitaries and high-ranking military personnel."

I wrinkled my forehead. "Translating?"

"Yeah. He's a linguist. He's fluent in nine languages—ten.

Maybe now it's ten. He said he's studying Mandarin. I don't know."

Jesus *Christ.* How had Brandon failed to mention that this joker wasn't some infantryman doing grunt work? He was smart, educated, and good-looking to boot?

Fucking Brandon. His penchant for understating things was killing me. I was completely unprepared for this guy.

So that's why the Ice Queen liked him. I looked like a damn fuckboy next to Tyler. No wonder Kristen didn't want anything serious with me.

"He wants me to marry him. We'd move overseas." Her eyes flitted up to mine.

My stomach lurched. "And you said maybe?"

"I said I would think about it."

I scratched my cheek, trying to act like none of this bothered me while inside I was losing my fucking mind. "What are your reservations?"

She didn't answer me.

"Sloan would miss you if you moved," I said. *Not to mention what it would do to me.*

But she just took a deep breath and looked away from me.

She gazed out the window, and I stared at her watching the road. When she turned back to me, her eyes were full of tears. Then she unbuckled herself, slid across the seat, and climbed into my lap.

My heart jumped at the unexpected affection. I pulled her in and tucked her head under my chin, breathing in the smell of her hair. The feel of her small, warm body in my arms was like home. There was no other word for it.

She was home.

It was hard to see how much he affected her. This was the

second time I'd seen her crying and both times had been over him.

The jealousy was almost more than I could handle.

This woman was mine. She was *mine*, not his. Why couldn't he have stayed away from her? Let her just get over him?

But then I realized the truth. She wasn't mine—she never was.

I'm hers.

And it's not the same thing.

I'd been fine being patient, because I was just waiting for her to come out of it. I hadn't been braced for him to come back into her life. And now, faced with the reality that I might lose her altogether, I realized what I'd known for weeks.

I'm in love with her.

And now this guy that I couldn't even begin to compete with might take her from me.

I felt helpless. Panicked. A fight response triggered inside and it had nowhere to go, because I couldn't do shit about this. All I could do was be me, and that wasn't good enough.

A sex thing. It will only ever be a sex thing.

She raised her head and planted a soft kiss under my chin, and it almost broke my fucking heart. She was never like this with me. And as much as I loved it, it was all fueled by her feelings for someone else. He hurt her and I was here, so I got to be the one to comfort her.

But it was something. At least I could do something for her beyond just scratching an itch.

She was with me, holding me. Letting me hold her. I needed to enjoy the moment because I didn't know how many more of them I'd get.

I squeezed my eyes shut and forced down the lump in my

throat, tried to focus on her breath on my neck, her cheek pressed to my collarbone—the vulnerability she was giving me that I only ever saw when she was sleeping curled up next to me on those nights when she let me in.

I vowed to make tonight fun so she'd forget.

And so I'd have something to remember when she left.

TWENTY-FOUR

KRISTEN

I stumbled off the stage, laughing hysterically. Josh caught me at the bottom of the steps as I collided with his chest. I felt the rumble of his laughter through his T-shirt.

He wore the shirt I'd stolen from him the day we met. The brewery one. It looked so good on him. His broad back, his tapered waist, the fabric tight over his contoured chest. I took a deep breath and tried to capture the scent I'd smelled that day when I wore it, that masculine cedar that was Josh. Once I had it, I held my breath, not wanting to let it go.

I'd had a smidge too much to drink.

We'd taken a shot before we went on, and I had already been two beers in. We'd just rapped "No Diggity" together, and I'd cracked up through half of it. Josh was pretty good. He did dance moves and everything.

I slipped my arms around his waist, hooking my fingers behind his back, and he held me to him, smiling down at me.

I put my chin to his chest. "I'm only hugging you because those cougars over there have their eye on you," I lied. "It's my duty as your friend to protect you from impending cougar attacks."

He chuckled. "Thanks for clearing that up. I was afraid for a second there you were hugging me for real."

I would do everything with you. For real.

"I have a confession," I said, gazing up at him. "I don't really think you're a bad driver."

He gave me an amused smile.

"What?" I bit my lip.

"I'm just thinking about something Shawn said the other day. That drunks and leggings always tell the truth."

I snorted. "I am not drunk. I'm just talking in cursive. And Shawn is an idiot. Have you ever had the urge to tell someone to shut the fuck up when they aren't even talking? That's how I feel literally every time I see his face." I narrowed my eyes. "Although, there *is* some truth to that legging thing..."

He laughed, the smile creasing his eyes at the corners.

I pushed my lip out into a pout. "Josh? I need hot wings."

He released me. "Yes, ma'am."

We walked back to our red booth to a poorly sung Lola Simone song, and he placed an order.

I took a long drink of my beer. "Why do guys always sit facing the door?" I asked, licking my lips.

He smiled at me. "Do we?" He looked over my shoulder at the entrance. "Huh. I guess we do. Maybe it's some protective instinct. So I can keep an eye out for danger. Keep my sword arm free to protect you." His dimples flashed.

God.

Tyler was handsome in a chiseled sort of way. Like a model in a black-and-white cologne commercial. But Josh. Oh God—*Josh*. He melted me. He was a teddy bear. A warm, gorgeous, delicious piece of everything.

I wished I could let him in. Let him be my boyfriend if he wanted to. He'd said the morning after we'd first hooked up that we could be exclusive. He would. He wanted to.

He would lock the house up before bed and kiss me good night. He'd throw his shirts on my chair and I wouldn't even complain about it. Stuntman could sleep with us because he likes Josh. And when he went to work, I could text him and tell him I miss him, and he would say it back, and if I got mouthy, he'd just laugh at me and handle me like he always did. He just let my moods roll off him, like nothing about me scared him, and it made me feel like I could be myself around him. Like the only time I really *was* myself was when I was around him.

Maybe I *should* marry Tyler.

I mean, why should everyone be miserable, right? If I married Tyler, he would be happy, Mom would be happy. Josh would move on to fertile pastures and have a million babies. And I'd be with someone that I cared about who could maybe distract me from the broken heart I was going to carry for the rest of my life.

Tyler and I got along. It wouldn't be bad. It wouldn't be me and Josh, but there wasn't going to *be* a me and Josh, so didn't I have to consider my alternatives? And Tyler knew I was in love with Josh. He knew what he was asking when he proposed.

My best friend would never talk to me again, and my dog would probably run away. With *Josh*.

I wondered if Tyler would eat hot wings and drink beer with me.

Probably not.

"You know what you need, Josh? One of those women who smiles when she talks."

He laughed. "What?"

"You know, one of those really sweet women who's always smiling. They make great mothers. They're supportive and they rub your back when you've had a bad day. They smell like cookies and they get laugh lines and wear scarves to the grocery store."

"I think you're drunk." His eyes sparkled.

I *was* drunk.

He grinned at me. "I like you like this."

"I have to tell you something." I made my face serious. "You can't make fun of me."

He sat up and made his face straight too. "What?"

"Earlier? Tyler took me back to his hotel room."

The humor in Josh's eyes evaporated instantly.

"No. Not that. We didn't do that." I waved him off. "He had this whole romantic setup. When we got there, he had champagne and rose petals and candles all over. *Everywhere*."

The levity returned to his eyes. "Ouch."

"Yup. I got outta there. It really freaked me out. Because you know why?"

"Why?" he asked.

"He should know. He should know I wouldn't like that, right? That means something, doesn't it?"

His expression grew a little serious. "Yeah, it does."

"Am I a bitch? I am, huh? That was really sweet, and I should have appreciated that. I *am* a bitch. I knew it."

He chuckled. "No. You're honest." He shook his head and talked into his beer. "And he did it all wrong."

I smirked. "Oh yeah?"

"Yeah." He put his glass down. "Let me guess—the ring was huge. Big rock?"

"Oh my God, Josh, you don't even know. It was *enormous*. He designed it and had it *made*. It had this red rope of rubies around the band and..." I took a deep breath remembering it. He'd spent a fortune on it and I'd hated it. It was so gaudy. "Why? What kind of ring should he have gotten me?"

"None. You'd want to pick your own ring. You'd probably

say something like, 'I'm the one who has to look at it for the next fifty years.' I would have taken you to buy it instead of just springing it on you."

"How do you know I wouldn't like a ring sprung on me?" I said, narrowing my eyes.

He scoffed. "The only thing you like sprung on you are snacks. You have an opinion about *everything*. You're also really practical. You'd probably pick something reasonable. No diamonds. I'm thinking an etched band. Nothing that would need to be repaired or cleaned or that you'd have to take off to do the dishes." He regarded me for a moment. "Something personal engraved inside. Something only the two of you would get."

He knows me. He knows me almost better than I know myself.

I had to press my lips together to keep my face straight. I changed the subject. "You know what I like about you, Josh?"

"My way with small, vicious dogs?"

I snorted. "I like that you don't do that guy thing where you try and solve all my problems. Guys do that. Sometimes we just want to complain. That's it. We don't want advice. We just want you to listen. You're a good listener."

He fiddled with a coaster and his smile sank a little. "I *would* try and solve all your problems." His eyes came back up to mine. "If you wanted me to."

God, yes, I want you to. But you can't and you never will.

The waitress delivered our wings.

"I'm double dipping," I said, grabbing a celery stick. "If you can't handle that, get your own ranch."

"I think we're slightly past that, don't you?" He dunked a drumstick, took a bite, and then dunked it again. "So when does he need his answer by?"

I nibbled on the end of my celery, not looking directly at him. "He's here for two weeks. So I guess before he leaves."

He spoke to the basket of wings. "What are you leaning toward?"

Someone started singing "Push It." "Josh! Let's dance. Will you?"

If he knew I changed the subject on purpose, he didn't let on. He wiped his hands with a napkin. "Sure."

We walked out into the thin crowd of people in front of the stage and started to dance.

He hadn't been kidding about having moves. He was as good on the floor as he was in bed. We danced for three songs, laughing the whole time.

Then someone started singing a really horrible rendition of John Legend's "All of Me." The woman singing it was even drunker than I was.

Josh and I looked at each other and wordlessly moved together. I wrapped my arm around his neck and he held my other hand over his heart. He was still a little out of breath, and his chest rose and fell against my palm.

I'm in love with you.

The impulse hit me so hard and fast, I didn't even see it coming.

I'm so in love with you.

How easily this came to me. With Tyler, the question was murky and confusing. But with Josh, it was clear. I was in love with him. And I was in love with him in a "we were made for each other" kind of way.

But we weren't though, right? Because how could I be made for him when my body couldn't give him children?

My eyes started to tear up, and he dipped his head to look at me. "Hey, shhhh. I know what happened today was hard."

He kissed my forehead, so tenderly, and I felt simultaneously better and worse.

I shook my head and buried my face in his chest. He didn't have the first clue.

When I looked back up, his concerned face hovered over mine. I wanted to stand on my toes and kiss him. Or let him kiss me. I wanted *him* to be the one to ask me to marry him. If I could be with him, I'd say yes to him in a heartbeat, even if he did it in some cringey, cheesy way. Even if there were rose petals all over the fucking house.

God, wouldn't we be something? If it wasn't for that one thing. That one thing that was everything.

For a moment, in my drunken state, I thought I could tell him. I could just blurt out the truth about everything. Get it out of me, put it in his hands, let him figure out what to do with it. And then maybe it wouldn't feel so heavy. Maybe he would be okay with it and he'd—

He'd what, Kristen? Settle? He'd give up his dreams for you?

"I'm so selfish," I whispered.

He put his cheek to mine and spoke into my ear. "You're not. You're wonderful. And you look really beautiful tonight."

I sniffed and tilted my head back to look him in the eye. "You know why I always looked like a slob around you? Because I liked you."

He pulled his face back a little and his eyes went wide.

"Yeah. I felt guilty that I liked you so much when I had a boyfriend. So I always tried to look bad in front of you so you wouldn't know."

He beamed down on me. "So the mud mask and the curlers and that nose strip thing—"

"All proof of my enormous lady boner for you."

My buzz made me careless.

And I couldn't care *less.*

"Wow," he said, looking reflective. "You must have really liked me. You didn't brush your hair for two days in a row once."

I launched into giggles and he laughed with me, putting his forehead to mine. "And I still thought you were the most beautiful woman I'd ever met."

I squeezed my eyes shut, breathing him in, feeling his breath on my face. I wanted to hold this moment in suspended animation. These tender stolen seconds. My forehead pressed to his, his warm hand over mine, his heart beating against my palm. Him slowly turning me on a dance floor, telling me I'm beautiful.

His deep voice spoke over me softly. "Can I ask you a question?"

"What?" I whispered, opening my eyes.

"What does Sloan think of him?"

I laughed, shaking my head. "Sloan hates him."

"Why?"

"Because she thinks I've settled."

He furrowed his brow. "Settled? How? Is something wrong with him? Is he a dick?"

I let out a long breath. "No. He doesn't want kids."

He scoffed. "Well, there you go. The kid thing is too important. Can't be with him."

It felt like a punch right to my uterus. A hard lump bolted to my throat, and I had to look away from him because I was going to cry.

There it was, straight from his own lips.

The kid thing is too important. Can't be with him.

He stopped turning us, and he put my face in his hands.

Once I was looking at him again, I lost it. My chin quivered and tears spilled over my cheeks.

His eyes moved back and forth between mine. "Don't marry him, Kristen."

My heart cracked in half.

"Don't marry him," he whispered. "*Please.*"

There was something desperate about the way he said it. I studied the look in his eyes. Distress. Longing. *Pleading.*

This wasn't the look of a man who just didn't want to give up his booty call. This was feelings. *Josh has feelings for me.*

The realization hit me like a deep, cancerous, soul-reaching sadness. These emotions I could see he had for me—they should have made me happy. I should have been ecstatic to know that what I felt maybe wasn't so one-sided. But instead, a bitter disappointment descended on my body making me so weak I worried my knees would give out.

I had to cut him loose.

This thing between us had gone as far as I could allow it to go.

I wasn't going to marry Tyler. I think I'd known that the whole time. After I'd said no, he'd begged me to think about it. So I did. But I wasn't going to be with either of them. I couldn't.

The kid thing is too important. Can't be with him.

I couldn't love Tyler the way he deserved, and I couldn't give Josh a family. I could never give either man what he really wanted.

TWENTY-FIVE

JOSH

Kristen told Tyler no to his proposal, and I hadn't seen her in two fucking weeks.

Shawn, Brandon, and I stood on the Vegas strip in front of the Bellagio fountains, waiting for the water show to start. It was Brandon's bachelor party weekend. It couldn't have come at a worse time. I was losing my fucking mind. I needed to see her.

I checked my phone again. *Nothing.*

Shawn saw me check my cell. "Man, she's not thinking about your ass. Fuck, you're sprung."

Brandon took a drink from his water bottle. "They're going into massages. Sloan just texted me."

Sloan was having her bachelorette party today back in California. I hated that I needed to hear about Kristen's day in the third person. I fucking hated it.

The morning after karaoke night, our crew had been sent as an emergency strike team to Sequoia National Park to fight a wildfire. We'd been there for twelve days, and Kristen only called me once the whole time I was gone. She wouldn't answer my calls or texts. She'd gone completely cold on me.

We'd gotten home just in time to leave for Vegas. I didn't have time to go to her house.

I rolled up my sleeves. It was 2:00 in the afternoon and the sidewalk radiated heat. Sweaty tourists streamed past us. Sunburned spring breakers drinking out of souvenir cups, a cluster of young women laughing as they passed, huddled around a friend in a white veil, two middle-aged women wearing backpacks and cameras.

Couples holding hands.

Shawn lit a cigar. "She's probably fucking somebody this weekend, bro. You should hook up too."

"Shut the fuck up, dick." I plucked at the front of my shirt, wondering offhand if Shawn was right, and getting irritable just thinking about it.

Brandon waved off a guy in sunglasses handing out flyers for a strip club. "No change at all with her, huh?"

I shook my head. "She's been off ever since karaoke night."

It was like an enormous tower had come up around her with a drawbridge, a moat full of piranhas, and machine guns on top. Compliments of Tyler, no doubt. I fucking hated that guy. I mean, I hadn't really been making progress with her before he showed up, but at least she spoke to me back then.

One minute she was sitting in my lap in an Uber and dancing with me, telling me she'd liked me, and the next I couldn't even get a text back.

I'd played that last night over and over again in my mind, trying to figure out what went wrong.

We'd been slow dancing. I told her not to marry Tyler. She'd obviously agreed I was right about that because she'd gone outside to call him and told him no to his proposal. Then she'd come back in a different person.

She'd made me take her home, cried the whole way there, and

wouldn't let me touch her. Locked herself in her room, kicked me out of her house, and she'd barely spoken to me since.

And I didn't fucking get it.

This morning I'd sent her a text I knew was risky. But if she wasn't speaking to me anyway, what was the harm? Things couldn't get worse. I'd typed the words "I miss you" and stood staring at it for a solid five minutes before I hit Send.

That was three hours ago. She left me on read.

Brandon leaned on his forearms against the concrete railing over the lake, squinting out over the blue-green water. "I hate to say it, but Shawn might be right. Maybe you should see what else is out there."

I couldn't even look at him. "I don't want to see what else is out there," I said through clenched teeth. "If this was Sloan, would you want to see what else was out there?"

Fuck, if anyone should understand, it should be him. What did it mean that even Brandon was telling me to get over it?

He put his hands up. "Okay. You're right. I'm sorry. It just doesn't seem like this situation is getting any better, and I hate to see you chasing someone who's not reciprocating. That's all."

"She's just not that into you, man. Take the hint," Shawn said, blowing cigar smoke. "Let me ask you something." He tapped ash onto the sidewalk. "How many of your hoodies does she have?"

I wrinkled my brow. "None. Why?"

"She's not into you, bro. Bitches love hoodies. If she's not stealing your hoodies, she don't want your ass."

This thrust me deeper into my dark place. As ridiculous as it sounded, it also rang true. Even Celeste had kept a few of my hoodies at the end and she fucking hated me.

Sometimes I worried Shawn was some sort of idiot relationship savant. Too much of what he said had a convoluted wisdom to it.

This terrified me.

Still, there *was* one thing. "If she's not into me, why did she check up on me through Brandon?"

This was weird. The whole time I was gone, she wouldn't return any of my calls or texts. But then, on day eight of clearing brush, I'd gotten moved to a different firebreak than Brandon. When he got off shift, he told Sloan he didn't know where I was, and within seconds of Brandon hanging up with Sloan, Kristen started blowing up my phone. It was the only time I'd talked to her. She'd sounded almost desperate to know I was okay.

Of course as soon as she realized I was alive and not burned to death, she hung up with me. But that's when I realized she'd been using Sloan's updates to keep tabs on me. Why? Why not just answer one of the many calls I made?

Shawn snorted. "Congratulations, motherfucker. She cares if you *die*."

I glared at him. But it wasn't just that. I caught her looking at me sometimes. Or when we were in bed, she would kiss me when she thought I was sleeping. Even at karaoke night, she was hugging me but she made a lame excuse about it. It's like she didn't want me to know she gave a shit. *Like she's pretending.*

Shawn jabbed his cigar at me. "This is what you get for being a thirst responder."

"A what?" I said moodily.

"A thirst responder," Shawn said, leaning his back against the rail and crossing his legs at the ankles. "A thirsty motherfucker who hits on a bitch the second she's single."

Brandon chuckled.

I scowled at Shawn and then turned to Brandon. "Has Sloan

said anything about it? Anything about Tyler? Or dating other people?"

Brandon shook his head. "No. Do you want me to ask her?"

"No." I wanted to know, but I didn't want Kristen to think I'd sent Brandon to sniff around. And Sloan would know if he was sniffing.

I dragged a hand down my face. I'd go right back to work at the fire station when I got back from Vegas, so that would be two more days. And then what? I'd come over and she'd ignore me in person? What the hell happened? I mean, I knew Tyler showing up had fucked with her, but I didn't see what that had to do with me.

I fucking missed her. I couldn't understand how she didn't miss me back. Even on a friendship level, she should miss me. We hung out every minute that I wasn't at the fire station. We were close. Could she really care this little?

"I just haven't seen her in a while," I mumbled, as if that explained it all.

"Good," Shawn said, grinning at the asses of a group of women walking past in short skirts and high heels. "Let her miss that shit. What up, ladies? Want to help a couple of firemen celebrate a bachelor party?"

They giggled and smiled at us but kept walking.

Brandon pulled a cigar from his pocket. "It's not the worst advice," he said, lighting a match and puffing on the end of his cigar until it lit. "Try to have a good time. Focus on something else."

Music erupted around us, and the fountains burst into life. An instrumental of "Ain't That a Kick in the Head." Water shot a hundred feet in the air and danced in time with the song, sending a cool mist over us.

It was a vibrant high-energy contrast to my shitty mood.

Brandon and Shawn leaned on the rail and watched the show, and I looked at my phone again.

Nothing.

I stared grouchily out over the congested strip at the black limos and taxis with their light boxes advertising shows I didn't want to see and steak houses where I didn't want to eat. What I wanted was to go home and see Kristen.

The ball was in her court.

It had always been in her court. This was *her* game.

Maybe she really *didn't* have feelings for me. She'd said that one night at the karaoke bar that she'd had a crush on me, and that was the last bone she ever threw me. Hell, it was the *only* bone she ever threw me. And I'd been gnawing on it ever since. At the time, I'd even been a little hopeful that maybe, if she gave Tyler the boot, it was the start of something more between us.

Every time I thought I was getting closer to more, it was ripped away from me.

Maybe she was telling the truth, that all it would ever be between us was casual hookups and no strings attached.

Maybe even the casual hookups are over.

When the water show was done, Brandon looked at his watch. "I want to check out that rare bookstore before it closes."

"Yeah, that sounds like a great fucking idea," Shawn said. "Hey, let me get a picture of you guys. You can send it to Sloan."

Brandon rummaged in his pocket and handed over his phone.

"Let me get one on your phone too," he said to me. "You can send it to Kristen. Maybe she'll print it and keep it where she keeps your balls."

"Dick." I put the phone in his hand.

Brandon and I posed against the railing in front of the lake, and I faked a smile. Shawn stood and held up Brandon's cell for the picture. Then he drew his arm back and chucked Brandon's phone over our heads into the water.

"Hey—" Before I could lunge for it, mine was next. Then he took his own phone, and like a fucking lunatic, he threw that too.

"What the fuck?!" I pushed him.

He laughed, taking the shove. "You two motherfuckers are in *Vegas*! This dude wants to go to a fucking rare bookstore, and your pussy-whipped ass is practically crying over some girl. I've freed you, bitches!"

Even Brandon looked irritated. "You're buying me a new phone, asshole."

Shawn pulled out a flask. "Yeah, yeah. We'll all get new shit when we win at the craps table." He shoved the flask into Brandon's chest. "No more Sloan and Kristen. No rare motherfucking books either. We're in Vegas, and we're gonna fucking do Vegas!"

TWENTY-SIX

KRISTEN

Sloan and I stood in a waist-deep pool of rust-colored water, slapping mud on each other's faces. I started her bachelorette party at Glen Ivy, a sprawling day spa in Corona.

Hot tubs, steam rooms, saunas. We rented a cabana by one of the pools and spent the first half of the day lounging and having mojitos. We'd just gotten out of massages and we'd made our way to the mud pit, a pond-size pool with a pedestal in the middle featuring a heaping pile of the spa's signature red clay. We were supposed to smack it on, let it dry, and slough it off to exfoliate our skin.

Sloan's mom, cousin Hannah, and Brandon's sister Claudia were already baking their mud into a crusty layer, lying under the sun in lounge chairs.

"Did Brandon say what they're doing today?" I asked, trying not to sound too interested.

Sloan smeared mud on her stomach. "They were walking on the strip the last time he texted me. And just so you know, that's the last update you're going to get from me. If you miss him, call him."

I pressed my lips into a line and wiped two muddy fingers on her cheek. She'd taunted me earlier with a picture of the guys on their motorcycles. Wouldn't let me see it. Told me if I wanted to see pictures of Josh, I should send him an Instagram request like a normal person.

"I can't call him."

She rolled her eyes. "Kristen, this is so stupid."

"It's not."

Ghosting him was for his own good. Josh and I needed a reset—especially after some of the things I'd said when I was drunk.

Josh was nursing a little crush on me—I was almost positive. And ultimately we needed to stop hooking up altogether. But I couldn't call off things with him just yet. Once I really thought about it, I realized there were complications with the timing. But his two weeks on a strike team were the perfect opportunity to put some much-needed distance between us. If he still wanted to see me when he got back, I'd see him. But for now this was the right move.

Sloan shook her head at me. "You can't be serious about this. You miss him. And I bet he misses you too."

I knew he missed me. He'd said it in a text not four hours ago. I couldn't stop thinking about it, wondering exactly how he meant that to be taken. Was he horny? Did he see something funny that Brandon wouldn't get and he wanted to tell me about it and it made him wish I was there? Or did he *miss* me, miss me.

No matter the answer, it reinforced my decision to back him off these last two weeks. He shouldn't be missing me. We were fuck buddies—he should only be missing the sex. I wasn't going to encourage him by engaging. Not talking on the phone or texting him had always been a hard-line rule for me, and I needed to stick to it, now more than ever. I didn't want to lead him on.

"He sees other women, you know. We date other people," I said defensively.

"Who are *you* dating?" She cocked her head to the side.

I rubbed mud on my arms, watching it smear over my skin so I wouldn't have to look at her. "I went on that one date with Tyler," I said lamely.

She scoffed. "That's what I thought. What if he's having sex with these other women? Doesn't that bother you?"

The very suggestion of it felt like she'd reached into my chest and squeezed my heart. Yeah, it bothered me. I tried not to think about it. Josh would have sex with other women, and one day he'd have babies with one of them. And that was just the way it was.

I shrugged. "He's single, so he can do what he wants."

"Hmm. And so why don't you do it too, then?"

She knew why I couldn't do it. I couldn't be with another man. I didn't want anyone else.

I stuck my finger in the pile of red mud on the pedestal. "I won't be having sex with anyone else until after the hysterectomy."

"How are you feeling?" she asked, eyeing my stomach.

I wore a T-shirt over my bathing suit to cover my belly. Even though it could be mistaken for a large lunch, I was too self-conscious about it. *I* knew what it was. And if even one person asked me when I was due, I would lose my shit.

"Well, the IUD kicked in. The doctor said it would take a few months to start helping with the bleeding, and I finally see the difference. It's been huge, actually. I only spot now."

Her smile was extra dazzling under the red clay on her cheeks. "Really? Could you live like this? Maybe put off the surgery?"

I shook my head. "No, I can't live like this. I'm still bleeding almost daily, the cramps are horrible, and I look three months pregnant. Look." I pulled my T-shirt tight around my waist and showed her my distended stomach.

She looked mournfully at my belly.

I think of everything, my swollen stomach was what made her get this. She had a beautiful hourglass figure, and what my uterus was doing to mine was her nightmare.

"I'm so sick of this being my normal, Sloan." I let the shirt drop. "Every day of my life for the last twelve years, this uterus has made me miserable. It's never done anything for me but give me grief, and it never will."

It occurred to me that pain was literally a daily part of my world. I took it for granted. I lived with it like someone learns to live with background noise. And I was done doing it.

My doctor had suggested writing a thank-you letter to my uterus before the surgery. To give me closure, he said.

Fuck my uterus.

I had nothing to thank it for. It had ruined my life a thousand times over in a thousand different ways. Every time I bled through my pants in public or vomited from the pain. All the times it stole my energy and robbed me of milestones and opportunities. It ruined relationships and vacations, special moments and dreams.

And it wasn't done. It would *never* be done taking from me. When it was gone, it would still take.

She sighed. "How do you intend to explain the surgery to Josh? I mean, the man works in your garage. He's going to know."

I looked away from her at the palm trees and birds-of-paradise that lined the mud pool. I did have a plan. I'd given it a lot of thought over the last two weeks.

"I'm going to fire him and break things off the day after your wedding."

Her eyes flew wide. "What?"

"I was going to end it after that night at karaoke. But then I realized if I did it before the wedding, it might make things weird, and I didn't want to ruin your special day."

With the wedding coming up, the four of us were going to be thrown together. Big-time. I couldn't vouch for how Josh would feel about the end of our arrangement, but I knew *I'd* have a hard time pretending to be happy once we were done, and Sloan would definitely pick up on that. There was no way that wouldn't affect her.

So why make things awkward or tense? What was one and a half more weeks? I'd just stick to my rules, like I always did—*when I wasn't drunk*—and it would be fine. It was just eleven days.

I looked at Sloan. "I figured we'd get through the wedding and then I'll tell him I can't see him anymore. I'm already putting out ads for carpenters. I need to find someone else anyway. He's been gone for two weeks, and I had to put my stairs on back order."

She sighed. "Oh, Kristen."

"What?" I shrugged. "I knew this was all part of it. I sold my soul, Sloan, for a few good weeks. At least I got to have him, even if it was just for a little while. I'll cut him loose before the surgery, but after your big day. Problem solved."

Hopefully he'd already have someone on the side he could slide into. It would be easier for us both when the time came.

Well, it would be easier for *him*.

He would have the women he'd been seeing besides me. He'd have his free time back. We wouldn't be able to have sex for months after the surgery anyway, so that would put an end to that.

Less than two more weeks until Sloan's wedding. Less than two more weeks of Josh.

Then it would all be over.

~

The phone woke me up at 4:23 in the morning. I didn't recognize the number, but I knew the Vegas area code. I sat up and hit the Answer Call button groggily. "Hello?"

"Hey... it's me."

My lips curled up into a smile. Josh. Drunk Josh by the sound of it.

"Tell me Brandon's not in need of bail money," I said, rubbing my eyes.

"No. He's fine," he slurred. "I managed to keep him out of jail. Best best man ever."

I lay on my side and tucked my pillow under my head. "Sloan's freaking out, by the way. Neither of you answered her calls."

The truth was *I* had been freaking out too. Sloan's talk about Josh sleeping with other people had haunted me all night. And without Sloan knowing where Brandon was, I didn't know where Josh was. I hated that.

"Shawn threw our phones in the lake in front of the Bellagio."

I snorted. "What?"

"Yeah. We're not even in our hotel. We're at—hold on. The Twisted Palm Motel. We couldn't make it back. Too drunk."

"Well, I'm glad you called. At least I can tell Sloan where Brandon is in the morning. He should have gotten to a phone. She worries." *And so do I.*

"He's too fucked up. Shawn made him take a shot every time he said 'Sloan.' We had to carry him to the room."

I cracked up and Josh chuckled with me, a leisurely, tired, intoxicated laugh.

It felt so good to talk to him. I'd missed him so much. I didn't realize how much until he was on the phone. I wished he were here, in bed with me instead of three hundred miles away.

"I had to go to the business center to call you," he continued. "I didn't know your number, so I looked up your website. I'm not sorry I woke you up."

I scoffed. "Oh, really? And why not? You should feel terrible. I need my beauty sleep."

"No you don't. You're perfect."

I smiled. "Why, thank you, Drunk Josh. That's very nice of you to say."

There was a hiccup in the pause. "What did you do today?"

I told him about the spa and the mud and the suck-for-a-buck shirt. "Sloan made sixty-seven dollars. She's not speaking to me, but we sold all her Life Savers."

He laughed. "Do you have pictures?"

"Yeah. I'd send you some, but you don't have a phone. If you're still in front of a computer, look me up on Instagram."

Sloan's insistence that I connect with him on Instagram finally made me fold. I didn't have any pictures of him. At least I could cyberstalk him if I followed him on Instagram, look at him when I missed him—which was all the time.

The phone shuffled. "Okay. Hold on."

I reached under the bed and pulled out my laptop. "Can I follow you too?"

"You can follow me anywhere."

He was flirty when he was drunk. It was cute. He didn't usually say things like this to me. I shut it down immediately when he did. But Drunk Josh wasn't really Josh.

"How come Sober Josh doesn't have all this swagger, huh?" I teased.

He snorted. "He does. He's just trying to follow your many rules. Drunk Josh doesn't live by rules. Drunk Josh does what Drunk Josh wants," he said, stumbling over the words.

"And what does Drunk Josh want?" I smiled, tapping his name into the search bar on Instagram.

"You."

I arched an eyebrow. "You're lucky you're not here. I'd take advantage of you. You sound too weak to fight me off."

"I consent."

I sent him a follow request, laughing at his comment. A second later I got his and approved it.

We got quiet as we looked at each other's pictures.

"I didn't know you rock climb," I said. There was a picture of him hanging off the side of a seriously high cliff face. He had on a harness and helmet, and he looked, as always, so handsome. "And you water-ski."

"Tyler," he said dryly.

I forgot I had those pictures on there. Tyler and me at the Marine ball. A few more goofy selfies during his leaves. One of him kissing me.

"Celeste's pretty," I countered, looking at picture after picture of them smiling together. She was a Sloan. The kind of woman who doesn't need makeup. The kind who glows when she smiles.

"You're prettier," he said.

"And your dick is bigger than Tyler's."

This garnered me a laugh. I could imagine the sparkle in his eyes and the dimples in his cheeks.

I missed him.

The ache ripped through me. I hadn't seen him in so long, and somehow the separation didn't lessen how I felt the way it had with Tyler.

Tyler faded. He always faded, even though we'd talk on the phone and Skype and write. But Josh just got brighter. The ache got deeper the longer I went without him.

Hopefully it was the opposite for Josh. I hoped the time away from me had cooled any feelings he might be having, because I didn't think I could keep my walls up when he got back. I missed him too much, and the time I was going to get with him was too short now.

How was I going to do it when things were over, when I told him after the wedding that I didn't want to see him anymore? It was going to kill me.

I went back to the photos, and my mood dampened.

There were a lot of pictures of him with his nieces and nephews. Him holding a new baby in a hospital. Giving piggy-back rides. One picture had him buried to his neck in sand on a beach somewhere, flanked by two little boys who looked a lot like him, holding red plastic shovels.

"You really love kids, don't you." It was a statement, not a question.

"Come to Vegas. Let's get married."

I snorted. God, he was fucked up. "And upstage Brandon and Sloan?"

"Come on. Why not?"

"How much have you had to drink?"

Another hiccup. "You're a unicorn."

I smirked. Yup. Wasted out of his mind.

He went on. "When you find a unicorn, you marry her. I think about you all the time. Do you ever think about me?"

Always. "Whenever I'm horny."

He got quiet. It didn't feel like a comfortable silence. It felt like a disappointed one. At least it was for me. I hated the lies I had to tell.

"Kristen…I think I'm gonna throw up."

I closed the lid of my laptop. The room went pitch-black again, and I sat there against my headboard in the dark. He wouldn't remember this call. He was too fucked up.

"Josh?"

It took a long minute until I got a slurred, "Yeah?"

I took a deep breath. "I think about you all the time. I miss you when you're not with me."

"You do?"

"Yeah. I do."

It felt so good to say it out loud. And to say it to *him*. Even if he was too wasted to retain it, it felt liberating to say just once how I felt.

I spoke low. "When you're not with me, it feels like I'm hollow. I wonder what you're doing. Who you're with. I read your texts a hundred times." My heart pounded. "I wanted to tell you I missed you back, but I can't say that stuff to you. But I *did* miss you. The last two weeks felt like torture."

He groaned and I heard the dragging of something metallic. Probably a wastebasket.

I sighed. "Josh, don't black out there. Go back to your room."

"No. I want to talk to you." He sounded like he was spitting. He didn't hear a word I'd said.

We sat in silence for a moment. I wondered if he'd passed out. "Josh?"

"Get Sloan and drive down here tomorrow. Let's get married. Come on."

I smiled gently. "I can't marry you."

Spitting. "Why? I would be a good husband to you. I would take care of you. I'd be a good dad."

I moved the phone away from my mouth as a sudden wrenching urge to sob bolted into my throat. I pressed my lips together and forced it back down. "I know you would," I whispered. "That's why I *can't*."

More silence.

Then he spoke into my darkness. "I love you."

My tears spilled down my cheeks and the lump in my throat threatened to suffocate me. "I love you too."

The line went dead.

TWENTY-SEVEN

JOSH

I love you too.

I imagined there were only so many events in life that could have made it through that level of intoxication. A murder. A horrible accident.

Kristen telling me she loved me.

I *remembered.*

Brandon was ready to be done with Vegas. We'd planned on staying an extra night, but Shawn's bachelor party experience was enough for a lifetime. So after we dragged ourselves, hung-over, back to our hotel, we showered, packed, went to the Verizon store so Shawn could buy us new phones, and we headed home.

We got back at midnight.

I couldn't wait to see Kristen. She wasn't expecting me and I didn't call. I wanted to show up tomorrow morning and surprise her. I was going to grab her and kiss her whether she fucking liked it or not, talk to her about what she'd said. Force her to stop playing these games with me.

My heart felt light and hopeful for the first time in months. I couldn't even sleep I was so excited to see her. I should have just gone straight there. I got up early and took off from my apartment before the sun was up, planning to just slip into bed with her.

But when I pulled up to her house and I saw the truck in the driveway at 7:00 in the morning, I was smacked back into reality.

I sat there, clutching the wheel with white knuckles. I couldn't believe what I was seeing.

I'd stayed the night enough times to know exactly how unlikely it was that a truck would be parked in her driveway at any time of the day, let alone this early.

Nobody came here. She never had visitors. And besides Brandon and me, she didn't have friends who drove trucks.

She was in there with some guy. She thought I was out of town and she'd brought home some guy.

He'd stayed the night.

Is this what she'd been doing while I was on the strike team? Is this why she hadn't answered my calls?

The reality of what I'd signed up for finally came full circle.

Disgust, anger, hurt, disappointment—they coursed through me and settled in my chest like a cinder block. My eyes pricked with tears and I pinched the corners, furious with myself for thinking she'd wanted me.

I put the truck in reverse and backed down the street and parked there, looking at the house, my mind racing. I wanted to kick in the fucking door and beat the shit out of him, whoever he was.

But could I really be angry?

She'd been clear. She'd been crystal clear with me that she was going to see other people. That she didn't want to be exclusive. We were fuck buddies. That was it.

I'd *agreed* to this.

But what about what she had said? She'd said she loved me. Hadn't she? She *had* said it, right?

Or had I said it first and then she'd said it back? Or had she said it like the way she told Sloan that she loved *her*?

She obviously hadn't meant it the way I'd meant it, or I wouldn't be looking at some fucking guy's truck parked in front of her damn house. I sat there, staring at the driveway for what felt like an eternity.

And then he came out. She stood in the door in her robe while he jogged down the steps. I breathed through my nose, trying to stay calm.

I couldn't get a good look. Early thirties maybe. Jeans and a T-shirt.

He got in his truck and drove off, and I wondered if she was taking a shower now. Stripping the bed. What if I'd shown up just an hour later? Would she have slept with us both on the same day? Did she lie there with him after like she did with me? Talking and kissing?

I put the truck in drive and went home before I did something fucking stupid.

When I got back to my apartment, the tower of boxes still standing in my living room taunted me. A reminder that I'd spent the last two months giving all my free time to a woman who didn't fucking want me, who could sleep with someone else without giving it a second thought.

I kicked the bottom box and the whole thing toppled over, spilling clothes all over the floor. I grabbed another box and flung it across the room and stood there, panting, in my shitty cube of an apartment.

Done. I was fucking *done*.

I didn't want any of this anymore. I didn't want this fucking life. I didn't want to live here. I didn't want my shitty job. I wished I could un-know her. Go back and never meet her, never come here.

I pulled out my phone and scrolled through until I found Amanda's number, the yoga instructor. I stood there, staring at it. I could call this woman. Do the same thing. See someone else too. Isn't that what I *should* be doing? Maybe it wouldn't have fucked with me like this if I'd kept my end of the bargain, if I'd actually been seeing other people like I'd said I would. Like she'd *pressed* me to do.

I typed in a text and was about to hit Send when my phone pinged.

Kristen: Hey, Sloan says you guys got home last night. Want to come over?

The irony was too much. She never texted me. Never asked me to come over. She never initiated *anything*—it was always me. She'd been totally cold to me for weeks. Her text sat there under my unanswered "I miss you" and a string of other ignored questions and efforts on my part, and the one time she finally did want me, I couldn't even stomach the thought.

Josh: Sick.

It wasn't even a lie. I couldn't even look at her. I didn't know if I could *ever* look at her. I couldn't even imagine walking her down the aisle at Brandon's wedding next week.

Kristen: You okay?

I shook my head at my phone and tossed it on the mattress.

No. I'm not fucking okay.

I'm done.

TWENTY-EIGHT

KRISTEN

I held a bag of In-N-Out and knocked on the door. I checked my watch: 1:15 p.m. It took Josh a while to open it. When he finally did, I saw he hadn't been kidding—he really *was* sick. He looked like shit.

His face was expressionless, like he felt too crappy to react to my unannounced visit. Red eyes and a rumpled shirt, like he'd been sleeping in his clothes. Messy hair, like I'd gotten him out of bed.

I smiled. "Hey. Surprise."

Ugh. I'd missed his face so much.

So much.

When Sloan told me Brandon was home, my heart had leapt in my chest. They were supposed to come home late tonight and Josh had work tomorrow morning, so I wasn't supposed to see him for three more days. Usually I'd just ride it out and wait for him to come back over. But I couldn't do it. I couldn't wait three more days to see him when I knew he was at home. So I broke my own rule and invited him over. And once I found out he was sick, I broke another one of my rules and went to *him*.

He didn't move to let me in. He just stared at me.

"Uh, can I come in?" I asked, looking around him into his apartment.

He stood there for another few seconds, then pushed open the door and walked silently back inside.

I followed him in, wondering what the hell was wrong with him. He couldn't still be hungover, two days later. Maybe the strike team and the trip had finally caught up to him. He must have been pretty worn down.

The apartment was dark and stale smelling.

"You didn't reply to my texts so I decided to make sure you were alive," I said, looking around, feeling an instant urge to throw open windows and start cleaning. "This place looks like you're losing a game of Jumanji. What the hell happened in here?"

He leaned against the kitchen counter and crossed his arms over his chest, watching me as I put the bag of food down. I walked over to him and put a hand on his cheek to feel if he had a temperature. He closed his eyes at the contact and breathed through his nose, grimacing like it hurt to have his head touched.

"You don't feel hot. Do you have a headache?"

He opened his eyes and stared at me.

I had to be honest—I'd hoped for a happier reunion. I thought...

I don't know what I thought. I shouldn't be thinking anything. I shouldn't be hoping for anything either.

"Stomach?" I asked.

Silence.

"Voice box?"

He flexed his jaw. "It's not a good idea for you to be here right now," he said flatly, his voice cold.

I gave him a crooked smile. There was nowhere I'd rather be. I didn't give a shit if he was contagious. "What hurts?"

It took him a moment. "Everything."

I snorted. "Wow. A man cold. Okay, I'm equipped to deal with this. Come on. Get in bed."

"Kristen, you should go. You should look for another carpenter," he said.

"Wow. Are you *dying*?" I laughed, opening up my purse and taking out my Aleve. I shook two into my hand and handed him the Coke I brought him.

"It's funny that you bring up getting a new carpenter." I handed him the pills, and he stood there looking at them in the palm of his hand, passively.

"Guess who showed up at the butt crack of dawn this morning begging for his job back. Miguel." I shook my head. He'd seen my carpenter ad on Craigslist. "Lost his job at Universal."

I put my hands on my hips and peered around his apartment. God, it was a mess. Clothes everywhere. His duffel bag from Vegas was still plopped next to the bed. He probably had two weeks of laundry to do.

Looks like it's my time to shine. This place was getting an exorcism. I'd get on it as soon as I got the patient in bed.

I turned back to him. "I don't even want to know what that dude did to get fired. He was always a little creepy. Like, *Silence of the Lambs*, 'it puts the lotion on its skin' creepy. And he came over, and I was in nothing but a robe." I shivered as it gave me the heebie-jeebies. "To be honest, it was too bad you weren't there. I could have used a bouncer."

His eyes bored into me, his messy hair over his forehead. He stared at me just long enough for it to be weird and then set his soda down. In a single fluid movement he gathered me in his arms and folded me into his chest, burying his face in my neck. It was so unexpected I froze.

And then I *melted.*

I'd missed him. *So much.* And I loved it when he held me. It was something I couldn't allow outside of sex because it made me want to never let go. But this hug took me by surprise, and once I was in it, there was no getting out. My heart just wasn't that strong.

He clutched me to him so hard that for a second I got worried something was wrong. *Really* wrong. I wrapped my arms around his waist and hugged him back, wondering if he'd gotten some bad news. He didn't look well, and he never broke my no-affection rules.

"What's wrong?" I whispered.

He shook his head in the crook of my neck. "I'm just glad you're here."

He dragged his face from my neck and looked like he might kiss me, but instead he put his forehead to mine and closed his eyes.

I gave him a breathless smile. "Well, we're friends with benefits, right?" I said, my lips an inch from his mouth. "This is the friends part."

And I missed you. Couldn't stand not seeing you today. Wanted to take care of you. Needed to make sure you were okay.

He put a hand to my cheek and ran a thumb along my lips. Then he leaned in and kissed me. It was tentative and soft, and I dissolved into it.

It was like the space I'd put between us made me need more of him to make up for it, and I couldn't get close enough or soak up enough of him.

I wrapped my arms around his neck and kissed him harder, pressing against him as he started to walk me backward toward the bed. We tripped over the mess, our mouths never breaking contact, our feet tangling in discarded clothes and boxes. I knocked into his lamp and it fell sideways with a crash, but we didn't stop. We peeled off each other's shirts, slamming back into each other before they touched the ground.

By the time we hit the mattress and he glided over me, I was ravenous. I tugged at his sweatpants, but he shook his head and dragged my hands up to hold them against the pillow. "No." His lips trailed down my jaw.

I tipped my head back while his mouth moved along my skin. "What do you mean 'no'?" I breathed.

He smelled incredible, his heady masculine cedar scent like an evocative pheromone. Heat came off his chest, and the way he had my hands imprisoned, I was cocooned in his body, nestled between his strong arms.

"You're in trouble," he said into my collarbone. "You've lost dick privileges."

I snorted. "What? *Why?*"

He came back up and ground himself against my core, shooting electricity through my body, and my need intensified.

"You didn't talk to me for two weeks." He sucked my lip between his teeth. "You're on punishment." His tongue plunged into my mouth.

I was practically panting. I tried to work my hands free, and he held them firmer to the bed, smiling wickedly against my lips. He shook his head. "No." He pressed into me, hard as a rock.

So it's to be torture, then.

I made an impatient noise. "Well...how do I get my privileges back?" I wiggled my hips seductively and his breath caught in his throat. I smirked and he squeezed his eyes shut, clearly struggling with his boycott.

"You have to apologize for ignoring me."

"I'm sorry." I nipped at his lip.

"And tell me you missed me."

I nodded. "Yes," I whispered. "I missed you."

He opened his eyes and looked at me. "Say it again."

I held his serious, brown-eyed stare. "I missed you, Josh."

His eyes moved back and forth between mine, like he was trying to determine if I really meant it.

I really *did* mean it. I missed him even now, and he was right here.

He nodded, something softening on his face, and he released my hands.

I went straight to his pants again, but he got off me, stripped, and kneeled between my knees. Then he grabbed the waist of my shorts and pulled them down. "Are you bleeding?"

His hooded eyes were dark with desire, his breathing ragged. He was *famished*. No way he'd slept with someone else these last two weeks. He was on the same sex drought I was.

I shook my head. "No, I'm not bleeding."

He lowered his face between my legs and gripped my hips, pulling me to his mouth. I gasped. His tongue went to work, and my hands flew to his hair.

Oh my fucking God…

He'd never done this before—I was usually spotting. And holy *shit*—he was an oral virtuoso. I don't know what he was doing down there, but it was obvious I was in the hands of a professional. *Fuck, is he good at everything?*

My knees started to shake. I moaned, and like he knew I was

about to lose it, he came up and lowered himself over me. "I don't have a condom."

Nooooooo! "What? *Why?* Where are they?"

His mouth descended my neck, kissing me roughly. "At *your* house, where I leave them," he said huskily.

I'm the only person he's sleeping with? I mean, I know he said his dates didn't usually…

My favorite plaything pressed against my stomach, teasing me, and I lost my train of thought.

Fuck it. "No condom—I don't care," I gasped. "You're the only one I'm sleeping with too."

He jerked up and looked at me, his shallow breath rolling over my face. He studied me for a second, something unreadable in his eyes. Then he crushed his mouth to mine and slid into me.

There was something deeper about the sex this time, more emotional, desperate. Both of us were frantic, like we'd thought we were never going to see each other again, and the lack of a condom, the absence of that barrier, elevated everything, made us hungrier.

Neither of us were going to make it very long. There was no way.

His forceful thrusts launched me into spasms within seconds. My moaning pushed him over the edge and he poured inside of me, growling and gasping.

He collapsed and we clutched each other, catching our breath, his forehead to mine in a light sheen of sweat. It took me a solid minute to muster the ability to speak. "I thought you were *sick*," I breathed. "Faker."

His chuckle rumbled against my breasts. "All part of my ploy to get you to come over."

I laughed and he squeezed his arms against my sides and smiled down on me, kissing me softly, his heart beating against my chest.

I love you, Josh. I wish I could tell you. I wish I could keep you.

With a twinge of dread, I wondered how I would live without these moments when it all came to an end. I'd have to enjoy every second of the next week and a half with him. Absorb it, store it up.

And then hope it was enough to last a lifetime.

We'd been in his bed for hours. We never did that at my house. There were always too many excuses I could come up with for why we had to go back to friends-only mode. Emails to check, deliveries to sign for, orders to work on. And once we left the bed, my rules dictated that the affection had to stop. But here, we had nothing to do but stay between the sheets. Josh didn't have a sofa or a TV, so we hung out under the covers, and technically, according to my own rules, that meant that kissing and affection were okay.

I was enjoying the loophole. I needed every second of it.

Josh didn't seem to object either. We'd been having sex *all* day. After our quickie, we'd had a long, slow marathon, full of deep kissing and gentle rocking, followed by a giggling and playful romp with Josh tickling me mercilessly before he took me from behind. After we wore each other out, we'd lain there, our legs tangled together, talking about everything we did over the last two weeks. He told me about the strike team and how much he liked being in the woods and not running medical calls. How beautiful Sequoia National Park had been and how much I would have liked a band that played in a bar they went to in their off-hours.

I told him all about the wedding errands I'd been on with Sloan and dropping off a large order at Dale's mansion and how Stuntman had bit the FedEx guy again.

He didn't bring up calling me from Vegas, thank God. He probably didn't remember.

He ran a knuckle along my cheek. "I'm going to get a drink. Are you thirsty? Want something?"

"Water."

He got up and I propped myself up on my elbows to watch him walk naked to the kitchen. You could bounce a nickel off the man's ass. God, he had a great body.

Mine, not so much.

I had to make my own naked walk to the bathroom in a minute, and my little stomach bulge had no business strutting around uncovered. My clothes were strewn all over the place. I had no idea where my shirt was.

I sat up, pulling the sheet to my chest to look for something to put on. Then I eyed a Burbank Fire hoodie draped over one of his unpacked boxes nearby. I leaned over and grabbed it before he turned around from the sink.

"Do you mind if I wear this?" I asked, pulling it on before he had the chance to answer. I tucked my nose into the neck and breathed in, closing my eyes.

He climbed back in bed, handing me a glass of water. "You can keep it if you want." He grinned at me.

"Really?" God, I would never wash it. I would wear it like a warm hug. "Are you sure? That's a slippery slope, Joshua. Hoodies are gateway clothes. Soon I'll be stealing your shirts and your jackets." I took a sip and then set the water down next to the bed and looked back at him.

He leaned in and kissed me, his smile enormous. "I'm sure," he whispered against my lips. "Take whatever you want."

I gave him a raised eyebrow. "Why are you so happy about me stealing your clothes?"

"I'm just happy because I like it when you call me Joshua," he said, smiling. His fingers brushed the hair at the top of my forehead and he kissed me gently.

There was something so intimate in the way he was with me I had to change the subject.

"What's this, Joshua?" I asked, looking away from him, picking up a dog-eared copy of *Under a Flaming Sky* from the upside-down box he used as a nightstand. I flopped onto my back. "I didn't know you like to read."

He scooted down to lie next to me and propped himself on his elbow. "I like to read about fires."

I held the book over my face. "Is it any good? What's it about?" I smiled at him. "Will you read me a chapter?"

He took the book from me and leaned over the other side of the bed. "It's about a firestorm in Minnesota, back in 1894." When he came back up, he was wearing glasses.

I blinked at him as he flipped to the dog-eared page, scooting to sit up against his pillows.

"Shut the fuck up," I said, staring at him.

He looked over at me. "What?"

"You wear *glasses*?"

"Just for reading. Why?"

Just when I thought the man couldn't get any more attractive, he goes and puts on motherfucking glasses.

"This is a joke, right? You are not allowed to get hotter than you already are. I forbid it."

He set the book down across his lap and grinned at me. "You like the glasses, huh?" He bounced his eyebrows. "Want me to keep them on the next time?"

I giggled. "Yes, please."

He pulled the glasses down and then put them back on. His eyes got wide. "Oh, wow. Look how pretty you are!"

I laughed and moved his book, climbing over his lap until I straddled him. His sweatshirt rode up my thighs. Then I held his cheeks in my hands and peppered kisses all over his face. He closed his eyes and let me, beaming like a happy little kid.

I smiled at his upturned lips. "You know, it's Tarantino Trivia at Malone's tonight. You wanna go? I'm getting kind of hungry." Josh had nothing in his fridge, and we'd eaten the burgers I brought hours ago. I looked at my Fitbit. "But we'd have to leave in, like, ten minutes."

"Sure," he said, his hands on my thighs. "Do we invite Brandon and Sloan?"

I shook my head. "They're going to Luigi's for dinner. It'll just be us."

He gave me a soft peck on the lips, his eyes warm. "It's a date—let's go."

It wasn't a date, but I didn't correct him. He'd just roll his eyes and say it was just an expression and he wasn't trying to slip a date past me, the way he always did. I didn't need the reminder.

I wished it *was* a date.

He followed me home in his truck so I could get ready and let Stuntman out. Then we took an Uber so we could both drink.

On the ride over to Malone's, I checked my emails.

He peered over at me as I tapped on my phone. "Wait until we're stopped. You're gonna get carsick."

"No I won't."

"Yeah you will. You get nauseous when you look at your phone in the car," he said.

"That's only when *you* drive, because *you* drive like a lunatic," I said, typing in an email about Pug Life sweaters on back order. "Braking, hitting the gas too hard, taking the turns too fast. And on top of that, you don't even swear."

He chuckled. "What does swearing have to do with driving?"

"If you're not pissed off when you drive, you're not really paying attention."

I gave him side-eye and caught a dimple on his cheek. I smiled down on my screen. Then I swallowed. I did feel a little dizzy, actually. I set my phone on my lap and closed my eyes.

"I told you," he said in the darkness behind my lids. "So stubborn, all the time."

"No. Sometimes I'm asleep. And anyway, you don't know my life."

He laughed. "Yeah, actually, I do. I know all about you."

I scoffed. "Mm-hmm."

"What? I do. I know you can eat a whole sleeve of Thin Mints by yourself."

I snorted. "Who can't?"

He went on. "I know your favorite thing is having your back scratched after you take off your bra. You're in a better mood when you go to bed at eleven thirty and wake up at seven than when you go to bed at twelve thirty and wake up at eight. You like purple. You love the smell of carnations but hate it when guys buy you flowers because you think it's a waste of money..."

I opened an eye and looked at him. He was talking to the window, watching the road.

"You like to argue when you think you might be wrong. When you know you're right, you don't bother. You hate sharing your food, but you pick at my plate every time. That's why I always order extra fries." He looked over at me and smiled. "And you'd rather give me shit for my driving than admit you get carsick when you're on your phone. See?" He arched an eyebrow. "I know you."

My heart felt like it might crack in half. He *did* know me. He'd been paying attention to me. And I knew him too. I knew him inside and out.

I could tell what work had been like by the set of his shoulders when he came over, and I knew it helped him to de-stress to talk to me about a bad call. I always listened, even though sometimes they were hard to hear.

When he got quiet, it meant he was tired. He'd choose pistachio ice cream at Baskin-Robbins every time, but at Cold Stone he got sweet cream instead. I knew he liked Stuntman, though he'd never admit it. And he secretly liked it when I gave him shit. I could tell by the sparkle in his eyes.

And I also knew he hoped he had more sons than daughters. That he liked the name Oliver for his first boy and Eva for his first girl. He planned on teaching all his kids to hunt and had a collection of camo baby clothes. He wanted to build the cribs himself from wood in the forest around his grandparent's house in South Dakota.

He wanted no fewer than five children, and he planned for nine. And he hoped all his kids got the signature Copeland dimples and cowlick.

I hoped for that too. I wanted him to get all the things he dreamed about.

Yes. I knew him. I knew him well.

~

We took first place in trivia. The prize was two Malone's T-shirts.

Afterward, we sat in a dim cracked-leather booth at the back of the bar, nursing our beers with a basket of hot wings and Malone's famous queso. A live band played "Wonderwall" on the beat-up stage. Malone's was a dive. There'd already been two bar fights since we got here. It was good entertainment—better than the band.

I'd gotten twenty dollars' worth of fake tattoos from a vending machine, and we were giving each other full sleeves and laughing at people in the bar.

"Okay," Josh said, pressing a wet napkin to my forearm to stick a tattoo. "If you could turn anything into an Olympic sport, what would you win a medal for?"

I lifted the napkin and peeled off the plastic backing, looking at my new rose tattoo. "Sarcasm."

He laughed, his brown eyes creasing at the corners.

"All right, my turn," I said, laying an anchor tattoo on Josh's impressive biceps. "Window seat or aisle?"

He watched me slap on the wet napkin. "Middle seat. That way I'm next to you no matter which one you want."

Gah. This man. So selfless.

He'd said it so casually it was like thinking about me first came naturally. Like it was knee-jerk for him. My lips twisted into a smile, and we gazed at each other for a moment.

He was having a good time. He was happy. I wondered if he was this happy when we weren't together. If he had this much fun with his friends, or the crew at work.

Or any of the dates he went on.

I didn't. Not even with Sloan. It was different with Josh. It just was.

How many good days like this did we have left? In a few weeks, I wouldn't be seeing him anymore. I'd be recovering from my surgery, and he would be long gone. The wedding wouldn't throw us together. I already gave Miguel his job back. Creepy or not, I needed to replace Josh. Miguel knew the work and had his own garage to build out of so I'd never have to see him.

Everything was already taken care of. Everything except how I'd feel when this all ended.

And there was nothing to do about that.

"I need to send Sloan a picture of this," I said, shaking myself out of my thoughts. I angled the camera to get my whole arm. Then I sat back in the booth and started texting. "I keep getting autocorrected from 'queso' to 'quest.'" I shook my head. "Trust me, phone, I'm never going to talk about a quest. It's queso. Always queso."

Josh snorted. Then he nudged me, nodding to a girl in a skirt way too short for her, teetering in heels on her way back from the bathroom.

I laughed. "Look at the guy she's with. He's resource guarding. Growling over her like a dog with a bone. He's eyeing every man that comes within ten feet of her."

Josh chuckled. "Want me to test your theory? Pretend like I'm gonna try and talk to her?" His eyes twinkled.

"Oh my God, yes. Please."

He set his beer down and slid from the booth, and I watched, grinning, as he made his way over to the bar, shooting me a wolfish look over his shoulder. When he got close, Dog Bone Guy puffed his chest and wrapped an arm across his girl's boobs. Josh veered left, laughing.

I put a hand over my smile. His boyish charm always got me. He was adorable.

He made his way back to our table and scooted in next to me, putting an arm around me. "You were right."

"That was fucking hilarious." I giggled, leaning into him.

His eyes gleamed and he drew his lower lip between his teeth, looking down at my smiling mouth. And like it was no big deal, like there weren't any rules, as if we were a couple just out on a date, having a good time, he leaned in and kissed me.

And I *let* him.

TWENTY-NINE

JOSH

She kissed me back. She didn't push me away and get pissed, she didn't object. She didn't remind me that we're just fuck buddies or tell me this wasn't a date.

She kissed me back.

I hadn't brought up the Vegas call—I didn't have to. She was so different with me today it finally felt like we'd turned a corner. Maybe she'd missed me all those weeks or it was me telling her I loved her that night on the phone. Maybe she was over Tyler. I couldn't be sure what finally opened her up to me. All I knew was it was a gift.

Her fingers clutched the front of my shirt, and I pulled her in, pressing her into my chest, loving the taste of hops on her tongue, inhaling her perfume.

The kiss was slow and full of emotion. And it was the first time we'd kissed when it wasn't about sex.

I cherished this small gesture, this tiny public display that I had any claim to her. This stolen contact that didn't adhere to any of her rules.

When we broke apart, her sideways smile was light and unguarded. She draped her arms around my neck. "You're my favorite monkey to throw poo with, you know that?"

I stared into her eyes. "Then why aren't we together, Kristen?"

And then like that, she was gone.

Her expression fell like a heavy curtain dropping.

I lost her.

She sat up straight and moved away from me. "It's time to go," she said flatly, looking around for her purse.

Disappointment cut into me, razor sharp and violent. My hope, yanked out from under me.

No. Not today. Not again.

I flexed my jaw. "Kristen, answer me. Why aren't we together?"

When she looked up, her face was cold. "I told you from the very beginning that this was just going to be sex. I never led you to believe that it was anything different, Josh."

I shook my head at her. "It *is* something different and you fucking know it."

She turned and slid out of the booth on the opposite side.

"Where are you going?"

"To get another drink," she said without looking at me. "A strong one. Feel free to leave. I'll Uber home alone."

"Kristen!"

She ignored me and walked to the bar. I raked a frustrated hand through my hair.

I can't do this anymore.

And I had to at the same time. I couldn't not take what little scraps she threw at me, but how could I keep living like this?

Weeks of this roller-coaster ride, of glimpses of… *something.* I chased it, ran after this elusive rainbow of a woman, never really catching up with her.

Why did she keep doing this?

She leaned on the bar and I sat, trying to calm myself down

a little before I went after her. I stared moodily at the business cards lacquered into the top of the table. I was glancing up from this when he approached her. Some fucking guy.

He put his hand on her...

I launched out of the booth in an instant.

THIRTY
KRISTEN

I had to get up, had to be somewhere where he wouldn't see the pain in my eyes. My mask could only hold up so long.

My boundaries had been wavering all day. I'd gotten sloppy—I'd gotten *stupid.* I'd just missed him too much, and with so little time left I couldn't help myself. I just wanted to show him how he made me want to be with him. Just today.

Just once.

And now I'd fucked everything up. I never should have started up with him. It was selfish and idiotic to think I could pull this off. And I shouldn't have gone over there today. I should have ended things after karaoke—I knew better. I *knew* he was having feelings.

"A shot of Patrón." I leaned on the worn wooden bar, imagining Josh's eyes on my back.

This was it. The last day. It was all over now. No more.

A lump bolted to my throat.

Well, it was a good day. It was. At least there was that. It came sooner than I'd hoped, but here we were.

A warm body edged up to me as I wiped a tear from my cheek and I turned, expecting Josh. But it was one of the frat guys from the table next to us at trivia.

He tossed his head back, flinging hair from his forehead. "Hey. Do you believe in love at first sight?"

He was wasted. Red eyes, reeking of Jäger. He leered at me, way too close.

I scooted away. "No, but now I believe in annoyed at first sight," I mumbled.

He snapped his fingers at the bartender. "She'll have another of whatever she's got." He pointed at me.

"Uh, no, she won't." I turned to him, irritated, and gave him my best sarcastic smile. "What's your name?"

He beamed under ruddy cheeks. "Kyle."

"Okay, Kyle. I'm trying to be a better person these days, so I'm going to tell you to fuck off in the nicest way possible." I gave him crazy eyes. "Fuck off. *Please.*"

He laughed. "Wow, okay." He blew a sour breath in my face.

The bartender slid my tequila in front of me, and Kyle dropped a bill on the bar. I slid it back to him. "No." I shook my head incredulously. "What is it about the look on my face that is encouraging to you right now?"

I never understood men who wouldn't take no for an answer. I opened my purse and paid. "Keep the change." Then I picked up my shot and gave Kyle my back, shaking my head.

He grabbed my arm from behind. "Hey, don't be fucking rude..."

I was looking down on his hand, ready to introduce him to my elbow, when suddenly Josh was there.

He pushed between me and Kyle, knocking him away from me. "Hey, get your fucking hands off her."

Then he lurched forward with a shove, crashing into me, sloshing my shot all over the bar.

Josh moved so quickly Kyle didn't know what hit him.

Josh was big, but he never struck me as someone who could be fast.

He was a viper.

In a split second he had Kyle shoved against the bar with his arm twisted behind his back, his cheek pressed into the counter.

The bouncer showed up out of nowhere. "You and you, *out*," he said, pointing at Josh and Kyle.

Josh let go of his drunk idiot and I grabbed my purse and jumped from my stool, making my escape before he tried to get me to go with him. I threaded my way through empty high-top tables toward the ladies' room, but Josh caught up and grabbed my arm.

"So you're just gonna run from me? We're not going to talk about this?"

I whirled on him and yanked my arm down. "No, we're not. There's nothing to talk about. I'm single, we're not a thing. You knew that from the beginning."

The pain rippled across his face.

I'd never seen him like this. I'd never seen him worked up before about *anything*. He was always so laid back, and all I could think was that I'd managed to hurt this sweet man. It gutted me. I couldn't keep looking at him.

I made to move past him to the ladies' room, desperate to hide from the damage I caused, but he blocked my way. "How can you act like today didn't happen, Kristen?"

"Josh, I don't want to argue with you. Move," I said, glaring at him.

His jaw set and I pushed past him. Then he picked me up

and threw me over his shoulder like I was a fire hose. Hooting and cheering erupted in the bar.

"Josh! Put me down!"

I struggled uselessly against his grip. He had seventy-five pounds on me, and he was on a mission. I wasn't going anywhere. His arms locked like a cage.

"You're not running from me anymore," he said. "You're talking to me."

He came out through the double doors into the parking lot, and he didn't set me down until we were on the grassy divider by the street.

As soon as I got my feet under me, indignant rage bubbled over. "Don't ever do that again. I'm not your fucking possession," I hissed at him.

His eyes flashed. "No, you're not my anything, are you? I'm allowed to touch you as long as I don't act like it means something, right?"

The emotion on his face twisted my insides. Anguish and despair swirled in his eyes.

I turned back for the bar to escape that look, and his arms were around my shoulders in a second, locking my back against his chest.

His lips went to my ear. "I can see the way you feel about me when you don't think anyone is looking. I fucking see it, Kristen." His voice cracked. "I remember what you said to me that night in Vegas. I *remember*."

All of the fight drained out of my body in an instant.

He breathed into my ear. "Why won't you just let me love you?"

A sob burst from my mouth, and I went limp in his arms. He held me up, hugging me to himself, absorbing my surrender.

I turned in the circle of his embrace and buried my crying in his shirt. He put his face into my neck and held me so tightly I couldn't breathe. But I didn't want to breathe. I wanted to be his prisoner. I wanted to never escape.

Tears poured out of me. "I can't, Josh." I gasped into his chest. "You don't know it all."

"Then *tell* me," he said. He pulled away from me and spoke to my eyes. "What is it? Because I know you want me. I know you're acting. Just tell me *why*."

How do you share something like that? How could I tell him that my body could never do the one thing he needed it to? I couldn't. I couldn't get the words out. I couldn't bear to see my value drop in his eyes, see him realize I wasn't actually what he wanted.

Less of a woman.

Damaged goods.

Barren.

Sterile.

I shook my head, biting my lips together. "Josh, you should just forget about me. Get serious with one of those other women you see. Have sex with them. Move on."

He let out a puff of exasperation. "What other women? There *are* no other women. There never has been. Do you know what I'm doing when you think I'm on dates? I'm at home, alone, wishing I was with you. This is what you've made me into. I pretend to see other people because I know if I don't, you won't see me anymore. *Why?*"

"You . . . you haven't been seeing anyone else?" I blinked at him.

"Of *course* not. I'm fucking in love with you."

And like he couldn't stand not to for one more second, he grabbed me and kissed me. His lips were pained and desperate, and I hopelessly kissed him back. I climbed him, combing my hands in his hair. I wished I could drown in him. I needed to extinguish the burning disappointment in my soul, and for a few seconds, I did.

And then I pushed him away.

He let me go and I staggered back in the grass, and he stood there, panting.

"Josh, I can't see you anymore, okay? This is over." I choked on the words.

I watched what I said hit him like a smack. "Why?"

I wiped my face with the back of my hand and blinked through the tears. "Because you're obviously taking this way more seriously than you should be. I told you. I told you from day one that this would only ever be sex. I never lied to you."

His jaw went rigid. "You're lying to me right now. I know this isn't what you want. You fucking love me, Kristen. Just stop—" He reached for me and I smacked his hand away.

He stood staring at me, confusion and hurt etched all over his handsome face. "Why aren't I good enough? Is it because I don't speak a dozen languages? I don't have a fucking master's degree? I don't make enough money? What is it?"

It's not you.

I let the tears run down my face, and I clutched at my facade. "You thought you could change me just like you thought you could change Celeste. You're changing the rules, just like you did to her. Don't put your shit on me, Josh. You said you could handle this. You said you could—"

"I'm not fucking crazy! Stop acting like I'm making this up!" He dragged his hands down his face and balled his fists over his eyes. He stood there, his breath coming out in gasps, and I wanted to run to him and dive into his arms. But I didn't budge.

"We're in love," he said, blinking at me through tears. "We *are*. Why are you doing this?"

My bottom lip trembled. "Fine. So we're in love. What do you want from me, Josh?"

He let out a shaky breath, and the relief transformed every inch of his body. His eyes softened into hope.

He closed the space between us and gathered my face in his hands. "I want what we had today, all the time. I want to be with you. I want to hold your hand on a walk and kiss you in a damn booth. I want you to answer my fucking calls and let me hug you. I want to make plans with you on New Year's and my birthday and tell people you're my girlfriend." His eyes begged me. "Please, Kristen. Just... *stop*."

"I can't have children."

I forced it from myself before I lost the ability to do it.

It had the desired effect. He froze.

"What?" he breathed.

"I can't have children. I have a condition. I'll never have them."

His hands dropped from my face. He stared at me with his mouth open, the color draining from his cheeks. "You can't... what do you... *what*?"

I took a few steps backward, giving myself a head start. He didn't move. He just stood there, shell shocked, gawking at me.

When he didn't reach for me again, I turned and ran.

THIRTY-ONE

JOSH

I got to the fire station early this morning. I had no hope of sleeping and needed the distraction.

Kristen never came home last night.

Fuck, I shouldn't have let her run off. I was just so shocked. It felt like she'd handed me a bomb and it detonated in my face, pelting me with emotional shrapnel. My ears had literally started to ring after what she'd said, and she'd bolted and jumped into the car of some girl she'd met during trivia, and she was gone in an instant. It happened so fast.

I'd stayed up, waiting for her in her living room. Calling her cell phone, sending her text messages, begging her to come home and talk to me.

She sent me a text around midnight saying only that she was okay, she wasn't coming back, and to please walk the dog.

Everything was finally clear. It all made sense. It was so obvious to me now I wondered how I couldn't have known. The severe cramps, the spotting. Her history of anemia. The long periods.

The walls she put between us.

And all the fucked-up things I've said to her.

That I wouldn't adopt. That I wanted a huge family. That I'd left Celeste because she didn't want children.

Karaoke night suddenly looked totally different to me, the weeks after it where she'd gone cold—I'd told her that if Tyler didn't want kids, she shouldn't be with him. That the kid thing was too important.

I'd actually told her that shit.

I'd been talking Kristen out of dating me almost daily since the day I met her.

Fuck, if only I'd known.

I'd had all night to think about what it meant, and it didn't change anything. I loved her. I couldn't not be with her. That's what it kept coming back to. I couldn't walk away from her—I wasn't even capable of it. The situation was fucked up and star-crossed, and I didn't give a shit. She was the woman I loved, so we'd just have to deal with it.

I stood in the kitchen making my second pot of coffee. The guys were napping. The wedding was in eight days, and Brandon was off for three weeks. We had a new guy named Luke we'd borrowed from another station. I was spooning grounds into the machine when I heard her voice.

"Joshua..."

I spun around and had her in my arms in a heartbeat. "Kristen, oh God, thank you," I breathed, kissing the side of her neck.

It was like a reprieve from a prison sentence, seeing her. I was stuck here for two days, two days that I wouldn't be able to get to her, and she'd come to me.

But she didn't hug me back. She put her hands to my chest and tried to make space between us. "Josh, I just came to talk to you, okay?"

I didn't take my hands from her waist. Her face was puffy, like she'd been up all night crying. Deep circles under her eyes. I leaned in to kiss her and she turned from me.

"I need you to stand over there." She nodded to the kitchen counter. "Please."

If she left, I wouldn't be able to go after her. I was on shift and couldn't leave the station. I didn't want to let her go, but I didn't want her to run off again, so I stepped back.

She wore leggings and one of her off-the-shoulder shirts that I loved, and even though she looked tired, she was the most beautiful woman I'd even seen.

And she loves me.

I didn't even know what I did to deserve her, but I knew I'd do anything to make up for the way I'd made her feel.

She took a deep breath. "I'm having a partial hysterectomy the week after the wedding," she said flatly. "I have uterine fibroids. They're tumors that grow on the walls of my uterus. Mine are imbedded. They can't be surgically removed, and they didn't respond to treatment. They cause heavy bleeding and cramping. And...and infertility." She said the last word like she had to force it out.

She tucked her hair behind her ear and looked away from me, tears welling in her beautiful eyes. "I'm sorry I didn't tell you. It was embarrassing for me. And I don't need you to say anything. I just needed you to know why. Because it was never my intention to make you feel unwanted." Her chin quivered and my heart broke. "I did want you, Josh." She looked back at me. "I always have. You didn't imagine anything."

The admission that she'd wanted me made my heart reach for her. I took a step toward her, and she took a step back.

I put my hands up. "Kristen, nothing has changed. My feelings for you haven't changed. I want you, no matter what. I'm so sorry—I didn't know. When I said—"

She shook her head. "Josh, this isn't open for discussion. I didn't come here to tell you so you could decide whether you want to date me. That's not even on the table. I just realized that for the last few weeks, I made you feel unloved. And I'm really sorry. I thought you . . . well, I didn't know you had feelings for me. I thought only I . . . Anyway, that's my fault. I should have never let that happen."

I scoffed. "There was nothing you could have done to keep me from falling in love with you. Even if I'd known this from the very beginning, it wouldn't have kept me away. You should have told me."

"No, I should have stayed away from you," she said. "I'm sorry I didn't."

The call bell went off, and the red lights started blinking. Three beeps and then, "Traffic collision, motorcycle down on the intersection of Verdugo and San Fernando Boulevard."

Fuck.

"You have to go." She turned toward the door.

I lunged after her, grabbing her hand. "Wait . . . just wait."

She looked up at me, her eyes sad. "There's nothing else to talk about, Josh."

"There is. Will you wait for me to get back? Please? Just wait here. Twenty minutes, so we can talk."

She pressed her lips into a line.

"*Please*, Kristen."

We stared at each other for what seemed like an eternity. She nodded. "Okay."

I breathed a sigh of relief and before she could object, I pulled her into me and kissed her. "I love you," I whispered. "Wait for me." Then I turned and jogged down the hall as the rest of the crew streamed out of the bedrooms.

Leaving her felt wrong. Everything between us was fragile and I knew how easily she could shut down on me. The timing of this call couldn't have been worse. I practically dove into the driver's seat, determined to get this over with as quickly as humanly possible.

The guys got in and Shawn put on his headset. "Kristen's here, huh?"

"Not now, Shawn." I turned on the lights and pulled out into the street. The accident was only a block over, thank God.

Javier opened the laptop. "Might be a DUI," he said, reading the notes from Dispatch.

Luke scoffed from the seat behind me. "Not even nine in the morning."

"Hey, it's five o'clock somewhere." Shawn snickered. "So, what's got her panties in a bunch now?"

I turned onto Verdugo and gave Shawn the finger over my shoulder.

I pulled up to the accident. The police were already on the scene, blocking traffic at the intersection, so I parked the engine behind a cop car with its lights on, and Shawn, Javier, and Luke hopped out to get the trauma kit.

A Hilton Garden Inn, newer-looking apartments, and an artists' senior living complex flanked the four-lane, tree-lined road. The brown, tired Verdugo Mountains loomed in the distance.

I checked my watch as I climbed out of the engine. If she was gone when I got back, I'd lose my fucking mind.

She'd said she'd stay, and she usually did what she said she would. But this thing had her shaken, and I couldn't wait forty-eight hours to run after her if she took off on me again. I'd go insane.

My mind was exhausted. I hadn't slept last night. I didn't fully absorb everything she'd said in the kitchen and some of it began to catch up to me now.

I didn't come here to tell you so you could decide whether you want to date me. That's not even on the table.

If Kristen thought I was going to let her go, she was fucking nuts. Not now that I knew she loved me. Not ever.

I finally understood the kind of love that made men give up everything. The kind that made someone change religions or go vegan or move to the other side of the world to be with the woman they loved. If someone had told me six months ago that I'd choose a woman who couldn't have kids, I'd have called him crazy. But being with her wasn't even something I had to think about. I did want kids. But I wanted her first. Everything else was just everything else.

Sure, a part of me grieved a life I knew I wouldn't have now. Kids that I'd never meet, a future different from the one I'd spent the last few years wanting. But I processed it like *I'd* been the one who just got a diagnosis. Because in a way, I had. This thing didn't feel like her problem. It felt like *our* problem, to figure out together. It was as much mine as it was hers.

I fell in next to the guys and we made our way onto the scene, our feet crunching over broken glass.

I stepped over a side-view mirror and nodded to a cop talking to a sobbing woman by the open door of her blue Kia. I assumed it was the other vehicle involved in the accident. The bumper had damage.

No skid marks. The lady blew right through a red light.

"Probably prescription pain pills," Luke mumbled.

Shawn scoffed. "She looks like vodka to me."

I shook my head. "I hope the accident didn't ruin her buzz. She'll need it where she's going."

We saw too much of this bullshit. And now I had to be here cleaning up this lady's mess instead of talking to Kristen.

Javier nudged Luke, and he veered off to check on the lady.

I tried to put myself into work mode, though most of it was autopilot at this point.

The motorcycle rider lay facedown twenty feet away. He'd been thrown. I knew walking up the injuries were bad. By the looks of his twisted leg, he'd been pinned between the car and his bike during impact. The mangled bike sat on its side next to a planter full of birds-of-paradise on the sidewalk in front of the hotel.

I stared at the bike as I walked.

The bike... *a Triumph, but with that new exhaust he just put on.*

I looked back at the patient, everything suddenly slowing.

The helmet... *a blacked-out Bell Qualifier DLX.*

The man's shirt... *from the gift shop at the Wynn in Vegas.*

Shawn and Javier must have noticed it at the same moment, because without speaking, we all began to run the last few feet.

Brandon.

It was *Brandon.*

I fell to my knees on the asphalt. "Hey! Hey, can you hear me?"

Oh my God...

He was unconscious. I put a hand to his back and felt the slight rise and fall.

Breathing. He's alive.

This is Brandon. How is this Brandon?

I picked up his hand and checked for a radial pulse in his wrist. It was weak and thready. I could barely feel it.

It meant blood loss.

I didn't see him bleeding heavily, so it had to be internal.

Internal bleeding.

He could be dying.

My mind raced. We needed to get him stable and into the ambulance.

Shawn dove into his trauma bag, kneeling in a rivulet of metallic-smelling blood. "Fuck, fuck, fuck! Come on, fucker, you're getting married! You gotta be okay!"

Sloan.

My heart pounded in my ears. "He's going to be fine. You're going to be fine, buddy."

I got out my pocket light, opened his visor, and pulled back his eyelids. His pupils shrank to small black dots. They were equal and reactive. Good. That was a good sign. He didn't have brain damage. Not yet. We needed to get him to the ER before his brain started to swell.

I gulped air. I had to stay calm. *Stay calm!*

The ambulance pulled up, and Javier jogged to meet them.

"I need a c-spine and a gurney!" I shouted.

Jesus Christ, his helmet was fucked. Dented from the impact. Covered in skid marks.

She didn't stop. The lady didn't fucking stop. It was a forty-mile-per-hour zone. A forty-mile-per-hour impact if she wasn't speeding.

And she probably was.

I pulled out my trauma shears and started cutting off his clothes. "Sorry, I know you like this shirt, buddy. We'll go back and get you another one, okay?" My voice shook.

As I cut away fabric, more injuries bloomed over his body before my eyes.

I grappled to make sense of it.

Where the fuck had he been going? Why wasn't he home with Sloan?

His tux. He had a final tux fitting today at 9:00 a.m. He told me about it.

Why couldn't he have been late? Or early? Why didn't he take his goddamn truck? Or a different street?

I cut his pants off. He had a break. Compound fracture, left leg. His femur pushed jagged through his skin.

I swallowed hard looking over his mangled body, and my brain ticked off injuries.

Serious.

Serious.

Serious.

I looked up at Shawn's wide, frightened eyes. "We'll have to log roll him onto the backboard. We can't pull traction on this leg. Let's get his helmet off," I said quickly.

Javier ran a backboard over while Shawn kneeled and cradled Brandon's head. I reached around and unclipped the strap, and we kept his neck stable while we pulled the helmet off. His brown hair was matted with blood.

Shawn was crying. "The bitch didn't even fucking stop."

"Keep it together," Javier said calmly. "Look at me, Shawn. He's a patient. He can be your buddy when this call is over. Right now he's a patient. Do your job and he'll be okay."

Shawn nodded, trying to collect himself. Javier snapped the cervical collar on Brandon's neck and we all put our hands on him, ready to flip him.

"On the count of three," Javier said, not looking up, sweat beading on his forehead. "One, two, three!" And in one fluid motion we turned him onto the backboard.

Brandon always wore heavy-duty pants when he rode. But he was in a T-shirt. It was eighty today. His bare left arm was torn to shreds by the asphalt. He looked like he'd been through a lemon zester. Blood oozed from the white streaks of the under layer of his skin. And this was the least of his worries.

Shawn, Javier, and an EMT lifted him onto the gurney while I felt his chest and stomach. He had rib fractures and rigidity in his abdomen. "A possible liver laceration," I said, a lump bolting to my throat.

Javier mumbled a curse word, and Shawn shook his head, his eyes red and glassy.

We needed to get him to the hospital.

The ambulance crew took over.

I rattled off what I knew as we ran him to the open ambulance doors, my voice professional and disembodied, like it came from someone else, someone who wasn't standing over his critically injured best friend. "Twenty-nine-year-old male, motorcycle rider struck by vehicle, thrown twenty feet from the point of impact. Helmet has significant damage. A weakened, thready radial pulse. Pupils are equal and reactive. Open femur fracture, severe road rash. Unresponsive."

I climbed into the ambulance and saw the woman from the blue Kia being slapped into handcuffs as the doors slammed shut behind us.

We'd gotten him in the ambulance in less than five minutes. I worried it was five minutes too long.

I leaned over him. "Hey, buddy." My voice cracked. "Hold on. You'll be all right. I'm going to get Sloan over here, okay?"

Tears stung my eyes, but my hands kept working, running on muscle memory. I set up his IV en route. The EMT put him on oxygen while the driver called it in.

We cycled his blood pressure. Put him on an EKG to monitor his heart. But none of this helped him. It was nothing but reassess. That's all we could do. Reassess. It was the longest ride of my life.

Finally the rig turned hard into the hospital parking lot.

The EKG flatlined.

"No!" I started chest compressions to the long, static beep of the heart rate monitor as the ambulance pulled up to the ER. "Come on, Brandon, come *on*!"

The ambulance doors swung open and I climbed the gurney and straddled him, pumping his chest with the palms of my hands. Javier, Shawn, and Luke were waiting, and I ducked as they lowered us both out of the ambulance and wheeled us into the trauma room.

"He's crashing!" I screamed between thrusts. "We're losing him!"

The emergency room team descended on the gurney.

The room was chaos. Shouting and barked orders, beeping machines and the squeaky sound of wheels rolling on a hard floor. I kept doing chest compressions until they ran over the crash cart. I didn't stop until I saw paddles.

A doctor in a white coat waited for me to clear the gurney and then he pressed the charge to Brandon's chest. "Clear!"

Brandon's body lurched with the jolt and everyone froze, staring at the lines on the monitor.

Nothing.

"Clear!"

He lurched again.

We waited.

The jagged V of a heartbeat launched the room back into action, and I breathed again.

I was backed out into the hallway by the throng of people working on him. They started a central line. They started X-rays. Neurology was called. And then a curtain yanked closed and it was done. There was nothing else we could do for him. That was it.

It was out of our hands.

I stood there panting, in shock, the adrenaline crashing into me now that I'd stopped moving. I looked down at myself, my hands trembling. I was covered in his blood.

Covered in my best friend's blood.

Luke spoke from behind me. "She was drunk."

My hands balled into fists, and Shawn started to wheeze.

Sloan. I needed Kristen to get Sloan. I walked outside, praying to God that Kristen answered my call, that she hadn't decided to ice me out again in the short time since I'd seen her. If she didn't answer and I had to text her, I wouldn't be able to do it. My hands shook so violently now that it was all I could do to unlock my phone and pull up her number.

It had been twenty minutes since I'd seen her. Twenty minutes that felt like a lifetime.

I pressed the phone to my ear, my hand shaking.

I wouldn't be able to stay with him. My station had mandated staffing. I couldn't leave until someone relieved me. I had to go back.

"Hey." Her voice gave me the first full breath I'd taken in almost half an hour. Just knowing she was on the other end of the line grounded me. Everything that had happened between us felt years away and unimportant.

"Kristen, Brandon's been in an accident."

I told her everything. I knew she would take care of the rest. She was capable—she'd get Sloan to the hospital.

When I got back, Javier paced the hallway, making phone calls to cover our shifts, a finger pressed to his ear. But there were fires up north. It would be hard to find someone. We were already borrowing Luke as it was.

Shawn breathed into a paper bag with Luke crouched next to him, looking worried. "They just wheeled him off to surgery," Luke said.

I slid down against the wall of the ER hallway as nurses and staff streamed by me. I put my palms to my eyelids and cried like a baby.

THIRTY-TWO
KRISTEN

I hung up with Josh, and the switch flipped in my head.

Sloan called it my velociraptor brain because it made me fierce and sharp. Something big had to trigger it, and when it did, my compulsive, laser-focused, primal side activated. The one that got me a near perfect score on my SATs and got me through college finals and Mom. The one that made me clean when I was stressed and threatened to launch into full-scale manic OCD if left unchecked—*that* kicked in.

Emotion drained away, the tiredness from staying up all night crying dissipated, and I became my purpose.

I didn't do hysterics. Never had. When in crisis, I became systematic and efficient.

And the transition was now complete.

I weighed only for a second whether to call Sloan and tell her or go pick her up. I decided to pick her up. She would be too upset to drive properly, but knowing her, she would try anyway.

From Josh's explanation of the situation, Brandon wouldn't be out of the hospital anytime soon. Sloan wouldn't leave Brandon, and I wouldn't leave her. She would need things for the stay. People would need to be called. Arrangements made.

I began to compile a list in my head of things to do and things to pack as I quickly but methodically drove to Sloan's. *Phone charger, headphones, blanket, change of clothes for Sloan, toiletries, and her laptop.*

It took me twenty minutes to get to her house, and I got out of my car ready for a surgical extraction.

I stood there, surrounded by the earthy smell of Sloan's just-watered potted porch flowers. The door opened, and I took in her blissfully ignorant face one more time.

"Kristen?"

It wasn't unusual for me to stop by. But she knew me well enough to instantly know something was wrong.

"Sloan, Brandon has been in an accident," I said calmly. "He's alive, but I need you to get your purse and come with me."

I knew immediately that I'd been right to come get her instead of calling. One look at her and I knew she wouldn't have been able to put a foot in front of the other. While I mobilized and became strong under stress, she froze and weakened.

"*What?*" she breathed.

"We have to hurry. Come on." I pushed past her and systematically executed my checklist. I gave myself a two-minute window to grab what was needed.

Her gym bag would be in the laundry room, already filled with toiletries and her headphones. I grabbed that, pulled a sweater from her closet, selected a change of clothes for her, and stuffed her laptop inside the bag.

When I came out of the room, she had managed to grab her purse as instructed. She stood by the sofa looking shaken, her eyes moving back and forth like she was trying to figure out what was happening.

Her cell phone sat by her easel and I snatched it, pulling the charger from the wall. I grabbed her favorite throw blanket from the sofa and stuffed that in the bag and zipped it.

List complete.

Then I took her by the elbow, locked her front door, and dragged her to the car.

"Wha... what happened? What happened!" she screamed, finally coming out of her shock.

I opened up the passenger door and put her in. "Buckle yourself up. I'll tell you what I know on the way."

When I got around to the driver's side, she had her phone to her ear. "He's not answering. He's not answering! What happened, Kristen?!"

I grabbed her face in my hands. "Listen to me. Look at me. He is *alive*. He was hit on his bike. Josh went on the call. He was unconscious. It was clear he had some broken bones and a possible head injury. He's at the ER, and I need to get you to the hospital to be with him. But I need you to be *calm*."

Her brown eyes were terrified, but she nodded.

"Right now your job is to call Brandon's family," I said firmly. "Relay what I just said to you, *calmly*. Can you do that for Brandon?"

She nodded again. "Yes." Her hands shook, but she dialed.

I drove fast and carefully while Sloan made calls. I scanned the road and went twenty over the speed limit on the freeway. I zipped around cars using my blinker and hand waves. When we got to the hospital, I dropped her off at the emergency room entrance and parked, then ran with her bag to meet her at the front desk.

"He's in surgery," she said tearfully when I jogged in through the automatic doors of the ER, my shoes squeaking on the white shiny floors.

I looked at the woman behind the check-in desk, like a robot gathering data. I could see everything. The age spots on her forehead, the gray wisps along her hairline. The sterile, white countertop and the shimmer in the petals of pink roses in a vase behind the desk. "Where can we wait? And can you inform the doctor that his family is here?"

We were sent to a private waiting area for the neurology department on the third floor. Brightly lit, plastic potted plants tucked in the corners of the room, serene blue walls, uniform gray tweed upholstered chairs, magazines and boxes of tissues on every end and coffee table.

Sloan scanned the room. Maybe it was the finality of it—the cessation of forward movement—but this was when she officially broke down. She buried her face in her hands and wept. "Why is this happening?"

I wrapped her sweater around her and put her in a chair. "I don't know, Sloan. Why does anything happen?"

I knew what things had to be done, what I had to do to make her comfortable. But I couldn't feel any of the panic or grief that I saw in Sloan. I felt like I was watching a movie with the sound off. I could see what was happening, but I couldn't connect to the characters.

We waited. And waited. And waited.

A police officer came in and asked Sloan some questions. Confirmed Brandon's name and address. Then he told us that the woman who had caused the accident had been arrested for driving under the influence.

Sloan sobbed again when she heard that.

I covered her with her blanket and got her a coffee. I plugged in her phone, made her eat half of a tuna sandwich.

Family began to show up and they huddled around the waiting room, whispering and crying. Brandon's mom prayed in Spanish over a rosary.

I sat next to Sloan, feigning emotion, doing all the motions. Looking somber and rubbing her back but feeling empty and removed because my crisis response was still in effect.

Now that the rush was gone, the velociraptor paced. I couldn't shut off my brain and the need to be doing something. But the only thing to do was wait. I bounced my knee and picked at my cuticles until they bled. I texted Josh and kept him posted. They'd found a replacement for him at work, but he couldn't leave until 8:00 p.m.

Then, ten hours after the accident, the doctor came out.

Sloan bolted from her chair and I followed, ready to absorb what he said with an accuracy that I would be able to transpose onto paper, word for word, two days later.

Brandon's mom wrapped her sweater tighter around herself and stood shoulder to shoulder with Sloan. Brandon's dad put an arm around his wife.

I tried to figure out the outcome from the doctor's lined, angular face, but he was unreadable.

"I'm Dr. Campbell, the resident neurosurgeon. Brandon is out of surgery. He's stable. We were able to stop the internal bleeding. I had to remove a large piece of his skull to alleviate the pressure on his brain."

Sloan gasped and started sobbing again. I put an arm around her, sandwiching her between Brandon's mom and me as she breathed into her hands.

The doctor went on. "The good news is there's brain activity. Now, I can't say what his recovery is going to look like at this juncture, but the tests we ran were promising. He's going to have a long road ahead of him, but I'm feeling optimistic."

The room took a collective deep breath.

"For now we're going to be keeping him on a ventilator in a medically induced coma to allow the swelling to go down and give his brain a chance to heal itself. We won't know the extent of his injuries until he comes out of that coma. But again, I feel optimistic. He's a strong young man."

"Can I see him?" Sloan wiped at her eyes.

"He'll be in recovery for the next hour. Once they get him set up in the ICU, he can have visitors. Fifteen minutes only, no more than two people at a time."

"When will he be off the ventilator?" I asked.

"That all depends on him. Could be days. Could be weeks. Weeks is the more likely scenario."

Dr. Campbell handed us off to the orthopedic surgeon, who went over the next steps to deal with Brandon's broken bones. Another surgeon told us about the repairs to the laceration to his liver. Then a plastic surgeon talked to us about the skin grafts he would need to cover the extensive road rash on his left arm.

By the time the doctors were done with us, Sloan was wiped. I put her back in her chair and called Josh.

The phone was still ringing when I heard it behind me. I spun and there he was.

The second I saw him, my emotional disconnect from the situation clicked off. My coping mechanism snapped away from me like a rubber band shot across a room, and the weight of what happened hit me. Sloan's grief, Brandon's condition—Josh's trauma. I dove into his arms, instantly withered.

I'd never trusted anyone else to be the one in control, and my manic mind gave it to him immediately and without reservation and retreated back into itself.

He clutched me, and I held him tighter than I'd ever held

anyone in my life. I wasn't sure if I was comforting him, or if I was letting him comfort me. All I knew was something subconscious in me told me I didn't have to hold the world up anymore now that he was here.

"I'm so glad you're here," I whispered, breathing him in as my body turned back on from being in suspended animation. The sound to the movie around me turned all the way up. My heart began to pound, I gasped into his neck, and tears instantly flooded my eyes.

He put his forehead to mine. He looked like shit. He'd looked bad this morning at the station—I knew he hadn't slept. But now his eyes were red like he'd been crying. "Any updates?" His voice was raspy.

I couldn't even comprehend how hard it must have been for him to see what he saw and stay at work, going on calls. I wanted to cover him like a blanket. I wanted to cover them both, Josh and Sloan, and shield them from this.

I put a hand to his cheek, and he turned into it and closed his eyes.

"He just got out of surgery," I said. Then I told him everything, my hands on his chest like they anchored me. He stood with his arms around my waist, nodding and looking at me like he was worried *I* was the one who wasn't okay.

It didn't escape me that we were holding each other and I didn't care what it meant or what wrong signals it might send to him at the moment. I just knew that I needed to touch him. I needed this momentary surrender.

For both of us.

THIRTY-THREE

JOSH

It was several hours before I got to see Brandon. The limit was strict on visitors in the ICU, and Sloan and Brandon's immediate family took first run.

It was night already. I had somehow managed to live through the worst day of my life. I checked my watch: 11:18 p.m. I sat in the waiting room with Kristen and Sloan and a fluctuating, thinning crowd of Brandon's relatives.

Kristen held my hand.

She hadn't stopped touching me since I got here. I was grateful. I needed her. Just being there with her soothed me. I'd been spinning at work, the images of Brandon running on a continuous loop through my head. The smell of blood, the crack of his ribs under my palms, every injury, replaying itself again and again, and me, questioning whether I'd done the right thing with each one. If I'd done enough to save his life.

But Kristen's fingers laced through mine quieted it all. I couldn't picture going through this without her. I didn't know how I'd be coping if it wasn't for her.

Sloan was a fucking mess. Kristen seemed to orbit around her in a constant stream of awareness, even when Kristen put her head on my shoulder and drifted off. Sloan got up to use the bathroom, and Kristen opened her eyes like she could detect the sound of Sloan moving, even in her sleep.

Kristen watched her friend walk from the room. When Sloan was gone, Kristen looked up at me with those brown eyes, one hand tangled in mine and the other on my chest, and I was whole just looking at her.

This crisis laid everything bare.

I'd found my person.

She was the foundation. She was the thing that all other things are built on. Everything was secondary to being with her. It didn't matter where I worked or if I liked my job, where I lived or how many kids I had. My happiness, my sanity, my well-being—it all started with her. And now that I knew that, I didn't want to just be her boyfriend—I wanted everything. I wanted her to be my wife. I wanted to wake up to her every day for the rest of my life.

We needed to talk. Not now. It wasn't the right place or time. But we needed to talk.

"You can go in now." A nurse broke into my thoughts.

Kristen sat up and gave my arm a squeeze. "Want me to go in with you?"

"No. Sloan will want to see him again. I'll be fine." I stood.

Brandon's parents had gone home to deal with their dogs and to take showers. Only Brandon's sister, Claudia, remained in the waiting room. She'd already gone in twice over the last two hours and was sleeping on a bench.

The nurse buzzed me into the ICU.

I peered into dim open hospital rooms as we made our way down the hall, the smell of antiseptic swirling around me as I walked.

We stopped at room 214.

His room was small. I could see why they limited it to two visitors at a time.

Like the other rooms, his was dimmed for the late hour. Brandon lay on his back. Hands at his sides, a pulse oximeter on the index finger of his right hand. His head was bound with thick white gauze, his left leg elevated in a sling and bandaged. He wore a ventilator over his face. Wires snaked from his chest under his hospital gown.

The gentle, quiet beep of a heart monitor and the in and out of the ventilator were the only sounds in the room. His cheek was purple and swollen, the bruising I'd witnessed on the scene blooming.

I just stood there, like I was looking at a mess too big to clean up and I didn't know where to start. I didn't know what to do. I felt frozen. This was a soldier in Iraq. A hunter. A strong and capable man.

And now he was broken.

Sloan slipped into the room behind me and slid into one of the bedside chairs, gathering up his hand. My legs unlocked and I took her lead, sitting in the chair next to her.

She looked at him, her chin quivering. Her hair was up in a loose bun, crooked and sloppy. Her face, blotchy and red. "They say he can hear us. We should talk to him, Josh."

I cleared my throat and leaned forward. "Hey, buddy. You look like shit, man."

Sloan did a laugh-cry. Then she put her other hand over his. "Your whole family was here today, babe. You won't ever be here alone, okay? Someone will always be in the waiting room for you. I'm not going to leave you. I can't be in here all the time, but I'll be just outside."

I wondered why someone wasn't allowed to stay with him.

When the fifteen minutes was up and the nurse came to get us, Sloan went back to the waiting room and I made my way to the nurses' station. I summoned my most convincing smile, the one that seemed to work on Kristen, and I walked up to the counter.

The middle-aged nurse manning the station looked up, eyed my firefighter badge, and gave me a warm grin. "Well, hello. What can I do for you, young man?"

I was grateful for my profession at the moment. Nobody was ever unhappy to see a fireman.

I put a thumb over my shoulder. "Yeah, I was just visiting my buddy, Brandon, in room 214." I looked over at the room and came back with a smile that I hoped reached my eyes. "I couldn't help but notice a lot of the other rooms had visitors that looked like they'd kind of set up camp. Is there any way his fiancée can just stay with him? He'd really like that."

My sister Amber was a nurse, and I knew that on the hospital floor, the nurses ruled absolutely. They could bend any policy they wanted to.

She smiled at me. "Well, it's against the visitor guidelines. But I think we can do that. I'll buzz her back in."

I made a case for Claudia too and got the nod.

When I came back out into the waiting room and gave Sloan and Claudia the news, they both hugged me before slipping back into the ICU.

I turned to Kristen. "We should go home. Get some sleep."

We were the last two left in the waiting room, and weariness started to take me down. I was emotionally and physically exhausted.

I put my hands on her arms. "There's nothing else you can do for Sloan at the moment, and sleeping in a chair isn't going to help matters. He's stable. Let's go home."

She folded herself into my chest, and I tucked her head under my chin and closed my eyes, wrapping her in my arms. I'd never seen her this vulnerable. Her guard was totally down, and it made me feel protective over her.

"Come on." I kissed her forehead, and she closed her eyes and leaned into it. "I'll drive."

On the way home she pulled her legs up to her chest and leaned against the door of the car. I held her hand.

We stopped at Del Taco, grabbed food, and ate while we drove. Both of us just wanted to get in bed. I don't think either of us had slept the night before because of our fight, and we were both spent.

When we got to her house, we brushed our teeth together and went right to sleep without talking. She curled up against me, and I held her to me all night.

In the morning, when the sun cracked through her window and I woke up next to her for the first time in weeks, my heart felt full, despite the events of yesterday. I nuzzled into her hair, breathing in the warm fruity scent that was her.

My hands wandered over her body and I pulled her close, kissing the back of her neck, waking her up slowly. I wanted to get lost in her, just for a little while, before the reality of what we had to go back to came into focus.

She stirred. "Josh, no."

"No what?" I breathed, moving against her, my hand sliding between her legs.

She wiggled out of my arms and sat up, her hair falling seductively over her eye. "No. We're not doing that anymore."

I slumped. I'd hoped we had moved past this. "Kristen, I don't care about the hysterectomy. I mean, I care. It's fucked up and I'm sorry it's happening to you, but it doesn't change how I feel about you. We can talk about—"

"*No.* And don't say you don't care, because that's bullshit. I didn't tell you about that so you could say it's fine, or figure out some sort of work-around." She flung the blanket off her and got up. "We're not seeing each other anymore. I let you stay with me last night so you wouldn't be alone. That's it."

She turned for the bathroom, and I got out of bed and followed her.

She stood in front of the sink putting toothpaste on her toothbrush, and I came up behind her and slid my hands over her shoulders. She shrugged me off.

I looked at her through the mirror. "Kristen, we're in love with each other. I want to be with you. Let's sit down and have a convers—"

She whirled on me. "No." Her face was hard. "I listened to you talk about having kids for *months*. We've already had the conversation. Plenty of times. And there is absolutely nothing you can say to me now to convince me that's suddenly not some major priority for you. I can't give you a family. I'm no different from Celeste."

"Celeste didn't *want* kids. It's not the same thing," I said.

She scoffed, waving around her toothbrush. "Isn't it? The outcome is the same. In vitro is only forty percent successful—did you know that? Do you even know what it costs? Or how hard it is to find a surrogate? We could try for *years*, go broke, and never even have *one* baby. Not even *one*."

"Then we can adopt, foster—"

She rolled her eyes and gave me her back as she ran her toothbrush under the faucet and put it in her mouth.

"Kristen, you're being ridiculous."

I put my hands back on her shoulders and she shrank away from me.

She spit in the sink and turned back to me. "Josh, it's not gonna happen, okay?"

My jaw flexed. "Why not? You have no right to make this decision for me. I want to be with you. If I say it doesn't change anything for me, then it doesn't."

She laughed. "It changes *everything*." She blinked at me. "Josh, I meant what I said. I do love you. I love you more than I've ever loved anyone. And I love you too much to let you settle." Her eyes softened slightly. "I know you think this is what you want right now. But in a few years, when you have a pregnant wife and kids running around, you'll see that I was right. I can't give you your baseball team. And I won't take it from you."

I reached for her and she pushed my hand away. "No."

"You are *not* Celeste. You're not even in the same league. And I'm sorry if things I said before I knew about this made you feel badly. I didn't know—"

"I know you didn't know. That's how I know you were being honest."

"I love you," I said, looking her in the eye.

She shook her head. "And what does love have to do with it? Love is completely impractical, Josh. It's stupid. And you should never use it to make decisions." Her eyes were determined and level. She pulled her hair from its ponytail and grabbed a towel. "We need to take showers and go back to the hospital. And I don't want to talk about this. Ever again."

THIRTY-FOUR

KRISTEN

It was twenty-one days after Brandon's accident and almost as long since I'd last spoken to Josh. The date of the wedding came and went, and Brandon hadn't woken up for it.

I spent my time between the hospital and Sloan's house where I watered her plants and brought in packages. I washed whatever laundry she left when she did her momentary stops at home to shower and change before heading back to the ICU. I checked her mail. I'd made all the calls to her wedding vendors to cancel the wedding until further notice.

At the hospital I brought books, magazines, coffee, and food for Sloan so she never had to leave her bedside vigil for anything trivial.

Then I went home to my empty house.

I cleaned for hours on end. I pulled out the contents of every cabinet in my kitchen and washed it all. I wiped out the drawers in the bathroom. I took apart my bed to vacuum underneath, and all the vacuum lines on the carpet had to be in just the right direction. I detailed the grout in my laundry room. I took a toothpick to the cracks in the stove, and I thirsted for relief from my own mind.

My perfectionism was something I harnessed and cultivated for my own purposes. Something useful that made me focused so I could get things done.

But now it was spiraling. None of the rituals made it better. Nothing shut off the urges or satisfied the feelings of incompleteness. Nothing gave me control again.

I missed Josh. I missed him like I missed my sanity.

It had become clear, almost immediately, that the burden of saving him from himself was going to fall on me.

After I'd told him it was over between us, he refused to drop it. So I'd stopped answering his calls. Avoided him at the hospital and refused to speak to him when I did see him. Since I gave Miguel his old job back, my garage was empty and lifeless. The smell of Josh's cologne on the throw pillows on my sofa was so faint it never puffed around me anymore when I sat down.

It was for his own good.

And the beast inside me roared.

Every day it got louder. Nobody could tame it. Josh could calm me, but I wouldn't let him close enough to try.

Nurse Valerie buzzed me into the ICU. I slid the container of cupcakes across the counter of the nurses' station. "Nadia Cakes."

She beamed at me. "You're too good to us, girl." She pulled the cupcakes down in front of her, looking over the assortment.

Sloan had assigned me the job of bringing thank-yous to the nursing staff. Donuts, cookies, flowers. I tried to bring something every couple of days. The nurses had made all the difference in this situation.

Valerie tapped her pen absently on top of the clear container and eyed me. "Can I ask you something?"

I leaned over the counter, sorting her pens by color. "What?"

I liked Valerie. She was my favorite nurse. She was no-nonsense. We'd hit it off immediately.

"What did that boy do to you? 'Cause I can't see any reason on my end why you're not all over that man like white on rice."

Josh. Somehow in the last few weeks, the hospital staff had gotten wind of the Josh situation.

"Valerie, we've talked about this."

She arched an eyebrow. "Have we? 'Cause you came off a little evasive if you ask me."

I shook my head at her. I wasn't getting into it.

She twisted her lips and gave me a knowing grin. "That man drives you crazy."

I snorted. "I don't need him to drive me crazy. I'm close enough at this point to walk."

She leaned back in her chair, chuckling. "Go on, girl. Sloan's been waiting for you."

I turned for Brandon's room. Sloan sat in her usual spot, a leg tucked under her. She looked good today. She must have gotten good news. She was pale and dark circles cradled her eyes, but she was smiling.

I hugged her shoulders and took a seat in the empty chair next to her.

"They're taking him off the ventilator tomorrow." She beamed.

"Really?"

"They took him off the ICP catheter. The swelling in his brain is gone. The doctor says he's really hopeful, that his scans lit up." She smiled down at Brandon, lying there as he had been for the last three weeks. "Kristen, he might be okay. Like, really, really okay."

Her eyes teared up and I hugged her. The beast retreated slightly.

She put a hand on his stomach. "He's going to have months of physical therapy. He might have to relearn things like talking. But he's still in there."

Valerie came in and Sloan grinned up at her.

"Ready for today's sedation vacation?" Valerie asked, fiddling with a drip bag.

Sloan was practically bouncing. "This is what I wanted to show you. Every day they lift the sedation a little to see how his vitals respond. Not too much, or he'll fight the ventilator, but just enough to make him a little aware."

We sat and watched him for a few moments.

"All right, baby girl," Valerie said. "Do your thing."

Sloan smiled and picked up Brandon's hand. "Babe, can you hear me? Squeeze my hand if you can hear me."

I held my breath and watched his fingers.

They squeezed.

Sloan let out a laugh that pushed tears from her eyes. "Did you see? Babe, squeeze twice if you love me."

Two squeezes.

Our laughter was the sound of relief. Hers was that Brandon was still in there.

Mine was that *she* was.

She kissed his hand. "One more day, babe. One more day and then I'm going to get to see you, okay? I love you so much."

When Valerie put him back under, Sloan's elation still lingered on her beautiful face. But she looked so, so tired.

"It's your turn to go home tonight, right?" I asked.

She and Claudia rotated nights in the ICU with the occasional help from Josh or Shawn so they could get sleep in a real bed now and then. Brandon's parents both had bad backs and couldn't sleep in a chair and Sloan refused to leave Brandon alone.

She never left longer than a few hours, but the night in a bed always transformed her. She looked like she hadn't been transformed in a while.

"No, Claudia had to go back to work," she said. "I've done the night shift for the last three days."

"Want me to do a shift?" I asked. Brandon and I were friendly, but we weren't close. For this reason, she'd never taken me up on my offer to stay the night. I guess she worried about awkward silences?

She shook her head. "Josh is staying tonight so I can go home. He should be here any second, actually," she said, looking over her shoulder at the door.

"I should go, then." I got up.

"Kristen." She put a hand on my wrist. "He misses you so much. Are you sure you're doing the right thing?"

"I'm doing the right thing for *him*."

Whether it's right for me isn't relevant.

I hugged her one more time and made my way down the hall. When Valerie buzzed me out, Josh was coming in.

It was the first time I'd seen him in over a week. We both froze.

His presence was a physical caress, like a gust of warm air.

My eyes pored over him. He had his hands in the pockets of his jeans, and he wore the shirt he'd won at trivia night—he wore the shit out of it too.

It was amazing how anything he had on looked sexy on him. The man could wear a burlap sack and look incredible. I knew just looking at it what it would smell like, and I wished I could put my nose to the blue cotton.

He'd lost weight. His muscles were more defined. His dimples didn't show, because he didn't smile.

He looked good—but he looked sad.

He'd get over it soon enough. A few babies from now and he wouldn't even remember me.

He didn't make any move to get out of my path. I looked away and walked past him, and he stood like a statue, eyes on me. Then suddenly a hand shot out and touched my arm. It trailed lightly down my forearm as I walked on, across the top of my hand, over my fingers, and then it was gone.

I didn't jerk away because that would have been acknowledging that he was even there.

But the few seconds of contact moved through my whole body.

I felt it the rest of the day.

THIRTY-FIVE

JOSH

I took off my glasses and pinched the bridge of my nose, setting the book down on the table by Brandon's hospital bed. "Sorry, I gotta take a break. *Shantaram* is long, man."

It would take me a month to read it to him, but it was the book he'd started at the station before the accident, and I knew he'd want to hear it.

It only took me a minute before my thoughts slid back to Kristen. My mind always slid back to Kristen.

At least at work I had distractions. I picked up extra shifts when I could so I wouldn't be at home, staring at the walls of my studio, thinking about her or worrying about Brandon. I went to the gym on my days off after visiting the hospital. I went all day sometimes. I'd unpacked my apartment, bought a couch and a TV. Tried to stay busy.

But inevitably, no matter what I was doing, I was thinking about her.

And now, without the book to read, sitting there with Brandon in the middle of the night, I had nothing to do but think.

I checked my watch: 2:12 a.m. I pictured Kristen, sleeping on her side under her flower bedspread. Her hand tucked under her favorite pillow—the one with the beige flannel pillowcase.

Stuntman Mike curled up on top of the blanket in the tangle of her legs. The clock on her nightstand giving me just enough light to see her long lashes across her smooth cheeks.

I mentally pulled the blanket up to her chin and kissed her forehead and saw her eyes flutter open as she smiled at me.

Fuck, I missed her.

"I wish you could talk to me," I said to Brandon. "Tell me what to do. I need you to wake up and straighten me out. Or even better, wake up and straighten *her* out."

I dragged a hand down my face. When I saw her today, it just confirmed what I already knew. I wasn't ever going to get over her. I wasn't ever going to *not* miss her.

She was punishing me for a crime I didn't even know I'd committed. For things I had said and things I wanted before I knew what they'd mean later. Every comment had been a nail in the board across the door she'd closed on me.

"I don't even know how to begin to convince her," I said. "She won't even speak to me." I snorted. "Leave it to me to be in love with the world's most stubborn woman."

I tried to think about what Brandon's response to this would be. He was always so level-headed. He would know what to do.

The more I tried to sway her, the further she distanced herself. The more I told her I loved her, the more she shut down. And I didn't know how to stop it.

I leaned forward, my elbows on my knees, and I peered around the cold, sterile room. Beige walls. Gray machines around the bed. Some I recognized, some I didn't. The only sounds at the late hour were the faint jingle of a phone ringing in the nurses' station, the ping of an elevator, the faraway sound of the wheels of a cart, and the gentle beep of Brandon's vital signs monitor.

They wouldn't allow any flowers or personal items in the ICU, but Sloan had snuck in an engagement photo. It sat on the table next to the bed. Her and Brandon on the beach, the surf crashing around their feet, her tattooed arm over his shoulder, them looking at each other. Both of them laughing.

I looked back at him and sighed. "You're going to have some gnarly scars, buddy." They'd started the skin grafts for the road rash on his arm. "But you'll get to do everything you planned to do with your life. One of us is going to get the girl. I'll help you any way I can. Even if I have to wheel your ass to the altar."

I could picture his smile. With any luck I'd see it in a few hours.

A knock on the door frame turned me around in my chair.

"Hey, cutie." Valerie came into the room for her vitals check. She turned the lights up, and I stood and stretched.

As if sleeping in a chair wasn't hard enough, the activity every two hours was the final kicker. I wouldn't call anything I did on these overnight shifts sleeping. Maybe napping, but not sleeping. Every two hours Brandon was moved. They checked his airways, changed out bags, looked at his vitals. I don't know how Sloan was handling doing this almost nightly for the last three weeks.

Sloan was a good woman. I'd always liked her, but now she'd earned my respect, and I was grateful Brandon and Kristen had her.

"Did you decide what day you want to bring the kids to the station?" I asked Valerie, yawning.

She cycled the blood pressure cuff on Brandon's arm and smiled. "I'm thinking Tuesday. You on shift Tuesday?"

"Yup."

She wrote down some notes on Brandon's chart and then gave me a raised eyebrow. "Any updates with your lady friend?"

I laughed a little. "No."

The whole nursing staff knew about my depressing love life. I'd gotten hit on a few too many times by some of the younger nurses. I couldn't claim to have a girlfriend, and I wasn't married, so it was either "I'm gay" or "I'm in love with that girl over there."

I'd gone with the latter, and now I wished I'd said I was gay.

They didn't know why Kristen wouldn't date me, just that she wouldn't. It had turned into the favorite topic of the ICU. A real-life episode of *Grey's Anatomy*. I rarely got through a Brandon visit without it coming up.

The drama escalated when Kristen had been hit on by the nurses' favorite single orthopedic surgeon. According to the nurses' gossip circuit, Kristen told him to go fuck himself.

And apparently she'd actually said, "Go fuck yourself."

After that everyone was sure she was holding out for me.

Only I knew better.

Valerie checked Brandon's temperature. "You know, I told that girl myself she's nuts. You know what she said to me?"

I arched an eyebrow. "What?"

"She said, 'Just because a man gives you the best sex of your life doesn't mean you need to date his ass.' Lawd, I just about died," she snickered.

I snorted. Yup, that sounded like Kristen.

Well, at least I'd done *something* right.

Valerie chuckled to herself while she checked Brandon's pulse. "He's coming out tomorrow. I bet you're all getting pretty excited."

I rubbed the back of my neck. "This has been a really tough few weeks."

"He's gonna do great."

She changed out the bag on his IV drip. Then she pulled out a small light from her breast pocket, clicked it on, and opened his right eye. "You know, a lot of the nurses are gonna miss the steady stream of cute firemen coming through he—"

She paused.

She opened his other eye and shone the light into his pupil. She cleared her throat as she clicked the light off and slipped it back in her pocket. "We sure are going to miss you guys." She picked up his chart.

She didn't look at me. Her tone changed. Her body changed. I'd done that change myself on the scene of a call.

Something is wrong.

"What is it?"

She didn't answer me.

I pulled out my cell phone and turned on the flashlight. I leaned over Brandon and opened his eye while Valerie watched me wordlessly.

My breath caught in my throat. "No. *No!*"

I looked at the other eye, and my hands started to shake. I stumbled back from the bed and knocked into my chair, dropping my cell phone to the floor with a clatter.

Valerie looked at me, and we exchanged a moment of understanding.

His pupils were blown.

They were large black marbles in his eyes.

THIRTY-SIX

KRISTEN

When the phone rang, I groped for it on the nightstand. It was the hospital. And it was also 3:57 in the morning. I brushed the hair off my forehead and sat up. "Hello?"

"Kristen."

It was Josh. But it wasn't. It wasn't any Josh I'd ever heard.

"Kristen, you need to go get Sloan. Brandon's had a stroke."

I threw off my covers. "What? A stroke? What does that mean?"

I tumbled out of bed and stumbled around the room, grabbing my bra and jumping into leggings.

He paused. "He's brain-dead. He's not coming back from this. It's over. Get Sloan."

The line went dead.

I stood in the middle of my dark room. The phone stayed lit for a moment. When the screen went back to black, I was doused in pitch.

The velociraptor roared, and the ground shook as it lunged forward.

As I drove to Sloan's, I had the surreal, almost out-of-body realization that I was about to tell my best friend the worst news of her life. That the moment she answered that door, I was going to break her heart and she would never be the same.

My altered state allowed me to process this in a compartmentalized way. I knew that I wouldn't feel the painful moment when it happened, but that I'd put it into a little box and take it out and look at it often for the rest of my life.

~

I watched Sloan die inside that night.

They called it a catastrophic stroke. A blood clot moved from the wounds in his leg up to his brain. It had probably happened while Josh sat with him. It was silent and final, and there was nothing anyone could have done.

Josh was right. Brandon was gone.

Three days after the stroke, an ethics committee made up of Brandon's doctors, an organization that coordinated organ donations, and a grief counselor called the family in for an 11:00 a.m. meeting at the hospital. I sat outside the conference room, bouncing my knee, waiting for Sloan to come out.

I hadn't left her side once since the stroke. Every night I slept in the chair next to her by Brandon's bedside. Only now he wasn't healing in his coma.

He was brain-dead.

Josh hadn't been back to the hospital since Brandon's diagnosis. He wouldn't answer my calls.

The shift was strange. Our text thread went from dozens of unanswered texts from him, begging me to talk to him, to dozens of unanswered texts from me, begging him to talk to me. I wanted to know he was okay.

His silence told me he wasn't.

I wore his sweatshirt today. I'd never wear it when I knew he might see it. I didn't want to encourage him. But based on his absence over the last three days, I didn't think I had to worry. And I needed to feel him wrapped around my body today. I needed to smell him in the fabric.

I just needed *him*.

This meeting wasn't going to be easy on Sloan. It was about the next steps.

The door to the conference room opened up, and Brandon's mom came out, speaking to his dad in tearful Spanish.

Sloan walked out of the meeting behind them, and I led her immediately into an empty waiting room.

Sloan was a zombie. She'd died three days ago when Brandon did. The light was gone from her eyes. Her legs walked, her eyelids blinked, but she was vacant.

"What did they say?" I asked, sitting her down on one of the cushioned chairs next to me.

She spoke wearily, her eyes rimmed a permanent shade of red. "They say we need to take him off of life support. That his body is deteriorating."

The wail of Brandon's mom came down the hallway. It had become a sound we knew all too well. She broke down at random. Everyone did. Well, everyone except for me. I was void of emotion while my predator and I shared space. Instead of feeling pain at Sloan's suffering, I spiraled further into my OCD. I slept less. I moved more. I dove deeper into my rituals.

And nothing helped.

Sloan didn't react to the sound of grief down the hall. "His brain isn't making hormones anymore or controlling any of his bodily functions. The medications he's on to maintain his blood pressure and body temperature are damaging his organs. They said if we want to donate them, we have to do it soon."

"Okay," I said, pulling tissues from a box and shoving them into her hands. "When are they doing it?"

She spoke to the room, to someplace behind me. She didn't look at me. "They're not."

I stared at her. "What do you mean they're not?"

She blinked, her eyelids closing mechanically. "His parents don't want to take him off life support. They're praying for a miracle. They're really religious. They think he rebounded once and he'll rebound again."

Her eyes focused on me, tears welled, threatening to fall. "It's going to all be for nothing, Kristen. He's an organ donor. He'd want that. He's going to rot in that room and he's going to die for nothing and I have no say in any of it."

The tears spilled down her face, but she didn't sob. They just streamed, like water from a leaky hose.

I gaped at her. "But... but *why*? Didn't he have a will? What the fuck?"

She shook her head. "We talked about it, but the wedding was so close we just decided to wait. I have no say. At all."

The reality suddenly rolled out before me. It wouldn't just be this. It would be everything. His life insurance policy, his benefits, his portion of the house, his belongings—not hers. She would get nothing.

Not even a vote.

She went on in her daze. "I don't know how to convince them. The insurance won't cover his stay much longer, so they'll be forced to make a decision at some point. But it will cover it long enough for his organs to fail."

My brain grasped at a solution. "Claudia. She might be able to convince them."

She hadn't been able to make the meeting. And she would side with Sloan—I knew she would. She had influence on her parents.

"Maybe Josh too," I continued. "They like him. They might listen to him." I stood.

She looked up at me, a tear dripping off her chin and landing on her thigh. "Where are you going?"

"To find Josh."

I went to the station first, but Josh wasn't there. I found him at home.

He opened the door after letting me pound on it for almost five minutes. His truck was in the carport. I knew he was here.

He pulled the door open and walked back inside without looking at me or saying a word. I followed him in, and he dropped onto a sofa I'd never seen before.

His face was scruffy. I'd never seen him anything but clean-shaven. Not even in pictures. He had bags under his eyes. He'd aged ten years in three days.

The apartment was a mess. The boxes were gone. It looked like he had finally unpacked. But laundry was piled up in a basket so full it spilled out onto the floor. Empty food containers littered the kitchen countertops. The coffee table was full of empty beer bottles. His bed was unmade. The place smelled stagnant and dank.

A vicious urge to take care of him took hold. The velociraptor tapped its talon on the floor. Josh wasn't okay.

Nobody was okay.

And that was what made *me* not okay.

"Hey," I said, standing in front of him.

He didn't look at me. "Oh, so you're talking to me now," he said bitterly, taking a long pull on a beer. "Great. What do you want?"

The coldness of his tone took me aback, but I kept my face still. "You haven't been to the hospital."

His bloodshot eyes dragged up to mine. "Why would I? He's not there. He's fucking gone."

I stared at him.

He shook his head and looked away from me. "So what do you want? You wanted to see if I'm okay? I'm not fucking okay. My best friend is brain-dead. The woman I love won't even fucking speak to me."

He picked up a beer cap from the coffee table and threw it hard across the room. My OCD winced.

"I'm doing this for you," I whispered.

"Well, *don't*," he snapped. "None of this is for me. Not any of it. I need you, and you abandoned me. Just go. Get out."

I wanted to climb into his lap. Tell him how much I missed him and that I wouldn't leave him again. I wanted to make love to him and never be away from him ever again in my life—and clean his fucking apartment.

But instead, I just stood there. "No. I'm not leaving. We need to talk about what's happening at the hospital."

He glared up at me. "There's only one thing I want to talk about. I want to talk about how you and I can be in love with each other and you won't be with me. Or how you can stand not seeing me or speaking to me for weeks. That's what I want to talk about, Kristen."

My chin quivered. I turned and went to the kitchen and grabbed a trash bag from under the sink. I started tossing take-out containers and beer bottles.

I spoke over my shoulder. "Get up. Go take a shower. Shave. Or don't if that's the look you're going for. But I need you to get your shit together."

My hands were shaking. I wasn't feeling well. I'd been light-headed and slightly overheated since I went to Josh's fire station looking for him. But I focused on my task, shoving trash into my bag. "If Brandon is going to be able to donate his organs, he needs to come off life support within the next few days. His parents won't do it, and Sloan doesn't get a say. You need to go talk to them."

Hands came up under my elbows, and his touch radiated through me.

"Kristen, stop."

I spun on him. "Fuck you, Josh! You need help, and I need to help you!"

And then as fast as the anger surged, the sorrow took over. The chains on my mood swing snapped, and feelings broke through my walls like water breaching a crevice in a dam. I began to cry. I didn't know what was wrong with me. The strength that drove me through my days just wasn't available to me when it came to Josh.

I dropped the trash bag at his feet and put my hands over my face and sobbed. He wrapped his arms around me, and I completely lost it.

"I can't stop cleaning and I have a monster inside my brain and I miss you and Sloan is falling apart and his parents won't take him off life support, so his organs are rotting. I can't get all the lines right on the carpet with the vacuum and Stuntman is

I blitzed the place. I stripped the bed, threw open the windows. I was washing dishes when the dizziness started.

Why are my lips tingling?

I pressed a shaking finger to my mouth.

And then my vision began to blur…

THIRTY-SEVEN

JOSH

I dragged a razor down my cheek for the first time in days and studied my face in the bathroom mirror. I looked the way I felt.

Lost.

It was good to see her. She filled me up. Even when she was giving me shit and bossing me around, it was like taking a deep breath just being near her. She charged my batteries, dragged me back to myself.

She looked beautiful—but she didn't look good. Pale. Thin. She'd lost weight—a lot of it. She wasn't taking care of herself.

I couldn't do shit for myself at the moment, but I could do anything for her. I would take care of her if she let me. But this was the first time she'd even spoken to me in weeks.

I hadn't given up. I could never give up on her. But I'd gotten tired. She was so stubborn, so implacable, and my heart was worn. Without Kristen and Brandon, I couldn't move anymore. I wanted to talk to him about her and talk to her about him. And both of them were gone.

The enormity of it was too big to wrap my brain around.

I was never going to see him again. Never sit with him in a

duck blind and bullshit. Never talk to him again about Kristen, or Sloan, or anything.

I wasn't going to be his best man. He'd never be mine. Our kids wouldn't play together.

Eleven years. We'd been friends for eleven years. And he was just gone. His life was over. He'd gotten all he was going to get. And I didn't know how to move on from that.

So I didn't move at all.

I half expected her to be gone by the time I came out of the shower. She ran. That's what she did with me. The half of me that expected her to still be here would have put money on her cleaning the place. But when I came out, she was on the couch. I knew immediately something was wrong.

I flew to her side. "Kristen, what is it?"

She panted. "I can't see. My . . . my eyes are blurry."

She was covered in sweat. Shaking, breathing hard. I pulled back her eyelid and she swatted at me.

Combative.

Hypoglycemic.

I ran to the kitchen, praying that she hadn't tossed all the trash. I spotted an old In-N-Out cup with Coke in it from yesterday and grabbed it, running back to the couch.

"Kristen, I need you to drink this. You're not going to like it, but I need you to do it."

It was flat, old, and room temp, but it was all I had in the apartment. I put the straw to her lips.

She shook her head violently and clenched her teeth. "No."

"Listen, your glucose levels are low. You need sugar. Drink this. You'll feel better. Come on."

She tried to knock the cup from my hands, and I protected it like it was the cure for cancer.

If she didn't get her blood sugar up, she could have a seizure next. Slip into unconsciousness. And her symptoms were already advanced.

Panic overcame me. My heart pounded in my ears. *What's wrong with her?*

"A few swallows, please," I begged.

She took the straw in her lips and drank, and my relief was palpable.

It took a few minutes and a few more sips, but she stopped shaking. I got a wet washcloth and wiped her face as she came back around. I peeled her sweatshirt off her—*my* sweatshirt.

"When's the last time you ate?" I asked.

She was still a little disoriented. When she looked at me, her eyes didn't really focus. "I don't know. I didn't."

I checked my watch. Jesus, it was almost 2:00 p.m.

"Come on—I'm taking you to get some food." I helped her up, putting an arm around her waist. She was so frail. The sides of her stomach were hard.

Something is wrong.

I helped her to my truck and went to the closest fast-food place I could find. It wasn't what she probably wanted. She fucking hated Burger King, but I needed to get food in her.

We went through the drive-thru and parked in the parking lot. I unwrapped her burger and watched her eat. She looked exhausted. Her skin was sallow.

"Are you diabetic?" I asked, studying her.

"No." She sniffed.

"Are you sure?"

She ate a french fry slowly. "Yes."

"Does diabetes run in your family? Do any of your relatives have it?"

"I know what 'runs in the family' means," she snapped. She shot me a glare and I smiled, happy she had moved from hypoglycemic to just plain hangry.

"And no, nobody has it. And neither do I."

I put the straw in the top of her orange juice and handed it to her. "How do you know?"

"Because I don't have time to be diabetic, Joshua."

I scoffed. *Of course.*

"Look, you need to go to the doctor and have a glucose test. Has this ever happened before?"

She shook her head.

I glanced down at her stomach. The tank top she'd worn under my sweatshirt was fitted. From what I could tell, her stomach hadn't gotten bigger than it was a few weeks ago. In fact, it looked a little smaller. I wondered if that meant the fibroids were shrinking. Could they respond to weight loss like the rest of her? It didn't seem likely.

I wanted to feel her abdomen, see if I could use my medical training to figure out what was wrong. But she never let me touch her stomach.

"When is your surgery scheduled?" I asked.

She took a sip from the soda. "Two weeks ago."

"When are you going to reschedule it?"

She shrugged. "I don't know. Not anytime soon. It's a six- to eight-week recovery. I have nobody to take care of me—"

"I'll take care of you."

She pressed her lips into a line. "I need to be with Sloan."

I sat back in the seat, shutting my eyes. I needed her to fucking take care of herself.

Did what she had going on have to do with her condition? But insulin came from the pancreas. What did uterine tumors have to do with a pancreas? I wondered if whatever caused this had been lurking for some time. If she never let herself get hungry, she'd never get hypoglycemic. She was always really good about eating. She might not have ever let it get to this point before.

"I'm okay," she said.

I opened my eyes. "No, you're *not*. You look sick. You're pale. Your pulse is weak. You almost passed out back there. You could have had a seizure. What if you had been driving?"

Protectiveness coursed through me. She was *mine*. I needed to be able to take care of her, and she wouldn't let me fucking do it. It defied all the laws of nature. It was wrong. We were in love, and I was supposed to be there for her.

She looked down at her burger. "Josh, I'm just a little run-down, okay? I'm sleeping with Sloan in the hospital every night. I'm living off of black coffee and whatever I can shove in my mouth. My OCD is manic—"

"You have OCD?" It didn't really surprise me. I'd seen a touch of it in her since I'd known her. One of my sisters had it. I knew it when I saw it.

"Usually it's not this bad, but it gets worse when I'm under stress." She finished the burger and balled up the paper like it was an effort to even do that. Then she lay back against the headrest and closed her eyes.

She was falling apart. She was deteriorating physically and mentally trying to keep Sloan together. And where the fuck was I in all this?

Failing her.

She wouldn't ask for my help. I knew her well enough to know this, and I hadn't even been to the hospital in three days to check in on her. I'd left her on her own with Sloan and Brandon's family and all the rest of it.

I should have been there. Maybe I could have gotten ahead of this life-support thing. Taken a spot on the overnight shift to be with Sloan so Kristen could get some sleep. Made sure she ate. Talking to me or not, Kristen never turned down food.

I blamed myself for this. But I blamed her too. Because if she had let me, I would have taken care of her. We could have taken care of each other, and neither of us would be in such bad shape.

I reached over and threaded my fingers through hers. She didn't pull away. She looked too tired to fight me. She squeezed my hand, and the warmth of her touch coursed through me.

"I'll go to the hospital," I said. "I'll talk to his parents, and I'll stay with Sloan today. I need you to go home and sleep. And tomorrow I want you to go to the doctor. Call to make the appointment tonight because you might have to fast before they do bloodwork."

She just looked at me, her beautiful face hollow and weary. She was always so strong. It was scary seeing her declining like this.

Love did this to her. Her love of Sloan.

And probably her love of me too.

I knew it wasn't easy on her. I knew she thought she was doing the right thing. But fuck, if she would just *stop*. If she would stop, we could both be okay.

She looked at me tiredly. "I bet you wish you would have kicked the tires before falling for this hot mess." She smiled weakly. "Aren't you glad I saved you from yourself?"

I shook my head. "No, that's not how that works, Kristen. Love is for better or worse. It's always and no matter what. The no-matter-what just happened first for us."

Her eyes teared up and she pressed her lips together. "I miss you."

My throat got tight. "Then *be* with me, Kristen. Right now. We can move in together, today. Sleep in the same bed. Just say okay. That's all you have to say. Just say okay."

I wanted it so badly my heart felt like it was screaming. I wanted to shake her, kidnap her and hold her hostage until she stopped this crap.

But she shook her head. "No."

I let go of her hand and leaned away from her against the door, my fingers to the bridge of my nose. "You're killing both of us."

"One day—"

"Stop talking to me about one day." I turned to her. "I'm never going to feel differently about this."

She waited a beat. "Neither am I."

We sat in silence for a moment, and I closed my eyes. I felt her move across the seat, and then her body was pressed against my side. I wrapped an arm around her and let her tuck her head under my chin.

The feel of her was therapeutic. I think it was for both of us. A warm compress for my soul.

I'd never had all of her at once. I'd only ever gotten pieces. Her friendship without her body. Her body without her love. And now her love without any of the rest of it.

But even with what little fragments I'd had, it was enough to tell me I would never stop chasing all of her. Never. Not if I lived to be a hundred. She was it. She just was.

"Kristen, you're the woman I'm supposed to spend the rest of my life with," I whispered. "I know it in my fucking soul."

She sniffed. "I know it too, Josh. But that was before."

"Before what?" I wrapped my arms around her tighter, tears pricking my eyes.

"Before I broke inside. Before my body made me wrong for you. Sometimes soul mates don't end up together, Josh. They marry other people. They never meet. Or one of them dies."

I squeezed my eyes shut and felt the lump in my throat get bigger. Just to have her admit it, to have her acknowledge that's what we were to each other, was the most validating thing she'd ever given me.

"Kristen, I know what I said, that I don't want to adopt, that I want my own kids and I want a big family. But you make everything different."

She was quiet for a long time before she answered me. "Josh, if you knew that being with me would take away the one thing I've always wanted, would you do it?"

I understood her reasoning. I did. But it didn't make it easier.

"What if it were me who couldn't have kids?" I asked. "Would you leave *me*?"

She sighed. "Josh, it's different."

"How? How is it different?"

"Because you're worth it. You're worth any flaw you might have. I'm not."

I moved her away from me so I could look her in the eye. "You don't think you're worth it? Are you kidding me?"

Her exhausted eyes just stared back at me, empty. "I'm not worth it. I'm a mess. I'm irritable and impatient. I'm bossy and demanding. And I have all these health issues. I can't give you babies. I'm not worth it, Josh. I'm not. Another woman would be so much easier."

"I don't want an easy woman. I want *you*." I shook my head. "Don't you get it? You are perfect to me. I feel like a better man just knowing that I can do anything for you—make you lunch, make you laugh, take you dancing. These things feel like a privilege to me. All those things that you think are flaws are what I love about you. Look at me." I tipped her chin up. "I'm miserable. I'm so fucking miserable without you."

She started to cry again, and I pulled her back in and held her.

This was the longest talk we'd had about this. I don't know if she was just too tired and sick to shut me down, or if she just didn't have anywhere to run to, stuck in my truck like she was, but it made me feel hopeful that she was at least talking to me about it.

I nuzzled into her hair, breathed her in. "I don't want any of it without you."

She shook her head against my chest. "I wish I could love you less. Maybe if I did, I could stomach taking this dream from you. But I don't know how to even begin letting someone give up something like that for me. I would feel like apologizing every day of my life."

I took a deep breath. "You have no idea how much I wish I could go back and never put that shit in your head."

Her fingers opened and closed on my chest. I felt happy. Just sitting there in my truck in a Burger King parking lot, I felt more peace than I'd felt in weeks just because she was there with me, touching me, talking to me, telling me she loved me. And then that joy drained away when I remembered that this wasn't going to last. She was going to leave again, and Brandon was still gone. But it was this temporary reprieve that told me that with her by my side, I could get through anything. I could navigate the worst days of my life as long as she stayed by me.

If only she'd let me get her through the worst days of hers.

She spoke against my chest. "You know you're the only man I've ever cried over?"

I laughed a little. "I saw you cry over Tyler. More than once."

She shook her head. "No. That was always about you. Because I was so in love with you and I knew I couldn't be with you. You turned me into some sort of crazy person."

She lifted her head and looked at me. "I'm so proud to know you, Josh. And I feel so lucky to have been loved by someone like you."

She was crying, and I couldn't keep my own eyes dry anymore. I just couldn't. And I didn't care if she saw me cry. I'd lost the two people I needed most in this life, and I'd never be ashamed for grieving over either one of them. I let the tears well, and she leaned in and kissed me. The gasp when she touched me and the tightness of her lips told me she was trying not to break down. She held my cheeks in her hands, and we kissed and held each other like we were saying goodbye—lovers about to be separated by an ocean or a war, desperate, and too grieved to let go.

But she didn't have to let me go.

And she would anyway.

She broke away from me, her chin shaking. "You deserve to give all that you are to your children one day. To have a little boy who looks like you who you can raise to be the same kind of man you are. You have to move on, okay? You have to."

We were back at the stalemate. I held her forehead to mine by the back of her neck, and I was desperate to know what to say to change her mind. But there was nothing I could do. She was so deep in this mind-set. And how could I even chip away at her when most days she wouldn't let me anywhere near her?

"Kristen, I'm never going to give you up. I'm just not. And you're hurting me. Please stop hurting me. I need you with me. Do you understand?"

And then I lost her again.

Her face took on that stony look that I knew so well. She

moved away from me, back to the passenger seat, the wall crashing back down, heavy and final.

I leaned forward and put my face in my hands.

I waited a few heartbeats before speaking again. "Can you at least start getting some sleep? If I go to the hospital, will you stay at my place and go to bed?" I looked back at her.

She nodded. "Josh?"

"What?"

"It's quiet," she said.

"What is?" I asked gently.

"My mind. It's finally quiet. It's only quiet when I'm with you."

It took a long, emotional discussion with Claudia and her parents, but they agreed to take Brandon off life support tomorrow.

After our meeting at their house, his parents hugged me goodbye, and Claudia followed me out to the driveway. The sun was setting. The freeway hummed nearby. I dragged open the heavy white wrought-iron gate that enclosed their tiny East Los Angeles property.

Claudia had volunteered to stay the night with Sloan in the hospital so I could go home. I just wanted to get back to Kristen. I wanted to slip into bed with her, feel the relief of the sleep that I only found with her next to me.

"Thank you," Claudia said as I turned back from the gate.

She was Brandon's carbon copy. They had the same expressions, the same eyes.

I'd never see my friend's expressions again. The thought hit me like a fist to the gut.

Claudia pulled her sweater around herself. "I don't think they would have done it if you hadn't come. It meant something to them that you said this was what he'd want."

She hugged me and when she pulled away, she wiped at her eyes. "It's hard to argue against faith. You can't see it, you know?"

"You should try arguing against logic," I said, clearing the lump in my throat.

She sniffed. "I'd argue against logic any day. Logic can be reasoned with as long as you have the facts. Good night, Josh."

On the drive home, I caught rush-hour traffic. I sat there thinking about the meeting with Brandon's parents. Horns honked. Red brake lights flashed.

I thought about Kristen, about how no matter how much I told her I wanted her, she didn't waver. I wanted her to believe in my love for her, to put all her faith in something intangible, the way Brandon's parents had believed in their prayers being answered. But Kristen wasn't like that. For her, feelings weren't grounds for decision making. She looked at this situation like she was a cool car that I couldn't afford. Something I wanted because of the way it made me feel, not because I'd considered the price tag and made an educated decision to buy it. She was pros and cons, facts and numbers, black and white. Common sense. She was practical, and there was nothing logical about being with me.

Or was there?

Logic can be reasoned with as long as you have the facts...

I stopped breathing.

Holy shit.

Holy fucking shit!

I'd been making the wrong argument!

Suddenly I knew how to get through to her. I knew what I had to do.

It would take some time to pull it all together—a few weeks maybe. But I *knew.*

I smiled the rest of the way home, until I got there and saw her car was gone.

Inside, my laundry was washed and folded. The apartment was spotless and aired out. And the hoodie I'd given her all those weeks ago was folded neatly on the bed.

THIRTY-EIGHT

KRISTEN

I parked in Sloan's driveway and used the key under the flowerpot to let myself in, like I did every day since the funeral two weeks ago. I kept saying I had to get a key made, but I never had the time. Between trying to run Doglet Nation while taking care of what was left of my best friend, my days were full.

I had begun to consider moving back in with Sloan. I didn't see her ever not needing me here. Her mom tapped in sometimes. She did what she could. But she had a sixty-hour-a-week job, and Sloan's dad lived two hours away. I was the last line of defense.

The house smelled like decaying flowers. I set Stuntman down and brought groceries to the kitchen and unbagged it all. Then I started tossing bouquets. She'd be able to start her own flower shop with all the empty vases.

Sloan's bedroom door was closed. I let her sleep. Getting her out of bed before noon was twice the struggle—I'd given it up. I used the earlier hours to do chores.

This was my life now. The second half of both our lives had begun. The before was over, and now we lived in the after. I came over every morning as soon as I woke up. Stayed until midnight. And I lived side by side with my velociraptor. We co-existed, taking care of Sloan.

I didn't try to clean up anything that was Brandon's. I didn't touch his dirty clothes. I didn't toss the beer bottle that sat in the garage. The only spark of life I'd seen from her since the funeral was when she'd lost her fucking mind on me because I'd removed and washed the almost two-month-old glass of water from Brandon's side of the bed.

At noon, I knocked on her bedroom door. When I didn't get an answer, I let myself in. She lay bundled in her blue comforter. I opened the blinds and then the window, hoping the fresh air would do her some good. I drew her a bath and sat on the edge of the bed to get her up.

"Sloan? Come on. Up. Let's go."

She groaned.

I peeled the blankets back, uncovering her. I took in her fetal position, her colorful tattooed arm tucked against her body.

I'd take her out today. Make her go to the park or for a short walk. Maybe I could get her to sit outside on the front porch. *Something.*

"Sloan. Get up." I wedged myself under her arm and hoisted her into a sitting position. With some effort I got her into the bathtub.

While she soaked, I stripped the bed and put it all in the washing machine. I washed her sheets daily, compliments of my OCD. If she was going to be in her bed for twelve hours a day, at least the sheets could be fresh. My endeavor was to keep her and everything around her clean and comforting.

As I put detergent in the machine, my cell phone pinged. I didn't even have to look to know who it was. Josh texted me every day. I looked at the message.

Josh: Just say okay.

I swallowed the lump in my throat and tucked my phone back into my pocket.

He kept a running correspondence with me. It was totally one-sided. Sometimes he said he loved me and missed me. He sent me emails that read like letters, with where he was or what he was doing, like he didn't want me to forget him—as if I could. And every day, one message was always the same.

Just say okay.

Last week he'd gone home to South Dakota for a few days, and I wondered if he was planning to move back. He had no reason to stay now. He hated his job, Brandon was gone, and I never responded to him. I hadn't seen him or spoken to him since the funeral.

I washed Sloan's hair while she hugged her knees to her chest. Then I got her out of the tub, towel dried her hair and brushed it into a braid on the sofa.

We'd watch a movie later. I'd choose it carefully like I did every day. Couldn't be a love story. Nothing sad.

I put the sheets in the dryer. Then I went to make lunch, badly, and when I came back out, she was on the sofa watching the music video. The fucking music video. *Again.*

It was the only thing that seemed to interest her. A viral video of "The Wreck of the *Edmund Fitzgerald*." A cover. She was obsessed with it.

I guess I should be happy that *something* interested her.

I set the food down on the coffee table. "Hey, are you sure you don't want to help me with lunch next time? You're a lot better at it than I am. I didn't know how much vodka to put in the rice."

She smiled a little, but it was mechanical. I went back in for the drinks. When I came out, she was watching the video again.

"How many times have you seen that?" I asked, sitting down next to her.

She shrugged tiredly. "I like it." Her voice was raspy.

I leaned in and watched the video with her. A Claymation thing of a shipwreck. A big freighter in a storm being tossed in the waves until it went down.

I watched it through to the end. Then she replayed it.

"Why do you like this so much?" I shook my head.

She stared at the screen for a moment. "Because I feel like those men. Like a storm came and sank something strong, and now I'm lost at sea. Drowning."

I didn't reply.

"I like his voice," she added.

"Why don't we buy some of his music?" *Hopefully it's not all fucking depressing.* "Let's see if he's got an album," I said, taking her phone. I was starting to scroll through Amazon Music when a message pinged and a text popped up on her screen.

Josh: 👍

"Uh... Josh just texted you." I looked up at her. I didn't know they talked. "He gave you a thumbs-up?"

She looked at me listlessly. "Kristen, why haven't you talked to him?"

The question surprised me. My best friend hadn't been my best friend in a long time. We didn't talk about me or what I was going through.

We didn't really talk about anything.

I went back to scrolling through the artist's album on her phone so I wouldn't have to look at her. "What's there to say?"

She laughed. It actually startled me it was so sudden, and I stared at her in surprise.

"Go home, Kristen."

I blinked at her. "What?"

She took her phone from my hands. "Go home. Talk to him. Be with him. Be happy."

I furrowed my brow. "Nothing has changed, Sloan."

She stared at me with red-rimmed eyes. "You don't think you're worth it."

I shifted uncomfortably. "What are you talking about?"

"Your mom. All your life she made you feel like you were never good enough. And so you don't think you're good enough for Josh either. But you are."

I shook my head. "No. That's not it, Sloan."

"Yeah. It is."

"Sloan, he doesn't know what's best for him. He's just thinking about right now."

"No. *You're* the one who doesn't know what's best for *you*. She ruined you. She spent your whole childhood setting a bar she knew you'd never reach, and now you think you have to be perfect to be good enough for anyone."

We stared at each other. Then Sloan's chest started to rise and fall in the rapid way that told me a breakdown was coming. I instinctively pulled tissues from a box on the end table just as her eyes started to tear up.

"Kristen? Brandon's accident is my fault."

I was used to this. She lost focus a lot. This time I was glad for the change of subject. "No, Sloan, it wasn't." I took the plate from her lap and put it on the coffee table and gathered up her hands. "None of this was your fault."

She bit her lip, the tears falling down her cheeks. "It is. I should have never let him ride that bike. I should have insisted."

I shook my head, scooting closer to her. "No. He was a grown man, Sloan. He was a paramedic. He went on those accident calls—he knew the risks. Don't you dare put this on yourself."

Her chin quivered. "How can I not? Shouldn't I have protected him from himself? I loved him. It was my job."

"No, it *wasn't*. People make their own decisions, Sloan. He lived the life he wanted to live. He was a twenty-nine-year-old man. He was capable of making choices."

She wiped her cheeks with the back of her hand. "So you can decide for Josh, but I shouldn't have decided for Brandon?"

I saw the trap, but it was too late.

She shook her head, blinking through tears. "You have no clue, do you? You think he's settling? For Josh, not being with you is settling. Don't you get that?"

"Sloan," I said gently. "You don't und—"

"Don't I?" she snapped. "Do you think if Brandon wouldn't have been able to have kids after his accident that I would have been settling to stay with him? I would have taken him any way I could have him. Disabled. In a wheelchair, without his fucking arms and legs. This thing that you're obsessed with doesn't *matter*. He loves you. He wants *you*." She breathed hard. "Don't be like me. Don't live the rest of your life without the man you love. Go home, Kristen."

"Sloan—"

"Go *home*! Get *out* of my house!"

Her shout shocked me into action and I stood.

"Go home." Her eyes went hard. "And don't you *ever* come over here without Josh again."

She picked up Stuntman and shoved him into my arms. Then she corralled me out of the house onto the front porch. She took the house key from the planter and slammed the door in my face.

The shock had me standing there staring at her door for a full minute.

She kicked me out.

She went off on me, and the crazy bitch kicked me out.

I hovered a hand over the door and knocked. "Sloan, open up."

The chain raked across the door and the bolt locked.

"Sloan! Come on!" I pressed the doorbell in quick succession.

Nothing.

Un-fucking-*believable*.

Well this was just *perfect*. Who was going to make her bed? She couldn't even wash the dishes. The ones from lunch would probably just get moldy in the living room. And what about dinner? She would starve to death without me. She was being completely unreasonable.

Stuntman looked up at me like he didn't know what just happened. Neither did I.

I walked out to the car and dropped into the driver's seat, crossing my arms.

Maybe the back door is unlocked.

Sloan and I had never had a fight before.

I let out a long breath. I got it. I understood her feelings—I *did*. My best friend was living her nightmare. She was in her own personal hell, and the man I loved was alive and here, and I wouldn't have him. Of course I could see how that hurt her, how trivial my reasons looked in the face of what she was enduring. It made me feel like shit that she thought I was being petty.

But it didn't change a thing.

Josh wanted to make a blind, emotional, knee-jerk decision that would alter the rest of his life, and I couldn't be a part of that. I just *couldn't*. Sloan could be pissed at me all she wanted. I was doing the right thing, and sometimes doing the right thing was unpopular, but that didn't make it *wrong*. Sometimes you had to be cruel to be kind, and I wasn't going to be bullied into changing my mind.

I drove home, Sloan's words pinging painfully around my mind like a ricocheting bullet. They didn't change anything. But they hurt.

When I got home, I dropped my car keys onto the table in the kitchen and looked around my immaculate house, feeling lost.

What did I do now? I'd always had Sloan. What if she was really serious about this and she wouldn't see me anymore?

I realized suddenly that I needed her almost as much as she needed me. Taking care of her helped me to stick to my guns with Josh, because even though she was a mess, a mess was something to clean up. And now, without the distraction, the emptiness was overwhelming.

I sat down at the kitchen table and pulled a stack of napkins in front of me and started to straighten them, lining up the corners and chewing on my lip, thinking about my next move.

Okay, maybe what she said about Mom *was* true. God knows I could spend the rest of my life in therapy working through the shit the Ice Queen put me through. Maybe Mom *did* fuck me up and I had some self-worth issues. But the cold, hard truth was that I came with too much baggage, and I *wasn't* worth the sacrifice Josh would have to make to be with me. I could never give as much as I would take from him. That wasn't lack of self-esteem. That was just a simple fact.

Maybe Sloan would agree to a deal. I'd talk to someone about some of my issues if she would agree to go to grief counseling. It wasn't me giving in to Josh like she wanted, but Sloan knew how much I hated therapists, and she'd always wanted me to see someone. I was debating how to pitch this to her when I glanced into the living room and saw it—a single purple carnation on my coffee table.

I looked around the kitchen like I might suddenly find someone in my house. But Stuntman was calm, plopped under my chair. I went in to investigate and saw that the flower sat on top of a binder with the words "just say okay" written on the outside in Josh's writing.

He'd been here?

My heart began to pound. I looked again around the living room like I might see him, but it was just the binder.

I sat on the sofa, my hands on my knees, staring at the binder for what felt like ages before I drew the courage to pull the book into my lap. I tucked my hair behind my ear and licked my lips, took a breath, and opened it up.

The front page read "SoCal Fertility Specialists."

My breath stilled in my lungs. *What?*

He'd had a consultation with Dr. Mason Montgomery from SoCal Fertility. A certified subspecialist in reproductive endocrinology and infertility with the American Board of Obstetrics and Gynecology. He'd talked to them about in vitro and surrogacy, and he'd had fertility testing done.

I put a shaky hand to my mouth, and tears began to blur my eyes.

I pored over his test results. Josh was a breeding *machine*. Strong swimmers and an impressive sperm count. He'd circled this and put a winking smiley face next to it and I snorted.

He'd outlined the clinic's high success rates—higher than the national average—and he had gotten signed personal testimonials from previous patients, women like me who used a surrogate. Letter after letter of encouragement, addressed to me.

The next page was a complete breakdown on the cost of in vitro and information on Josh's health insurance and what it covered. His insurance was good. It covered the first round of IVF at 100 percent.

He even had a small business plan. He proposed selling doghouses that he would build. The extra income would raise enough money for the second round of in vitro in about three months.

The next section was filled with printouts from the Department of International Adoptions. Notes scrawled in Josh's handwriting said Brazil just opened up. He broke down the process, timeline, and costs right down to travel expenses and court fees.

I flipped past a sleeve full of brochures to a page on getting licensed for foster care. He'd already gone through the background check, and he enclosed a form for me, along with a series of available dates for foster care orientation classes and in-home inspections.

Was this what he'd been doing? This must have taken him weeks.

My chin quivered.

Somehow, seeing it all down on paper, knowing we'd be in it together, it didn't feel so hopeless. It felt like something that we *could* do. Something that might actually work.

Something possible.

The last page had an envelope taped to it. I pried it open with trembling hands, my throat getting tight.

I know what the journey will look like, Kristen. I'm ready to take this on. I love you and I can't wait to tell you the best part... Just say okay.

I dropped the letter and put my face into my hands and sobbed like I'd never sobbed in my life.

He'd done all this for me. Josh looked infertility dead in the eye, and his choice was *still* me.

He never gave up.

All this time, no matter how hard I rejected him or how difficult I made it, he never walked away from me. He just changed strategies. And I knew if this one didn't work he'd try another. And another. And another.

He'd never stop trying until I gave in.

And Sloan—she *knew.* She knew this was here, waiting for me. That's why she'd made me leave. They'd conspired to do this.

In her grief, when she needed me the most, when she couldn't even feed or wash herself, she was willing to give me up in the hopes of forcing my hand because she wanted this for me. She wanted me to be happy.

Because that's how much she loves me. She loves me as much as Josh does.

They thought I was worth it.

I still didn't believe it. I might never truly believe it.

But *they* did.

Something inside of me broke in that moment. I gave up. I no longer had the strength to stay away from him. I just couldn't do it anymore—there wasn't any reason to. His eyes were open.

Stuntman pressed against my side, looking up at me. I wiped my eyes with the top of my shirt. "I'm gonna bring your daddy home."

His tongue stuck out of the front of his mouth, and he looked like he was smiling. I picked up my phone and sent Josh a text for the first time in weeks.

Kristen: Okay.

I waited, looking at my phone with my heart in my throat. The doorbell rang.

I laughed, leaping off the sofa, tears pouring down my cheeks. Of course he was waiting for me. That's all Josh ever did.

He'd never have to do it again.

I threw open the door. He stood on the porch beaming with his dimples and his messy cowlick hair. I dove into his arms, and his cedar scent crashed into me, the familiar shape of his body wrapped around mine, instantly making me whole. He laughed with relief and lifted me off the ground, holding me so hard I couldn't catch my breath. "Okay," I whispered. "Okay."

Josh is mine.

The happiness was almost too much. And then just as deeply, as it settled in that my struggle had all been in vain, I felt the loss of the last few months without him. The weeks we could have been taking care of each other, carrying one another through this tragedy. "Josh, I'm so sorry. I'm so sorry for hurting you." I clutched him, crying. "Thank you for never giving up."

"Shhhhhhh." He squeezed me. "I would have fought for you for a lifetime. I'm just glad you didn't make me wait that long." He smiled with his forehead to mine, his eyes closed. "Are you ready for the best part?"

I sniffled. "Did you steal a baby?"

He laughed, running a knuckle down my cheek, his brown eyes creasing at the corners. "No. But it's almost as good." He held my gaze. "I already have a surrogate lined up."

I jerked back. "No. Sloan is not in any place emotionally or mentally to do this. I don't know if she'll ever be in a place—"

"It's not Sloan." He gave me a smile. "It's my sisters."

I blinked. "What?"

He grinned at me. "I went home to have a family meeting. I met with all six of my sisters and their husbands. I told them I was head over heels in love with a very practical woman who wouldn't have me unless I figured this out."

A laughing sob choked from my lips, and I put a hand over my mouth.

"All six of them volunteered. They even argued about who gets to go first. It's no fun unless they get to argue."

I snorted, rivers spilling over my cheeks.

He pulled me in, thumbing tears off my face. "Kristen, I need you to know that if none of these options were available to us, I would still want you. I want you no matter what. I want you first before I want anything else." His face was earnest and steady. "I have no chance of happiness if I can't have you. None."

I buried my face into his neck, and he held me to him.

"It's hard for me, Josh. It's hard to feel like I'm enough," I whispered.

"Well, I'll just have to spend the rest of our lives working on that, won't I? Which brings me to the next thing. Look at me."

He tipped up my chin. "I think we should get married." His eyes moved back and forth between mine. "Today."

THIRTY-NINE

JOSH

We stood on her porch, and she looked up at me with those brown eyes. "You want to marry me *now*? *Today?*"

The tower was gone. The drawbridge, the piranhas, the machine guns—*gone*. She was happy and open wide and her love was in everything. It *poured* out of her. It was in the way she looked at me. The tone of her voice. It was in her hand on my chest and her kiss, the smile that reached her eyes and the set of her mouth.

All these weeks I'd planned and prayed for this outcome. I didn't even know what I'd do if I failed. It was something I'd refused to let myself think about.

But I *hadn't* failed.

And now, seeing her love me like this was a relief for my soul. I had all of her for the first time. She was mine. She was *finally* mine.

But it wasn't time to celebrate yet.

I'd thought long and hard about this over the last few weeks. We still didn't know if she had some underlying health issues, and I'd bet my life that if she did, she'd leave me again to spare me having to take care of her.

Kristen believed in marriage. She believed in better and worse and sickness and health, and if she made that commitment to me, I knew she'd honor it. Even if *she* was the one who was sick.

I needed to seal this deal before she changed her mind. I'd seen time and time again how quickly I could lose her, and I had no intention of letting that happen by putting more time between us while we planned a wedding. Not while she was one bad doctor's visit from bailing on me.

"Hear me out," I said. "The fact that I'm crazy in love with you doesn't play into this. I promise. I know how much you'd hate it if I wanted to marry you in any sort of romantic sense, right?"

She laughed. *God, I missed her.*

"You're about to have a major surgery, and your insurance isn't as good as mine. You could see any doctor you want. You'd have access to any specialist you want to see, without a referral. I don't want to end up like Sloan and Brandon. I don't want to die not being married to the woman I love. And I want us to be able to make medical decisions for each other in the event that something happens to us."

She bit her lip. "The thought of my mom having total say does scare me a little bit, actually."

I grinned. I knew it would. "Also, the tax benefits for married couples are pretty generous."

"That is true." She smiled at me, her beautiful face light and open. "I have to say you make a pretty good argument. Do you need citizenship? Or maybe you need me to help you move a body and you don't want me to be able to testify? Because if you did, I think that would clinch the deal."

I pulled her closer. "Marry me. Now. Today. Let's go down to city hall and just do it."

Say yes. Please, say yes.

She shrugged. "Okay."

My heart exploded in my chest. "Yes?"

She bit her lip and smiled. "Yeah, I can't really argue with the pros list." Her brow wrinkled. "But what about your family? They won't be mad you've run off and married some random woman?"

Fuck my family—and I meant that in the most loving possible way—but my family was the *last* thing I was thinking about at the moment. I wouldn't be able to relax until Kristen was my wife. None of this was real or certain until we were married.

This first, family and taking deep breaths later.

I shook my head. "My parents already married off six daughters. They're relieved they don't have to do another wedding. I already told them what I planned to do. We can go home for a party whenever we're ready."

"Oh!" She bounced up and down. "Can we get our wedding rings at the *Pulp Fiction* pawnshop?"

I smiled, a cautious excitement seeping in. "Anything you want." I checked my watch. "If we want to do this today, we have to get going. You can probably take a few minutes to change."

"Okay, and I'll call Sloan," she said, reaching for her phone.

My stomach dropped. I knew this was coming, and my heart ached preemptively with what I had to tell her. I put a hand to her wrist. "Kristen," I said gently. "Sloan knows that I was going to propose to you. She doesn't want to be there."

Her happiness bled out in front of me, and my own joy at the situation sank. I hated to see her hurting. I wished I could give her all the things she wanted today. But Sloan wasn't for sale.

I looked at her softly. "She's supportive. She was rooting for me. She asked me to text her with your answer. But she can't go to a wedding."

She swallowed hard and nodded, her brown eyes glossing just enough to make my heart break. "No. She wouldn't be able to handle it. Of course." She smiled up at me, weakly this time, trying to put on a good face. I loved her for it. But I knew how deeply this hurt her. It hurt me too.

We finally had each other, but both of us had lost our best friends.

FORTY

KRISTEN

We sat on brown wooden benches on opposite sides of the hallway of the courthouse, waiting for our names to be called. We'd gotten our marriage licenses and rings and managed to get the last appointment of the day for a civil ceremony.

It cost thirty-five dollars to be married by a justice of the peace, plus an extra twenty bucks for two court-assigned witnesses we didn't know to sign our marriage certificate.

I didn't have flowers or a cake. I wasn't in a wedding dress. My ring was so loose I'd had to put tape around it to keep it on. It rained on us in the parking lot. We wouldn't have a first dance or photos or the mawage guy. My best friend wouldn't stand next to me and neither would his.

It was the lamest, saddest wedding in the history of weddings—and I was so excited about it I couldn't stop smiling.

Now that I'd let it go, I realized how exhausting my crusade had been. Like fighting to stay awake when you want to just let go and slip into a dream.

Letting him love me was natural and easy—it was keeping him away from me that was hard. It had drained me to the core, taken everything out of me, and I was relieved that it was over.

Josh wore the brewery shirt from the day we met, under a

sport coat, and I wore the black dress from Sloan and Brandon's party, by Josh's request.

I glanced at him, and he looked up from the paper in his lap and grinned at me, his dimples flashing. We were writing our own vows.

This man was about to be my husband.

He'd been my boyfriend for about three minutes, my fiancé for the last two hours, and he was about to be my husband for the rest of my life.

I was going to be Kristen Copeland.

I don't know what he was thinking as he watched me from across the wide courthouse corridor, but I'd never seen him look so happy.

"Kristen Peterson and Joshua Copeland?"

Our names being called shook us from our private moment. Josh got up and gave me his hand. Then, just before we went inside, he pulled me into him. "Are you ready?"

God, I was so ready it wasn't even funny.

"Yes." I drew my bottom lip into my mouth and smiled.

He caressed my cheek. "You know you're the best thing to ever happen to me, right?" His eyes blazed with emotion. "I love you, Kristen. You are the one great love of my life."

His words gripped my heart. "I love you too, Joshua. Forever."

~

The ceremony was in an office. We stood in front of the desk as a gray-haired clerk confirmed our names and checked our IDs. Our witnesses stood against the back wall as the ceremony started. We were a few minutes into it and I was just about to read my vows when the door burst open and Sloan spilled inside.

My jaw *dropped*.

She looked like a zombie bridesmaid. Her braid was frizzy, and her red lipstick was crooked. She wore the pink bridesmaid's dress from her mom's wedding three years ago, and she'd buttoned the dress wrong. Her hands clutched the half-dead flowers from her kitchen that I'd been picking through earlier. She must have taken them out of the trash. She had deep, dark circles under her eyes, and she looked pale, even with the blush.

But she was *here*.

I threw my arms around her.

"I couldn't not be here," she whispered.

I couldn't even imagine the strength it must have taken for her to pull herself out of the house to be here for me. The emotional anguish she would feel, watching me have the wedding she never got.

But she *came*.

Josh hugged her, and for the first time, I saw Brandon's absence etched on his face. He'd been doing a good job trying not to dwell on it, I think. But with Sloan here, Brandon was a void.

This wasn't the way any of this was supposed to go. Sloan and Brandon would have been long done with their honeymoon by today, at home and settled in. I don't know where Josh and I would be, but I realized now there was no world in which the two of us didn't end up together. And Brandon and Sloan would have been in our wedding, supporting us.

Instead, it was just her. And she wasn't really *her* anymore. I didn't know if she ever would be again.

But at least she was here.

Sloan stood next to me and I sniffled, picking up the Taco Bell receipt I'd jotted my vows down on.

I looked up at Josh. His chest rose and fell a little too fast. He had this look on his handsome face—a touch of anxiety, worry, and anticipation around his brow, like he was afraid at any minute all this would be taken from him, like I might suddenly change my mind.

I deserved that.

This was a shotgun wedding. Josh was the one holding the shotgun.

This whole thing was some flash-bang-chaos campaign to hustle me into marriage before I got my bearings. He wanted to lock me down before I freaked out on him and ran. That's why he'd rushed this. Only, the joke was on him—I *wanted* to be locked down, and I'd never change my mind. I'd never leave him again. If he wanted this rust bucket of a body so badly, he could have it, and I'd just have to spend the rest of my life making sure he felt secure and loved.

I looked at him, my eyes steady, and I took a deep breath. "Joshua, I vow to text you back."

Everyone in the room laughed, my fiancé included, and his face relaxed.

I continued. "I will answer every call you make to me for the rest of my life. You'll never chase me again."

His eyes filled with tears, and he seemed to let go of a breath he'd been holding.

"I promise to always go to family day at the station so you know that you're loved. I vow to support you and follow you anywhere until you've found the place that makes you happy. I'll be your best friend and try and fill that hole in your heart. I'm going to take care of you and cherish you, always and no matter what." I smiled at him. "I'll orbit around you and be your universe, because you've always been my sun."

He wiped at his eyes, and he had to take a moment before he read his own vows.

While I waited, I let his face anchor me. I soaked him in, let his love remind me again and again that I was worth it.

He looked at his paper and then seemed to decide he didn't need it, setting it down on the desk. He gathered up my hands. "Kristen, I vow that no matter what health issues lie ahead, I will love and take care of you. I will show you every day of your life that you're worth everything. I will carry your worries. All I ask is that you carry your own dog purse."

The room chuckled again.

"I promise to love Stuntman Mike and slay your spiders, and keep you from getting hangry."

Now I was laughing through tears.

"I will always defend you. I'll always be on your side." Then he turned to Sloan. "And I vow to protect and care for you, Sloan, like you're my sister, for the rest of my life."

This did it. The tears ran down my face, and I was in his arms and weeping before I knew I'd closed the distance.

We were both crying. We were *all* crying, even the witnesses who had no idea how hard the journey had been to get here, the sacrifices that were made for this union.

Or who we'd lost along the way.

FORTY-ONE

KRISTEN

Doctors' offices are never warm enough. You'd think they'd keep the heat up in a place where you're expected to sit and wear nothing but a paper gown.

Josh leaned next to me against the examining table where I sat with my bare legs dangling. He held my hand so I couldn't fidget.

"Does it always take this long?" he asked, checking his watch.

His wedding ring was on his watch hand and I smiled at it, despite being cold and nervous. The inscription inside his ring said "okay." I'd had my ring sized, and Josh had it inscribed with "my universe." We were adorable.

We were also hungry.

It had been almost a half an hour since the ultrasound tech finished taking images. Nobody had been back since, and I'd had to fast for a glucose test. Josh hadn't eaten in solidarity, so we were both starving.

I sighed. "I don't know how long this takes. I've never had a pre-op for a hysterectomy before."

We'd been married four weeks. It had been a hectic month.

Josh had moved in with me, but we realized almost on day one that we needed a place closer to Sloan. Both of us were there more than we were at home.

We asked her to move in with us and she'd flatly refused. We asked to move in with *her* and she refused that too. So we'd been house hunting in addition to merging our lives, launching our new line of doghouses, and taking care of my best friend.

Josh had taken on all the home repairs that Brandon hadn't gotten to. He cooked most of our meals, and I spent almost every day still getting her out of bed, cleaning her house, trying to cheer her up.

She wasn't getting any better.

The only time I could get her to leave the house was to visit Brandon's grave or for the occasional visit to Starbucks. She refused to go to the doctor for counseling or antidepressants to help get her through. I didn't know what else to do.

Josh nuzzled me and I closed my eyes, leaning into him. "What should we bring to Sloan's for lunch?" he asked.

"Um, she likes tacos. We can stop at the taco truck on the way over."

He cupped my cheek with his hand. "Sounds good. Remind me to fix her bedroom door. The lock has been sticking."

I tilted my head and he kissed me. He was always kissing me. Touching me, hugging me, holding my hand. We didn't get a honeymoon, but it didn't matter.

Every day was our honeymoon.

Last week Sloan's mom came and spent a few days with her so Josh and I could fly to South Dakota for me to meet his family.

He was not kidding. His sisters were crazy.

I loved those bitches.

It was like running with a pack of female alpha wolves fighting for the pack leader position. It was so much fun.

When we were there, we decided his sister Carmen was in the best place to be our first surrogate. She was a stay-at-home mom with her toddler and her seven-year-old, and she'd had the easiest pregnancies.

I'd have to do daily injections before they could harvest my eggs, and my fibroids never responded pleasantly to hormones, so even though we were busy with Sloan and my recovery was going to be a long one, we decided to schedule my hysterectomy.

It was time. My cramps had been horrible, and I was still spotting almost daily. The fibroids had started pushing against my bladder, and I couldn't sleep on my stomach anymore because it was too uncomfortable. And no matter how many times Josh told me I was sexy, I didn't feel like it with my potbelly.

I was ready to be done.

Josh was kissing me when the knock came on the door, and we jumped away from each other like teenagers who just got caught making out.

Dr. Angelo let himself in, looking at my chart. "Well, we have all your tests back. Mr. Copeland, you were definitely right to be concerned." He flipped a page, scanned it for a moment, and then turned to me. "You've got a few things going on that unfortunately are going to make the hysterectomy out of the question."

His face was grave.

I closed my eyes and let out a long breath. Something was wrong with me.

I knew it.

They say you're only as old as you feel. I was beginning to think I might be some kind of ancient relic or something.

For the last few weeks, I'd been getting headaches and I was really run-down. And I'd been losing weight like crazy. I kept having dizziness that I didn't dare tell Josh about because he would have dragged me straight to urgent care. He'd already been riding me relentlessly to get my glucose levels tested. I didn't have time to be hauled off to the hospital. I had shit to do.

And now I had diabetes or cancer or some rare heart condition, and Josh was going to have to take care of my dying ass.

This was *just* my luck. Not only was I going to have to keep my stupid, bleeding, bulging uterus, but now I'd have to deal with whatever else was wrong with me.

I seriously didn't have time for this. Sloan was a full-time job. My *job* was a full-time job.

And poor Josh. I just wanted to be a good wife to him. I wanted to be normal and healthy. And if I couldn't have a hysterectomy, could my eggs be harvested for in vitro? I mean, how far-reaching was this? And if I couldn't do in vitro, would my health keep us from being able to adopt? They had rules about that, didn't they? If you were dying, you couldn't bring a kid into it?

My velociraptor scratched at some inner door. But Josh put a hand on my shoulder and gave me a reassuring squeeze, and the monster went back into hibernation.

I knew my husband wouldn't leave me, no matter what bomb was about to be dropped. And the thing that sucked was I'd let him put a ring on this, and now I couldn't leave *him* to spare him a lifetime of my health issues. Well played, Josh. He was stuck with me.

I sighed and braced for the news.

Dr. Angelo pulled his stool up and sat, his clipboard balancing on his thigh. He twined his fingers in his lap. "You're pregnant, Mrs. Copeland."

Everything stopped.

Josh's hand went slack on my shoulder.

I stared at the doctor. "I'm *what*?"

"A little over four months along." Dr. Angelo gave us a grin.

"*What?*" Josh breathed.

Dr. Angelo swiveled his stool in front of the ultrasound machine. He typed into the keyboard, and a black-and-white image came up on the monitor.

He tapped a pen to a spot on the screen. "There's Baby." He tilted his head. "There's a foot. We have Baby's head here. There's a hand..."

Josh and I gawked at the screen. I don't think either of us breathed. My ears started to ring.

A black-and-white paper printed out under the monitor, and Dr. Angelo handed it to us. "Your first baby picture."

Josh and I looked down on the thin paper in shock, each of us holding a corner.

Dr. Angelo pushed his glasses up his nose. "Your glucose tests did come back a little off. Gestational diabetes. You'll need to be vigilant with your diet from now on, and you'll have to test your blood sugar." He talked to his clipboard. "That's what caused that bout with hypoglycemia that you mentioned." He nodded at Josh. "I'll give you a dietary printout. Your ultrasounds look good. Your baby appears to be healthy. Everything looks fine."

"*How?*" I breathed. "I have an IUD. And the fibroids! I've been bleeding this whole time!"

Dr. Angelo shook his head. "You mentioned spotting when we spoke earlier. Spotting and cramping are not unusual during pregnancy, especially after intercourse. And from what I can see, your IUD is, well—" He laughed a little. "It's not there. I didn't see it. My radiologist didn't see it either. It was likely expelled during a heavy menstrual flow. If your period is heavy enough, the IUD could have dislodged and passed completely undetected."

Josh was shaking. I could feel the tremor in his hand. I looked up at him and his eyes were wide. I started to laugh manically, and as soon as I lost it, he did too. The doctor waited patiently for us to get ourselves together.

"How is this happening? Things like this just don't happen." I looked up, wiping at my cheeks. "Why don't I feel it moving? Is it okay?"

I was processing all this at a rate of a thousand what-the-fucks per second. I couldn't believe it. I literally couldn't believe it.

The doctor smiled reassuringly at me. "You're still a little early yet. And if you're not anticipating being pregnant, it's not unusual to disregard the fetal movement and symptoms as something else."

"I just thought this was... the fibroids. I was so used to feeling like crap..." I put a hand on the small, rounded bulge that was my stomach for the first time in months.

A baby.

My swollen stomach was a *baby*. Not a belly full of tumors, but a *baby*.

I was *pregnant*.

"Your fibroids don't seem to be causing any problems for the pregnancy. The tumors actually appear to have shrunk quite a bit since your last visit," Dr. Angelo said, flipping through my chart. "It's not uncommon for the pregnancy hormones to have this effect."

The last four months began to come at me in flashes. "But I drank. And I didn't take vitamins and... and..."

"The occasional drink won't harm the pregnancy. Even getting a little tipsy once or twice won't hurt the baby. And while prenatals are ideal, you can get most of what you need in your normal diet."

I gasped for air. I was getting dizzy. I covered my mouth with my hands, and then I broke down. Body-wrenching sobs. I clutched Josh again, and he buried me in his chest.

Neither of us could contain our emotions. You could probably hear us through the whole clinic, laughing and wailing like lunatics.

The doctor handed Josh and me tissues. "I'm recommending you take it easy, and we'd like to see you gain a little weight. You're about ten pounds from where you should be. A pregnancy requires an extra three hundred calories a day. It'll take everything you have if you don't eat properly, and we want you nice and strong for the delivery, Mrs. Copeland."

The room whirled around me. I couldn't catch up to it.

Pregnant. Me. Me and Josh.

When the doctor finally left the room after I'd asked all my questions and I got to see the baby again on the ultrasound and hear the heartbeat, Josh and I sat hugging.

"It was that night," I said. "The night of Sloan's party."

He laughed and wiped a wet strand of hair off my cheek. "The first time. It was the only time we didn't use condoms back then. One shot and I knocked you up."

I snorted. "It was your super sperm. Thank God you made an honest woman out of me. Dragged me right down for a civil ceremony, befitting my scandalous condition."

He laughed. Then he hovered a hand over my stomach and looked at me for permission.

He'd touched every inch of my body but there. I nodded, and he set his warm palm over my belly button, and it was the most intimate moment of my life. He leaned over and kissed me, holding our baby under his hand.

And then the terror took over. I jerked back, suddenly frightened. "Josh, what if I miscarry? My mom lost my brother. What if it comes too early? What if it's a girl and she has the same issues I do? What if I'm a shitty mom like my mom and I don't know how to raise her or tell her how much I love her or... or..." Hysterics bubbled out of me.

I was now a woman who got hysterical.

"Hey, hey. You're not going to be a shitty mom," he said, holding my face in his hands. "You're nothing like Evelyn. Don't think about the what-ifs, because there's nothing you can do to stop any of it. Let's just enjoy this. And if things don't go the way we planned, we'll deal with it. Always and no matter what. Together."

I nodded, the shaking in my hands slowing the tighter he held me.

I closed my eyes and calmed my breathing, focusing on my husband's hands on my face and his familiar presence. My rock. The calm in my storm. The whisper to my scream.

Then I looked up at him, the final reality coming into focus. "Josh. You're going to be a daddy."

He gave me a sideways grin, tears and joy twinkling in his eyes. "Kristen... *you* are going to be a mommy."

EPILOGUE

JOSH

2 years later

I leaned into the back of the SUV and unbuckled Oliver Brandon from his car seat. Kristen stood next to me, a diaper bag slung over her shoulder. "You're sure you want to do this? What if she eats him?"

I smiled, lifting the baby into my arms and grabbing his sippy cup. "Evelyn's trying. She deserves a chance." I closed the door and turned to her.

My wife eyed me. "She called you a rapscallion."

I laughed. "Yes—yes she did."

Kristen and I had good fun with that one. It was Kristen's favorite nickname for me.

I gave Oliver his sippy cup. "But in all fairness, you told her you were married and pregnant via Potatogram. She had a right to be upset. Give me this." I took the diaper bag from her. "You shouldn't be lifting more than you need to."

She scowled at me. "It's been four months since my surgery. I can carry a five-pound diaper bag."

I kissed the side of her stubborn head.

After Oliver was born, we'd tried for over a year to get pregnant again. But lightning didn't strike twice.

We'd gone to a fertility specialist and done three unsuccessful rounds of in vitro, but her fibroids kept the embryos from implanting.

Kristen had been miserable. Her periods were a nightmare. She was in pain and borderline anemic. That, coupled with the fertility treatments and caring for an infant, had been really hard on us both.

I'd hated to see her suffering.

She was reluctant to pull the trigger on the hysterectomy this time because we'd gotten lucky once. But after over a year of it, we saw Oliver for what he was—a miracle. And one that wouldn't repeat itself.

So with lots of reassurance from me that it was okay and that I just wanted her to be healthy, she'd had the hysterectomy at twenty-six.

And she was a new person.

I don't think I truly realized how strong my wife was. Kristen didn't like to tell me when she wasn't feeling well. She did a good job hiding it and putting on a happy face. But when the cramps and bleeding were no longer a daily part of her life, she bloomed. She slept better, she had more energy. It transformed her. Even her hangry was less terrifying.

Seeing her like this was a gift.

"You know, Mom will probably have him potty trained by tomorrow," she said.

"Good." I peered up at the front of Evelyn's 1940s-era Simi Valley mansion. "I'm liking this better and better by the minute."

We made our way up the steps, and Evelyn opened the door before we knocked.

I still couldn't get used to seeing this lady smiling. But she did. Not at Kristen and me, of course, but she loved her grandson.

"There's my grandbaby!" she said with a flourish.

She leaned in and gave Kristen and me an air-kiss and then took Oliver from me in a flurry of Chanel No. 5.

Maria, the night nurse Evelyn had on staff to get us to agree to a sleepover, took the diaper bag.

Oliver knew Maria. Evelyn had hired her for us to help out for the first few weeks after he was born and again when Kristen was recovering from her hysterectomy.

Evelyn had become very helpful as of late. She'd gone to being all carrot and no stick now that the stick had stopped working.

Sloan was doing as well as could be expected. I wouldn't say she was thriving, but she was functional again. And some of that was Evelyn's doing. In addition to helping us with our son, Evelyn had also stepped in to represent Sloan in probate court to help her keep her house. Not that it was much to hang on to. I was over there weekly trying to keep it standing. But the gesture had meant the world to all three of us. And after that, I found it very hard to rebuff her attempts at being in her grandson's life.

Kristen was still leery. But I didn't worry about it. Oliver was the first thing Evelyn ever acknowledged that Kristen had done right.

Kristen bit her lip nervously, and I put a hand on her shoulder.

"Are you sure you can handle this, Mom?" she asked.

Oliver had always been with at least one of us at any given time. It was his first sleepover. But today was a special occasion, and we needed the house empty.

Evelyn waved her off, a diamond tennis bracelet flashing on her wrist. "Yes, yes. You two go. Happy birthday. Enjoy your night, dear."

Evelyn turned back into the house, whispering to Oliver that they were going to see his mommy's piano. The plinking sound of baby hands on keys followed as we closed the door behind us.

We stood on the porch. "Free at last," I said, slipping my hands around her waist.

She wrapped her arms around my neck and kissed me. "We're gonna do that thing we like, all night, right?"

I cupped my hands under her ass and nipped at her lip, smiling. "It's been so long..."

"I know—can't wait to get you in bed," she whispered.

I grinned. "We're talking about sleeping, aren't we?"

We laughed against each other's lips, and I kissed her deeply, right there on Evelyn's porch.

Fuck, I never got enough of my wife. She was the sexiest woman alive. I loved every inch of her. I loved her stretch marks and her scars, the specks in her eyes and the birthmark on her neck. All her flawless imperfections.

I was grateful every moment of every single day that Brandon brought me to her. She was my everlasting gift from a man I'd never forget for the rest of my life.

I broke away and put my forehead to hers. "So you want In-N-Out for lunch and steaks for dinner, right?"

She nodded and put her hand over my heart where the tattoo of her name was. "Josh? I think I could be ready again to keep trying. Should we start talking about surrogacy? Carmen is still down for it, right?"

I knew why she was asking. She still wanted to give me my baseball team. But my dreams had changed.

Seeing the strain of the in vitro process and how much it took out of her emotionally and physically—I just wanted her to be happy. I wanted her to enjoy our son. She never complained, but I knew she was tired of the doctor's visits and the hormone injections and the disappointment. If she was up for it in a few years, maybe we'd try again or look into the other options. We were young—we had time. But I didn't want her to do it for me because she thought she owed it to me. She'd done enough.

I put my hands on her face. "Let's take a break, Kristen. I'm happy where we are. And if this is our family, I'm good with that."

The relief was visible in her eyes. "Are you sure?"

My mouth curved up into a smile. "I'm very sure. I have everything I need."

A NOTE FROM THE AUTHOR

When I sat down to pen this novel, I knew I wanted to write a story that felt real—a story that could include hangry, neurotic women who actually get periods, and the men who love them (lol).

With infertility being a serious and prevalent issue, I felt like I had a responsibility to tell this not only compassionately, but also authentically. So for this I went to someone who lived it.

While Kristen's love story with Josh is fiction, her infertility journey is inspired by real events.

Kristen's character is based on my best friend, Lindsay, and her struggle with infertility. I talk about it now with her full permission, the same way I wrote about it.

Lindsay had a full hysterectomy at the age of just twenty-nine after dealing with debilitating reproductive issues for years. While she was able to conceive her two children naturally (and much like Kristen, without medical intervention and to her complete surprise), she dealt with secondary infertility due to severe uterine fibroids. She had all—if not more—of the physical and emotional challenges Kristen experiences in my novel. Much of what I wrote was verbatim, as Lindsay described it to me.

You may or may not have seen your own infertility journey in these pages. The thing I realized doing research for this book—and the truth you might already know if you're going through this yourself—is that there *is* no universal story to tell. No two experiences are the same, and any measure of this challenging diagnosis is heartbreaking to endure.

What does unify these stories are the feelings of hopelessness, worthlessness, guilt, and despair that come with this very common, but often not discussed, health issue. And so that is what I strove to tell in *The Friend Zone.*

Just one final note.

Kristen's happy ending was never about getting pregnant. It was about her allowing herself to be loved, despite what she felt were shortcomings. It was about her recognizing that she wasn't defined by her ability to have children, and that her worth went beyond the state of her uterus. That was her happily ever after.

ACKNOWLEDGMENTS

There are so many people to thank for this book becoming a published reality.

First and foremost I have to acknowledge my crit buddies and beta readers. These people trudged through some seriously awful shit before it became the book you just read. A special shout-out to my very first beta reader, Kristen McBride, who was reading my stuff before it was cool. And yes, my main character is named after her in thanks. You took one for the team, gurl. You've earned it.

Thank you to Joey Ringer, Hijo, Tia Greene, Shauna Lawless, Debby Wallace, J. C. Nelson, Jill Storm, Liz Smith-Gehris, G. W. Pickle, Dawn Cooper, Andrea Day, Lisa Stremmel, Lisa Sushko, Michele Alborg, Amanda Wulff, Summer Heacock, Stacey Sargent, George, Jhawk, Abby Luther, Patt Pandolfi, Bessy Chavez, Mandy Geisler, Teressa Sadowski, Stephanie Trimble, and Kristyn May.

To Naomi, my oldest daughter, who loved to hear my story ideas and encouraged me to write them down and then in typical teenager fashion rolled her eyes and said I'd probably not even mention her in the acknowledgments—I showed you, you salty bitch.

Thank you to the people who lent their expertise so that this story could be authentic: Valerie Hales Summerfield (ICU nurse), Terry Saenz (emergency room nurse), Suzanna and TJ Keeran (California firefighter paramedics), and my OB-GYN who answered some really random reproductive health questions without any explanation on my part.

To my best friend, Lindsay Van Horn, who seriously didn't read shit because she only does audiobooks but who was the inspiration for Kristen and the cheerleader I needed along the way. Also, she sent me a congratulatory Potatogram upon the news of my book deal, with zero knowledge that I'd written that into the novel. Damn if I don't know her.

I can't express enough gratitude and appreciation for my literary agent, Stacey Graham. She took one look at that email from an unknown, first-time author, read the dick joke I'd put in my query, and said, "This girl is going places." She was honorable, supportive, encouraging, and generally just an amazing human being right from the onset. She talked me off ledges, was an advisor, and most important, a friend. Thank you for taking a chance on me.

Thank you to Dawn Frederick for letting me be a part of Red Sofa Literary.

A thanks to my editor, Leah, who saw something in me and wanted to bring my stories to the world. Your mad skills and guidance unleash my creativity, and I can honestly say my books are better because you're a part of them. Thanks, too, to the entire Forever team, who's supported this book from the beginning: Estelle with her amazing publicity, Lexi, Gabi, Cristina, and to Elizabeth for the awesome cover.

And lastly, to my long-suffering husband, Carlos, who sacrificed time with me and my attention so I could focus (compulsively, I might add) on my passion. If it weren't for him, I wouldn't know what a happily ever after looks like. People ask me if Josh is my husband. All the best parts of any man I ever write will always be something I've seen in my own. No fictional character will ever be him—he's better.

Don't miss Abby's second novel,
The Happily Ever After Playlist,
featuring Sloan's heartbreaking and
romantic story, coming in spring 2020.